CIRCUMPOLAR!

OTHER BOOKS BY RICHARD A. LUPOFF

Fiction:

One Million Centuries
Sacred Locomotive Flies
Into the Aether
The Crack in the Sky (in England: Fool's Hill)
Sandworld
The Triune Man
Sword of the Demon
Lisa Kane
Space War Blues
The Return of Skull-Face (with Robert E. Howard)
The Ova Hamlet Papers
Lovecraft's Book
Sun's End

Criticism:

Edgar Rice Burroughs: Master of Adventure
Barsoom: Edgar Rice Burroughs and the Martian Vision

Edited by Richard A. Lupoff:

What If? Vol. 1
What If? Vol. 2
All in Color for a Dime (with Donald A. Thompson)
The Comic-Book Book (with Donald A. Thompson)

CIRCUMPOLAR!

Richard A. Lupoff

TIMESCAPE BOOKS
Distributed by Simon and Schuster, New York

A Timescape Book
Published by Pocket Books, A Division of Simon & Schuster, Inc.
Simon & Schuster Building
Rockefeller Center
1230 Avenue of the Americas
New York, New York 10020

Designed by Eve Kirch
Manufactured in the United States of America

1 3 5 7 9 10 8 6 4 2

Library of Congress Cataloging in Publication Data
Lupoff, Richard A., 1935–
Circumpolar!
I. Title.
PS3562.U605 1984 813′.54 83-18085
ISBN 0-671-49941-6 (Simon and Schuster)

Anything is possible. *Everything* is possible. Somewhere in God's infinite universe there may be a system of planets sharp-edged and square-faced as ice cubes. There may be a solar system where worlds are hollow and illuminated by tiny interior suns. There may even be a family of spherical planets as solid as baseballs!

Who can say? All we know is that there's no reason to assume the planets of other suns are flattened toroids just because our sun's planets are so formed.

Think of it! Somewhere, an earth like our earth, complete with a Minnesota and a Morocco, a Pennsylvania and a Peru, an Emperor of Australia and a President of Japan. And yet that world is as round and solid as a baseball!

Everything is possible.

—Stanley Grauman Weinbaum
December 14, 1946

Chapter 1

The glittering colored lights atop the new El Cortez Hotel winked like beacons in the black subtropical sky. Making a low-level overland approach, Lindy banked his spunky little Pitcairn biplane and swung the craft past the hotel tower. He gunned his engine and waved at startled celebrants, fashionably garbed for dinner atop San Diego's newest landmark, as they gawked at the *Mailwing*. They could actually look down at the biplane as it swept past them, headed toward the city's Mission Bay wharves.

Lindy fed fuel to the Wright Whirlwind radial to pick up a little extra altitude. He shot a quick glance at the airspeed indicator, nodded, then cut his engine. With a couple of desperate pops the Whirlwind quit. There was sudden silence in place of the steady drone that the radial had provided on this last leg of Lindy's flight, since his refueling stop at Vegas.

Now the engine's roar was replaced by the whisper of cool night air whipping through the open cockpit. The whine of the slipstream over the Pitcairn's fabric-covered wings and taut guy-wires created weird harmonies that sounded like a chorus of disembodied spirits.

Guiding the biplane through a long, graceful glide, Lindy passed over mast-studded Mission Bay and Coronado Island with its posh resorts, then curved briefly over the inky Pacific waters. He swung the *Mailwing* back over North Island, pulled his goggles down over deep blue eyes, and searched for the flares that should mark the landing strip. He'd spoken via long-distance trunk wire with his friend Howard Hughes before taking off from Vegas, and Hughes had promised to see to it that the landing strip would be prepared for a night arrival.

As promised, the flares were there, sputtering their lurid glare in twin rows.

Lindy dipped the nose of his plane, kicked the flaps to hold his airspeed down. The Pitcairn's rubberized wheels kissed the hard-packed grassy runway once... twice... then settled and began to roll. The tail-mounted landing skid scraped. Lindy permitted himself a sideways glance as the plane rolled smoothly to a stop. He pushed himself erect, stiff from the long cross-country flight.

Even as Lindy stepped from the open cockpit of the *Mailwing* he flinched at the sudden glare as a pair of bright lights blazed into life. A self-starter whined, a powerful engine caught with a throaty roar, and the lights sped onto the runway, leaping forward eagerly. The twin glares were blinding, the engine's roar deafening.

Lindy squinted, trying to shade his eyes from the glare. The car roared closer and closer.

At the last moment Lindy made his move. He dived sideways, slid under the fuselage of the Pitcairn. He grabbed a wooden landing brace, swung upright and thrust himself forward, peering across the fuselage of the plane.

The car swerved to a halt with brakes screeching, its tires skidding on the grass runway. With the glaring headlights no longer blinding him, Lindy could see the car's driver leap to his feet, vault over the roadster's closed door without bothering to lever it open, and hit the runway at a sprint, headed for the Pitcairn.

The man was almost skeletal, close to half a foot taller than Lindy, with narrow shoulders and huge rawboned hands that stuck out past his cuffs. He headed straight for Lindy. The flier recognized him and clambered back over the aircraft, hitting the wing-mount braces with one boot, the cockpit with the other, and landing with both feet firmly on the hard-packed grass.

The taller man halted. In the confusing illumination of the auto's headlights and the still-sizzling flares, Lindy could see the man's face break into a grin that suggested a laughing, moustachioed skull. The man yanked off his felt hat and flung it into the air with a joyous whoop. The two men flew together, embracing and thumping each other's leather-jacketed backs.

"Lindy, you nut! What kind of landing was that? You didn't take off light on fuel and run out again, like the other times?"

Lindbergh drew back from Hughes's embrace, laughing. "Nothing like that. You know what it's like up there, Howard—just you and the sky. Especially the sky! Just you in a sweet little ship like the *Mailwing!*"

"Sure I do." Hughes retrieved his battered hat. He jammed it back onto his dark head and led the way to his Marmon roadster. "But what's that got to do with a deadstick landing?"

Lindbergh halted with one foot on the roadster's running board. He drew off his flying helmet and turned his eyes skyward. A Pacific breeze tossed his curly sand-blond hair forward and he shook it away from his eyes.

"Up there, Howard, with no one but God for company, with the moon in disk and ten thousand stars all around—somehow I don't want the sound of a mill reminding me that I'm in a machine. That I'm an intruder in thc sky, that I don't really belong there."

He paused and shrugged. Laughed at himself. "I guess I'm a poor poet, ain't I?"

Hughes put the Marmon into gear and released the hand brake. "Compared to me you are. But I guess I savvy. You still gave me a scare coming in that way, though!"

Lindy changed the subject. "How are things here? Is the big ship ready to fly? What do the Ryan boys have to say?"

Hughes threw Lindy a grin. "I've been breathing down their necks so hard they cringe every time I walk into the hanger. But they're good workers there. Bill Bowlus runs 'em like Trojans. The mono's ready to take off. I've been testing her for a week with Don Hall. She's one sweet ship, Lindy."

"You haven't had her up, though?" Lindbergh's dark eyes showed concern.

"By God, Swede! You act like a nervous bridegroom afraid some sheik's going to deflower his virgin sweetie before he can do it himself!"

Lindy's face grew hot. "You needn't be vulgar!"

Hughes let out a guffaw. He'd manhandled the Marmon off the impromptu landing strip now, and was guiding the roadster through the black palm-lined streets of Coronado toward the shingled ferry building.

"I'm sorry, Swede. I keep forgetting your northern reserve. But no"—he paused—"don't worry. Nobody's had your sweet ship into the air. And I've warned 'em all down at Ryan's that nobody's to give her an air trial till you arrive and do it yourself."

Lindbergh grunted his thanks coolly.

Hughes guided the Marmon onto the ferry and locked its wheels. The two men climbed from the roadster and walked to the ferry's bow. The lights of the city danced on the water like fireflies.

"Don Hall ordered everything himself. Tach, airspeed indicator, altimeter, fuel gauge, oil pressure..."

Lindbergh looked up from the water where the ferry's prow was throwing a wedge of foam before the craft. "Both compasses, as I specified?"

"Hall thought the magnetic would be best."

"We've been over this before," Lindy insisted. "We don't know what it's going to be like on the other side. I want the earth-inductor, too!"

"Relax!" Hughes started to clap Lindbergh once more on the shoulder, then held back. "I told him you want both, so he had 'em put in both. They've even got the fuel and oil drums ready. Everything's set. We should be on our way next week."

Lindy grunted again, satisfied. The ferry pulled into her slip and both men climbed back into the Marmon. Within a few minutes Hughes was guiding the auto through darkened streets, past shuttered haberdasheries and closed filling stations. He turned the roadster up a steep hill, dropped it into second gear and gunned the powerful V-12 engine.

"She's got a sweet mill in her, Swede."

"The Ryan?"

"I meant the Marmon. But the Ryan has, too. Hall and Bowlus over at Ryan's wanted to put in a high-powered Pratt and Whitney. They doubt that the Wright has the horses to lift the ship over those ice walls down at the rim."

"You didn't let 'em, did you?"

Hughes shook his shaggy head. "Not a chance. I told 'em that you knew what you wanted and you had confidence in the Whirlwind."

"That's right. Three-twenty horses is plenty enough, and it's a sweet-running, reliable engine. Gets the best range out of a tank of juice, too, and that's going to be crucial. Not like this boat of yours, Howard!" He grinned and slapped his palm on the outside of the Marmon's alloy door. At last his good humor was returning.

Hughes agreed. "Don't I know it, Swede! Especially once we get across the ice wall and onto the other side. Who knows what we'll find there?"

"That's half the fun of going." Lindy smiled. "Not that I'll mind collecting my share of Mrs. Victoria Woodhull Martin's fifty thousand! That money's been there a long time, and I aim to see that it doesn't gather dust any longer than it has to!"

Hughes guided the Marmon into the curving driveway of a hotel and set its parking brake. He tossed the keys to a smartly uniformed bellman and vaulted from the car. Lindy followed suit.

"I've got a surprise for you," Hughes said. "Glad to see you're still peppy after all that flying tonight. You feel up to meeting a friend of mine?"

Lindbergh said, "Great with me."

They made their way up a tiled walk and into a stucco-covered, Spanish-style building. Above the entryway curved a graceful arch spelling out *El Cortez* in turquoise blue letters.

Hughes led his companion across the glittering lobby and into a filigreed elevator cage. "Sky Room," he grunted to the operator. Then, to Lindbergh, "Wait till you lay your eyes on her!" Hughes grinned broadly.

"Her!" Lindy echoed. "I thought you'd chosen another aviator to make the try with us. You didn't say anything about a woman."

"That's right, I didn't! But I didn't say I'd picked a man, either,

Charlie. You assumed it. But you'll—whoops, we're here."

The elevator swayed a couple of times, then settled. The operator slid the gate open and Hughes and Lindbergh stepped out. "There she is," Hughes announced.

They crossed the Sky Room, dodging waiters and tables. The room was glassed in, overlooking San Diego, Mission Bay and Coronado.

There was a stone fireplace in the center of the room. A young woman sat beside it in an overstuffed leather chair. The air was chilly here, high above the city, and the blazing wood fire made the room comfortable. As Lindbergh and Howard Hughes approached, the young woman lifted her gaze from the flames. A look of recognition crossed her face and she advanced to greet the two aviators.

As she did so she was momentarily backlit by the dancing flames. The unusual lighting turned her circle of curly, light red hair to a halolike nimbus.

She held one hand out to Howard Hughes, the other to Lindy. "You must be Charlie Lindbergh," she cried. "I'm Amelia Earhart. Howard's been filling my ears with the most wonderful yarns about you! He thinks you're the grandest airman in the world! If you're anywhere near as good as Howard says, we can't lose this race."

Lindbergh thought he could feel electricity flowing from the woman's hand. He surveyed her, found her almost as tall as he, and if anything, even slimmer. She dressed unconventionally, forsaking the customary skirts for a pair of aviator's jodhpurs and boots. She wore a white satin blouse open at the neck, and a grin that illuminated the lounge.

Lindy looked down at the hand that he still held, noticing its strength. "Well, I shall try and live up to my billing," he managed to stammer.

Hughes laid his huge hands on their shoulders and guided them back to the chair Amelia had vacated. "You'll have to forgive me, Swede. I knew you'd love Amy once you met her, but I was afraid you'd object to flying with a woman if I told you in advance."

Lindbergh crouched on the edge of a leather chair close to Amelia Earhart's. Hughes had plunged his lanky form deep into another. An octagonal table with a tooled-leather top stood in the center of the trio.

The sandy-haired Lindbergh gazed seriously at the woman. "Please don't be offended, Miss Earhart. But this is a very serious enterprise. There's a prize of fifty thousand dollars at stake. And more than that—our very lives will be on the line throughout this flight."

"I quite understand," the woman replied. "I know all about Victoria Woodhull and her prize."

"And you understand what we have to do to win it?"

"I know the terms that Mrs. Woodhull Martin set. We can either travel to the Arctic, traverse Symmes' Hole there, make our way all across the bottom of the world, and climb back over the ice barrier at the South Rim to complete our journey..."

Lindy nodded in affirmation.

"Or," Amelia resumed, "we can make our way over the ice barrier first, and perform the circuit in the opposite direction. South to north instead of north to south."

"That's exactly right," Lindbergh agreed.

"And Mr. Bowlus down at the Ryan company is just finishing up a monoplane that Mr. Hall designed for us to use," Amelia finished.

"*The Spirit of San Diego*," Lindbergh breathed proudly.

A cynical smile crossed Howard Hughes's rugged face. "Courtesy of our sponsor, the *San Diego Union* newspaper."

Lindbergh leaned back in his chair, stretched his long legs toward the fireplace, steepled his fingers beneath his chin. "I'm sorry to put you through this grilling," he said. "But before we can sign you on as a member of the crew, I'll need to know something of your qualifications."

"Let me at the controls of that Ryan Special and I'll show you my qualifications!" Defiance sparked in her eyes.

Lindbergh rubbed his chin.

Howard Hughes laughed out loud.

"But if you're afraid that I'll ground-loop your precious monoplane and delay your departure for the ice wall, let me reassure you, Mr. Lindbergh. I've done plenty of flying. I learned on a little Kinner *Canary* up in Santa Monica. I've handled Jennies and a dozen other kinds of aircraft since."

Lindbergh sat up, interested. "Could you name a few?"

"The Stinson biplane, the Curtiss *Carrier Pigeon*, the Douglas M-2—"

"I was pretty fond of the M-2 myself," Hughes interrupted. "I like the Liberty mill. Four hundred horses, Charlie!"

"Horses, horses! That's all you think about!" Lindbergh made a fist and smacked it on the arm of his leather chair. "It isn't just horses that make a good craft, it's a subtle balance of design and power. And if we're going to beat our rivals..."

The fire crackled in the silence that he left.

"Do you want me to go?" Amelia pursued. "I was in England last year during the Russian Tsar's visit to his cousin George the Fifth, and toured the British aircraft works. Alliot Roe has taken out a license on Señor Cierva's autogyro, and I took up his experimental model. A fascinating craft—flying her was a real challenge—but what grand fun it was!"

Lindy flung his hands in the air. "I surrender!" he yelped. "Unless you're a prize liar, young woman, you've flown more kinds of machine than ninety-nine per cent of the male aviators alive. And if you can handle the Ryan as well as you can talk about aircraft, you'll make a fine member of our crew."

"We'll need every bit of flying talent we can get!" Hughes put in. "Not only is it a terrific task to make this trip at all—the competition is getting damned hot! Or haven't you been keeping track, Charlie?"

Lindbergh said, "No, I've been too busy trying to earn a living. I know there are others after the Woodhull prize. But flying the mails between Chicago and St. Louis, you know, with barely time for a shower and a shave between flights..."

He paused.

"...who else looks ready to make the jump?"

Hughes unzipped the front of his leather jacket and reached inside for a much-folded newspaper. He laid it on the tooled leather table top, spreading the creased pages to make them lie flat. Lindbergh and Amelia Earhart leaned forward, the woman's fluff of flame-tinted hair brushing the lean Swede's sandy waves.

The newspaper had a large photo on its front page. It showed two men and a woman in flying costume standing before a huge four-engined monoplane.

Lindbergh's eye went directly to the plane. "Look at that," he whistled. "Strut-mounted radials. But where are the props? Oh." He grinned. "Shaft-driven pushers."

"I know those men," Amelia Earhart said. She touched two graceful fingertips to the gray images. "Those are the famous German aviators, the von Richtofen brothers. But I don't recognize the woman." She indicated the slim figure standing between the two men.

The woman in the photo wore an aviator's costume of white leather, a startling contrast to the black flying suits of the two men. The white leather costume was generously trimmed in matching fur.

"Interesting configuration," Lindbergh added. "Unconventional design, but she looks airworthy. Powerful craft. Huge. Hmph. Looks like the kind of thing Ernst Udet would come up with."

"Combined German-Russian crew"—Amelia read the caption aloud—"pause during tests of their airliner *Kondor* at Tempelhof Aerodrome near Berlin. The aviators plan to attempt the circumpolar flight via Symmes' Hole in competition for the Woodhull Martin Prize."

Howard Hughes signaled to a waiter while Lindbergh and Amelia Earhart studied the photo. The waiter brought three glasses filled with a rich concoction of coffee and liqueurs topped with whipped cream. As he set the glasses out, Hughes gathered up his newspaper and slid it back inside his flying jacket.

"Paper doesn't say who's behind the *Kondor* flight. Don't suppose you'd care to guess. Swede? Amy? Okay."

He looked around cautiously, leaned over the table and lowered his voice. "Friedrich Wilhelm is sitting there in his palace, far above politics, where a proper monarch is supposed to stay nowadays."

The others nodded.

"And the old Kaiser is cooling his heels on the other side of the border in Holland, all guilty and contrite over setting off the One Year War back in ought-twelve."

"I almost wish that war had gone on a few years longer." Lindbergh sipped slowly at his glass. "Or else started a few years later. Man, I'd have loved to fly a Sopwith or a Spad or one of those little Curtiss Tripes we were building. But as soon as Roosevelt got back into the White House in '13, he got our side so revved up, the Hun never had a chance. And I was too young to fly!"

A wry grin crossed his face.

"Just as well," Amelia said. She laid her long fingers across his wrist. Lindbergh started to flinch away, then left his hand where it was.

"I was working in a settlement house," Amelia said, "when we got into the war. It was quite an experience, helping those little children. A real melting pot. I think I picked up a smattering of every language from Chinese to Choctaw—not omitting Russian and Rumanian.

"But when the wounded boys started coming home, I switched over to an army hospital and—Charles, you wouldn't have wanted to live through some of the things I heard about. Or come home like some of those boys. Believe me."

Howard Hughes cleared his throat. "What this all has to do with the Woodhull Martin Prize..."

Amelia Earhart withdrew her fingers from Lindbergh's wrist, lifted her glass and leaned back in her chair. Lindy laughed nervously and turned to Hughes.

"What this has to do with the prize," Hughes repeated, "isn't just the prize. I have a feeling that Friedrich Wilhelm is up to a lot more than patronizing scientific advancement. He and his old daddy are still as thick as thieves, and the pair of them are huddling with their cousin Alexei in Petrograd every chance they get.

"They're using the *Berliner Staats-Zeitung* as a conduit, but you can bet that the marks come out of the imperial treasury one way or another! Big Willy and Little Willy and that Russki Prince Lvov are out to get control of the Hole, and to get ahold of whatever's on the other side of the disk. If they can do that they can come down on any country in Europe or Asia or North America and then we'll be in for a rumpus that'll make the One Year War look like a pigskin pep rally!"

"Oh, come on, Howard," Lindbergh scoffed. "You're seeing spies under every bed and conspirators around every corner. All that political stuff is over my head. I want to fly! I want this flight for the adventure of it. And for the glory, too. I won't deny that.

"I won't deny wanting the money, either. But don't pull us all into international intrigue, that's not our game!"

"Okay, Swede, okay. But what I'm saying is, with the *Kondor* that close to takeoff—I don't think the newspaper photo was a put-up job—we'd better get airborne as quick as we can."

"I was hoping for some air tests," Lindbergh said. "I don't like the idea of a cold flight."

"Me neither. We all need to get used to flying the *Spirit*. Especially you, Amy."

"I'll make myself useful," she said.

"I know." Hughes smiled. "I picked you 'cause we can use a hot navigator as well as a third pilot. Two could probably do the trick, but three'll make it a lot easier. But we *really* need a navigator."

"I can handle both jobs."

"This all sounds fine to me," Lindy said. "But if we're going to push up our departure, and do our familiarization as we go, then we'd better get in a map session right now. You have the charts, Howard?"

Hughes rose from his chair. The others followed him toward the elevator, Lindbergh casting a look behind to see the city once more through the Sky Room's tall windows. "We're checked into a suite a couple floors down," Hughes rasped. "One room for us, Charlie, one for Amy, and a sitting room. The charts are there."

They rode downstairs. Hughes led the others to their suite, unlocked the outer door and swung it open. Charles Lindbergh and Amelia Earhart stepped past Hughes, into the lighted sitting room.

Simultaneously they gasped.

Clothing and papers were strewn about, empty bureau drawers lay on the thick carpet, even the pictures had been torn from their places on the walls.

The suite had been ransacked!

Chapter 2

Princess Irina Lvova shrieked with mock alarm as the bullet-headed driver swung the huge, powerful Maybach onto the bridge. "Lothar," Irina cried, "Lothar, not so fast!" She clung desperately to the leather arm-rest, her long, platinum hair flying in the chilly springtime afternoon.

Lothar von Richthofen geared down from seventh to sixth as the heavy automobile jounced along the ancient, cobblestone-paved bridge. He was bare-headed, his warm astrakhan cap lying unheeded in the empty rear seat of the car. He was bundled in a gray military greatcoat with mouton collar. Although the afternoon sun shone pale and watery through a low sky, beads of sweat like drops of glycerine shone on his naked skull and forehead.

The rumble of the Maybach's more than twenty-five hundred kilos across the Spree Brucke drowned out the Princess's laughing protests and the loud music pouring from the saloon's radio speakers.

Von Richthofen shouted angrily and sounded the horn of the Maybach as a farmer's cart hove into sight a few car's lengths ahead. The farmer turned his head, his eyes popping. He jerked back and shouted frantically at his nag, trying to pull his wooden cart to the side of the roadway.

The Maybach swerved, nearly avoiding the farmer's cart. Only the front fender of the auto struck the rear of the light cart as

Lothar swung the vehicle around and back. The wooden slats of the cart flew before the impact of the saloon like a bundle of straws in a winter storm. The cart lifted off its crude axle and spun once in the air, then landed with shattering impact on the roadway. Farmer and horse alike lay on the cobblestones, moving their limbs feebly.

Princess Irina slid around so she could see the scene behind the still-moving saloon. Other vehicles had halted and a man had jumped out of a car and run to the aid of the injured farmer.

Von Richthofen gunned the Maybach through busy streets, settling at length to a steady rate of progress along a broad, tree-shaded thoroughfare. A steady string of curses hissed from between his teeth. He clasped the steering wheel tightly in leather-gloved fists.

"Fool," the Princess sneered. "He should be whipped for that! Why did you not stop and beat the mongrel, Lothar? Oh, you soft *Mitteleuropeans!*"

"We have no time," von Richthofen snapped back. "We are expected at the *Reichskanzlei.*"

The Princess sniffed angrily. "I hope you will at least send a messenger back for the man's name. I am sure that the paint is scratched and he may have smashed a lamp on your automobile. One must not let them get away with vandalism, Lothar."

"Petty details." Von Richthofen geared down to fourth, ran one gloved hand across his brow wiping the sweat away before it could drop into his eyes. "You are right, Princess, but I have no time for such pettiness. Here—here is the *Kanzlei.*"

He pulled the Maybach to the curb behind a glittering Graf und Stift SP8. "You see? Manfred is here waiting for us. Now we'll hear about promptitude and keeping the *Kanzler* waiting."

A gray-clad soldier leaped from his post at the entranceway of Wilhelmstrasse 75. He opened the door for the Princess Irina and helped her from the car. Von Richthofen let himself out of the driver's door, ignored the soldier's snappy salute and hustled the Princess up the steps of the *Kanzlei.* A second saluting soldier stood at the front door while a liveried lackey pulled the door open for Lothar and Irina.

Inside the *Kanzlei* a tall red-bearded man, properly dressed, paced impatiently. He whirled at the entrance of the Princess Irina and her escort, hurried across the marble floor to meet them.

"Your Highness." The equerry bent over Irina's white-gloved hand.

"Bodo," she replied, nodding.

"Captain von Richthofen." The equerry made a quarter bow.

"*Graf* Alvensleben." Von Richthofen returned the gesture curtly.

"Please to follow me. The others are already assembled. The meeting has already commenced. You should understand, Captain—we do not keep the *Kanzler* waiting."

Lothar did not offer a response.

The equerry, *Graf* Hans Bodo von Alvensleben, ushered Lothar and Irina through a high doorway into a huge room. The chamber was dominated by a single gigantic desk. Chairs, tables, windows, were all cut to larger-than-human scale. They dwarfed all who stood or sat in the room.

Over the great dark desk hung two portraits done in dark oils and framed in ornate gilt. One showed a thin, sharp-featured, prematurely white-haired man of early middle years. He wore a hussar's dress uniform, bearskin busby on one arm, the other hand resting on the hilt of a dress sabre. His tunic was covered with colorful orders and decorations.

The other portrait was of a huge, heavyset man with white muttonchop whiskers and black, piercing eyes sunk deep into a fleshy yet powerful face. His garment was a spartan field-gray military greatcoat. He wore a military cap and a single military decoration suspended by a ribbon from his collar.

The chamber was hot and stuffy despite its cavernous dimensions. Great stone hearths dominated either end of the room, and logs were piled high and burning fiercely in both.

Beneath the two portraits a thickly built man sat behind the great mahogany desk. He wore whiskers like those of the gray-clad man in the second portrait, but these whiskers were a rusty brown. His features, too, resembled those of the painted figure.

Seated across the desk from him were two more men, one in conservative civilian garb, the other in a trim uniform bearing the insignia of an aviation squadron officer.

The newcomers halted a few paces from the desk. The equerry, Count von Alvensleben, bowed to the heavyset man. "*Herr Kanzler*, I regret the tardiness with which—"

The chancellor waved him to silence. "All right, Bodo. Let us just go on."

"I regret, *mein Kanzler*... unavoidably detained..." Von Alvensleben bowed deeply. "I am sure that the *Hauptmann*... your most valuable time... our most gracious Russian guest, the Princess Lvova, the young Tsar's cousin..."

"*Bodo!*" the chancellor roared. The equerry quivered into silence.

"Bodo," the chancellor repeated softly. "Bodo, I'm not my father, you know." He gestured significantly at the portrait hanging behind his desk. "They called Otto von Bismarck the Iron Chancellor for good reason, Bodo. But what do they call Herbert von Bismarck?"

He held up one hand, gesturing to the equerry. "No, don't tell me. I think I know already, and I don't want to hear it. Let's just get on with our business."

The chancellor stood up and leaned forward, putting his weight on his two hands. "*Herr* Udet, here," he nodded his heavy head, "tells me that his aeroplane *Kondor* is ready to depart. Our two pilots, Major Baron von Richthofen and Captain von Richthofen. And our most gracious guest and passenger, the Princess Lvova."

"*Ja, mein Kanzler.*"

"And I will bring to your attention, Your Highness." The chancellor bowed slightly to Irina. "And Captain." He nodded frostily toward Lothar. "Two most important communications that were received by me this morning."

He shuffled the papers on his huge desk, found the two he sought and held them one atop the other. "The first is from His Majesty the Kaiser." The chancellor turned and looked up at the portrait of the white-haired man. "'The undertaking upon which you depart will reflect glory upon two great empires, will carry the names of Germany and of Russia, of two great dynasties, the Houses of Hohenzollern and of Romanov, to a *terra incognita*, virtually to another world. We know that you will vanquish all rivals and return in triumph and glory. May God go with you!'"

The chancellor looked at the two brothers and at the Princess. "His Majesty also sends you, as personal mementoes of himself... these." He snapped his fingers to von Alvensleben. Von Alvensleben snapped his fingers to a lackey. The lackey approached with a heavy coffer of polished wood and held it open before the chancellor.

Herbert von Bismarck took from within the coffer three short, glittering scabbards, one shellacked scarlet, the others black. He presented them to Irina, Lothar, Manfred.

With a sudden gesture Lothar yanked the dagger from its polished scabbard, hefted it once, whipped it forward so it glinted momentarily with reflected firelight before it struck the mahogany desk. The blade thudded home. The hilt swung back and forth in the room's sudden silence.

"Good," Lothar giggled, "good! It isn't a toy! Tempered steel, with a keen edge and point. Good."

He strode forward and retrieved the dagger. He slipped it back into its scabbard, and the scabbard inside his uniform.

The chancellor, pale-faced, remained seated in his chair. "The other message I have received..." he recommenced. He looked significantly at Udet and Manfred von Richthofen. They placed themselves to either side of Lothar and urged him quietly into a chair. He twisted angrily from their grip and seated himself.

"... the other message arrived from America via diplomatic code. It is from San Diego, California. Our man there has obtained information concerning the Ryan flight." The chancellor bent over his desk, bringing his eyes within inches of the scrap of memorandum paper. "The Ryan crew have assembled in San Diego." He turned his face upward, presenting the appearance of a predator crouched over its prey. He swiveled his head as if to warn interlopers away from his feast.

"Their aeroplane is complete and the mechanician Hughes has been testing it for some days. The *Spirit of San Diego* is expected to depart for the southern circumpolar route within ten days at most. Their itinerary is via Ecuador, the Chilean islands of Juan Fernandez, and Tierra del Fuego." The chancellor placed both his hands on his desk and heaved himself heavily upright. He scanned the others' faces with his deepset eyes.

"The ill effects of the One Year War will never be overcome as long as our dynastic empires live in the shadow of the western colossus. Your triumph will signal a renaissance of the imperial ideals. *Meine Herren . . . Mademoiselle . . .* I can only add my own wishes to those of His Majesty Friedrich Wilhelm."

The chancellor made a gesture indicating that the interview was at an end.

"*Ein Minute,*" Manfred von Richthofen interrupted.

The Princess Irina turned her eyes toward the older of the brothers. His features resembled those of Lothar but were of a leaner and grimmer cast. Where the younger von Richthofen's scalp was free of any hair, the elder wore his fine hair slightly longer than was customary in the imperial service. His thick eyebrows in contrast with his sallow complexion appeared as two vivid slashes. His hands were almost preternaturally long and thin. They moved continually as if with an independent life.

"*Ja?*" the chancellor blurted, surprised. "*Ja, mein Freiherr?* Baron?"

"Have we no sappers?" von Richthofen demanded. "A single bomb could assure our victory." As he spoke his hands crawled back and forth over each other like blind adversaries feeling for one another's weaknesses. "Or—have we no friends in America who could eliminate this Hughes and his crew?"

Herbert von Bismarck let out a breath like an overinflated balloon venting hydrogen. "*Ach*, Baron." The chancellor permitted himself a condescending smile. "Your father, *Freiherr* Oswald, understood the complexities and shadings of politics. You boys have been raised in a more direct manner."

"From Boelcke we learned, *mein Kanzler*," Manfred returned.

"Pounce upon the enemy!" Lothar asserted.

"From the sun!"

"From anywhere!"

"Rip him to shreds!"

"*Ach*, you're two good boys." Bismarck smiled paternally. "But you don't understand diplomacy."

"Diplomacy is the extension of war by peaceful means," Manfred quoted.

The chancellor pushed his bulk away from his desk, leaned back laughing. "*Ach*, Bodo, Bodo, you see what fine boys we are raising here? *Ach*, if only the war had lasted, what fine hunting falcons they would have grown into, hey? Well, and now instead they must train themselves as racing peregrines. *Aber*, one way or another, the dynasty will triumph.

"And the Romanovs, Your Highness." Bismarck directed this to the Princess. "All is well with Friedrich Wilhelm's dear cousins, one trusts?" Bushy eyebrows rose.

The Princess smiled icily.

"Do not pretend, Herbert. As *Kanzler* well knows, weakling Tsar alternates between doctors and priests, between priests and toys. That Alexei has lived until now is miracle of some sort. Give thanks to saints that Dowager Empress Alexandra gets along with father Prince Lvov. Together have saved crown and throne, as did from day monster Ulianov murdered poor Uncle Nicky."

"*Ja*," Bismarck sniffed, "poor Uncle Nicky."

"Well, and truckling weakling Kerensky tries to make Duma new Tsar. And if Kerensky ever goes, who will replace weakling as premier? Weasel Bronstein? Pah!"

"My poor, poor dear." Bismarck actually stood up and walked around his desk to stand beside the Princess's chair. He reached toward her with one puffy spotted hand and patted her white, carefully manicured fingers. "I think the climate of Russia is too hard for so delicate a flower as Your Highness."

"Charlottenburg would be more salubrious," the Princess conceded.

"*Ja*," Bismarck nodded. "I believe the *Prinz* Joachim was speaking recently of how charming he found your portrait, Princess."

Irina sneered. "Pewling child. What about Eitel Friedrich?"

"The Kaiser's closest brother? Princess, you are being unrealistic!"

"Lvova thinks not."

"What about Oskar, then?"

"Do not make joke, *Kanzler*. Why not Prince Eitel?"

"I am saving him for a more direct connection, Your Highness. We have to strengthen our ties with the Saxe-Coburgs. Germany is an Atlantic power as well as a continental one!"

"All right. Adalbert, then. Although Lvova does not care for way Adalbert sits to horse."

"*Nein*. Adalbert I have slated for Scandinavia, as the Princess Viktoria Luise despises cold climates and insists on my securing an Iberian husband for her." He rubbed his face. "*Aber*, Princess, then what about August Wilhelm?"

"*Kanzler* jokes again. Augie Willie lisps. Princess thinks that one wears dresses in private apartments. Will settle for no less than Adalbert!"

Bismarck blew his breath. "Let us see how this race concludes, Your Highness. If the *Kondor* returns first your dowry will of course be increased with a share of Mrs. Woodhull Martin's money."

"Oh, come, *Kanzler*, do not talk like Hebrew lender!"

"I apologize, Highness. We stood here haggling so, I must have made a mistake."

"Enough, *mein Herr!*" Furious, her cheeks paler even than her nearly white hair, the Princess stood and made for the exit. The *Kanzler*, flaming-cheeked, let her go. *Graf* von Alvensleben ran after the Princess while engineer Udet and the elder and younger von Richthofens conferred anxiously with Bismarck.

Von Alvensleben managed to reassemble the quartet of Irina, Lothar, Manfred, and Udet in his own chambers within the *Kanzlei*. The chancellor had been called away on a mission of state, Bodo apologized. It remained vital that the *Kondor* leave from Tempelhof with utmost dispatch. He would personally accompany the three who were to traverse the terrestrial disk, along with engineer Udet, to the aerodrome.

Manfred von Richthofen volunteered the use of his Graf und Stift automobile for the purpose. He swung himself into the driver's seat and sparked the powerful Austrian-built engine into life.

At Tempelhof the Baron propelled his automobile past guardposts, horn blaring. The equerry waved frantically from the rear window to dissuade guarding soldiers from firing after the automobile. Von Alvensleben kept reaching blindly to grasp Manfred's shoulder while pleading with him to slow the Graf und Stift. Von Richthofen merely laughed.

With a screech of brakes the Baron brought the auto skidding to a halt before the hangar where Udet's *Kondor* was being fitted for the circumpolar dash. Shortly the two brothers inspected the aeroplane's mechanical features while the Princess Irina, von Alvensleben at her elbow, toured its cabin.

The engineer Udet dashed between the two parties, proudly explaining a mechanical detail to the brothers, pointing out a luxurious appurtenance to the Princess.

The party reassembled in the cabin of the *Kondor*. Lothar von Richthofen grumbled angrily. "I do not know why we agreed to this flight at all, *Bruder*."

"What!" Manfred returned. "For the glory of the Reich!"

"*Ach!*" Lothar spat. "What glory? To fly this fancified contraption, this plush aerial omnibus? Rather would I pilot at least a Gotha bomber, or even—*Gott im Himmel!*—a Zeppelin, provided it should carry bombs and guns. But my heart is in the killer aeroplane. *Ach*, to get back into a Pfalz or a Walfisch or a Fokker, with some foreign swine in the sights of my guns! The joy of seeing an enemy spin away in flames!"

Ernst Udet shook his head. "I would gladly take your place sharing the duties with *Freiherr* Manfred, Lothar. The chancellor himself chose the crew for this flight. The chancellor—in consultation with an even more illustrious personage! But if I had been permitted . . ."

He shook his head.

"Lvova will not be burden," the Princess volunteered. "And will add, Lothar, having experienced such management of automobile, that Princess is not eager to enjoy such piloting of Monsieur Udet's obviously excellent aeroplane."

"Now," Udet took over in a businesslike tone, "let us make one more check of the loading of the *Kondor*, before we study again the projected route."

He marched to the rear of the cabin and tugged open a door to a large storage compartment.

"In here," he indicated, "will be carried extra fuel, clothing, propellors, spare mechanical parts. Of course, tools. Also, food and potable water."

Manfred von Richthofen brushed against Udet and stood gazing into the compartment. "I will personally oversee the stowage of weapons and ammunition. Such may be needed—eh, Lothar, *Bruder?*" The Baron chuckled. "One never knows who—or what—one will encounter in *terra incognita.*" He fingered the black-scabbarded dagger that the Kaiser had sent. "His Majesty's personal memento is most appreciated" (this to Bodo von Alvensleben), "but one might run up against anything from a polar bear to a tropical reptile, hey? Not to mention savages in need of a demonstration in the art of civilized warfare."

Udet nodded agreement. "*Gut!*" The engineer ducked his head and stepped carefully into the stowage compartment of the aeroplane. He laid his hand on a very large carton. "And this—is my proudest innovation. Come ahead. You can all fit in here with a little effort.

"This carton," he beamed, "contains a Zeppelin!"

Both von Richthofens roared with laughter. "Wonderful, Udet, wonderful! You remind me of the fellow who expected a second deluge and built an ark in his basement. When the water came, there was no way to get the ark outside!"

Udet shook his head. "I am quite serious, von Richthofen. There is presently no way to carry enough fuel in an aeroplane to complete the circumpolar voyage. We have already allowed for all the petrol that *Kondor* can lift. To carry any more, I would have had to build an even larger aircraft. That would require still more petrol, and so on, *ad infinitum.*"

"So?" The Princess shook her head scornfully. "Are telling crew that passage is impossible?"

"By no means, Your Highness." Udet bowed slightly. "Your Highness graciously brings us back to the need for an auxiliary transport." Again he patted the carton. "You may find a source of petrol once you reach the other side. The *Kondor* will leave Tempelhof with enough petrol to reach Novaya Zemlya.

"Once there you will make landfall and be greeted by the staff of our base. The joint co-imperial installation there will provide replenishment of your petrol supply, and you will again depart. The *Kondor* possesses enough range to carry you through Symmes' Hole and well onto the far side of the terrestrial disk—but not sufficient to reach the South Rim and return!

"It is my hope—and that of the chancellor, not to mention a still more illustrious personage—that the natives of the far side will possess enough civilization to supply you with petrol for your continuing voyage. But in case they do not, you need merely uncrate this Zeppelin.

"I have anticipated Your Higness, *Freiherr* Manfred, *Hauptmann* Lothar, and have already furnished the Zeppelin with a name, that of the noble order to which a successful race will assure your elevation. It is called the *Black Eagle*.

"You will assemble the Zeppelin. It is lifted by hydrogen gas, of which a large cylinder is provided. It is propelled by a system of aerial screws turned by an electrical motor. The battery is provided with a generator that you may operate by manual or pedal effort, to maintain the charge."

The Princess shook her head in cold disdain. "Why, Monsieur Udet, do racers not simply travel in Zeppelin to start with, if balloon is superior to aeroplane?"

Udet bowed again. "Because, Mademoiselle, there is no way that a Zeppelin could survive the swirling air currents of Symmes' Hole. Otherwise—perhaps. Although you must be aware that aeroplanes are far faster than Zeppelins, and you will be in competition with the *Spirit of San Diego*."

Irina nodded her understanding. "May Princess propose motto for party. To cite words once spoken by Imperial Majesty, father of present All-Highest Kaiser. Majesty said, 'Whosoever opposes me—I shall smash!'"

Manfred von Richthofen, Lothar von Richtofen, Ernst Udet, Hans Bodo von Alvensleben responded in unison—

"*Viel Glück!*"

"*Alles Gute!*"

"*Gott mit uns!*"

"*Hals und Beinbruch!*"

An English-speaker might have summarized their wishes—*break a leg!*

"Are you sure, Swede?" Howard Hughes asked the question, but he already knew the answer. If he hadn't, he would not have been settled in the copilot's seat, however unhappily, strapped in and running his dark eyes over the instruments for the hundredth time.

"Amy—all set?" Lindbergh asked. He had not bothered to answer Hughes.

Amelia Earhart looked up from the navigation chart tacked to the flimsy board in her lap. "Ready as I'll ever be, Swede! Things were never like this in Kansas!"

Lindbergh leaned from the window of the Ryan and signaled to the business-suited man standing in front of the plane. Don Hall had personally come down to the field to swing the prop of the plane he had designed. Lindy pulled himself back into the cabin, rocking the plane slightly. Hall reached as high as he could, grasped the polished duralumin propellor, flung one leg waist-high for leverage and swung the blade.

The switches were already set... the cylinders primed... the fuel lines open.

The Whirlwind radial coughed once and then roared into life. Don Hall jumped away from the scythelike duralumin blades. Ryan workers knelt beside the monoplane's fuselage, waiting to pull the chocks from under her tires. Two more ground-crewmen stood at the rear of the plane holding its tail.

Lindy eyed the tach and oil-pressure meter, adjusted the carb to lean out the mixture as the Whirlwind warmed up. When the engine had settled into a smooth drone Lindy again leaned from the window. He shouted to the ground crew, pulled back and let in the throttle.

The Ryan seemed to strain at its handlers, quivering with eagerness to roll across the tarmac.

At Lindy's wave the crewmen pulled the chocks, released the *Spirit*'s tail. The plane rolled forward, gathering momentum with every yard as it accelerated toward the end of the runway.

Lindy pulled back on the stick. The *Spirit* lifted her nose into sparkling Pacific morning air. Her wheels rose from the tarmac and she headed up, up into the early sunlight, banked to set a course southward and settled to a steady pace.

"Better take the wheels up, Howard." Those were the first words spoken since the Ryan had lifted from her runway near the factory-hangar minutes before. Hughes unbuckled himself from the copilot's chair and knelt at the side of the cabin. Amelia Earhart leaned the opposite way to keep the plane balanced.

Hughes seized a polished crank that was clamped to the bulkhead. He inserted it into a socket and began to turn. "I wish we'd had more time," he grunted as he turned.

"Can't be helped," Lindbergh snapped.

"Ground tests are all good and well," Hughes panted. "But this ship has too many new gadgets to make me happy. These retractable wheels are cute but what if we forget to take 'em up—or worse yet, to put 'em down again? And the boat-hull fuselage. Bill Bowlus says she's watertight. Hell, I sat through the tests and I *know* she is. But we never actually ran the *Spirit* in the bay. And the folding wings—I know they work, but they still worry me a little."

Amelia looked up from her charts. "Nothing we can do about that now, is there, Howard?" She called to the pilot, "Lindy."

Lindbergh grunted.

"I've got our bearing for Guayaquil." She called out the compass setting for him.

"All right," Lindy replied. "I'll put up the earth inductor." He reached forward and adjusted the instrument. "Might as well settle back now. We've got a lot of hours of flying to do."

Howard Hughes clamped the wheel crank back against the bulkhead. He slid carefully into the copilot's seat and belted himself in. Amelia leaned back and turned her face toward the ceiling. Through square mica panels the sky shone a spotless, brilliant blue. Over the Mexican mainland to the east the sun was a perfect dazzling globe.

"I wish we could see straight down." Amelia lowered her eyes and checked the charts. "As long as we're on this side, at least, it'd be nice to take a visual check. There ought to be plenty of landmarks."

"Next time," Hughes grunted. "We should've told Hall to put windows in the floor, too."

Relaxed now at the controls of the Ryan, Lindy grinned broadly. "You know, that's not a bad idea. But we can get a look anyhow. Hang on!" He kicked the plane into a slow, banking circle and pointed from the window. "There's Baja!"

"For sure," Hughes grunted.

"Okay." Amelia held her pencil point against the chart, looked out the window, then back at the chart. "That little inlet has to be Bahia Magdalena. There's a good-sized fishing fleet down there. Yep! See the sails?"

Lindy dropped the plane a few thousand feet and circled over the fishing boats. A few fishermen stood gaping at the unfamiliar sight. Others waved, then went back to their nets. Lindy set the plane back onto a level course and slowly began regaining altitude.

"Anybody hungry?" Amelia asked.

Hughes said he was ravenous. Lindy said he could stand a little snack.

Amelia broke out a basket of provisions and handed each of them a sandwich. She settled back in her own seat and took a healthy bite of chicken salad on rye.

Lindbergh leaned over slightly, put the Ryan into a gentle bank. "Nothing but water, folks. The coast of Ecuador should be coming up pretty soon. You think you can get our position again, Amelia?"

Amy peered up through the mica squares. "Sure thing. Just hold her steady while I get the sextant ready, and I'll shoot."

Less than a minute later she was jotting figures on the edge of her chart, then reading them out for Lindbergh.

"Fine," the pilot gave back. "The earth inductor compass is right on line. Ecuador should come in sight any minute. Howard, you want to try the superhet? I don't know if anybody's listening, down in Guayaquil, but it should be worth a try."

Hughes flicked a switch on the control panel and warmed up the *Spirit*'s radio. He reached under the panel and pulled out a pair of earphones and a mike.

Lindy kept the Ryan steadily on her course while Hughes alternately spoke and listened. After a little bit Lindy reached behind him and tapped Amelia with one hand. She followed his gesture as he pointed. The coastline of South America loomed on the horizon like a long black storm-front.

Hughes flicked the superhet into silence and put away the earphones and mike. "Guayaquil's expecting us," he said. "No word from San Diego, though. But the consul wants to give us a fancy dinner and put us up overnight while the *Spirit*'s refueled."

"Oh, boy," Lindbergh grumbled. "What'd you tell 'em, Howard?"

"What would *you* have told 'em?"

"I would have said, Thanks a lot but we'll settle for a handshake and a candy bar at the airport. We're in a race, not making the grand tour. And besides, every minute the *Spirit* sits on the ground she's vulnerable to—let's say, some suspicious accident."

"Yup," Hughes answered huskily. "Makes sense to me, Swede."

"What do you mean, makes sense? What did you *tell* 'em, for Pete's sake?"

Hughes laughed boisterously. "That's exactly what I told 'em. The consul was standing right there and he told the radio op to say he was let down but he understood. He'll meet us at the airstrip with candy bars all around."

Lindy grinned. "What's the strip like, did he say?"

"Yep." Hughes turned in his seat. "Amy, if you can bring us

in right over the harbor at Guayaquil, Swede here can lift the *Spirit* a bit and we'll be right on line with the local soccer field. There's a schoolboy game going on right now. We ought to get there—*hmmm*—let me check my wristwatch. Right at halftime.

"Charlie, all you have to do is bring 'er in and drop 'er over the goalposts. Consul says there's a nice headwind for us to land against. Three hundred feet should be plenty of roll, eh?"

Lindy nodded. "Sounds good. They'll clear the field for us?"

"Unless some of the local goats wander onto it."

"Say, I've dodged everything from haystacks to longhorns in different kinds of crates. Guess I can avoid a couple of billy goats if I have to."

"Hah! And what if they want to butt?"

Lindy shrugged. "We can always share our candy bars with 'em."

Amelia called an azimuth and approximate distance to the harbor. She leaned between Lindbergh and Hughes and checked the compass readings against her charts, humming with satisfaction. She laid her chart-board aside. "Everything's right on target!"

"Say, Howard." Lindy tapped his copilot on the shoulder. "Guess what! Don't forget to wind the wheels down before we land or we're going to ruin a lot of Billy Bowlus's hard work!"

"You know, we could just leave 'em down, Swede. Don Hall put in the retractor gear mainly so we could keep 'em out of the water when we use the boat hull. Doesn't hurt the wheels to have 'em down when we're flying."

"Adds to drag, Howard. You know that—you've flown racers. That would slow us down, burn up fuel..."

Hughes grumbled an *okay* and bent to crank the landing wheels into position.

The *Spirit of San Diego* swooped low over the harbor at Guayaquil, took one trial pass over the soccer field while boys in bright shirts and short pants scattered to the sidelines, then circled and came in for her landing. Lindy brought the monoplane low over a stand of tropical vegetation, dropped nearly to ground level, hopped over the white-painted goal posts and dropped softly onto thick grass.

The Ryan rolled half the length of the field, slowed and stopped. The metal propellor whirled to a halt.

The three fliers climbed from their cabin onto the green soccer field, welcoming the change from their little plane's confining cabin. They looked up to see a dignified man in a business suit advancing across the grass, a broad grin on his face, a few of the soccer players trailing in his wake.

The consul shook hands with the fliers and said he was sorry they couldn't spend the night. "You know, we don't get many visitors here. The white community isn't very large—a few traders, a little French shipping concern left over from the old de Lesseps days. Couple of Yankee import-export offices. That's my real job, you know. The consular thing is mostly honorary.

"And a little German bakery *cum* restaurant and candy shop. *Herr* Hentsch was going to do up a banquet in your honor, but he understands your need to get off. He sent this with his compliments."

The consul produced an elaborately wrapped box of candy, presented it to Amelia with a half-serious bow. She accepted it with similar ceremony. "Thank you—and please thank *Herr* Hentsch for us."

Behind the consul she could see some of the soccer players pressing forward. A couple of tame goats struggled between the boys, curious or perhaps attracted by the odor of the candies even through their heavy wrapping.

Amelia looked at the boys and the goats. To Howard and Lindy she stage-whispered, "I suppose we could save these for later, but they're so cute." She inclined her head toward the youngsters and the animals. "Why don't we share the treat?"

She opened the fancy paper wrapping and lifted the lid. "Oh, what lovely candies!"

Without warning she was sent flying, the box knocked from her hand. She sprawled on the grass. The consul leaped to help her back to her feet, babbling apologies and regrets.

The goat that had knocked the box from Amelia's hand and sent her tumbling onto the grass was standing over the spilled candies, his head lowered, eyes darting challenge. His horns were mute warning to anyone who thought of trying to take away his prize.

"Okay, Billy, you win," Amelia laughed.

As if he understood her words, the goat lowered his head and picked up the largest bonbon, paper cup and all. He chewed meditatively while his audience looked on. Suddenly the goat raised his head as if he heard some distant summons. He lifted his tail. His legs stiffened.

He arched his back, looking astonishingly like a frightened but angry alley cat. A strange sound emerged from his throat, something half a growl and half a moan.

Without another sign he toppled sideways, twitched once and lay stiff and still on the ground.

Howard Hughes knelt beside the motionless animal. He rolled back the goat's eyelid, felt its chest, listened for a sign of heartbeat with his big ear pressed against the animal's bony chest.

The consul fluttered his hands, circling the others, chattering senselessly.

The nearest schoolboy, still wearing his soccer uniform, had picked up the confectioner's box and was carefully retrieving the spilled chocolates, fitting them back into their places. He came to a particularly fancy and inviting confection and instead of placing it in the box conveyed it toward his mouth.

Like a rocket Howard Hughes launched himself from the grass. He plummeted into the boy with one shoulder, striking out at the candy at the same time. The box tumbled, the succulent piece of candy flew through the air. The boy doubled over, his wind knocked from him. Hughes and the boy tumbled to the grass in a tangle of arms and legs.

"*Qué pa-pasó?*" the boy gasped, struggling to regain his breath.

"That goat was poisoned!" Hughes shouted.

"*Las dulces,*" the boy stammered. "*Me dió un golpe solamente por las dulces!*"

"What's the kid saying?" Lindy asked the consul.

"I don't know." He wrung his hands. "I don't speak Spanish."

"You don't sp—?"

"Never mind," Amelia interrupted. "We got a lot of Spanish and Portuguese at the settlement house. The boy is frightened.

He says he hit him just because he was taking the candy. I think he's afraid of being branded a thief."

"That candy was poisoned," Hughes blurted. "One bite and the kid would've been dead as a doornail. Or as that goat." He jerked his thumb over his shoulder.

Amy squatted in front of the boy and spoke a few sentences in Spanish.

The boy's eyes popped open and the blood drained from his face. "*Ponzoña!*" the boy gasped. "*Las dulces son venenosas! Ay!*" He jumped to his feet, ran to stand where candy lay scattered and ground the largest piece into the grass with his foot. He ran from the field shouting to the other soccer players.

"I suppose the game is canceled," the consul moaned. "Too bad. Our boys were trouncing Santa Isabella. Such a pity."

Hughes's dark-browed countenance grew crimson. "Listen here, Mr. Yankee Trader!" He towered over the dumpy consul, his great fists planted on his hips. "What the hell's going on? You come out here and greet us like butter won't melt in your mouth. And then you hand us a box of poisoned goodies! If it hadn't been for that poor dumb billy goat Miss Earhart would be dead by now. Or maybe we all would."

Charles Lindbergh joined the confrontation. "Maybe the idea wasn't to poison anybody—here! Maybe we were supposed to take the candy up in the *Spirit of San Diego* with us. Imagine two of us dozing in the night, the third one piloting the ship, reaching for a taste of candy for a pick-me-up. And—*zzzt!*" He drew his finger across his throat.

The consul flapped his hands. "I'm dreadfully sorry. But you surely can't imagine that we would try to . . . to *murder* you! Really! It must have been some sort of dreadful accident or mistake. Are you sure the poor goat is dead? Maybe it died from natural causes. There are diseases here in the tropics. Maybe it had a heart attack. Maybe—"

"Smell its mouth," Hughes told him.

The consul took two steps sideways, toward the goat. He stood looking at it, shook himself and turned back to Hughes. "I'll—I'll take your word. But what killed the beast? How do you know it was poisoned?"

"Odor of burnt almonds on its mouth. Here." Hughes bent and picked up another large bonbon. They clustered around while he turned it slowly in the bright afternoon sunlight. "Let's see if this one's been doctored," Hughes said.

"You—you aren't going to—to—" The consul made motions of popping a sweet into his mouth. His expression was that of a man who had bit into a lemon thinking it a tangerine.

"Now just look," Hughes said. "If anybody wanted to poison the person who ate this chocolate, he *might* spread the poison on the outside. Not a good idea, though. It might rub off. Or the intended victim might notice it by sight. Or..."

He passed the candy beneath the noses of the others.

"...by smell." He shook his head. "No. Better to inject the cyanide with a hypodermic. But that would leave a hole in the chocolate. A tiny one, sure, but why take the risk? If the poisoner is the candy-maker, he could simply add the cyanide to the filling, then add the chocolate coating. No sign. No smell, even: the chocolate seals the filling completely. Let's check."

He broke the candy in half, exposing purple gummy stuff. "Too bad, I love raspberry." He raised the candy to his nose, nodded in satisfaction, then held it for the others to sniff.

The consul shook his head in distress. "I don't understand. We have such a close little community. Who could have done this?"

Charles Lindbergh offered a wan smile. "As they say in all the mystery novels, the finger of suspicion seems to point at *Herr* Hentsch."

"But—but he is a pillar of the white community!"

Lindy shrugged. "Your problem, then. Handle it your way. But I don't think I'd take my dinner at *Herr* Hentsch's wiener-schnitzel parlor. At any rate, what I think we'd better do..." He put his hand on Howard Hughes's shoulder. "...is get the *Spirit* refueled, and get out of here. I don't think the climate at Guayaquil is good for aviators."

"Right!" Hughes nodded vigorously. "You and Amy can try and rest a little. You did all the work getting us here. I'll superintend the refueling. Very closely."

He turned once more to face the consul. "*Herr* Hentsch doesn't run the local gasoline concession, too, does he?"

"No, oh, no," the consul fluttered. "That belongs to, er, a consortium. There's a Standard Oil representative for the region, and the local manager is a Frenchman from the de Lesseps interests. I'm afraid, in fact, that Monsieur Chirol and *Herr* Hentsch are the only members of our little community who don't get along with each other. Something about the One Year War. Really quite beyond me."

"Okay. Sounds promising. Lindy, Amy, why don't you just take it easy. We still have some food in the *Spirit* if you don't like the local grub."

He turned back again. "Okay, Mr. Consul. Where's this Monsieur Chirol and his gas station?"

Lindy spun the prop himself when they were ready to leave Guayaquil. Howard Hughes sat at the controls of the *Spirit;* Amelia sat in the copilot's seat studying the instruments. A group of soccer-uniformed schoolboys working under Lindy's supervision had lifted the *Spirit*'s tail and turned the monoplane 180 degrees.

Hughes patted Amelia's hand. "So far so good. I feared the Swede would have a conniption fit when he met you."

"I don't think he had a chance," Amy grinned. "He's been too busy to get upset over flying with a woman." She leaned from the cabin window and waved to Lindy standing with his crew of volunteers.

To Hughes she said, "I think I'll just taxi back to the other end of the field. If I'm going to fly this plane—"

"That's great with me!" Hughes assented.

"—I'll feel a lot better about it if I've handled her a little first. Even from the second seat. You're sure Charles can handle navigation?"

"Oh, yeah. He went to army flight school. They really bang that into the cadets. I don't know how *happy* he'll be, playing third fiddle. But we'll vote him down, hey?"

Amelia looked around to make sure the ground-crew were safely away from the Ryan's prop. She gunned the Wright Whirlwind and the monoplane rolled along the soccer field. Three-quarters of the way to the goalposts she cut the engine to an idle and let the plane roll to a stop.

The soccer players again turned the tail, prompted by much shouting and waving from Charles. He shook hands with each boy and climbed into the cabin.

He stood by the doorway, staring at Howard Hughes in the pilot's seat and Amelia Earhart in the copilot's.

For seconds the only sound was the low drone of the Whirlwind and the occasional coughing quiver of the powerful engine at idle.

Hughes reached forward and ran up the throttle.

"Better close the door and have a seat," he called over his shoulder. "We don't want to lose you on takeoff, Swede!"

Lindy nodded. After a few seconds he said, "I see I've been elected navigator."

"Say, you're not going to let me down, are you, Swede? I told Amy here that you could handle the job. Don't make me out a liar, will you?"

Lindbergh chuckled ruefully. "All right, Howard. I guess I can handle the charts."

Chapter 4

The Udet *Kondor* circled over Tempelhof Aerodrome a single time. From the ground her designer watched through field glasses as the great four-engined aircraft leveled from its bank and turned northward, toward Prussia, the Arctic Ocean, and Novaya Zemlya. Once the *Kondor* was out of sight, Udet returned to the hangar. He placed a telephone call to the *Kanzlei* and reported that all was well.

Aboard the aeroplane, Manfred von Richthofen, clad in a flying suit of gray leather and mouton fur, handled the controls. Behind him his brother Lothar and the Princess Irina Lvova engaged in conversation. "Can imagine, Lothar," the Princess complained, "fool upstart *Kanzler* offering Lvova, *Prinz* Joachim for husband! Such insult! As if Princess were younger daughter of petty nobleman. Princess is sole offspring of Prince Lvov!"

"I never mix in politics," the younger von Richthofen replied lackadaisically. "Just give me a good machine! Let me get my hands on the controls of a fighting aircraft or a powerful motorcar. Or let me caress the cold steel and polished wood of a fine firearm. *That* is life!"

He reached to his side and undogged the holster that hung at his hip. He wore a flying suit similar to his brother's. Each wore also a gunbelt with holster and clips of ammunition. Lothar pulled his automatic pistol from its holster and caressed the polished barrel.

The Princess watched through narrowed eyes. The sun had set but with the moon in full disk bright light reflected from the snow-covered territories beneath the *Kondor*. The aeroplane droned ever northward, its four Siemens-Schuckert engines singing a song of dedication and efficiency. Through the *Kondor*'s broad wings they transmitted a steady vibration to the plane's metal fuselage.

The cabin was lighted by small electric bulbs placed so as to make possible the reading of the aeroplane's instruments even at night. By carefully monitoring the *Kondor*'s altimeter, airspeed indicator, and compasses, Manfred von Richthofen defied the hands of the clock and guided the aircraft as confidently by darkness as he did by daylight.

"You were sorry that *Einjahrkrieg*, One Year War, ended, Captain." Irina dug at Lothar von Richthofen, prodding for an answer that she could store away and save for an occasion to use it to advantage. "All men profess hatred of war, but in hearts, all love war."

"*Nein*, Princess. I do not pretend to hate war," Lothar replied. "You may be right about most men. *Nur Gott weiss*, there are peacemongers aplenty. But not I. Every Prussian is a soldier in his heart. From the Kaiser downward. This is our tradition. This is our pride.

"When the *Krieg* began, I was a little *Kadett*. My brother Manfred," he gestured carelessly with his pistol, "was already *ein Leutnant*. He was already learning to fly from the great Boelcke. I was practicing close order drill, Mauser on my shoulder and spiked helmet on my skull. *Aber*, every soldier an infantryman, hey?

"Well, but when the old Kaiser gave word to march, in 1912, we were not ready. Another two or three years and the war would have come out differently. Today the emperors would stand atop Europe, rather than the parliaments. *Ach*, Princess! A mistake in timing! And it could have been a better war, and a longer one. Why, by the time I had my own *Dreifachdecker* the war was nearly finished. I am a better pilot than..."

He looked past the Princess to his brother at the controls of the *Kondor*. Lothar lowered his voice and leaned closer. "I am a better fighter pilot than *Freiherr* von Richthofen. An accident of birth gives him the title. As it gave him opportunity to win his spurs in combat, while I still flew trainers. I had so few chances against the enemy—but I used them well! I won the title of *Fleischer*. The butcher! Yes! I wore it with pride! I struck terror in the hearts of the enemy!"

"And big brother? Was brother not known as *Jäger*, hunter?"

"He was."

"Yet little brother preferred other title."

"Rather than *Freiherr?* Baron? Oh, I see, Princess! You mean, butcher rather than hunter. *Aber, ja! Freiherr* Manfred kills always with coldness and precision. He misses the point of war, the point of killing. To kill with a red rage, not a cold calculation, that is the meaning of war. Our line descended from the berserkers of the north, not the calculating Caesars of Rome who could issue a command and wash their hands of responsibility. The hands of a killer must be red with the blood of his victim!"

He raised his fingers before his eyes, still clutching the pistol in one hand. The Princess raised her glance, as if the butcher's hands actually dripped with gore. She fixed her eyes on a point above his head.

"Lvova is cold," the Princess announced. She stood and drew the fur-lined hood of her heavy flying coat over her nearly white hair. In the dim illumination provided by the instrument lights she seemed a pale, almost ice-blue silhouette, slender and graceful as a translucent stalactite in a frozen cavern.

Lothar von Richthofen seemed to forget the Princess and all his surroundings. He lowered his pistol to the lap of his thick flying suit and gazed at the weapon. His abstracted expression seemed tinctured with affection, the first he had exhibited since the takeoff of the *Kondor* from Tempelhof.

Princess Irina flapped her arms a few times to warm herself. She crossed the cabin and plumped her form into the seat beside that of Manfred von Richthofen. He turned his face toward her and nodded, then returned to flying the aeroplane.

The Princess looked out the window. The moon was past its zenith but still rode high in the night sky. Beneath the plane rugged mountains reached upward as if to tear at the *Kondor*'s belly with jagged claws of granite.

"You will explain to Princess, please, *Kondor*'s progress, Baron."

Von Richthofen made a sound deep in his throat, as if he were suppressing an expression of anger. After a moment of silence he spoke.

"We have passed over the Baltic Sea and the Gulf of Bothnia. Finland is behind us. We are crossing now the Kola Peninsula. If Your Highness will look down you will see shortly some lights."

She shook her head. "Do not see lights."

"Very shortly. *Herr* Udet arranged for the lighting of a beacon at Murmansk. That will be our last overland transit mark. From there we will cross the Barents Sea on the last leg of our flight to Novaya Zemlya."

"*Freiherr* forgets," Irina demurred. "Murmansk is not property of Imperial Majesty Kaiser Friedrich Wilhelm. Is territory of Tsar. Baron should have arranged for beacon through embassy of Majesty Tsar Alexei."

"I am sure *Herr* Udet did so."

"Princess should have been informed."

"Perhaps the arrangement was made after we were airborne, Princess. Or perhaps Your Highness was too busy to notice, riding around the countryside in a butcher's wagon."

Irina hissed at the insult. "All shall be resolved when *Kondor* returns to Europe!"

Manfred von Richthofen did not respond to the comment. Instead he leaned forward and peered through the corner window of the sealed cabin. Looking down, he swung the heavy aircraft into a smooth bank. "Have a look, Lothar," he called to his brother. "Our Junker precision did not fail us! Murmansk is below!"

Lothar slid his revolver back into its holster and strode to the side of the cabin. He peered downward at the huge bonfire glowing in the midst of a field of white.

"Why don't they use an electric beacon?" he muttered.

"Probably they don't have one. Primitive technology. A half-civilized empire, *mein Junge*. Be grateful that a telegraph line reaches to this Godforsaken city, or there would have been no beacon at all."

"So?" Lothar shrugged.

"So? Then we couldn't see the city, we could not check our course for precision!"

"*Ach!*" Lothar threw back his head and roared with laughter. "*Bruder! Bruder!*" He shook his head. "You lack the confidence of a Junker. You're lucky that poor Oswald Boelcke didn't survive the war to hear you speak so.

"If your navigation is competent, you need no beacon to tell you that Murmansk is below. Don't fly like a weakling! The *Kondor* needs no beacons!"

"Enough quarreling," the Princess interjected.

"Perhaps!" Manfred leveled the plane and straightened its course to the northeast. "All that we will pass over for several hours is frozen sea. The next land will be Novaya Zemlya, and no question of their being prepared for us. There are German as well as Russian forces manning the station there. They will be ready with fuel and supplies when we arrive."

"Your confidence is comforting."

"The Kaiser's fleet will have received word by wireless, even if the Tsar's has not."

"Lvova possesses good appetite," the Princess announced. "Will accept small serving of caviar if gentlemen please."

"We have no servants on board, madame. You will have to serve yourself."

The Princess stalked to the *Kondor*'s tightly furnished galley.

Manfred von Richthofen summoned his brother to the copilot's seat. He pointed to the surface of the Barents Sea. "Pack ice, *Bruder*. Amazing that our fleet can operate here at all! But Admiral von Tirpitz sent word by wireless of successful passage."

"*Ja.*" The younger von Richthofen nodded. "A wonder, also, that von Tirpitz did not send an *Unterseeboot* force to attempt the circumpolar achievement. Of course," his face moved in a rictus that might almost have been a grin, "I have no complaint. If the

U-boats had been used for this voyage, we would have lost our opportunity. Still . . ."

Manfred shook his head. Too much ice near the *Nordhoehle*. "*Ach*, Lothar, you too should have spent more time studying the reports and less time wooing that Slavic icewoman." He tossed a gesture with his head. He kept his voice low. "And at the Hole itself—the mad Russian Sikorsky flew across it with his great *Mourometz* bomber. He even took photographers with him, and returned with reports and pictures."

"*Ja, ja, ja, Bruder.*" Lothar's right hand toyed absently with the latch of his holster. "I have seen the reports furnished by the Tsar's ambassador. Where the *Symmeshoehle* opens there is a steady rush of water spinning that would destroy a ship. Including an *Unterseeboot*. Nor could a Zeppelin live in the endless storm inside the *Hoehle*. So we must travel in *this*." He struck the inner fuselage paneling with his open hand.

"I would prefer to fly in a Fokker or a Pfalz."

"*Ich auch, Bruder*. I also."

At Novaya Zemlya they landed safely on a field cleared by squads of German and Russian sailors pressed into duty using shovels and spreading bucketsful of cinders.

The base commander was a captain in the naval service of the tsarist empire. His opposite number was a commander in the navy of the Kaiser. They personally greeted the *Kondor*, standing beside the temporary runway as the aeroplane dropped from the Arctic sky and rolled deliberately to a halt, its four powerful engines kicking up clouds of ice crystals and cinders in its wake.

A squad of sailors unrolled a carpet to the door of the *Kondor* and raised salutes as the two officers marched together to the aeroplane. The door of the *Kondor* opened and a bulky figure, unrecognizable in massive dark flying suit and fleece-lined helmet, clambered out. The figure was followed by another, slightly smaller and dressed in a bulky white suit, then a third, in a dark outfit matching that of the first.

The three travelers, looking like bloated Martians, stood at the end of the red carpet. The Russian naval captain stepped forward.

The Princess Irina extended her thickly gloved hand and the officer bowed over it, then rose and returned the salutes of the brothers von Richthofen. The ceremony was repeated by the Prussian *Fregattenkapitän*.

Without an audible word the party of five turned and passed between ranks of Russian and German sailors, who closed in behind them, rolling up the carpet as they trudged through the frigid night to the shack where the naval officers had awaited the *Kondor*'s arrival.

Inside the hut the newcomers doffed gloves and helmets but kept on their bulky suits and fleece-lined flying boots. A potbellied stove, stoked to the full with precious coal, struggled in vain to warm the interior of the shack. Enlisted men in tsarist and imperial German uniforms stood at attention, waiting to obey the commands of their respective officers.

"Princess," the Russian officer spoke, bowing low. "The Little Father himself has communicated his greetings. We admire the incomparable courage of one such as yourself, in this great undertaking for the glory of Mother Russia. If there is anything I can offer for your comfort, or any requirements for the performance of your staff..."

The Princess nodded. "A glass of tea, please. And some *piroshkies*. All I have eaten for hours is a meagre portion of somewhat stale eggs."

The captain snapped his fingers and two sailors disappeared to prepare the Princess's repast.

The captain turned to address his Prussian associate. "Perhaps these two aeroplane-drivers need nourishment also. Do you want to send them to the sailors' mess?"

The *Fregattenkapitän*'s eyebrows rose and his pale skin flushed. "Captain," he said, half under his breath, "these 'aeroplane-drivers' are nobles of the German empire and officers of the King and Kaiser's army! I present Major *Freiherr* von Richthofen and *Kapitan* von Richthofen. Both heroes of the *Einjahrkrieg!*"

The Russian officer nodded. "Very well, they may remain with us. I suppose this is as near to an officers' wardroom as we can obtain in such a place."

The *Fregattenkapitän* smiled at the brothers. "*Etwas Schnaps, Flie-*

ger. And some good German food. Come!" He repeated the Russian's gestures and this time two German sailors left the room. "*Freiherr*," he continued, "we have wireless contact with our ships, standing as far north as they can travel."

Manfred nodded.

"They report snow and wind. I suggest, *Freiherr*, that you depart as quickly as you can. Your aircraft is now being fueled. A few minutes to warm yourselves and eat. Or else, the storm is coming up, you will have to stay until it passes."

The brothers conferred briefly.

"How long will the storm last, *Fregattenkapitän?*"

The officer rubbed his chin. "Probably one day. But sometimes, so near the *Symmeshoehle*, *Freiherr*—two, three days. Even longer."

"Then we must leave."

"I can order the men to protect your aeroplane. They can draw tarpaulins over it, tie down to protect from winds."

"*Nein*, *Fregattenkapitän*, *danke*. We have no time."

The door opened revealing returning sailors. A man in the Tsar's uniform carried a tray with a steaming silver pot of tea and a dish of hot *piroshkies* for the Princess. Two German sailors carried bowls of potatoes, red cabbage, sauerbraten.

"I keep the *Schnaps* under lock and key," the Kaiser's officer said. He opened a small safe, pushed aside fat envelopes and carefully rolled charts, drew out a bottle and poured drinks all around.

The three travelers ate quickly and prepared to leave the hut.

An orderly entered the room, saluted the tsarist officer and handed him a paper. He read, cursed, turned the paper over to the *Fregattenkapitän*. Moments passed while the Kaiser's officer compared the message with a small code book he drew from an inner pocket.

A sailor entered the hut, garbed for the chill outdoors. His hood and shoulders were covered with snow. He reported that the *Kondor* was ready and fueled for departure.

Manfred von Richthofen downed the last of his *Schnaps* and wiped his mouth. He thanked the *Fregattenkapitän* for his hospitality. The Princess extended a hand to the tsarist naval officer, who bent over it formally. The three moved to depart.

The *Fregattenkapitän* stopped Manfred with a small gesture. "A mere word, if you please, *Freiherr*. I apologize to delay your party for one moment."

Manfred instructed Lothar to warm up the *Kondor*'s engines while he dealt with the naval officer.

"*Freiherr*." The *Fregattenkapitän* looked around suspiciously. His Russian counterpart was still ushering the Princess from the hut amidst bowing and ceremony. "A message from our wireless station. Relayed from our fleet. Received by them from Berlin."

Von Richthofen nodded. "So? Yes?"

The *Fregattenkapitän* shook his head. "I tried to find the meaning, *Freiherr*. The code book shows no equivalent. I do not in the least understand this message."

Von Richthofen held out his hand and received the slip, reluctantly yielded by the officer. The Baron's eyes sharply scanned the precise inscription. *Hentsch brand sweets have failed to win their market. Guayaquil shop may have to close.*

Von Richthofen handed the slip back to the naval officer. He shook his head angrily. "I do not know, *Herr Fregattenkapitän*, why you waste my time with reports of some petty shopkeeper. Now if you will excuse me, I must join the others in the *Kondor*.

"*Auf Wiedersehen.*"

The Princess Lvova and Lothar were already in the cabin of the aircraft. A few of the sailors must have known something of aviation, or had at least been lately coached. The four radial pushers had been started by the time *Freiherr* Manfred crossed the cindered field from the hut to the *Kondor*. Beneath his fleece-lined boots snow crunched loudly at each step.

In other circumstances, he thought, the sound would be a cheerful one. Even now it summoned up recollections of winter holidays in the Black Forest. Hunting lodges, days spent tracking and slaying game in the woods, nights before a roaring fireplace, drinking, singing, sharing tales of the heroes of old and bragging of one's exploits. Then the ancient spirits seemed to rise from the very earth, the stern and disciplined strength of knighthood returned to the sacred land.

* * *

The sting of ice crystals blown by the *Kondor*'s propellors recalled him to the present. To this Godforsaken Russian island that was the last bit of land he would stand upon before plunging northward and into the tempestuous *Symmeshoehle*.

He grasped the handle beside the door to the *Kondor*'s cabin and pulled himself up into the aeroplane, ignoring the salute of the sailor who stood stiffly beside the fuselage in the biting wind. He slammed the door shut behind him, dogged it firmly in place.

"So, *Bruder*," Lothar called from the pilot's seat, "what was the little delay?"

"Come, begin the flight. Enough time for talk in the air!" He plunged into the copilot's seat, nodded curtly to the Princess sitting stiffly at a window looking back toward the hut.

Lothar let in the throttle and the throb of the four engines rose to a roar that could be heard even over the growing arctic storm. The *Kondor* rolled down the makeshift runway, then lumbered into the air. Manfred watched Lothar take his compass reading and set the big plane on its course. It was now headed due north, virtually on the seventieth meridian of east longitude. Already they were above seventy-five degrees of north latitude, and were droning steadily northward.

Northward, toward *Symmeshoehle*.

Again Lothar asked his brother the reason for his final delay at the hut.

"*Ach*, that damned stupid Hentsch. Somehow he bungled. The Americans escaped and have left Ecuador. Perhaps something will prevent them yet from reaching the *Südrand*. But I doubt it, I doubt it."

"Still—how can they cross?"

Manfred shrugged. "How can *we* cross?"

The Princess entered the conversation of the brothers.

"Aircraft can penetrate Symmes' Hole, brave flying-men. Once through, can cross whole world to return to South Rim. Somewhere on other side, can find way to cross back. But *enemy*..."

She smiled narrowly at the word.

"...enemy must cross South Rim from *near* side!

"That is *Kondor* team's ace in hole!"

Lothar grunted agreement. He hunched forward to study the

progress of the aeroplane. Outside the giant ship, even the whiteness of the storm was lost to sight. Running lights on the aircraft's wings and fuselage cast little pools of colored luminescence in the air. Swirling flakes like swarming insects clustered about each light, making kaleidoscopic patterns of red, green, or yellow-white.

More flakes ran down the *Kondor*'s windscreen, streaking the pilots' view. Manfred leaned forward to examine the altimeter and airspeed indicator. He nudged his brother, pointed to each dial with a thick-gloved finger, then turned to gaze out the side window.

The fuselage of the *Kondor* was of light metal construction. The wings were of plywood laid over a frame of aluminum. They were beginning to ice up. The coating represented a double peril to the aircraft. The extra weight could strain the *Kondor*'s engines, force her to expend extra fuel, even drag her down toward a forced landing. Here in the frozen Arctic that would be almost certainly fatal.

Beside that peril, the ice threatened the craft's wings. Already it was distorting their airfoil shape, reducing the lift provided and adding still more to the strain on the engines. If the weight on the wings became too great, they might fracture and drop off, spelling quick death rather than the slow one that would follow an involuntary landing.

The brothers von Richthofen leaned together, conferring.

Their exchange was interrupted by the Princess's cutting voice. "Lvova hears great crashing, air-men. Like frozen Yenisei River breaking ice-jam in summer."

Manfred leaned forward and wiped the inside of the windscreen with his glove, trying desperately for vision through the blowing flakes.

"Look," Irina nearly screamed. "Look! Is great roaring river! Is great glowing light shining from ocean! Holy Virgin!" She fell to her knees. The *Kondor*'s engines roared. The storm swirled. Frigid winds buffeted the *Kondor*. The great river beneath them seemed to swirl sideways while the flames of hell itself poured straight upward through a fissure in the ice.

"Holy Virgin!" Irina screamed again. "Is end of world! Is Gehenna. Aeroplane is Satan's prey!"

Chapter 5

The United States cruiser *Topeka*, Captain Irwin Jarrold commanding, stood off the Argentine city Ushuaia, a full head of steam up, her crew standing to. Captain Jarrold, field glasses in hand, observed operations from the bridge. The watch officer, Lieutenant Wright, was at his elbow.

"Look at those youngsters," Jarrold urged the watch officer, pointing. "What do you think, Lieutenant—wouldn't you love to trade places with one of them?"

The younger man shook his head. "Not for me, Captain! This is as far south as I ever hope to get! Fifty-five degrees south latitude is plenty!"

The elder man shook his gray head. "No, Lieutenant. I can't agree with you. Why, just think of it—in only a few hours they'll be working their way over the Rim. Or through it, if they can find a path. If they succeed, they'll reach a whole new world. They'll see wonders no human eye has ever beheld."

"Are you sure of that, sir?"

"Well," the captain hesitated, "you've a good point there, Mr. Wright. Some may have made it to the other side before now. As far as we know, no one has ever returned to tell the tale. But some may have died in the attempt."

"And some may yet be alive on the other side, don't you think, Captain?"

Captain Jarrold rubbed his jaw. "Could be, I suppose. You don't think the other side is Hell, Mr. Wright? Or all a boiling sea inhabited by man-eating serpents? You don't think these fliers will wind up in somebody's belly over there?"

He leaned on the railing and focused his glasses on the refueling activity off the stern of the *Topeka.* The sea was fairly smooth—a lucky break, for otherwise the metal airplane would never have had a chance. As it was, the *Spirit of San Diego*, her landing wheels carefully wound back into her hull, sat rocking on the ocean's face, her wings held high above the wavelets, her exposed engine cylinders and propellor a trifle lower and picking up a coating of cold brine. She couldn't stay on the water too long or the engine would be soaked. As it was, there would eventually be corrosion if she wasn't carefully cleaned. But the airplane *could* stay down for a short time: time enough to refuel from the supply of aviation-grade gasoline that *Topeka* carried for her own catapult-launched observation craft.

"I think they'll make it back, Mr. Wright," the captain reiterated. "To the plaudits of the whole world!"

"To collect the Woodhull Martin Prize money, also," the younger man put in.

"Yes, yes, of course. You boys are all so cynical." He pointed. "Look, Lieutenant! They've finished refueling. The line's coming back in and our boat's returning. Ah, what an adventure! What an opportunity! Well, the boat has cleared their aircraft. Let's see what kind of start they get. Where are they going to stand to swing their propellor?"

While Lindbergh sat at the controls and Amelia Earhart occupied the copilot's seat, Howard Hughes swung out through the *Spirit*'s cabin door and lodged his feet carefully on a pair of D-rings bolted to the fuselage. He edged toward the front of the plane, moving his feet from ring to ring, searching out handholds as he moved.

He halted behind the engine, looked back into the cabin and exchanged hand signals with Lindy. As Lindbergh set switches on the instrument panel, Hughes reached high with one hand and gripped the propellor blade. He kept his other hand on the fuselage and one foot on a D-ring, raising the other leg for extra oomph.

With all his strength he swung down on the prop, barely avoiding losing his balance and plunging into the icy water. The engine sputtered and roared. A cloud of gray exhaust swept over Hughes, leaving him coughing. As quickly as he could, he inched back to the door and was pulled into the cabin by Amelia. She dogged the latch behind him and helped him to the navigator's seat. He fell into it gasping.

"Wow! Never again! Talk about scared!"

"You looked absolutely confident." Amelia smiled. "I'd have thought you started engines that way all the time."

"Jehosophat! Why did we ever work out *that* loony way of goosing up a mill?"

Over his shoulder, Lindbergh interjected, "Because it works. Better hang on. I don't want to sit on these seas any longer than I have to."

Amelia plunged into the copilot's seat just as Lindy gunned the Whirlwind. The Ryan monoplane lurched forward, picked up speed, then began slowly to rise. She was again carrying a maximum load of fuel and her ascent was agonizingly slow. For a hundred yards or longer, the boat-hull fuselage slapped the top of each sea wave sending a shudder of apprehension through the cabin.

Finally the *Spirit* won free of the water and Lindbergh lifted her into the gray air above the narrow straits. He circled once over the cruiser *Topeka*, then headed south toward Cape Horn and Drake's Passage. An indicator flashed on the control panel and Amelia Earhart lifted the earphone from its cubbyhole. She held it to her ear for a few seconds, then picked up the microphone and acknowledged the message.

"That was *Topeka*," she said. "Captain Jarrold wishing us godspeed."

Lindbergh grunted. "We're really on our own now. I don't imagine we'll see another face or hear another voice except one another's till we get to the other side."

From the navigator's position Howard Hughes, recovered from

his exploit on the D-rings, spoke up. "Maybe not then either. We may find nothing but wilderness."

"Or ocean," Amelia put in.

"Or ice," Lindbergh murmured.

"What a cheery bunch we are!" Amelia turned in her seat so she faced both Lindbergh and Hughes. "The worst that can happen is that we'll be killed having a grand adventure. Isn't that better than living out our three score and ten in factories or taking dictation in an office? And if we make it—just think, if we make it! The circumpolar voyage! We'll be the greatest explorers since Christopher Columbus!"

The Ryan monoplane droned southward, southward, her radial engine never missing a beat. The sky was gray and threatening, the sun hidden. But they were lucky. No storm struck, no aerial ice accumulated on their wings and propellor.

Blocks of sea-ice began appearing, though, bobbing on the soft swells of the Southern Ocean. The sky grew steadily darker. There was no one moment at which they realized that the sun had fallen beneath the western rim of the earth. But now it was dark, and in the light of the moon—still near its full disk—and the uncounted stars, the ice floes seemed to shine with a dim luminescence like great chunks of phosphorescent fungus bobbing slowly on the black face of the water.

Soon, the airplane's charts indicated, they would approach the final circular channel that lapped against the base of the South Rim, that towering wall of ice that surrounds the terrestrial disk and blocks the southern route of would-be travelers to the far side of the world.

There seemed no chance for the *Spirit of San Diego* to fly over the South Rim unless some sort of fissure or channel could be found. There were old sea-dogs' tales of ancient tall ships sailing too close to the Rim and being caught up in the dreaded Circumpolar Swell, the mighty rush of water along the base of the Rim. The eternal spinning of the earth carried the water of the Southern Ocean with it, and wherever ridges in the sea bed, jagged elbows of the Rim itself, held back the flow of brine, a huge head of icy water built up, and was whipped around the base of the Rim faster and faster, growing ever more massive as it made its way around the entire circumference of the planetary disk, until it towered up and then toppled with the crash of millions of tons of mass.

The ancient tales told of ships that had been caught in the Circumpolar Swell and lifted to the top of its towering crest. When the crest broke and went crashing back to the face of the ocean, the ships could be flung incredible distances. Most were smashed against the wall of ice, then to fall like matchwood to the surface of the sea. Others crashed directly back onto the water and were demolished as thoroughly.

But a few—a very few—were thought to have lodged in fissures high in the Rim. They were never seen again, except as remote, shimmering mirages. Of survivors little was known. Certainly men could not survive for long on the Rim itself. There had been stories of some few sailors making their way back down the Rim face, hailing passing ships and returning to civilization.

There were tales, yes. But they seemed always to concern someone who knew someone who had met someone who claimed to have...

Firsthand reports seemed ever to elude investigation.

But the vague rumors, at their strangest, told of men who had trekked on into the fissures in the Ice Rim. They were supposed to have frozen there, in a graveyard of the ages. Or, perhaps, to have found a shimmering city of ivory towers and perfumed fountains. Or even to have made their way to the other side of the earth and found—or founded—countries of incredible beauty and unmeasured wealth.

But these were only stories.

Charles Lindbergh sat stolidy in the pilot's seat, guiding the Ryan southward. Amelia Earhart and Howard Hughes had traded places, and Hughes now sat in the copilot's seat, dozing. Amelia had resumed her post in the navigator's position, her chart-board in her lap.

But the charts were forgotten. Amelia sat with her chin cupped in one hand. The cabin was chilled, but her bulky flying outfit did a good job of keeping her warm. She was gazing out the side window abstractedly, her mind lulled by the steady drone of the

Whirlwind engine and the barely perceptible vibration of the airplane.

She could see somewhat ahead of the Ryan. The view was of an almost complete wall of blackness punctuated by myriad twinkling lights. The bottom of the sky was cut off by the distant horizon. Slowly that horizon was approaching: a towering wall of ice.

Over the drone of the Whirlwind Amelia became gradually aware that a second sound was becoming audible. A deep, throaty, rushing noise. It was almost like lying abed with her sister back in Kansas, whispering in the dark about this or that bit of excitement. The slide they were going to build, the horse their uncle was going to buy for them, the wonderful pilots who had come through town, walking the wings of their Jennies, leaping off with parachutes, taking people up for rides.

Five dollars for a short ride, ten for a long one.

She'd dreamed, then, of getting off the farm someday. Of being someone important someday, of doing some great thing that would make people line up just to shake her hand.

She wouldn't go through life being just someone's daughter, someone's wife, someone's mother. She'd be famous if she had anything to do with it.

On a dark Kansas night the autumn rains and winds would pummel the Earhart farmhouse. And far off, while Amelia and Muriel lay listening, there would come a low, lonely sound, the whistle of a distant locomotive. The sounds were mixed with the sweet, sad memories of childhood. The water sounds of moist wind and of rain thrumming on a shingled roof.

Amelia blinked.

"Look!" she exclaimed.

Lindy, in the pilot's seat, leaned forward toward the windscreen. Beside him, Howard Hughes started in his seat, grunted—*hunh!*—and peered through the windscreen.

"There it is!"

Straight ahead, across a broad stretch of black water, the ice wall rose as high as they could see. The bright moonlight gave the wall, like the floating floes, an eerie pale glow.

* * *

The black waters of the Southern Ocean lapped at the base of the wall.

The Ryan drove steadily forward, approaching the ghostly cliffs. For a moment it appeared that Lindbergh was going to ram straight into the ice, ending their expedition with a single spectacular impact.

But quickly it became apparent that the ice was still far off—perhaps a hundred miles or more. It was the astonishing height and the sheer massiveness of the barrier that had created the illusion of proximity.

"There's no way, is there, Swede?" Hughes shifted sideways in the copilot's seat. "We've been fools. We can't possibly get over that wall. It makes as much sense as flying this crate to the moon!"

Lindbergh shook his head. "I don't know. It *is* a mighty impressive sight. But—wait a minute."

"What?"

"I just want to check a couple of things. Plenty of fuel. Oil pressure's up where it belongs. How do the wings look?"

Hughes shifted around. "Not bad far's I can see. There's a little icing, not much. We've been in dry air, mostly."

"Huh. Good. It'll take us forty, fifty minutes yet, to reach the wall. So let's consider our options."

"Sure, consider this," Hughes offered. "We have enough gasoline to get back to Tierra del Fuego."

Lindy and Amelia said nothing. The silence stretched and the Ryan's radial engine droned, droned.

"Nah." Hughes made a face. "I could never look in a mirror again."

"That's the spirit!" Lindy reached over and patted Hughes on the shoulder. "All right. We can try and climb. That's a little dangerous. Might ice us badly. But if there *is* any way over the wall, that's how we'll find it."

"It's after midnight," Amelia put in.

"Hmm? So what?"

"So—if the water is smooth enough, we could set down and wait for morning. It's tough enough to face that wall anyhow. If we have daylight to see by, it might be a little easier to cope."

"Good point. All right, what else could we try?"

"How's about exploring a little before we land? Aren't there any features on that wall?"

"You haven't been doing your homework, Howard. You should have investigated that before now."

Hughes said he'd been too busy working with Hall and Bowlus on the Ryan . . . while Lindy had been too busy flying the mails, trying to eke out a precarious living, to take time to study.

"Would anybody like to hear from the navigator?" Amelia asked. "There are plenty of features on the ice. The top is uneven. It's been observed from ships, it's been explored by Zep—Tom Baldwin and Lincoln Beechey both made long flights and charted the wall. I have it all here on my board."

Hughes laughed triumphantly. "Okay, Swede—how's my little lady aviator doing now?"

Lindbergh ignored the taunt. "All right, Miss Earhart. I'll admit that Howard and I haven't kept up with you on that score. Are you still recommending that we set down on the ocean here, and wait for morning?"

"Better than that. If we can turn west and fly another few hours, we'll reach the Shackleton Ice Shelf. We can land on the shelf. It's—let me figure a little." She measured distances on her chart, computed their speed against the miles to be covered.

"We can be there, I think, by two o'clock. Three at the latest. We can land and wait for daylight in comfort."

"Done!" Lindbergh exclaimed. He swung the Ryan slowly into a turn.

There are few sights ever observed by human eyes to compare even remotely with sunrise as the *Spirit of San Diego* crew saw it a few hours later.

The earth's complex motions—spinning around Symmes' Hole like a gramophone disk on its spindle, at the same time that it rotates through space like a flipped cartwheel coin, all at the same time that it falls endlessly through its orbit around the sun—brought sunrise this day directly over the Shackleton Ice Shelf.

One moment there was black Antarctic night. The moon had set in the west. The Shackleton Shelf for the time being represented due east. The only light came from the brilliant sprinkling of stars.

Inside the *Spirit of San Diego*, Charles Lindbergh slept on a makeshift bed, resting from the hours he had spent at the controls bringing the monoplane in from Tierra del Fuego, paralleling the Ice Rim over the Southern Ocean, and landing smoothly on the ice. Even if the plane had skidded on the smooth surface, there was plenty of room and there were no nearby obstructions against which it might have crashed.

But in fact, Lindbergh had landed the Ryan as if the ice shelf had been a perfect packed-grass runway.

Howard Hughes, refreshed by his nap in the copilot's seat, was methodically working over the Wright Whirlwind engine. "There's only two times to worry about an airplane mill," he'd explained as he picked up his tool kit and started to climb from the cabin. "When there's something wrong, and you know you'd better worry, you'd better see about getting it fixed.

"And when she's running smooth as clockwork, then you figure she's getting *ready* to blow, and then you better worry twice as hard 'cause you never know when she's goin' to let go—or how!"

Outside the Ryan he'd set up a semicircle of lanterns and was now happily tinkering with the Whirlwind.

Amelia Earhart checked her padded clothing, pulled her hood close around her face, and climbed down from the Ryan. She walked to Hughes's side.

"You all right, Amy?" he asked.

She smiled. "Isn't it beautiful? All of this whiteness around us. The sky and the stars perfectly clear. And it isn't nearly as cold as I'd expected."

Hughes snorted. "You check the thermometer?"

Amelia nodded. "Twenty below. Inside the cabin it's five above. Poor Charles. He must be roasting in there." She turned away from Hughes and the monoplane, gazed across the ice shelf stretching away to black water along one edge and to a ghostly white wall on the other. "I'm going to take a little walk," she announced.

"Don't get lost," Hughes grated.

She stepped away from the plane, walked slowly along the ice shelf with her eyes fixed on the vertical face that marked its southern limit.

She stopped.

Somewhere deep within the ice there was a dim, flickering radiance. Amelia stopped and stared, her hands, even in their fleece-lined gloves, plunged into her coat pockets. The glow seemed to grow in intensity, then to lapse back again; to grow, then to lapse. But each time it increased a little more, and each time it fell back a little less.

Soon, it seemed, the whole ice wall was alive with a faint radiance. The lights shifted and flickered, then rays of pastel began to dance.

A shaft of delicate rose flickered through the ice, then disappeared, replaced by a cone of pale blue that shimmered from the base of the ice wall, upward and upward until it faded into the darkness overhead. A shaft of pale yellow glowed within the ice, then one of faint lavender.

Amy stood enchanted, then inhaled deeply and started running back to the airplane. She grabbed Hughes by his elbow and shouted, "Leave that for a little bit. Look, Howard! The whole wall is turning to a diamond of flame!"

Together they stood watching as the entire wall of ice, its internal crystalline structure acting like a latticework of mirrors, began to flash with brighter and brighter colors. Strange forms drifted toward them. Ice mirages, images of random patterns formed within the crystal, or of actual beings and objects long frozen in the ice, trapped now fathoms, or miles—or thousands of miles—away, projected for them by the growing light.

A great, shaggy animal form shimmered into being, deep within the ice. It glided forward silently, silently, its mighty trunk and long, curving tusks upraised in defiance of the band of barely human creatures that circled around it brandishing stone axes and crude spears.

A tall sailing ship, its masts broken and its canvas shredded, loomed overhead, thousands of feet in the air—upside down.

Crewmen in tattered garments, their features haggard and their beards long and ragged, moved listlessly across its decks.

An exotic village, its lavish architecture suggestive of the styles of classical Egypt and imperial China, swam into view. Nearly naked men and women moved through its streets. Strange beasts and vehicles proceeded through passages of dizzying geometry.

Surrounded by incomprehensible flowing reflections, a gigantic four-engined monoplane battled winds and driving snow in total silence. The craft grew larger as it approached, buffeted by gales Amelia neither heard nor felt.

"Do you—can you see those things too?" Howard Hughes gasped at Amelia's side.

"I don't—I mean, what did you see?"

He shook his head and stammered half-coherently. "I think they're mirages," he managed. "We got 'em in the desert sometimes." He rubbed his eyes. "Look now!"

The entire glacial wall before them blazed with a spectrum of light, gleaming with a brilliance that brought tears to eyes unable to bear the splendor. The light was so vivid that it was almost audible. A wind seemed to sweep across the top of the wall, uncounted miles above them, and send clouds of glittering ice crystals pouring over the cliff, rushing across the ice shelf in a blue-gray river that engulfed Amelia and Howard and the *Spirit of San Diego*, then plunged hissing into the Southern Ocean.

Then the sun itself appeared. It slid up, edging over the ice wall. The sky had turned a blue of incredible depth. The sun presented only a gleaming section of disk over the top of the wall, but its rays were scattered and shifted as they swam through the ice, turned to a million variegated rays. Amelia spun on her heel and watched her own multicolored shadows jump and waver across the shelf.

And from the distance was heard a roar that grew and grew in volume until it was louder than a hundred thunderclaps in one. And yet it continued to grow and continued to grow.

Awestruck, Amelia stood with the sun and the ice wall behind her; her still-weaving shadows and the Ryan monoplane and the black waters of the Southern Ocean before her.

She felt a hand clutching her by the elbow, through the thick layers of her flying costume, and shaking her violently.

"What is it?" she shouted. Even at the top of her voice she was barely able to make herself heard. Again she screamed, "What is it? What is it?"

Howard Hughes cupped his gloved hands around his mouth, held them up to the opening of her fur-lined hood to get close to her ear, and shouted.

"It's that circular tide, the ocean swell! It sounds as if it's going to get here in a few seconds!"

Chapter 6

The Princess Irina Lvova, only daughter to the Prince Georgi Ivanovich Lvov, *de facto* regent for the feeble Alexei, Tsar of All the Russias, crouched in the corner of the passenger cabin. The brothers von Richthofen sat side by side in the pilots' seats of the *Kondor*, their faces beaded with the perspiration of effort, tension, concentration.

The Princess, behind them, hid her face in soft gloves and muttered incoherent prayers to the Blessed Virgin.

The *Kondor*'s four radial engines roared. The aeroplane swung to the left and to the right, soared, tipped its nose and zoomed like a fighting plane engaged in dogfight in the *Einjahrkrieg*.

The surface beneath the plane was a sheet of gray, glistening ice that stretched away to both east and west, gradually curving upward until it disappeared in mist. The sky overhead was similarly misty, scintillating and gray. Like a thick fog bank it was utterly intangible, completely lacking in features, and to the eye might have been a few hundred metres in thickness—or a thousand kilometres.

Strangest of all was the prospect directly behind the *Kondor* and that ahead of the plane.

Behind, the titanic funnel of ice gave way to a vast vortex of swirling water. And visible in the center of the vortex was a gigantic perfect circle of night sky. The storm had begun to abate, but its strength was not yet totally exhausted.

Great shards of heavy black cloud spun and shifted. Showers of snow still fell from them, only to be caught in the winds that buffeted about the mouth of *Symmeshoehle* so that they were swept eventually into the eternally swirling waters of the *Hoehle*.

Between the ragged edges of the clouds appeared bits of remote blackness dotted with twinkling multicolored stars.

Ahead of the *Kondor* the ice-tunnel stretched for what appeared to be hundreds of kilometres. Whether there was a similar water vortex to be encountered at the remote end of the ice-tube, it was as yet impossible to tell from within the cabin. But an almost blinding brilliance was reflected from the curving sides of the tunnel, while at the far end a perfect circle of daylight could be seen, and in the center of the blue circle gleamed the sun, set like a bull's-eye in a target.

Manfred von Richthofen dropped his fascinated gaze from the astounding sight ahead of the *Kondor*. He leaned forward, tapped the airspeed indicator with his knuckle, then glanced sidelong at his brother. The needle was stuck at its maximum. The *Kondor* acted and felt as if it were in a vertical power dive.

The brothers exchanged an almost telepathic glance.

Manfred reached for the row of throttles and cut back each of the aeroplane's engines until all were running at idle.

Still the needle remained jammed at its maximum. The aircraft seemed still to be gaining, rather than losing, speed. The air flowing over the wing surfaces and the fixed landing gear set up a shrieking sound. Within the cabin a few loose objects began to float into the air.

The Princess began to scream.

The von Richthofens turned in their seats, their legs and lower torsos held in place by safety belts. The Princess was floating effortlessly in the center of the cabin, screaming at the top of her lungs in barbaric Russian.

Manfred signaled to his brother to take control of the plane—or, more accurately, to take charge of monitoring the instruments. The elder brother unclasped his lap-belt and pushed himself out of his chair. Like the Princess he found himself floating. He was gripped by a momentary access of nausea, then fought down the sensation. He braced his boots against the back of his pilot's seat and shoved himself toward the rear of the cabin.

The Princess shrank from the onrushing pilot but he shot out one hand and grasped her elbow. They swung around each other, floating and tumbling. The Princess let go a great sob and subsided into silence.

"Princess!" Manfred shouted. "Irina! Princess!"

"Is end of world!" she screamed. "*Kondor* is flying into Gehenna! Pray to Virgin, quick!"

"*Nein!*" von Richthofen shouted. "I have felt this before at the top of a loop. Everything is falling freely. It is a time without gravitation!"

"No! No! Is end of world!"

As if to settle the disagreement their weight returned slightly—but they drifted toward the rear of the cabin rather than toward its floor.

"See, see, is end of world!" The Princess Irina reached insidc her white flying costume and extracted a set of opal rosary beads and a glittering double crucifix of obsidian. With pale lips she began to pray.

Slowly she and Manfred von Richthofen drifted across the cabin. They landed with a soft thump against the rear bulkhead.

"Lothar!"

The younger von Richthofen glanced over his shoulder.

"You understand what has happened?" Manfred shouted.

Lothar shook his head. "The world is mad!"

"*Nein, Dummkopf!* We have passed the *Mittelpunkt*. We have been through the *Symmeshoehle*. We now are halfway through. We must now climb again. In a few minutes the *Kondor* will lose its momentum and we will stall."

"*Ja?*"

For a few seconds there was only the whine of wind, the low drone of four idling engines.

"The engines cannot lift the aircraft in a vertical direction for—*ach*, I understand!"

"*Ja*, *ja*. Bring her over into level flight. Swing around *Symmeshoehle*, climbing steadily. We can continue!"

"Good, yes!"

Lothar bent over the controls. Slowly he increased the throttle, eased forward the stick so that the *Kondor* altered its attitude. The sun was soon overhead rather than before the aeroplane; the disk of night and storm was directly beneath rather than behind the craft.

Freiherr von Richthofen and the Princess Lvova slid from the rear bulkhead of the cabin and sat with a soft thump on the floor. There they struggled to their feet and walked on trembling legs to their seats, Manfred von Richthofen beside his brother and the Princess behind them.

"Now what? Now what?" the Princess demanded.

"Now, Your Highness, we climb through the *Symmeshoehle* until we emerge in the very center, the *wirkliche Norden*, the true north of the world. But—we on the other side of the earth will arrive!"

"Manfred! Irina!" Lothar exulted. "Now we will be successful!"

Steadily the *Kondor* climbed. Overhead the tunnel grew less bright rather than more so, as the sun passed its zenith and sank toward evening on the new side of the earth toward which they labored. The walls of the *Symmeshoehle* remained of glistening ice. For the first time they had the opportunity and the interest to gaze through the windows of the *Kondor* and try to study the icy tunnel.

It was impossible to calculate the depth of the ice. It seemed to be transparent, but when one gazed into its deeps it merely faded to darkness. Shadowy shapes were embedded in the wall, of sizes and shapes conducive to wild imaginings.

"Look!" the Princess exclaimed. She pointed at a huge form that moved on the surface of the ice rather than standing still beneath it. "Is demon, as Princess said!" Irina cried.

Lothar shook his head. "Look! That is no demon! Some sort of white grub. *Ugh!* A giant worm that lives in ice! What can it eat? So huge!"

Manfred made a sound in his throat like a growling panther. "Polar bears. Seals. Whales. Whatever creatures are caught in the vortex of *Symmeshoehle* and dragged here by mad gravity."

"And water?" the Princess Lvova demanded. "Why is no water dragged, also? Why is no wall of water in middle of *Symmeshoehle* if—pull of earth—"

"*Schwerkraft*—gravitation."

"Yes. Why is no water here in middle?"

"Too much spin. *Umdrehung. Ach!* Centrifugal force."

The Princess shrugged. "Royalty does not understand such things. Are not interesting. Princess will now take nap. Drivers awaken Princess when aeroplane reaches ground again." She did not wait for them to answer.

The two pilots turned back to their tasks. The fuel indicators showed sufficient petrol in the *Kondor*'s tanks to carry them easily to the top of the *Symmeshoehle* and some distance beyond, onto the surface of the earth. But by no means was there enough petrol in the tanks to carry the heavy ship the thousands of kilometres across the unknown face of the world and back to the Ice Rim at its far edge.

There would, eventually, be the problem of crossing the Rim itself. But that was a matter to be faced in due course. Perhaps the enemy party had found a solution in their own efforts to make the circumpolar journey. Perhaps the two parties, one making its way via the Ice Rim and the other by *Symmeshoehle*, would cross paths somewhere on the far side. The chance of that was remote. If each party sought the shortest route of travel, the European crew would trek across the hemidisk opposite to Europe and Africa, while the Americans would travel on the reverse hemidisk of their own continents.

Still, no one knew what events would befall on the far side of the disk. It was only a short time now, a few hours or even a matter of minutes, and the *Kondor* would emerge through the far opening of *Symmeshoehle* and make her way toward—the von Richthofens hoped—a safe landing. Once that was accomplished they could reconnoitre. Perhaps they could even take the *Kondor* up once more, this time by daylight, to make observations. And then they could lay their plans.

Outside the ship the tunnel had grown very dark. Ahead was still the gray, icy wall. Above them, the disk of the opening had grown large but now showed only a dark, twilight gray. Behind them the tunnel disappeared into blackness.

With a final transition that took only a matter of seconds the disk above also turned to blackness. The *Kondor* was circling in a world completely dark. A few stars shone overhead, but failed to define the outline of the *Symmeshoehle*'s mouth.

As if startled into wakefulness by the sudden loss of light, the Princess sat up sharply in her seat. "Is time of doom!" she cried. She began weeping and telling her beads.

"Quick!" Manfred commanded.

Lothar reached to the instrument panel, flicked switches.

Spotlights blazed into life from the wings and nose of the big aeroplane. A trio of lights reflected blue-white from the glimmering inside of the ice-tunnel. The lights picked out a huge ice-worm that had detected the oncoming aircraft, perhaps by the vibrations it set up in the air. The worm dug into the smooth surface of the ice with half-metre-long, daggerlike claws that ran in pairs along its segmented belly.

It reared its front end away from the cold surface and groped blindly toward the *Kondor*.

Lothar von Richthofen left his copilot's seat and rummaged for his high-powered rifle. He assembled the barrel and stock, rammed home a clip of heavy-calibre shells and returned to his seat. He slid open a window and extended the muzzle into the slipstream.

He fired a round at the ice-worm. The report of the rifle crashed through the cabin. The Princess covered her face with her hands, the opal-and-obsidian rosary dangling against her flying coat. Manfred von Richthofen did not flinch at the controls of the aeroplane, but a grim smile touched one corner of his mouth.

Lothar watched as the heavy round blew a hole in the chest—or what would have passed as a chest—of the ice-worm. The worm was knocked backward by the force of impact. Several pairs of its claws were ripped from the frozen surface. A shudder rippled through it. There was a ruin where the round had struck; white ichor oozed from the wound.

The worm regained its balance and again groped eagerly toward the *Kondor*. Manfred von Richthofen maintained the course of the aircraft, a steady, banking spiral. As the plane completed 360 degrees of its course and passed over the worm again, the creature extended itself vertically to its full height. Only its hindmost pairs of claws maintained their hold on the ice.

Lothar ejected the spent round from his rifle and shot home another. He sighted carefully down the worm. With a final effort the creature launched itself at the aircraft. By an astonishing exertion of its muscles the worm managed to bring its face level with the cabin of the aircraft.

For one instant the great, pallid face stared through the window of the aeroplane. It was fully a metre in width. A row of pale eyes stretched across the top of the face, staring weirdly into the cabin. Beneath the eyes a great mouth-orifice gaped. The knifelike claws lining the creature's belly waved and clicked.

A strange sound came from the ice-worm.

Lothar carefully squeezed the trigger of his rifle. For a second time an explosion crashed through the cabin. The perfectly aimed round entered the monster's throat and blew away the back of its head. The worm tumbled back, a final terrible wail following the *Kondor* as it continued its climb.

Lothar leaned out to watch the death-throes of the animal. When he finally slid the pane shut and slumped into his seat his brother reached to clasp his hand. "Good shooting," he offered.

"It should not have taken two rounds," Lothar commented.

"Then why did it?"

Lothar shook his head. "I thought I would get it in the heart. That should have done the job, hey?"

"*Hmm*. Primitive creature. Maybe it does not have a heart. Or it was so stupid, it didn't know you'd killed it." Manfred burst into laughter.

His brother joined him. "Too *dumm* to know it was dead! *Haha!* A good joke, that! What do you think, Irina?"

The Princess sat hugging herself. "Creature might have killed fliers! Should not have disturbed monster! What if monster had crashed into propellor or wing, Lothar?"

"*Nein*, *nein*. First law of life, Princess. If in doubt, kill enemy.

If you are wrong, apologize to survivors. But if enemy kills you first—*enemy* gets to apologize!"

Again, both brothers burst into gales of laughter while the Princess sat white-faced, biting her lip.

Manfred pointed ahead of the plane. "Look!"

The *Kondor*'s triple spotlights showed that the wall of the tunnel had changed from a solid, glistening sheet of ice to a broken curve where greenish brine washed the chunks. The plane continued to rise, its spotlights illuminating alternately the wall of the tunnel and the mist-shrouded center of the *Symmeshoehle*.

The brine grew deeper, its motion more obvious. Pale figures wriggled or darted through the translucence. As the *Kondor* turned away from the wall on its endlessly circling course, vague forms began to appear in the mist as well.

Something faint and gelatinous and huge appeared for an instant in the *Kondor*'s lights, then disappeared again into the gray murk as the aeroplane spiraled past and above it. The plane trembled in a sudden downdraft from the flapping wings of something larger than itself.

A creature darted before the monoplane, something like a great, leathery bat with jaws metres in length, jaws lined with rows of triangular teeth. The whole creature was a pallid gray-white. It plunged into the water and there was a great thrashing and spray as it locked in mortal combat with some pale fish-thing.

The *Kondor* flew on.

There were no further encounters with the flying or swimming inhabitants of the *Symmeshoehle*... except once. The *Kondor* shook and nearly collided with the watery surface beyond its wingtip as something crashed into it from above. There was a rending, screeching sound.

A claw as long and as sharp as a honed sabre swept through the cabin-roof and traced a line from above the pilot's seat to the rear bulkhead. Then it was withdrawn. There was a shaking of the entire plane and a scrabbling of clawed feet on the roof. A single thrust downward that made the wings scream with strain, and then the monster—whatever the thing was—was gone.

Steadily the engines droned on.

The *Kondor* banked away from the mist.

The watery wall had disappeared.

The aeroplane was circling above a titanic hole in the earth, a huge maelstrom that swirled and sucked at the waters of an arctic sea.

Briefly the pilot von Richthofen kept the Udet monoplane on its spiraling course. Then he let out a yell of triumph: "We are through! We have reached the other side of the earth!"

He leveled the course of the aeroplane, gained a bit of additional altitude, then tilted the *Kondor*'s nose ever so slightly downward so that the spotlights illuminated the terrain around them.

It was a vast waste of ice, indistinguishable from the territory north of Novaya Zemlya on their home side of the disk.

The Princess Lvova ran to the windscreen and peered downward. Before her eyes stretched kilometre upon kilometre of ice. Great glacial peaks thrust jagged pyramidal tips upward. Huge white birds, startled by the noise and size of the *Kondor*, deserted their nests and swept away on broad wings, their mouths opened in alarm or in hostile cries that could not be heard above the drone of the four pusher engines.

"Is all same!" the Princess cried. "Is no purpose! Only ice and water and birds! Is useless trip!"

"Don't be stupid!" Manfred von Richthofen hissed. "Don't be so damned *dumm*. You are as brainless as the worm!"

"Pig!" she screamed. "German pig insults imperial Princess! When party returns, Baron will suffer penalty for insult!"

Manfred turned control of the *Kondor* to his brother with a single angry gesture. He thrust himself from his seat and whirled to confront the Princess.

"Listen to me, you stupid woman!" he commanded.

She cringed before him, but with eyes slitted with hatred rather than with terror.

"Use your mind! The earth we know is all ice and desolation at the North Hole. And so is this earth! But a few thousand kilometres from the *Symmeshoehle* are Berlin and Moskva, and a few thousand farther are jungles and burning deserts! What makes you think this world will prove different?"

He stood with his feet spread wide, clenched fists planted on hips, his bulky flying suit failing to conceal the contempt he felt in every muscle of his body.

"We will fly to a safe landing place. We will leave the *Kondor* protected—concealed—with a few parts missing so no one else can use the aeroplane. And then we will proceed by means of the *Schwarze Adler*—the *Black Eagle*. Do you recall?"

"Yes," she conceded. "*Herr* Udet's little Zeppelin."

"*Ja*. Von Richthofen nodded contemptuously. "The little Zeppelin. We will proceed, and we will find a way to cross the hemidisk from *Symmeshoehle* to South Rim, and return to our own side of the planet."

"How? How? If *Kondor* has not fuel to cross world and *Schwarze Adler* cannot cross Rim, how can party return? Is death of all! Was madness to travel! Party will die in Gehenna-ice!"

Von Richthofen roared with laughter. "We will triumph and we will survive to glory in our triumph!"

"How, *Freiherr*, how? Is madness!" With trembling hands she fumbled for her rosary.

The von Richthofens exchanged glances. "*Bruder Freiherr*," Lothar said. "Shall we tell her of Bodo's plan? She cannot let slip any longer. She cannot betray our secret."

Manfred assented.

"Irina," Lothar said. "Irina." His voice contained—for him—a degree of softness.

The Princess looked up, tears brimming from her eyes. She pulled a heavy glove from one hand and retrieved a dainty kerchief from a pocket of her flying outfit. She dabbed at her nose, then wiped away a tear. She turned away so that neither man could see her expression.

"Princess," Lothar commenced again. "Our Zeppelin *Schwarze Adler* can carry us across this hemidisk. I am confident of that. The problem is to cross the South Wall and return to Tempelhof to win the Woodhull Martin Prize. And to set the feet of our two empires back upon the path of greatness that was denied them by the One Year War."

"Is true. But is not answer to question, How? How, Lothar? How?"

Von Richthofen shot a glance again at his brother, received an almost imperceptible nod in response.

"Hans Bodo von Alvensleben," von Richthofen said, "is a man most resourceful. Along with the admirable *Herr* Udet, he helped to plan our journey. He helped to conceive the idea of concealing the Zeppelin *Schwarze Adler* within the *Kondor*.

"No rule of Madame Woodhull forbids Zeppelin," the Princess asserted.

"True enough, but the contest rules require our party to complete our journey in our own vehicle."

"So?"

"So—no one is to know this, Princess! No one! Bodo and Ernst have constructed a second *Kondor*. It has been shipped to Argentina and is being reassembled even now. We must somehow reach and penetrate the South Rim, and transfer to the second *Kondor*. None will be the wiser, and we will triumph over the stupid enemy."

A new light came into the Princess's eyes. Nodding her satisfaction, she reached with both hands and placed her fingertips softly on the faces of the brothers von Richthofen.

Chapter 7

Amelia shouted at the same instant she started back for the *Spirit*. She moved at a dead run. "Is she ready to start?"

Hughes followed at a lumbering sprint. "Set!"

"I'll grab the controls. You spin the prop." Amelia was already hauling herself into the cabin. She ignored the slumbering Lindbergh, vaulted into the pilot's seat and hit the magneto. At the same moment she glanced up and saw Howard reaching for the propeller. He swung it with all the strength in his wiry torso. The Whirlwind caught on the first spin. Hughes grabbed his tools and headed for the cabin.

Even as he pulled the door shut, Amelia throttled the Whirlwind to its top speed and the *Spirit* rolled forward. "Come on, you good baby, don't die on us now!"

Charles Lindbergh sat up and looked around. "What's going on? Why are we—"

"Just pray!" Hughes snapped.

The Ryan lurched across the ice shelf on her rubber tires. The great tidal swell was surging toward them, a rolling mountain of black water and shattered ice floes dotted with fragments of driftwood and seething patches of foam. Great wild birds soared above the swell, screaming shrilly at one another: *tii-tii-tii!*

A wall of ice loomed directly in front of the Ryan. Amelia tugged back on the stick, lifting the monoplane's nose, then shoved the stick to the left and hit the rudder pedal to send the *Spirit* into a roaring, climbing bank and turn.

Howard Hughes steadied himself in a crouch near the door. Lindy had planted himself in the navigator's seat and was clutching the wickerwork for dear life.

The Ryan climbed, slipped past the ice wall into clear air.

The circumpolar tidal swell was roaring forward, a huge wave miles across and hundreds of feet in height. It swept along the ice shelf at express-train speed.

Amelia kept the Ryan in as steep a climb as the straining monoplane could handle without dropping into a fatal power stall. Simultaneously she kept the Ryan's controls shoved over, struggling to turn the plane's nose away from the swell.

There was a doubled chance to survive the onrushing millions of tons of brine. If the Ryan could climb high and fast enough to overtop the swell, she need merely circle until the wall of water had roared past and the sea returned to normal. Or if she could swing away and simply turn tail before the water arrived, a full-powered aerial sprint might outdistance the onrush, and the plane could then climb to safety, or even cruise northward a few miles and then circle back to safety.

The *Spirit of San Diego* almost made it.

The circumpolar swell caught her under the belly.

Her nose was still lifted, and pointed some 45 degrees away from the mountainous wave. Howard Hughes had crawled forward and was cranking in the landing wheels.

"Steer her! Steer her like a boat!" Lindbergh shouted from behind Amelia.

Amelia kept the engine throttled up to maximum RPMs. The plane's boat-style hull caught hold and she straightened. The world was divided between Antarctic sky before the *Spirit* and a raging watery abyss beneath her nose. Amelia stifled a moan and looked back. Behind the plane, spray jounced high into the air.

A huge bird swooped low over the propeller and hovered facing the windscreen. For an insane moment Amelia found herself staring into a beady black eye while the bird stared weirdly back at her. In the midst of peril that could spell death at any instant Amelia laughed. It was not the shrill, tense shriek of hysteria but the contagious laughter of tension released.

The bird nodded, seemingly in understanding. It opened its beak and gave out a piercing, grating, echoing *tii-tii-tii!* It pressed down with its broad wings and rose above the *Spirit*'s windscreen, swept overhead—Amelia saw it swoop over the Ryan's vertical observation windows—and soared away.

Amelia heard Howard Hughes shouting at her. He had pulled himself into the copilot's seat and turned sideways to face her.

"Where's this thing go?" he shouted.

Amelia shook her head.

Hughes cupped his hands around his mouth and leaned toward her. "I said, where's this thing go? Where's the damned tidal wave headed for?"

"I looked on the charts," Amelia shouted back. "It just builds up until it collapses. But there's rough coast ahead. Look!" She pointed through the windscreen.

"I think that's Great Halley Bay," she said. "See that ice cliff? I think the wave will break on it! I'm going to try and get us airborne when it does!"

The tidal swell swept them onward. The windscreen was running brine, the engine coughing but still managing to stay alive. The sky was a dark and impenetrable gray. More birds circled the Ryan. How fast can they fly? Amelia found herself wondering.

The Great Halley Bay ice cliff loomed ahead, gleaming a milky white, rising thousands of feet into the tormented air, presenting a knife-edge to the onrushing water.

The tidal swell encountered the first, underwater ridge of Great Halley Bay. The entire mountain of roaring brine lurched. Amelia felt the Ryan tilt, start to tumble onto her port wingtip. She wrestled the stick, managed to right the plane.

A giant gleaming scimitar of frozen brine slashed at the Ryan.

Amelia swung the stick, kicked the pedals.

The plane swerved, its starboard wingtip literally brushing the sheet of ice. But it passed safely to the left.

Instantly the water was tumbling away beneath the Ryan. The tough plane's roaring prop caught purchase of air. All of the controls became suddenly responsive, like a strong-willed horse that has tested its rider to the ultimate and found her not wanting.

"Now look ahead." Amelia pointed with one gloved hand.

Hughes leaned forward in the copilot's seat.

Charles Lindbergh moved cautiously forward from his position, standing behind the pilots' chairs and holding to the back of each.

"It's a canyon," Lindbergh exclaimed. "No—it's more than a canyon. It's a valley. We can fly up it. This is our passage through the South Rim."

Amelia shook her head, more in puzzlement than disagreement. "I don't remember seeing any channel. Is that chart handy?"

Lindy hauled the board forward. Hughes took over the controls while Earhart and Lindbergh studied the map. "It shows Great Halley Bay, all right," Lindy said. "But it just shows a pointed inlet from the Southern Ocean. It doesn't show this cleft running back into the wall. Can you climb out of here and circle once, Amy? Maybe we can get a better reading. Maybe this isn't Halley after all."

She complied, pointed back toward the mouth of the channel. "Look at that! There's some kind of natural ridge at the end of the cleft. A glacier must have blocked off the passage from Great Halley Bay."

Lindy nodded. "Makes sense. Nobody could see this route from the sea or even from the Shackleton Shelf. That tidal swell must have—well—*thrown* us over the ridge!"

Howard Hughes lifted one hand from the controls and rubbed his rapidly darkening jaw. "Do you think that ridge has always been there?"

"Always? Why?"

"Because—it might not have been there forever. If that channel used to be open—then there might once have been a clear route through the ice. People might have traveled through there by boat or dogsled or God knows how, for centuries. Until that ridge popped up."

The Ryan monoplane droned steadily southward, penetrating ever deeper into the Great Halley Cleft. Walls of ice thrust skyward to either side. The floor of the cleft shone the same clean and glittering white. Whether rock, soil, or water lay beneath the frozen floor, or whether the ice stretched all the way to the far hemidisk of earth, there was no way of telling.

Amelia Earhart, drained by the labor and tension of piloting the *Spirit* from the Shackleton Ice Shelf, through their nearly fatal encounter with the circumpolar tidal swell and into the Great Halley Cleft, munched on a sandwich provided courtesy the USS *Topeka* wardroom. Charles Lindbergh sat at the controls once more, with Howard Hughes at his side.

"The problem, I think, is this," Lindy said calmly. "It's just possible that this cleft stretches all the way. If so, we're in clover. All we have to do is beware of strange gravitational effects and we'll wind up, eventually, on the other side. We just have to keep an eye on the compasses."

"We're still bearing south," Hughes offered.

"But if this cleft doesn't go all the way..." Lindbergh said softly. He reached with one hand and ran his fingers through his curly hair.

"Yeah?" Hughes prompted.

Before Lindy had his answer ready, Amelia asked, "How are we doing in the fuel department?"

Hughes checked the gauge. "Over half a tank. That's the main tank. We haven't even cut in the reserve supply yet."

"Sounds good to me." Amelia smiled. "Don't you agree, Charles—we can just turn back if this cleft is blocked. But I don't think it is. I have a feeling we're going to get through."

Lindy smiled, too. "I think you're right, Miss Earhart."

"And find what?" Hughes demanded.

With a straight face, Amelia said, "Colonel Fawcett."

"Colonel Fawcett?" Hughes's face reddened. "He disappeared in the Amazon jungle! How come you think he's on the other hemidisk?"

"How should I know? I'm just a little Kansas farm-girl."

Hughes made a disgusted sound.

"Well, really, Howard, while you and Charles were so busy with your he-man activities—"

"Listen, somebody who knows machinery had to superintend

the Ryans. And the Swede was out makin' a few fish. What was he supposed to live on, air?"

"Well..."

"Besides, who picked you for this job? You know how many bozos'd give their eye teeth to be in your boots?"

"Now, be calm. I was merely saying, while you two men were so busy with your male obligations, I *did* study up a bit on the whole history of circumpolar exploration."

"There ain't no setch annimul, lady."

"You mean, no one has returned to tell the tale—convincingly! There are plenty of people who *claim* to've traveled there and returned."

"Fruitcakes."

"And some of their stories are pretty convincing."

"Banana oil!"

"What about the people who claim they've had visitors from the other side?"

"I put 'em in the same crate with Conan Doyle and the rest of the loonies who've played pat-a-cake with ghosts."

"You don't think there could be people on the other side? People with civilizations as advanced as ours? Or even more advanced? Look at the development of aviation, Howard. It's less than thirty years since Samuel Langley first flew. If some nation on the other side of the disk is even ten or twenty years ahead of us, they might have aircraft that have been visiting our hemidisk for years."

"What a lot of hooey!"

"What about natural passages, then? People have explored caves that go deep into the earth, and have been lost and never come back. What if they found their way through the earth?"

"They'd never clear customs. Besides, there's one thing you can't explain, with all your fancy ideas, Amelia." Hughes made a hideous leering grin.

Lindbergh, sitting beside him, shrank away. He knew that one of Hughes's infrequent and horrible jokes was emerging.

"There can't be any civilization on the other side," Hughes gritted, "because everybody over there has to walk around on his hands, and they're all too busy hanging on to invent anything!"

* * *

The sun continued in its daily spiral across the sky. Its path was dictated by the complex interplay of the earth's rotation around the North Hole and its twirling, coinlike, on its axis.

Less than two hours after the *Spirit of San Diego* started its flight up the Great Halley Cleft, the walls began noticeably to close in. Howard Hughes was seated at the controls. Charles Lindbergh and Amelia Earhart were huddled together over the chart-board. The Halley Cleft was of course not marked on the printed charts, and they were penciling in its position for later editions of the charts.

"Better come up here," they heard. There was apprehension in Hughes's tone.

"What is it, Howard?"

Hughes said, "I think I smell trouble."

They laid aside the chart-board. Lindbergh slid into the copilot's seat and Earhart crouched between them.

Hughes pointed to one side, then to the other. "This place is getting crowded."

Amelia darted a glance in either direction. "Just like Poe. Remember 'The Pit and the Pendulum'?"

"Nope. But what're we going to do?"

"I don't think we're in imminent danger," Lindy said. "The cleft may widen again in a while, but of course we can't count on that."

"You bet your britches we can't!"

Amelia slid one of the plane's windows open. She peered at the surface beneath the *Spirit*. "That ice doesn't look so bad. I wonder, do you think our wheels could get any purchase on it? It looks as much like old snow to me as slippery ice. No glare, not very translucent."

"You mean, you want to *land* here? Maybe so—but why?"

"Well, didn't you and Ryan design this plane so the wings fold back?"

"Sure. But that was just for convenience. We didn't know but what we'd have to ship the plane by rail, or pack it aboard ship. What's that have to do with—*oh!*" A broad grin spread across his face.

Lindy complained. "I don't get it. What are you two plotting?"

Amelia reached up and placed her hands on the shoulders of the two pilots. "If the wheels can get a grip on that snow, and the cleft is too narrow to fly through, we can just go through it like a sort of ice-boat. We can land, stow the wings, and *roll* the rest of the way. Won't our propeller pull us along?"

Lindy conceded that it would. "Not very efficiently—taxiing is hardly the ideal way to travel in an airplane."

"But it *would* get us through the narrow part."

"Yes. If the pathway doesn't get *too* narrow."

Within half an hour Amelia's plan was put to the test. The ice walls of the cleft gradually narrowed. The demands on the pilot of the moment grew increasingly severe. Finally it was impossible to keep the *Spirit of San Diego* in the air.

They landed on the snow, rolled to a stop. The engine was cut.

They climbed from the plane. Amelia took observations of the sun, and Hughes and Lindbergh folded back the monoplane's wings. Hughes stood beside the fuselage, studying the wheels, a worried expression on his elongated face.

"I don't like this," he grunted.

The others joined him.

"Look." Hughes pointed at the wheels. "It's in too deep. Have a gander at this." He picked up a handful of snow, cupped it in his gloves. "It's too soft. Almost slushy. We'll never taxi in this goop. The wheels'll just dig in. We'll either nose over in this stuff, or just sink where we are. When night comes, we'll get frozen in!"

"You think we can get out of here?" Lindy asked. "What if the three of us pick up the tail and swing the *Spirit* around?" He studied the ice cliffs. "I think there's still room. Maybe we could take off and fly back out."

Amelia squatted beside the plane, her slim form made clumsy and massive by her bulky flying suit. "The wheels are sinking into the slush—that's the problem, right?" She looked from Lindbergh to Hughes, then back. "Why don't we just retract the wheels? The *Spirit*'s fuselage is shaped like a boat hull anyway. We did fine landing and taking off at sea, at Tierra del Fuego. Wouldn't the hull skim along this slush just as well?"

Lindbergh's blue eyes widened. "I think it would. Howard,

you're our engineer—as close to one as we have. What about that? Would it work?"

Hughes squatted beside Amelia. He ran one hand along the bottom of the Ryan's fuselage. He thought about it, pulled off a glove and felt the consistency of the soft snow beneath the plane, then rapped the metal with his knuckles. "If we don't hit any rocks. Or any sharp chunks of ice sticking up through the slush. Yeah. It should work."

"Well then. No point in waiting around. Let's give it our best."

The Whirlwind started without hesitation. Lindy, in the pilot's seat, turned toward Hughes. "Try the superhet, would you? Let's see if we can get a message back to Captain Jarrold. Let him know our position and plans. Just in case."

"That last reading," Amelia supplied, "was twenty-eight degrees, thirty minutes west, eighty-nine degrees plus south. This is just about it. If we get any farther south, we'll be through!"

Hughes relayed the news to the USS *Topeka* and signed off. He put away the radio gear and nodded to Lindbergh.

Lindy ran up the engine speed, then throttled down again. "I'm going to try for a little roll. I want the *Spirit* moving before we retract the wheels, to discourage the hull from bogging down. But the second she starts to dig in or the ship tries to nose over, Howard, I want that crank going like crazy!"

"Check!" Hughes knelt at the crank.

Lindy ran up the RPMs.

The *Spirit of San Diego* quivered, leaned over almost imperceptibly, then began to edge forward. The airspeed indicator, functioning now as a makeshift speedometer, read *five miles per hour*. The needle edged to the right, passed *eight*... *ten*... held. The *Spirit* settled a little in the snow. Lindy ran up the throttle farther. *Twelve*... the *Spirit* settled, the needle vibrated at *twelve*, then started to slip back toward *ten*...

"Wind 'em up, Howard!"

Hughes began furiously to turn the crank.

The needle continued to slip. The Ryan's tail surfaces caught at the air and the rear of the plane lifted. The nose dipped. With a heave Hughes got the wheels retracted.

The plane leaped forward. The boat hull thudded onto the

slush, slowing the *Spirit*. The engine roared. The plane resumed acceleration.

"Look at that!" Lindy shouted. His finger quivered as he pointed at the airspeed indicator. The needle hovered at *twenty miles per hour*... crept to *thirty*... *forty*... finally steadied near *sixty miles per hour*.

"This is some nutty snow-boat!" Howard Hughes slapped his leg. "Wait till I tell Bowlus and Hall about this! They'll have Ryan in the speedboat business in a week! Hah!"

The *Spirit of San Diego* zoomed forward. The icy walls of the Great Halley Cleft loomed threateningly above but drew no closer than fifteen feet apart. It was a challenging job, keeping the *Spirit* centered between the cliffs, sliding along on her hull and occasionally hydroplaning over a slippery area. Lindbergh had only the airplane's tail empennage for control, but he managed to make it do.

Gradually the ground—or rather, the snow-covered ice—seemed to dip away beneath the nose of the Ryan. "This must be the very edge," Amelia gasped. "The rim of the Rim! Look up!"

Charles Lindbergh cast a quick glimpse skyward, then returned his concentration to the task of keeping the *Spirit* on her course.

Amelia Earhart and Howard Hughes stared straight up through the Ryan's roof windows. The sky was a bright blue behind them. Directly overhead it deepened to a richer shade. They couldn't see directly ahead of the Ryan because the irregular walls of the Halley Cleft blocked their line of sight, but the occasional patch of sky that flashed before them was black and dotted with stars.

"We've made it!" Amelia exulted. "It's daytime on our side of the disk and nighttime on the far side. And here we are—it's night!"

She reached forward to give Charles Lindbergh a hug. He permitted her the briefest contact, then shrugged away so he could concentrate on his task. Amelia drew back, found Howard Hughes grinning at her side and yielded to his bear-hug.

"We're going to be in trouble again," Lindbergh said over one shoulder. "It's getting dark in here. If we have to stop, we might freeze in. Damn!"

The Ryan continued forward. Lindy throttled down and the

makeshift snow-boat slowed. But she continued forward through deepening twilight. Within the Great Halley Cleft the illumination turned from a blue-white to a deep purple, then all but ceased.

"My God!" Howard Hughes pointed through the windscreen. "Look at that, will you? The walls are glowing!"

They stared.

"No, not the walls," Hughes corrected. "Not the ice. There's something *in* the ice. Look—there's another! And on the other side, too! There are more of them! It's a whole row—two whole rows!

"Look at the things, all of 'em are deep blue-purple on one side and green like radium on the other side! I seen pictures of things like them in the paper, from those archaeologists digging up the old pharaohs. I know what them things are!

"They're sphinxes!"

"Not so big, eh, as the bombing dirigible *Doktor* Eckener was working on! Or even the old *Deutschland*. But it flies! It flies, and with the generator operating, we can recharge the batteries and make our way to the Rim!

"Well, good-by, *Kondor!* We will see your likes again!"

Von Richthofen waved at the tarpaulin-covered Udet monoplane. With its canvas covering staked out against permanently frost-covered ground, it was almost invisible. Aboard the *Schwarze Adler* were carried key parts of the Udet's four engines, along with notations of the aeroplane's latitude and longitude. The three Europeans fit into the gondola of the little Zeppelin with scant room to spare. Their weapons and supplies were laid out carefully.

A cast-iron tank of compressed hydrogen gas was, ironically, the heaviest single item in the balloon. Without it the *Schwarze Adler* would have flown farther and more easily than it did. But also, without it the Zeppelin would have been helpless to rise again, once its present fill of hydrogen had been vented.

With the extra tank, it would be possible, by careful use of ballast, to descend and rise again a number of times.

A light snow had begun to fall. The sky was a shining wall of pearl. Dry flakes were already covering the canvas that was stretched over the *Kondor*. Lothar von Richthofen manned the controls of the *Schwarze Adler*. *Freiherr* Manfred took the small chart-pad that contained the latitude and longitude data for the *Kondor* and scanned the landscape—or icescape—for some distinguishing features to use in locating the aeroplane, should they ever wish to return to it, or should a later imperial expedition seek to recover the machine.

"What planning to do now?" the Princess demanded. She had managed to arrange herself with a degree of dignity in the gondola of the *Schwarze Adler*. She was annoyed that the brothers paid more attention to their work and to each other than they did to her.

"Your Highness." Manfred bowed ironically. "We will fly due south for the time being. I have in the pad marked landmarks to return us here, should we desire. You see the saddle-back mountains to the west, the crown-shaped projection in the opposite direction."

"Yes. Am seeing clearly, Baron. And next? Is party flying to end of journey?"

"*Nein*, *Prinzessin*. We shall have to stop for supplies. Also, our batteries will not carry the *Schwarze Adler* to our destination without recharging. I hope we will see signs of civilization. Or even of savages. Some sign of human habitation.

"Else—who will work mines and farms for us, eh? Unless we send good German stock to settle. Here is plenty of *Luft zum Atmen*, plenty of air to breathe."

He gestured expansively.

"Mother Russia has not our crowding, eh? Not our need for living space."

"Tsar and Kaiser are allies, Baron. Great empires can be allies, also! Not needing more space, needing more soldiers! Needing more ships! Needing more aeroplanes!"

The *Schwarze Adler*'s propellers turned silently, powered by quiet electric motors. The absence of engine noise and vibration made the *Schwarze Adler*'s progress contrast emphatically with that of the abandoned *Kondor*. But the little Zeppelin also moved more slowly through the ever-leaden sky.

By midafternoon the dirigible encountered her first problem.

The three imperial aviators had eaten a light lunch and had

consumed glasses of tea kept hot in vacuum bottles. Aboard *Schwarze Adler* there was an absolute prohibition against the use of flame—a single spark could set off the Zeppelin's hydrogen in a disastrous explosion.

Even the use of firearms had been strongly discouraged by Ernst Udet and Bodo von Alvensleben. The chance of a gunpowder flash igniting the hydrogen bags was remote, but real.

Manfred and Lothar took turns guiding the Zeppelin southward over endless fields of ice and broken patches of black water. As one brother piloted the airship, the other would mount watch from the gondola's prow, scanning the ice with binoculars, high-powered rifle at hand but unloaded to discourage precipitous firing.

The Princess Irina kept her own counsel, sitting regally and seldom speaking to the men.

As the sun spiraled lower in the sky, clouds grew thicker and darker. Shadowy forms, pale white against the white of snow and ice, moved ghostlike across the mottled field beneath the airship.

"Ice!" Manfred von Richthofen, at the pilot's station, spat the single word. His brother Lothar turned from the mica window and looked questioningly at Manfred. The Princess Irina turned her pale face toward the pilot also.

"The snow is too wet now." Manfred gestured toward the gas-bag overhead. "It is freezing on the ship. We are losing altitude. Lothar, take a look. How high are we now?"

Lothar groaned. "Fifty metres, *Bruder*."

Manfred nodded grimly. "We could rise by dropping ballast, but higher would be colder even. Better to make camp and wait for morning. Then we can clear the ice and proceed."

Irina flared angrily. "And Americans? Are making camp also?" She snorted. "*Black Eagle* must fly on!"

"*Unmöglich*. Impossible. If we continue even a little, we will be in danger of losing control. If *Schwarze Adler* is destroyed, Princess, we have little hope. To win this race—or even to survive!

"So—we land!"

He peered through the mica windows, selecting a suitable place to bring down the Zeppelin. Small as it was, it did not require much area for landing. But von Richthofen needed to avoid sharp projections that might snag in the fabric of the airbag. Repairing tears under Arctic conditions would be sorely difficult, and reinflation would expend irreplaceable hydrogen.

The sharp-nosed Zeppelin circled slowly and silently over a patch of open ice. A nearby glacial range offered protection from what seemed to be a steady prevailing wind. Von Richthofen vented hydrogen into the atmosphere. The airship dropped closer to the ice.

Gray shadows slid across the white surface, yet there were no living creatures apparent on the ice. "Are ghosts!" Irina exclaimed. "Demons of frozen hell!"

"Foolishness!" Lothar snapped.

"In Russia, is knowledge of cold regions. Are souls of damned, racing to catch fliers."

At the Zeppelin's helm, Manfred laughed. "At *Symmeshoehle* you said we were going to flames of hell. Now you say hell is icy. Which, Your Highness, is the genuine Hades?"

"Are both, Baron! Is Gehenna-fire, is Gehenna-ice! Below airship are souls of damned!"

"Then they had better get out of our way!"

Again he reached for the lever that opened the airship's gas valve and vented hydrogen. "Lothar—you must be ground crew, hey?" von Richthofen ordered.

Lothar closed up the flaps of his flying suit. He pulled a fleece-lined helmet over his bullet head and knelt beside a trap in the floor. Beside the trap stood a coiled line with razor-sharp hooks at its end.

Manfred turned the rudder, putting the *Schwarze Adler* into a narrow spiral, dropping her steadily.

Lothar pulled back the trap door. He swung the grapnel through the bottom of the cabin, attempting to snag it upon irregularities of the ice. Again and again the grapnel bit, only to pull free as the *Schwarze Adler* circled away.

"No use," he grumbled, "dead slow, *Bruder*, *bitte*."

Manfred cut the airship's speed to its minimum. "Lothar, *mach schnell!* Quickly—we are vulnerable now. One puff of breeze and . . ."

Lothar perched on the edge of the trap. "Lower yet," he demanded. Manfred vented hydrogen still again. The ship floated less than five metres above the ice. The grapnel and line dragged behind the gondola.

With a muffled grunt Lothar heaved himself through the trap. He held both hands on the sturdy line, slid down it until his feet were near the ice surface and dropped. As the line swept past him he grasped it again, half a metre from the grapnel. He set his feet on the ice, shouted at the top of his voice, "Cut engine!"

His brother, aboard the airship, could hardly have heard the words. But he was watching, and at the correct moment he cut the engine; the propellers windmilled to a stop.

Lothar lifted the grapnel in both his hands, found an outcrop of solid ice. He swung the grapnel at the end of its line. Snow was still falling onto his flying helmet and suit. He shook his head to clear his vision of accumulated flakes. With his full strength he swung the grapnel at the base of the outcropping. Sharp prongs bit deep and held.

Within the hour they had secured the *Schwarze Adler*. The gondola rested lightly on the ice, the gasbag exerting hardly the lift needed to hold itself above the gondola.

"Not a good way to make camp," Manfred mourned. "But the best we can do on this ice. *Pah!* How far can it go? Is this whole hemidisk a frozen waste, lifeless and worthless?"

"Is Gehenna." Irina revived her theme. "Bible says Hades is beneath earth. Travelers have come to icy Hades."

"Unlikely. And if we have, we shall to earth above return." Manfred stood beside her. "Come. *Schwarze Adler* is secure—as much as possible. Let us eat dinner, warm ourselves, try to rest." He turned. "Lothar. We must set watch. Turn and turn about."

The younger man grinned sarcastically. "To guard against Her Highness's spirits of the lost, *Bruder?*"

Manfred frowned. "One never knows, *Bruder*. Probably we will be as safe as if were in our father's *Schloss*. A castle on the ice, eh? But still, to take no needless risk..."

The Princess graciously agreed to take a turn in the night. She preferred four hours of sleep first, and the brothers took the first two watches, each of two hours' duration. Irina slept inside the gondola. Her flying outfit provided sufficient warmth, even with the Zeppelin resting on ice, although the Princess was impatient at being unable to change her costume.

She was awakened by Lothar. "Irina," he whispered.

She frowned and mumbled, half asleep.

"Irina! You now have the watch." As she sat upright he held the high-powered rifle toward her. "You should be armed. You are familiar with firearms?"

She nodded. "For hunting. Also—in Russia, bodyguards can betray masters. Poor Uncle Nicky!" She brushed a tear away.

Lothar handed her the rifle. "If danger appears, sound the alarm, Highness. If you fire the rifle, be certain it is pointed *nowhere near the airship!* A bullet could set the hydrogen gas afire. And—*bitte*—no heroics!"

The Princess made no reply. She accepted the rifle from Lothar, tried the action, practiced sighting, lowered the weapon to her side. She drew the hood of her costume around her face. Climbing from the gondola she tested her footing on the ice and moved cautiously a few steps from the *Schwarze Adler*.

Outside, there was bright moonlight. The snowfall had ceased and a heavy formation of clouds had broken into drifting, scattered patches. As long as the moon was unobscured, the ice-landscape was illuminated in a ghostly imitation of day. The plain of ice stretched in all directions, interrupted at random intervals by jagged protruberances of white.

Irina held the heavy rifle across her chest, as the Tsar's soldiers carried their weapons. She walked slowly toward the prow of the Zeppelin, crossed to the far side and continued her patrol. The ice-boulders cast dim shadows on the flat plain. Their shapes were wildly suggestive. In the pallid light they cast chiaroscuro images: a mammoth, a walrus, a roosting eagle, a giant rose such as grew in the imperial greenhouse at the Winter Palace, a spired and turreted fairy-castle.

The Princess halted and lowered the heavy rifle, leaning its butt on the solid ice. In the lunar glare a shape had seemed to shift, almost beneath her feet. She knelt and wiped away loose snow.

She peered down through gray ice. Perhaps there was water farther down. How deep the ice extended was a mystery.

As she knelt, a vague shape appeared beneath the ice. She could almost believe that it was a living thing. It halted and appeared to gaze up at her.

Could it see her through the ice? Did it have any idea of what a human being was? Was the thing an Arctic fish? A seal? Was it any kind of animal or was it in truth a demon from the icy depths?

Was there even anything there?

She pressed a gloved hand to her eyes, shook her head to clear her vision, peered once more into the ice. She could not see anything looking back at her. She wasn't certain that there had been anything. Perhaps it had been only a shadow all along.

She felt herself shudder violently. The reaction was in part attributable to the cold, but it was a response, also, to the thing she had seen—or not seen—underneath the ice.

Carefully the Princess pulled herself erect and resumed her walk around the encampment, the heavy rifle held across her body. She halted with her back against an uneven ice-boulder the size of a peasant's hut. She lowered the rifle, studied the *Schwarze Adler*. It was silent and dark. The two brothers were within, sleeping. The bright moonlight cast strong shadows of the Zeppelin and the icy outcroppings.

The Princess let her gaze rise from the airship. In the distance was the *Symmeshoehle*, the North Hole of the world. At this very moment, on the other side of the disk, it must be broad daylight. It was noon, or close to it, in St. Petersburg and in Berlin.

She strained her eyes in the direction from which the *Black Eagle* had floated, wondering if she would be able to see Northern Lights, the reflection of daylight through the *Symmeshoehle*. But it was too far. There was only the ghostly whiteness of the ice field, punctuated with patches of black water.

Above her was the similar pattern of sky and cloud—black sky instead of white ice, gray clouds instead of black water.

Stars blazed in the blackness. The Princess wondered if the remote stars were truly suns, as the astronomers claimed, and if they possessed planets and people who were at this moment gazing into *their* skies, even gazing at earth's sun, wondering if there were planets here and if they had people. Were the men and women of other worlds Christians? Did they speak Russian? Did they have a tsar of their own? Were their cities as great as—

The weight struck her from above.

It sent the Princess tumbling to her knees. The heavy rifle skittered and jounced across the ice. Irina struggled toward it but the weight landed on her a second time and sent her sprawling.

She struggled to regain her feet, got as far as her hands and knees and caught her first sight of the thing that had knocked her down. It was a ghost or demon of some sort. Squat, ugly, vaguely similar to a man in shape. Its features were grotesque and its hands were huge and clawed.

It was completely naked.

It was utterly hairless, and as pallid as the ice.

It made no sound.

A wind had risen, and was moaning around the ice outcroppings. Irina screamed once for the von Richthofens. It was unlikely they would hear her, in the *Schwarze Adler*, over the wind.

The demon leaped forward, knocked Irina down again, passed over her and landed with a horrible plop. She managed to scramble to her feet despite the interference of her clumsy flying outfit. The demon had turned and faced her again. It was between her and the heavy rifle. Its eyes were ablaze with cold fire.

Irina crossed herself in the Russian fashion. She backed away from the demon, praying silently that the holy sign would make it disappear in a puff of smoke. Or at least that the ritual would hold it at bay, as the crucifix was supposed to hold *vrikolaki* at bay.

The demon hunched itself together, squatting menacingly.

The Princess backed away from it, repeating her holy gesture. She halted when she jolted against the edge of a mass of ice. The demon crept slowly toward her, belly down on the ice. It used its thick, pale legs to propel itself with a horrifying hopping motion.

Irina pulled the glove from one hand and reached inside her heavy coat, feeling frantically for her opal-and-obsidian rosary. Her gesture had not dispelled the demon, but the monster had slowed its advance. Perhaps the holy object itself... She moved her lips in silent appeal to the Virgin, searched inside her coat for her crucifix.

Instead of beads and cross, her searching fingers closed upon—the Kaiser's gift to her. The dagger.

She drew it from her coat and held it before her. Ever since the assassination of Nicholas and the nearly successful revolution that had set off the One Year War, every Russian aristocrat and every member of the royal family had received training in the use of weapons.

Girls as well as boys.

The Princess Irina held her hand wrist-up, the dagger gripped loosely in her fingers, her thumb across the hilt. If the demon did not respond to supernatural defenses, it might yield to arms.

She fixed her eyes on it, flexed her knees, shifted her feet to gain balance on the dangerous ice.

The demon gave a low call, the first sound it had made. It braced itself, the claws of its feet and hands making a scratching sound on the ice. The demon hopped forward once. Twice. Then it halted and drew itself up and glared at Irina.

Without warning a shadow swept over the Princess, encompassing the distance between herself and the demon. Then it advanced and took in the demon as well. She took her eyes from the demon for a moment to glance upward. A dark snow-cloud had obscured the face of the moon and darkened the outcropping and the frozen plain.

The demon made a different sound, a horrid croaking noise from deep in its throat.

Irina looked back at it quickly. The demon had launched itself through the air, straight at her. Its powerful legs carried it to the level of her face.

She dodged frantically aside.

The demon swiped at her with the claws of one hand; it missed her. Its body thudded against the ice and its claws embedded themselves in the outcropping where Irina's face had been.

The monster tumbled back to the frozen surface and Irina backed away. She kept her free hand behind her, guiding herself relative to the hill of ice. The Kaiser's dagger she kept before her at the level of her waist.

The demon leaped once more. Again the Princess managed to dodge its bulk, but this time the clawed hand drew a row of parallel slices in her coat. At the same moment Irina lunged upward with her dagger. She felt it scrape roughly along the monster's ribs.

The monster flopped back onto the ice, a gray-white mass that stared up at her through hate-filled eyes in a parody of a human face.

The eyes bulged.

There was no visible nose or ears. The mouth was broad and flat and narrow-lipped. It flicked its tongue at her obscenely: a long, disgusting member, as pale as the rest of the monster. The tongue was coated with some viscous liquid.

A drop of it flew across the intervening space and spattered on the ice-mound beside the Princess. It sizzled there, melting a bowl-shaped depression into the ice. A disgusting stench arose from it.

The Princess glanced briefly at her shoulder. The edges of the marks made by the demon's claws were singed as by hell-fire.

The demon crept across the ice, renewing its attack on the Princess. It heaved itself up onto its haunches and struck at her with its claws. She managed to escape and struck down at it with her dagger, but she also missed. The demon flicked its tongue and a blob of its loathsome spittle struck her heavy coat. It hissed and foamed and sent caustic fumes rising.

The Princess started to run across the ice toward the heavy rifle and the *Schwarze Adler* beyond.

The thick cloud passed at last from the face of the moon, and the ice-plain was once more brightly illuminated. Beyond the rifle but short of the Zeppelin, the Princess could see a dark patch on the ice. It was roughly circular. It glinted with moonlight and she realized that it was a hole, that the glint of light was off the surface of black water.

It was the portal through which the demon had reached the upper world from the cold and watery Gehenna beneath.

Irina was just steps from the rifle. Again the demon crashed into her; again she tumbled to the ice as a white form flashed above her body. She caught herself on hands and knees, retaining her grasp on the Kaiser's dagger.

The demon flopped on the ice, slid until it caught itself by digging in with the claws of hands and feet alike. For the briefest moment it squatted unmoving, its back turned to the Princess.

Irina thrust herself forward, unconsciously imitating the hopping, bounding movement of the demon. She hurled herself onto its back, reached with her left hand and tugged its loathsome head upward. The demon's bulging eyes stared into her own with an almost hypnotic power.

She gasped but moved without hesitation. Still tugging toward herself with her left hand, she reached far forward with her right, plunged the Kaiser's dagger into the demon's throat beneath the spot where a man's left ear would have been. She drew the dagger sideways, feeling its razorlike blade slash through the demon's stringy tendons and soft, almost jelly-textured flesh.

The demon made a final sound, a wailing moan like that of a soul at the realization of damnation. Its body flexed in a meaningless, thrashing convulsion, throwing the Princess sideways, her dagger still in her hand, dripping with a horrible green-white ichor.

The Princess crouched, horrified, on the ice. The demon, trailing gobbets of white jellylike stuff, struggled across the surface. It was no longer able to hop, but instead dragged itself by its claw-tipped hands. It ignored her, struggling through puddles of its own insides, to the black hole in the ice. With a soft splash it disappeared into the depths.

The Princess Irina Lvova carefully cleaned her dagger in a handful of wet snow. She slid it into its scarlet scabbard beneath her flying coat, drew her glove onto her exposed hand, retrieved the unfired hunting rifle and walked to the *Schwarze Adler*.

She tugged the door open, slid the heavy rifle into the gondola, and hoisted one foot onto the lintel. She glanced back over her shoulder. The moon was low in the sky now. The sun was not yet visible, but the clouds had almost all disappeared, and the stars shone brightly against the solid blackness.

The Princess Irina drew a deep refreshing breath and hauled herself into the gondola.

Chapter 9

At noon they saw the great city.

The Avenue of Sphinxes proved a tantalizing mystery but little more. They would not stop the *Spirit of San Diego* if stopping were at all avoidable. There was the danger of the makeshift snow-boat's hull becoming frozen if they halted; there was a slight but significant risk that the Ryan's engine, once switched off, might be difficult to restart; there might be a shifting of the ice that would trap the *Spirit*, even crush it.

Howard Hughes "piloted" the Ryan between the towering rows of sculptures. Through the crystalline ice the features of the glowing beasts were clearly visible: classic human heads dressed in archaic ceremonial style, set with convincing naturalness on the bodies of muscular quadrupeds. As with the Great Sphinx at Luxor, these mighty sculptures held between their massive legs entrances to buildings apparently lodged within the torsos of the creatures.

Incomprehensible inscriptions surmounted the portals.

As Hughes manned the controls of the Ryan, Amelia Earhart and Charles Lindbergh sketched the hieroglyphics as rapidly as they could.

"We should have brought along a Kodak," Amelia mourned. "I don't know why none of us thought of it. What opportunities we're missing!"

Lindbergh shook his head ruefully. "But once we get back, Amy... Once we get back, this should open routes to the other side. People will want to come here. If we find any nations there'll be trade. Explorers will want to see everything. There'll be plenty of photographers later on."

The channel through the ice dipped again. This time, upward.

"Hey," Hughes called from the pilot's seat. "Trouble. Time for a council."

"I think we've passed the halfway mark," Lindbergh said.

Amelia agreed. "If those sphinxes were built by some ancient people who traveled between the hemidisks as a matter of course—"

"We don't know that," Lindbergh interrupted.

"No, we don't. But I can't think of a more likely explanation, can you?"

"Guess not."

"Then the statues might have marked the halfway point." Amelia gestured out the cabin window. "It seems the kind of thing people would do. Build some sort of markers to show travelers they were halfway to—wherever they were going."

"Some milestones!"

"Milestones, customs houses, temples."

"Tourist hotels," Hughes gritted.

"They just might have been that, yes. When in the South Rim, stay at the luxurious Sphinx Hotel. All the comforts of home. Fresh ice available at all hours. Exotic dancing in the Blizzard Room."

Lindy shook his head. "Why build inside the ice like that? I can't see how anybody could get in or out of those things."

Hughes said, "Maybe they're just beacons. Nobody's *meant* to get to 'em!"

"Then why have doors?"

"You win."

"And how did they build 'em anyway? Did they melt the ice away, build the sphinxes, then pour back tons of water and let it freeze in place? *Why?*"

Amy said, "Maybe the climate changed."

"What?"

"We don't know that the South Rim was always here, was always icy."

"Come on," Hughes challenged. "If the Rim wasn't here all the water would squirt off the edge of the world. Then the rest of the oceans would pour down here and they'd *all* spray off. The whole disk would become a desert. It isn't—so we know that the Rim has always been here!"

"Nope!" Lindbergh joined the debate again. "We don't know how deep the ice is, Howard. The Rim might be a few hundred feet of ice, and all the rest of it rock. If that's so, then if the climate was different at one time, people might have been able to sail ships right around the Rim. Right over it. Maybe there *were* Egyptians here!"

"Yeah? Then how come nobody remembers that?"

"Who knows? How far back does our history go? A few thousand years? And how old is the earth, and how long have there been people on it? A million years? Ten million?"

Hughes shrugged.

"When I was a nurse in Boston," Amelia volunteered, "I met an odd man who wrote stories with all sorts of monstrosities and weird notions in them. Said his idol was Poe. The man gave me one magazine with a story of his in it, about an ancient city.

"In fact, he described the city as being under the ice, just about where we are. I'll have to send him a note about it when we get home. Anyway, this story of his has the city being built millions and millions of years ago, by people who weren't people."

"Hold it, sister," Hughes snapped. "People who weren't people? How's that again?"

"I'm sorry. I wasn't clear. Well, despite poor old William Jennings Bryan, you know, Mr. Scopes was right. The species of the earth are all related to one another, and the more advanced developed from the less advanced, over a long period of time."

"I'm not so sure of that. But so what?"

"Oh, my." Amelia shook her head. "This was only a story that my friend showed me. He'd been wounded in the One Year War and I was his nurse. Maybe I shouldn't have mentioned it. But his idea was that a very advanced, very scientific race had emerged on the earth millions of years ago. And built a great city at the South Rim but then died off. But their city was still there, and there was even a way for them to communicate with us by telepathy, even over millions of years."

"Sounds like a lot of hooey to me," Hughes said. "But anyhow, it looks like it's gonna be all uphill from here on. You think we can make it, Swede?"

"You were with Bowlus and Hall, Howard."

"Yeah, but you wrote the specs."

"True enough." He put his head in his hands. "Hold on a minute. I *think* we're all right. The engine's running smooth, oil pressure's good. I don't know how much to trust the fuel gauge when we're, uh, 'flying' uphill like this. But I think we have a fair supply left."

He turned in his seat, gave Amelia a rather strange grin and said, "Besides, we don't have any choice, do we? The cleft isn't wide enough to turn around in, and if those sphinxes marked the halfway mark—seems sensible to me that they did—then it would be farther to go back than to push ahead, anyhow!"

"So, as Columbus said..."

The channel was lighted, now, by a faint suggestion of daylight that filtered down from the sky, and back to them from the ice.

Then the channel ended with startling suddenness. Howard Hughes was still at the controls when the *Spirit of San Diego* left behind the oppressive walls of ice and surged onto a brightly reflecting plain.

Hughes cut the engine back to idle and the Ryan skidded to a halt.

"Okay, time for a rest stop," Lindy announced. "Then we set the wings back into place and fly again. What's the matter, Howard? You look worried!"

Hughes stroked his stubbled chin. "Don't like the idea of taxiing on the boat hull, Swede."

"Huh! We came through the Rim that way."

"Number one, we had no choice. Number two, we were lucky, and let's not push Lady Luck. And number three, that was nice soft slush. This stuff looks a lot harder and rougher. Suppose we stroll around and check it out."

Lindbergh nodded thoughtfully. "How're your muscles? Think you can crank the *Spirit* back onto her wheels? Let's fly the crate—that's what she's for!"

It was difficult, but they got the Ryan airborne again, Lindbergh babying along the controls while Hughes grunted and strained at the wheel-crank. For the first time on their trip Amelia Earhart felt useless and consequently miserable.

As soon as Hughes called that the wheels were fully lowered Lindy gunned the radial Whirlwind and the monoplane sped along the farside ice shelf. Lightened by the weight of expended fuel, the *Spirit* leaped into the air, her takeoff as different as night and day from her lumbering rise from the waters at Tierra del Fuego.

It was her first flight in the circumpolar hemidisk. As far as her three crew members could know, it was the first flight ever made by an aircraft on this side of the disk in all the history of the planet.

As far as her crew could know!

The morning gray of the Rim region gave way to skies as blue as the crisp vista off the San Diego shoreline on a May morning. The white wall of the Ice Rim receded behind the *Spirit*. Soon it shrank to a low, glistening line that separated sky from dark sea. The broken floes that clustered at the base of the Rim grew fewer until the *Spirit* soared over unbroken ocean.

Amelia sat with the chart-board in her lap, a blank sheet fastened to the board and push-pins and drawing tools at hand. The blank map comprised nothing more than two concentric circles laid on a square of heavy paper. The outer circle represented the Rim; the inner one, Symmes' Hole. The great swath of blankness that lay between was a whole hemidisk of *terra et mare incognitae*.

The only sound in the cabin was the steady drone of the Whirlwind's nine powerful cylinders. There was no need for Lindy, Hughes, or Earhart to speak of the Ryan's fuel supply. Or of the need to find a landing space before it was expended. If this hemidisk was covered entirely with water, the *Spirit* could land safely on her specially built hull. But her crew would be doomed, trapped in their aircraft until rough weather sank the *Spirit*—or until their supply of drinking water and food gave out.

If they could find land, there was a chance they could find people as well. They might then obtain fuel for the Ryan and food and water for themselves.

The Whirlwind engine droned on.

"Don't see no sign of a welcoming committee," Hughes finally grumbled.

That broke the tension. Suddenly they all could speak.

"A committee would be swell, but I'd settle for a sight of the nearest continent."

"Continent! I'd be grateful for a two-bit atoll!"

"Would you settle for a sandbar?"

"A sandbar? Listen, crank down the wheels and I'll put this baby down on a pool table!"

"Would you settle for a fishing smack?" Amy asked.

"I'd settle for a garbage scow!"

"Or a rowboat!"

"How about a fishing smack?"

"You used that one. No repeats!"

"I'm not joking. Look over there. There—to starboard. Can you see it? The sun is glaring on the water, but..."

Hughes pressed against the window. "Holy cow! She's right! It's a boat! Swede, it's a little sailboat!"

Lindbergh swung the monoplane into a bank and spiraled down to starboard.

The boat was small and white, with a single mast and a fore-and-aft rigged sail gently bellied by the breeze.

The monoplane circled over it, dropping closer to the water. The fliers could see the crew of the boat laying down their work to gaze at the airplane. They seemed surprised, but neither awed by the aircraft nor uncomprehending of it.

"Looks like they've seen big silver birds before," Hughes said. "We won't get away with any gods-from-the-sky stunts with these guys." He slid back his window and waved to the fishermen. He yelled a greeting and one of the men shouted back.

"Hey," Hughes grinned, "they're friendly little devils. Funny-looking, though. Look at their skin—red men! But they don't look like Injuns. *Really* red! And they ain't got a hell of a lot of clothes on 'em neither! Better cover up your peepers, Amelia!"

"I *was* a nurse," she snapped. Hughes roared with laughter. Amy flushed as red as the fishermen. She joined in the amusement. "All right, you got me that time."

"I'm going to give this a try," Lindbergh broke in. He leveled the Ryan, then banked to the left and circled the fishing vessel again.

He slid his own window open and shouted at the fishermen.

They waved and shouted back. One of them pointed.

Lindbergh shook his head. He set the Ryan on a steady course and began to pick up altitude. In a few minutes the fishing boat was lost behind them.

"What was that all about?" Hughes demanded.

"I'm not sure." Lindbergh checked the compasses and nodded. "I *think* he was telling us the way to land. I certainly hope he was."

Hughes grunted. "I think the guy was saying, 'Whatever you do, don't head *that* way, that's where the sea-serpents and the killer cyclones are!'"

"Yeah. Only one way to find out, though. What do you think, Amy? Our lives are *all* on the line."

Amelia looked up from her chart. The map was still mostly blank, but she had carefully sketched in the location of the Great Halley Cleft and the Farside Ice Shelf, and their location when the fishing smack had appeared.

"I don't think they'd send us to the serpents. They looked pretty friendly."

"Hmm. And?"

"And on the face of it, you'd be more likely to show a stranger the way to safety."

"That's my point," Hughes insisted. "You show 'em the way to safety—you show 'em the way to avoid getting crunched."

"No. You'd show strangers the way to *go*, not the way *not* to go."

"Anyhow," Lindbergh announced, "we can't circle indefinitely.

Those fishermen may not return to port till night—maybe not for a week. We don't have the fuel."

"We could land on the water."

"Sure. But what for? We'd have to take off again."

"Okay," Hughes gave in. "I know what's coming. *As Columbus said...*"

"Right."

The water beneath the *Spirit of San Diego* remained smooth. A few fluffy cumulus clouds drifted slowly above them like wads of cotton tossed into the air.

The sun reached its highest point, then began its slow, complex spiral down the afternoon sky, toward some point on the Ice Rim where it would create a simultaneous nightfall for one side of the earth and dawn for the other.

But now it was early afternoon. At least, where the *Spirit* drove steadily through the air. In Atchison, Kansas, Amelia thought, it was past midnight. There was probably not a light burning, not a soul awake in the entire town.

Hughes shouted and pointed. "As Christopher Columbus's lookout said, '*Land ho!*'"

It lay on the horizon, a narrow strip of featureless black. A dark, thick line separating ocean from bright sky. But it was land.

Amelia set up her instruments, shot the sun, jotted rapidly on the margin of her chart.

Lindy checked his altimeter, fuel gauge, said, "Looks like an easy jaunt. We'll get there with juice to spare." He leaned toward the windscreen, as if moving even a few inches closer to the approaching land-mass could make its features clearer. "Wish I could see the land better. What kind of place will it be?"

Each of them had his own thoughts on that point, but none spoke. There was no real choice but to wait.

Soon the shoreline drew near. There were a scattering of light patches, natural beaches where the ocean washed onto pale sand.

"Our fishermen certainly didn't come from here," Lindy said.

"How so?"

Lindbergh pointed. "No harbor. No piers. No sign of a town at all."

"They could of come off the beach."

Lindbergh shook his head. "Not with that boat. Cloth, woodworking, tools, and that far at sea—those people came from a country with some industry. Some technology. They're not woodsfolk."

Amelia put away her gear. "Then they're civilized."

Lindy grinned. "I guess so. I'm not really so sure. Depends on your definition."

"Sure," Hughes said sarcastically. "Just look at the wonderful civilization down there. All of them wonderful cities and busy factories and roads. Why, tonight we'll have a fancy dinner in some posh roadhouse and dance the black-bottom, then ride back to town in a Stutz Bearcat and catch the midnight talkie.

"Only how come I can only see trees down there?" he continued. "I think maybe we're over this world's version of Africa. I hope we don't get invited for dinner and discover it's us for the main course."

Lindbergh held the stick in his left hand. He turned halfway in his seat and laid his right hand on Hughes's arm. "Howard," he said evenly, "I really think you ought to try the radio. Why don't you just try the radio. They may be calling us right now."

"Who might, Swede? Chief Waziri? Mowgli the jungle boy?"

"Just try it, Howard!"

Lindy and Amelia didn't have to hear a word. Hughes's jaw dropped, his eyes bulged, he bounced up and down until the Ryan shook in midflight.

"Okay," Lindy said. "What did you pick up?"

"What?" Hughes looked startled. "Oh. Oh, I don't think they're really talking to us. Must be some kind of stuff, uh, for home receivers. Like KDKA or KPO and them stations. It's *music*. I think it is, anyhow!"

He pulled the earphone from his head and held it to Lindy's. The Swede listened for a few seconds and shook the phone away.

"Some kind of music, I guess. Sounds like an organ. Do you think it's picking up a church broadcast? Maybe even from home? Who knows if the signals can come through the disk itself?"

He offered the earphone to Amy. She reached for it, held it to her ear. Her forehead creased in concentration. Abstractedly she made a notation on her chart. "There's a voice now."

The drone of the Whirlwind engine filled the cabin. Seconds passed. They seemed like minutes.

Finally she said, "This is strange. I can *almost* understand what they're saying. She closed her eyes as if she could shut out the drone of the engine.

Moments passed.

She shook her head, handed the earphone forward again. "It's maddening. Most of the words sounded familiar to me. But I couldn't quite get the meaning." She pounded her fist on the chart-board in frustration.

"Wait a minute."

Hughes turned around. There was an almost feverish light in Amelia's eyes.

"Let me hear that again!"

She reached for the phone, sketching figures on the margin of her chart.

Lindbergh, ignoring the byplay between Earhart and Hughes, leaned forward. He peered from the window. The thick growth of trees had given way to a range of gently sloping, meadowy hills. He pointed excitedly.

"Look! There are buildings down there! Roads! We're in some-body's country, that's for sure. There are *people* here!"

Hughes looked out the window on his own side of the plane. He nodded in agreement with Lindy. "They must be them red-skins we saw out fishing. Look at that—they got some pretty good houses. Ain't no dinky fisher-shacks down there."

Amelia lowered the earphone. "I think I've got it now."

"If that's their shanties, what's their big houses like?"

"There has to be a city."

"It's a mixture, that's what it is. That's why it was so hard to follow."

"At least, I *think* there has to be a city. If this is just a farming country, maybe they only have scattered houses. Maybe they haven't *invented* cities yet!"

"I don't care."

"I wish I'd paid more attention at Columbia."

"I wish I'd paid more attention at Wisconsin."

"I can taste the hot cookin' now!"

"Damn, who was that language prof. Said that mixed cultures produced mixed languages every time. You get a *patois*. A pidgin. Oh, damn me, why didn't I listen more!"

"I should have taken some sociology courses. All I paid attention to was engineering. Do they *always* build cities? Look at those fields. Everything's beautiful. Can that advanced a people run their culture without trading centers, ports, *anything?* Don't they have a capital?"

"Oh, boy, a hot shower and a clean bed. That's for me! Wonder if they have shaving cream."

"I'm sure I could figure it out if I had a chance. It's so crazy—I'm sure some of the words were Spanish and some were Syrian and some were Chinese. Does that make any sense at all?"

"Look! There *is* a city! Look up that road. And what a burg! They don't have to give no ground to Broadway or the Loop!"

They dropped the tangled conversation and peered forward. The cultivated fields gave way to a rectangular track of rich green grassland, and in the midst of that a magnificent array of massive structures. Each was built upon a square, heavy-looking base. Twenty feet up the base was set back and roofed, and another wall rose to another level.

The buildings mounted that way, level upon level, hundreds of feet into the air.

Each was constructed of mighty stones, each building of a single color: ochre, brick-red, clay-blue, olive. Great tangles of leafy vines grew from the upper levels and extended thick creepers to the lower steps.

Oddly shaped machines stood on the roofs, and at the corners were great rounded objects that might be lights.

"Are they pyramids?" Hughes said. "They look like 'em, only kind of—different."

"Like—they're more like the ones in Yucatán." Lindy shook his head. "I barnstormed down there with Leon Klink and Bud

Gurney, before we got the mail service contract. They have pyramids there too, like Egypt, only they have steps like these. Only they're dead. The ones in Yucatán and the ones in Egypt. They're all dead. And these look like people live in them!"

Figures were scurrying around on the roofs of the giant structures. Some were climbing into the machines that stood in precise patterns. Others swarmed over the rounded things at the edges of the roofs.

"They're not exactly pyramids," Amelia said. "They're—oh, help me remember! They're *ziggurats*, that's what they are! The vines are the tip-off, they're like the hanging gardens of Babylon. Those things are ziggurats!"

A dozen or more of the machines had lifted from the roofs of the huge buildings, and moved gracefully through the air toward the *Spirit of San Diego*. Clearly, they were piloted aircraft, although of a type that the Ryan crew had never encountered before.

Each consisted of a square platform with strange contrivances at the corners and midpoints of each edge. The pilots sat in transparent enclosures at the center of the flat area.

From this distance it was clear that the pilots manipulated controls, but their nature was unclear. With each movement by the pilot, the small devices along the perimeter of the aircraft would revolve, rise or fall, or glow a different color.

The machines rose swiftly toward the Ryan as the monoplane approached the city. If they made any sound it could not be heard over the droning of the Whirlwind engine.

Amelia was the first to look away from the approaching machines and down again at the city.

"Look—they're moving those things! Aiming them at us!"

The flying machines had now formed a perfect ring, well above the *Spirit* and with the *Spirit* equidistant from the square flyers.

Amelia gasped. "Those curved things—they're glowing! Look, they're making colors like the flyers!"

The Whirlwind engine gasped once, then lapsed into silence. The only sound aboard the Ryan now was the rush of wind past the cockpit and over the braces. Lindbergh tried the magneto.

"It's no good. Our mill is dead."

"We ain't fallin', though," Hughes grated.

Lindbergh nodded. "You're right. I can't figure it out. Look!" He moved the stick forward. "Nothing. No controls. No power. Yet we're flying as smooth as silk."

"That's what's happening," Hughes returned. "There." He pointed. "Look at them babies glowing at us! They're pullin' us in as smooth as an angler lands a sock-eye salmon!"

Chapter 10

"Was real! *Was real!*" The Princess Irina Lvova beat her fists in rage against the wooden framework of the *Schwarze Adler*'s gondola.

"I am sorry, Princess." Manfred von Richthofen tried to soothe her. "I cannot believe in demons. They are the product of superstition. The product of ignorance. Such creatures do not exist."

"Fool, look!" The Princess pointed scornfully to the scratches in her flying costume. "Who did? Who did? Also—how? See cuts and burns in leather, Baron. Did Princess do this to self?"

The *Freiherr* examined the damaged costume, shaking his head. He glanced briefly over his shoulder, saw the back of his younger brother's shaven head as Lothar carefully steered the *Black Eagle* over the ice-fields. "Something happened, Princess. This of course it is necessary to concede. You met some wild creature perhaps."

"Was demon!" Irina insisted. "If Baron saw demon, *would* believe. Creature's face—oh! Great eyes, bulging, like so! No nose! No ears! And mouth was broad, flat thing, like so!" With long fingers she pulled at the corners of her mouth, imitating the face of the monster.

Manfred von Richthofen turned away so the Princess would not see the laughter in his expression. When he regained his composure he turned back. "And your demon—from Hades, of course. You can solve a great problem for theologians. Was the demon black in color, or red?"

"Was *white!*" she spat. "White like ice! White like death! Was lost soul, wandering from Gehenna, seeking home on earth. In Russia have them also. *Vrikolaki*. What word in German, oh—is *Vampyr*. Knowing *Vampyr*, Manfred? Lothar?" She called past the Baron. "Knowing *Vampyr*, Lothar, *vrikolaki?*"

Lothar grinned over one shoulder. "*Vrikolaki? Vampyr? Ach, ja, Prinzessin. Nosferatu, ja? Manfred, nosferatu, hah?*"

"*Ja*," Manfred nodded.

"Not real," Lothar averred.

"You see, Princess?" Manfred resumed. "Impossible. But perhaps a beast. A polar bear cub, maybe." He held his hand to her shoulder, placed restless fingertips at the end of the slashes and traced the damage. "You see—the claws of a cub could these marks have made."

Without waiting for further comment from the Princess he strode and stood beside his brother, gazing out the front window of the gondola. The Zeppelin's electric motor purred softly, spinning the silent propellers, driving the airship southward.

Impatiently, Manfred took over the helm from his brother. He pushed the Zeppelin to the limit of its speed. It still moved with frustrating slowness. "*Ach*, for a Pfalz or a Roland! This rotten gasbag is as fast as a hippopotamus! That would be a better name for it. *Das Flugflusspferd. Ach!*"

"Bodo and Ernst planned everything, *Bruder*." Lothar grinned ironically. "The *Kanzler* himself placed his seal upon our plan. Have you complaints?"

Manfred's hands scurried over the Zeppelin's controls like creatures with independent wills. He glared at Lothar. "Boelcke would spin in his grave. His greatest pupil, I who outdid my master, standing at the helm of a *Flugflusspferd*. A flying hippopotamus. What a disgrace!"

The broken ice-field beneath the airship had given way to a band of threatening black water that smashed against even blacker, towering cliffs.

Only where a broken wave rained back onto the black sea was there any change of color. There the spume shone sickly greenish-white. Occasionally a ray of sunlight caught the flying spray and created a feeble rainbow that hung hopelessly against the gloomy cliffs and the gloomy sea.

The sky that had lightened with dawn was darkening again, this time with a thick overcast of depressing gray.

The Princess, standing at one side of the gondola and peering into the distance, came suddenly alert. "Will crash!" she screamed. "Will die! *Schwarze Adler* will smash on cliffs, will fall into sea, will fall into demon-land!"

She sobbed disconsolately. "Should never have left Petrograd! Should have stayed with father, Regent Lvov, and Cousin Tsar!"

"*Sag ihr, dass sie schweigen soll!*" Manfred commanded. Across his shoulder, he repeated, "Silence her! I can stand no more of these complaints!"

Lothar tried to comfort the Princess. She resisted his efforts, telling her beads noisily and beseeching the Blessed Virgin to protect her from the demons beneath the sea. "Is victim! Is dead demon calling for *Schwarze Adler!* Is wanting our lives!"

"We are safe, Princess," Lothar insisted. He tried to take her hands but she jerked them away from him.

"*Bruder*." He turned his bullet head toward the pilot. "Those cliffs are very high. Can this flying hippo climb them?"

Manfred barked his scorn. "I am waiting merely for the proper moment to drop ballast, *kleine Bruder*. There is no cause for fear."

He spun the Zeppelin's helm a few degrees, so the airship approached the cliffs obliquely instead of head-on. The overcast had thickened still further, turning from a solid blanket of gray to a roiling body of cumulonimbus masses with ragged, frightening streamers of stratus clouds whipping beneath them like angry serpents.

Bolts of lightning slashed between the clouds and the peaks of waves. Others seemed to explode within masses of dark cumulus, giving forth an eerie, malevolent glare.

"Look!" the Princess burst forth again. She pointed ahead of the airship toward the menacing granite rampart. "Is palace! Is castle of lost souls! Is palace of Lucifer, Prince of Underworld!"

She fell to her knees, pressing the double-barred obsidian crucifix to her bloodless lips.

A bolt of lightning crackled and smashed into the peak of a granite cliff thirty metres from the *Schwarze Adler*. A massive shard of jagged stone slowly split away from the cliff and tumbled toward the Zeppelin. There was no time to steer the airship away from the looming mass of granite. Each occupant of the gondola instinctively reacted to the sight of the onrushing mass.

The Princess Lvova curled into a ball in the corner of the cabin, shrieking prayers.

From the throats of the brothers von Richthofen there emerged inarticulate growls. Lothar's lips tugged away from his teeth, exposing a feral threat. Manfred raised his hands, fingers waving with a life of their own, seeking some enemy to throttle.

But the massive shard of granite tumbled past the *Schwarze Adler*, passing like the stony club of a murderous giant in some tale of the brothers Grimm.

The massive rock smashed into rough water beneath the *Schwarze Adler*. The sound of its impact reached the ears of the travelers simultaneously with a crashing thunderclap. The doubled roar of thunder and water was overwhelming. The three travelers involuntarily clamped their hands to smitten ears.

Before they could recover from the blast of sounds, the entire Zeppelin was rocked again, this time by a single massive rush of water sent rocketing upward by the impact of the granite. The gondola tumbled. The airship tipped, nose-downward, so that it nearly plunged into the sea. The three occupants were sent rolling around the floor of the cabin, colliding with walls, with furnishings, with one another.

Desperately Manfred von Richthofen scrambled to the control column, levered himself back to his feet, spun the tiller to send the *Black Eagle* heading away from the cliff. He hit the peglike switch to start dumping ballast. He shoved over the lever that controlled the Zeppelin's electric motor and the propellers ran up to maximum speed.

The airship raised its nose from the brink of doom. It turned away from the cliffs and began to battle for altitude. For anxious minutes the contest was in doubt. Angry winds were whipping the *Schwarze Adler* toward granite walls with knifelike projections.

Greedy seas lashed upward, eager to pull this strange prey from the troubling sky.

The gasbag barely cleared the top of the cliffs. The toe of the gondola smashed against granite, was jolted away and nearly torn loose from the gasbag. The bottom of the gondola scraped across a sharp edge of rock. Floorboards were ripped clear and angry storm-winds whistled through the cabin.

But the *Schwarze Adler* rose. The airship survived, and those within her.

"Splendid piloting!" Lothar von Richthofen clapped his brother resoundingly on the back. "Now can Oswald Boelcke rest happily in his tomb, *grosser Bruder!*"

"*Ja, ja, kleine Bruder. Und—*" he looked behind him for an instant "—and the Princess. What is she doing now?"

Lothar made his way gingerly through the half-wrecked cabin. The Princess had staggered to her feet and stood trembling against the outer wall of the gondola, staring with horror-stricken eyes at the landscape below.

It was dark, windswept, rocky. The storm hid whatever illumination might have fallen from the night-darkened sky, but an almost continuous series of lightning flashes threw a flat, deathlike glare over the scene.

The *Schwarze Adler* had turned again so that its course now ran parallel to the crest of the escarpment. To seaward, black masses of water yielded up roaring, foaming waves that shattered on the rock, casting back tons of green-white spume. To landward, the terrain fell away briefly, then rose again toward a range of jagged mountains. Another wing of the storm—if not a separate front—roiled and flashed among those peaks, illuminating their sides and summits fitfully.

Directly beneath the Zeppelin the land appeared grim, lifeless and black. The edges of the cliffs were ragged and sharp. There were few signs of life. The occasional hardy trees that managed to survive in the thin soil stretched gnarled limbs achingly as if to draw desperate sustenance from the very air.

The Princess Irina, after staring in fascination at the horrid vista, turned toward Lothar von Richthofen. She reached for his hands and inclined her head toward his massive chest.

The aviator pulled away from her. "Your Highness," he hissed slowly, "seems uninjured. *Mein Bruder* and I are most relieved that you escaped from harm in the little incident that our airship experienced."

He made a shallow bow.

She grasped the rim of the gondola's window with both her hands, pressing her cheek against the cold pane. Her breath formed an oval of frost against the darkness. A drop of moisture ran from the place where her cheekbone contacted the isinglass and formed a miniature puddle on the window's rim.

She drew a deep breath and pressed her hand against her chest.

A great flash of greenish white illuminated the countryside.

The Princess gasped and pointed. "See! See, Lothar! Is castle again! Is palace of Lucifer! O Holy Virgin!"

She grasped Lothar by his arm and spun him so he faced out the window. He barked a word but the thunderclap that followed the huge flash of lightning drowned it out. Another flash of illumination—this one, if anything, even brighter than the last—dazzled their eyes.

The stench of ozone filled the air and a tree whose limbs reached upward like the fingers of a skeletal hand burst into lurid, crackling flame.

"You see!" Irina shrieked at Lothar. "Lvova is not mad! Is palace of Lucifer! Is! Is! O Virgin, save daughter Lvova!"

"*Gott!*" Lothar crossed the cabin in two long strides, his flying boots spanning the rent in the gondola floor. He held his brother's arm with one hand, pointed with the other to the louring, massive structure beneath them.

Manfred stared through the front window of the cabin. "*Bruder! Bruder! Vater! Vater!* The Princess was right! Look! It is Lucifer's palace!"

The castle stood darkly, its northerly wall a vertical continuation of the granite escarpment, its southerly rampart facing the distant mountains.

In the lightning flashes it appeared deserted at first, but as *Freiherr* von Richthofen swung the *Black Eagle*'s helm to put the airship into a circular course above the towers, it became apparent that flickering lights like smouldering cressets cast a dull luminance from the windows.

"Fly away!" Irina ran from the rear of the cabin to the controls. "Fly away airship! Not to stay at Satan house! Not to stay at devil place!" Tears coursed down her cheeks.

She reached for Manfred's hand to force him to swing the airship's helm. He shoved at her viciously. She struck the cabin's wall. Weakened by the earlier near-crash, the gondola swayed and creaked. A gust of wind swept wetly through the rent in the floorboards.

Manfred leaned over the instrument board, concern etched on his features. He ran long, restless fingers through disheveled hair. "Altitude!" he growled at his brother.

Lothar reached and set the levers that would dump whatever ballast remained in the airship's tanks.

The needle on the altimeter swung to the right briefly, then halted, quivered, began its slow but steady drift to the left.

"The gas is leaking, *Bruder*."

"*Ja*."

"I can release more hydrogen into the bags."

"*Nein*, Lothar, *nein*." Manfred shook his head despairingly. "What use would that be? To gain a few more metres of altitude. To stay aloft another few minutes, to travel a few kilometres from this *Palast*. And then what? Stranded on this vacant plain—we would have to trek back to seek assistance anyway. Let us instead land under our own power, now, at our control."

"*Ja, ja, mein Bruder*. You make sense. Very well." He turned toward the Princess Irina. "Be seated. We are landing here. We will obtain assistance from the palace."

"No! No! Is evil place! Fly away airship!"

Lothar shook his head, then turned his back.

Manfred slowed the propellers to little more than an idle. The airship continued its slow headway, spiraling down into the courtyard.

A gust of hostile wind swept the *Schwarze Adler* horizontally just before it touched down in the courtyard. The gasbag slammed into the inner wall. The gondola itself, all of bamboo construction with iron fittings, scraped on naked stone. A spark was struck, flew upward into the rapidly emptying gasbag.

There was a flash, then at once a loud thump.

Three figures, one of them carrying a high-powered express rifle, scuttled away from the Zeppelin seconds before it exploded. Even so, the force of the suddenly combusted hydrogen gas hurled them flat onto the flagstones. Lothar von Richthofen tumbled, his body wrapped protectively around the rifle. Beside him his brother Manfred and the Princess Irina Lvova scraped their flying suits on the roughly hewn stone.

Agile as a tumbler, Lothar rolled to a crouch, cradled the rifle with one hand and pressed the other to the flagstone. He sprang to his feet and studied the *Schwarze Adler*. The gasbag, framework and skin of the balloon had burned within seconds of the explosion. Only the gondola remained, and that was now burning furiously despite the wind-swept, icy rain that drenched the courtyard.

"*Schnell! Schnell!*" Lothar ran to Manfred and the Princess Irina, tugged them to their feet. He hurried them away from the fire. "Quickly! Waste no time!"

The Princess tried to hold back. "My belongings! Are in airship! Wait!"

"*Nein! Kommen her!*" The brothers grasped her by her elbows and hustled her away from the remains of the Zeppelin. The courtyard was huge, perhaps as much as a hundred metres across. They managed to cover most of the distance before the reserve hydrogen tank, heated to a red glow by the flames, exploded.

The metal cylinder itself burst with a violent *crack!* Almost instantly the compressed hydrogen within it, liberated into the burning air, combusted with a deep *whump!*

Tongues of flame rose twenty metres into the air.

Liberated hydrogen gas, burning with ambient oxygen, formed a miniature rainstorm of its own above the burning wreckage. Raindrops hissed into steam on contact with the heated shambles and made a bank of thick, hot fog.

With the hydrogen exhausted, the combustible materials of the Zeppelin burned more slowly. The rain continued to fall upon the fire. Soon the flames died out and the remaining chunks of metal and cinder lay hissing on the flagstones.

Lothar looked to Manfred. "What now?" he asked.

Before the Baron could reply the Princess burst in, sobbing. "Now comes Lucifer! Now come devils to carry three souls to master. Now is end!" She stood trembling, making the sign of the cross in the Russian fashion, again and again.

Dragging the Princess Irina between them, the von Richthofens struggled to a portal that led from the courtyard into the castle proper. "We must find help now," Manfred said. "We must obtain transport.

"Do you think we can regain our monoplane? How far did we travel from *Kondor?* There was some fuel left in the tanks. If we cannot continue, perhaps we can return via *Symmeshoehle* and refit."

"Nein, Bruder, Nein."

"Why cannot we do it?"

"You forget, *kleine Bruder.*" The fingers of his free hand, animated with a life of their own, seemed to scurry across the chest and shoulder of his flying suit and tug nervously at his cheek and ear.

"Forget what?"

Manfred von Richthofen smiled ruefully. "The engine parts and control of *Kondor*. We arranged so no one else could steal *Kondor*. Now it is useless to us, too. Even if we could survive these cliffs, cross sea and ice, and make our way back—we could not fly the aeroplane!"

"Gott! Manfred, you are right. All is lost!"

The Princess burst into hysterical laughter. "See! See!" she shrieked between gales of horrid merriment. "Lvova makes no mistake! Are lost! Are doomed! Come, brethren, bid God Jesus farewell. Prepare for welcome of Prince Lucifer!"

As if on cue the heavy door blocking the portal swung open, its iron hinges screeching in protest. Beyond lay only darkness. The sole illumination within the portal had been the last flickering flames of the dying *Black Eagle*. Now there appeared new light from within the stone castle, wavering, lurid light cast by the smokily burning pitch of hand-held torches.

"Come!"

The voice was deep with authority. The intonation was that of the German language as it had been spoken in the days of Frederick Barbarossa. The three battered fliers obeyed, Manfred leading the way, followed by Irina and Lothar.

They found themselves standing within a vestibule. The one who had spoken was flanked by four torchbearers. In turn, a squad of men with crude halberds stood ready to protect their commander or to enforce his authority.

"*Grosser Bruder*," Lothar whispered hoarsely, "*Das Gewehr*." He gestured significantly with the high-powered rifle.

"*Nein!*" Manfred hissed. He shook his head. "We have one weapon only. And—they seem to be Germans, eh? Better willing allies than restive foes."

He drew himself to his full height and strode forward. The halberdiers shifted nervously but von Richthofen halted before their leader and glared at him commandingly. The man was of stocky, Germanic build. He wore a suit of tight-fitting chain mail with attached hood and foot-coverings. Over it hung a cloth doublet with a coat-of-arms stitched on the breast.

"You will lead us to the *Kommandant* of this castle," the *Freiherr* commanded.

The guard officer frowned uncertainly.

"*Schnell!*" von Richthofen shouted. There remained a trace of hesitation. Von Richthofen backhanded the man viciously, the *Freiherr*'s long, restless fingers leaving a row of welts on the other's face.

A thin stream of blood ran from the man's nose and into his thick, ruddy moustache.

He ducked his head and murmured, "*Ja, ja mein Herr.*" He turned to the other guards, singled out the slightest of the torchbearers and landed a solid blow with his fist against the man's cheekbone. "Stand up properly, dog! Torchbearers, comport yourselves as a guard of honor! Light the way properly for my lords and lady!"

They scurried to obey. "Halberdiers," the officer resumed, "form ranks! What sort of Esquimaux peasants do you think you are! Quick-step, now. *March!*"

Bowing and scuttling in circles, he gestured the fliers ahead of him through the stone-walled hallway. In minutes they reached an ornate double door and halted. The guard commander cocked his head, listening worriedly to the loud voices that came from within. He reached for the halberd of the nearest guard and pounded its butt against the door.

The noises ceased. The double doors were drawn back and the lights within blazed out.

The Princess Irina, standing between the two brother aviators, screamed and slumped toward the floor.

Chapter 11

The dozen square flying platforms remained hovering above the ziggurat while the *Spirit of San Diego* settled smoothly to the flat roof of the great structure. Charles Lindbergh, seated helplessly at the controls of the Ryan monoplane, watched the dish-shaped machines slowly return to their former metallic hue, their variegated radiant colors fading.

"Listen," Howard Hughes shot at Lindy and Amelia, "one of us got to make a sacrifice. I wish to hell we had one of them self-starters on this bird. I'll run around to the front of the *Spirit* and throw the prop. Swede, you hit the magneto and fly this ship out of here! I'll stand off them siwashes as long as I can!"

"No, Howard!" Lindbergh reached past Hughes and held the cabin door shut. "They brought us down as easy as could be. Those flying picture-frames are still up there. Lord knows what kind of weaponry they're fitted with! And even if they don't stop us, these ray machines could just bring us back again."

"Well then?" Hughes's face darkened with anger. "What do you want to do? Crawl out of here and surrender? Not me, palsy! I'll go down fighting first!"

"Please!" Amelia burst in. "Let's just be calm. Howard, Charles is right. We couldn't get away from here if they didn't want to let us. And besides..."

She hesitated.

"Yeah! And besides, besides *what?*"

Amelia smiled. ". . . we're going to need assistance anyway. We haven't the fuel to fly to the Hole, as it is. Maybe these people will help us."

"They're a bunch of savages. All they want to do is probably eat us for dinner!"

Lindbergh shook his head. "This city is hardly the work of savages. And those flying machines and ray machines aren't either. I'd give my autographed Shoeless Joe Jackson baseball for a chance to tinker with one of those gadgets."

"Yeah. Well, maybe you'll get your chance, Swede. Take a look outside now." He hooked a thumb toward the Ryan's windscreen. "It looks like the official welcoming committee, and it sure don't look like they're bringing us the key to the city, neither!"

The party advancing across the roof of the ziggurat were arrayed in archaic splendor. Their skins were uniformly brick-red, their hair black and cut straight across the forehead and the back of the neck. Men and women dressed alike, with waving feathered plumes in their headdress, ornate kirtles cinched at the waist by jeweled metallic bands, glittering necklaces and brilliant enameled gauntlets.

The leader carried a long object, pointed at its tip, blunt at its base. To the first glance, it was an ornate ceremonial spear no longer than a pygmy's throwing stick. As he approached the *Spirit of San Diego* it was obvious that the resemblance was deliberate. The slim object was made to look like a spear, but it was in actuality—something else. Its tip was not a blade of sharpened metal or stone, but a polished lens. The engravings along its shaft were not mere ceremonial markings but were meters and controls.

"What now?" Hughes rasped. "We going to sit here and wait for them bozos to take us out of the ship?"

"Right, Howard." Lindbergh stood away from the controls. He strode to the door, but Hughes got there first.

"I dunno what that bozo has in mind, but if anybody's going to get stuck with that pig-sticker, I'll take the risk. I got the toughest hide of us three, anyhow."

He undogged the cabin door and hopped to the roof of the ziggurat.

The chief greeter stared at Hughes. The plumes rising from his headdress created the illusion that he was eight feet tall.

The man's eyes were as black as his hair. His skin was as red as the brick-colored stone of the ziggurat. The plumes that dipped and swayed above his head were bone-white and as graceful as those of an ostrich.

Hughes stuck out his big hand. "Howdy! Name's Howard Hughes. Just in from San Diego with my friends. What's your monicker?"

The other took a half-step backward as Hughes extended his hand. He raised his spear a fraction.

Hughes started to say something but his mouth wouldn't work. Nothing would work. His whole body was tingling as if it had fallen asleep the way a foot might. He tried to turn and signal the others for help, but he couldn't move at all.

All he could do was breathe, and move his eyes a little. That was all!

Inside the Ryan monoplane, Lindy and Amelia crouched, flying-helmeted heads close together, watching the proceedings outside. "Something's wrong," Lindbergh whispered "They've done something to Howard. I'm going to help him."

Amelia started to lay her hand on Lindbergh's arm, to stop him from acting on impulse. But he was gone, out of the Ryan and onto the roof of the ziggurat, charging to Howard Hughes's side.

As Lindy drew alongside Hughes the chieftain raised his stick. Amelia, watching from the Ryan, saw a ruby-tinted glow at the tip of the spear.

Lindbergh froze in his tracks. His hands were chest-high as if he'd intended to grab the red man. Even the chin-strap of his leather helmet stood flying in the breeze.

The chieftain stepped closer to Lindbergh and Hughes, looking them up and down studiously. His followers scurried forward, closing the semicircle that pinned the three men midway between the Ryan and the nearest dish-shaped ray machine.

Amelia took a deep breath. She stood straight, squared her

shoulders, climbed deliberately from the Ryan. Without haste she carefully closed and dogged the aircraft's door, then strode toward the red chieftain.

Half a pace beyond the statuelike Lindbergh and Hughes she halted, planted her feet on the brick-red stone and her fists on her hips, like a drill sergeant preparing to chew out a squad of hapless recruits, and angrily shot her words at the chieftain.

"*Qué malo es con Usted! Déjalos a mis amigos o lo lamentará!*"

She breathed a silent prayer of thanks at the slight widening of the chieftain's eyes. It was all the response that he made, but it was a sign of some degree—some degree—of understanding.

And he didn't raise that electric spear or whatever it was. Amelia could still speak and move.

She pointed sternly at the man, repeated her demand in broken Syrian, then in stumbling Mandarin. The language of these people seemed a polyglot of those tongues and others, but Amelia had no notion of how they had mixed to form the *patois*.

The best she could do was repeat her statements in each language, and hope that the red people would pick out the words they recognized and reassemble the message: *What's the matter with you! Let my friends go or you will regret it!*

What a bluffer I am, she thought. Might as well drive home one final shot. She tugged her helmet from her head with a dramatic sweep of her hand, shook out her hair and barked, in all the languages she knew, *Now!*

To Amelia's startlement, the chieftain staggered backward as if she had struck him a belly punch like the Manassa Mauler. He swung on his heel, gestured to his followers and uttered a short sentence of command.

Universally, they knelt.

The chieftain swung back. He raised his face and his arms to the sky. The dozen flying platforms that had escorted the *Spirit of San Diego* over the city of ziggurats still hovered in a rectangular formation above the *Spirit*. The pilot's station in each of the square platforms was a perfect cube of transparent material set in a cutout in the center of the platform.

The cube extended as far above the platform as it did below, so the pilot was able to see in all directions, above and below the machine.

At the chieftain's signal the pilots of the platforms adjusted their controls. Devices at the perimeters of the machines glowed. Slowly, silently, the dozen machines settled to positions on the roof of the building. The pilots climbed from their cubes and formed a row behind the semicircle of kneeling people. In unison they, too, knelt.

Now the chief faced Amelia once again. He muttered a formula in the *patois* and laid his yard-long spear at her feet.

Amelia suppressed a grin. She said to the man, "Your homage is touching, but above all you must still release my friends." She wasn't sure that the message was getting through so she emphasized it by pointing to the futuristic spear, to the kneeling chief, and to Lindbergh and Hughes.

The lens glowed again.

"Cripes-a-mighty!" Howard Hughes exploded. "Ain't that bozo never seen a woman before? You okay, Swede? What'd you do to put the Indian sign on that guy, Amy? All I done was stick my mitt out and he kayoes me with one wave of the joystick there. You okay, Swede? You ain't talking any!"

"Yes, sure," Lindbergh managed. "That *was* pretty amazing, though!" He stood rubbing his hands together, then slapped himself softly on the cheeks to get his blood circulating.

"You aren't hurt, are you?" Amelia looked into the faces of the two men, Lindbergh's pale ascetic visage and Hughes's darker, rough-hewn features.

Lindbergh shook his head. "No, there was no pain. Just a sort of tingling. But I was helpless. I could see and hear everything going on around me, but I couldn't lift a finger."

"Yeah." Hughes rubbed his nose with his knuckles. "Same here."

"Well, look." Lindbergh swung a long arm in a circle around them. "Here we are in some fine-looking country. Look at this city—there must be a score of these huge buildings. How many people do you think one of these can hold? I'd guess they use them for living quarters, I didn't see any suburban districts on the way here."

"Hundred thousand," Hughes ventured.

Lindbergh computed. "That makes a city of two million. Bigger than St. Louis. Close to Chicago in size. And look at the splendid farmland out there. It stretches off for a hundred miles or more. And those thick forests. And those hills. This could almost be Wisconsin!"

Hughes made a wry face. "There was never no town like *this* in Wisconsin!"

"I don't know, Howard. I suppose you never heard of the old Indian mound-builders."

"Nope."

"Let it pass."

"Listen," Amelia said, "I don't think our hosts here want to spend the day waiting for us to make a move. What are we going to do now?"

"I say, let's amscray astfay while you got 'em aredscay, Amy."

"Huh? Oh, igpay atinlay. They don't speak English, I'm certain."

"Then let's get the hell outta here while the gettin's good!"

"No." Lindbergh shook his head. "I can't agree. Look, we've a little fuel left but we'll need to refill in a few hundred miles. We don't know whom or what we'll find if we just keep going. If they'll let us keep going, anyway. I think we'd better stay here and get these people to help us."

"Amy," he continued, "can you ask the big bonz there who these people are, and why they've treated us this way?"

She turned back to the chief and ran through a series of questions in all her languages.

With each repetition the chief nodded his growing comprehension. Finally he unleashed a stream of *patois*, backing up and repeating, rephrasing, and explaining when Amelia asked.

Finally she nodded, turned back to her companions and said, "They seem to think we're the fulfillment of a prophecy. A prediction that their ancestors brought to this land from, ah, *the older land*, I think. Or maybe it's *the other world.*"

"You mean they're from our side of the disk?"

Amelia shrugged. "Their language is tough for me. I'm not really certain of the meaning. And some of his phrases—oh, I just can't tell. It's possible."

"Uh-huh. So how come Lindy and me got the mummy treatment and you get the great white goddess show? Bigshot here fall in love at first sight, or what?"

"I think it had to do with my hair," she smiled. "And with the way I acted, a little. The chief here... I don't think he's exactly a chief, either. The way he talks, he's more like the chief scholar, I think. Certainly not a king."

Hughes snorted.

"Anyway," Amelia resumed, "they have some sort of belief that their people, their ancestors, were visited by a light-skinned, light-haired hero or god. He or she was supposed to return some day, and the people were worried all this time that their hero would come back to their *old land* and not find them there.

"That's why they're so happy that we came *here*, you see. And they'll be thrilled, Charles, when you take your helmet off."

Hughes glared at the chief. "That makes some kind of screwy sense, I guess. But how come he did his stuff on the Swede and me and then made like a good boy for you—*before* you pulled your helmet off?"

"I think the old man is sacred," Amelia said. "You don't just touch him, Howard. When you offered your hand, you were making a very threatening move, by their lights. As for Charles, I think he really was going to hit the chief. All I did was speak to them. In languages close enough to their own that they could understand me. A little bit, at least.

"Then, once they saw my hair, they decided that I was their long-awaited hero. Or heroine, I suppose. They don't seem to mind, so I surely don't."

The old man stepped closer and held his spear shoulder high, gesturing. He spoke a few words in *patois*.

Amelia smiled. "We're invited to his place. He used some odd terms again. I think it comes out literally as the chief librarian's office. But the way he used the term, it means more like the ruler's court."

They started across the rooftop, the old man showing the way. "You know," Lindbergh commented, "if they make their scholars their rulers... and if the head librarian is really the top dog of the whole country..."

They had reached the edge of the ziggurat and stood for a moment looking over the city. The vista of differently colored ziggurats, their flat roofs blending into the distance, produced an effect like that which a small child sees, lying on a floor of linoleum squares and looking across a room that seems—to the child's eye—miles in extent.

Flying platforms moved above the city. They came in all sizes, from the little single-pilot craft that had intercepted the *Spirit of San Diego* to huge machines that must carry heavy cargoes of passengers or freight. The only sound they made was an occasional soft hum as fixtures around their edges glowed to an incandescent blue, green, yellow, or rose.

The sky itself was a perfect blue with only tiny puffs of cloud marking it. The smell was that of spring.

A large rectangle beneath their feet glowed and began to descend into the ziggurat.

"Hey, an elevator!" Hughes exclaimed.

Lindbergh looked worried. "We left the *Spirit* on the roof. Do you think these people will tamper with it?"

Amelia shook her head. "Look at their machines. They must know plenty about aviation—and a lot else! I wouldn't worry about anything happening to the plane."

The head librarian's office resembled a royal audience hall more than it did an administrator's work space. The floor was of black polished marble, veined with white. The ceiling bore ornate decorations and was supported by gold-leafed columns. The walls were heavily hung with tapestries.

"Say, I know what that stuff is," Hughes blurted. "Some Mex gal I knew in Texas explained that to me. She said that was old siwash writing. But she said nobody knew how to read it any more. All the knots mean things—what kind of knot, how far apart they are, everything is part of the writing. I guess these bonzes still know how to read it."

The old man bowed them through the elaborate chamber and into a smaller one beyond. They sat on cushions. There was a low table in the room. The old man sat at the table and lifted something from it—a miniature replica of his elaborate mechanical spear.

He inclined his head toward Amelia and spoke in *patois*. He took a string from the tabletop and began knotting it, using the miniature spear as a knotting tool.

"Well I'll be swatted!" Lindbergh exclaimed.

Amelia and Howard stared at him.

"Look at that! If those knots are really their way of writing, and the string is their paper—then that little gadget isn't a spear at all. It's, uh, a kind of pencil! Whatever kinds of gadgets the old man has built into the big one, what it really is, is a giant pencil, that's all!"

He burst into laughter.

"Grand," Hughes rasped. "Lookie here, Amy. If these bozos are going to give us a hand, we better know some more about 'em. Can you ask him again... what's his monicker? Who are these siwashes? Can they let us have some air-grade fuel? And when can we hightail it out of here?"

When Amelia frowned, Hughes added, "You high-brows can parlay-voo all you want to, later on. But right now we've got a race to win with a fifty-thousand-smacker prize on the line, winner take all. *I* don't want to hang around here playing amateur anthropo-something-or-other!"

"He's got a point," Lindy agreed.

"All right," Amelia gave in. She shot a stream of questions at the old man.

The old man nodded, lowered his head and stroked his chin. He reached behind him and ran his hand down a tapestry of knotted strings, reading them with his fingers.

"I *think* I asked him right," Amelia said softly.

"If you didn't," Hughes husked, "don't worry about it. Just get ready to eat six kinds of potatoes. *Hah!*"

The old man rose stiffly and walked to a far corner. He reached high above his head, drew his hands slowly downward, mumbling and nodding as he read the long strings that had hung there for uncounted years.

He returned to his seat. He bowed his head to Amelia and launched upon a narrative. Although Hughes and Lindbergh couldn't understand his words, they could tell that it was a rhythmic recitation, some sort of litany designed to be passed on by oral repetition even if the knotted strings should be lost.

When the old man finished, Amelia asked him questions in Syrian, Mandarin, Spanish. He answered in *patois*, sometimes repeating sections of the recitation.

Finally Amelia said, "I think I've got most of that. His name is Icheiri. It comes from an old medicine god, now the head librarian gets it every generation.

"The people came here because they were attacked by evil monsters, half-human, half-horse, with skins of iron, who stole their gold, killed their warriors, raped their women, enslaved their children, and imprisoned their king."

"Sound like nice folks," Hughes said.

"Sounds like the Spanish *conquistadores*," Amelia said. "And they did it all in the name of God. Anyway, the people took their great treasure to the bottom of a sacred lake—"

"I thought the evil monsters stole their gold."

"Maybe that wasn't their great treasure."

"Huh!"

"Well, that was how they left their other land, their old country. They came here."

"At the bottom of a lake?"

"I couldn't follow that either. Maybe they had submarines."

"You're kidding. What about those little sailboats we saw?"

Amelia shrugged. "Don't *we* have submarines and sailboats? Anyway, here they are. And they're worried about other enemies in the new country, or that the monsters will follow them here."

"They seem able to take care of themselves."

"Nonetheless—they were pleased to see us."

"Yeah."

Lindbergh asked, "Did he tell you the name of this country? Or is it just, the New Country?"

"No, he told me. It's something like Muiaia. The name of their country. And their city. It's the same. And the people are Muiaians."

"Hah!" Hughes said, "Like Mayans? I thought they were from Yucatán."

Lindbergh said, "You don't think he meant something like Muvians, do you? As in Colonel Churchward's books?"

"I don't know," Amelia shook her head, "I never read Colonel Churchward's books."

"Weird stuff," Lindbergh said. "When my Dad was in Congress we always met these odd folks coming to Washington to plead their cases. This Churchward wrote books about a lost continent called Muvia, or Mu, or Lemuria. It was something like Atlantis, only it was out in the Pacific Ocean."

"Muvia!" the old man echoed. "*Muiaia, Muvia, sí, ésto es.*" He rattled on in *patois.* The word he kept repeating in different forms was Mu, Muiaia, Muvia.

Chapter 12

Prinz Nikolauz turned from the writhing sub-man and handed the smoking poker to his head torturer. He accepted a soft towel and wiped the sweat from his face and chest. A page stood by, ready to take the towel the moment the master was finished with it.

Another stood by, holding in his hands the *Prinz*'s luxuriant chamois shirt. The *Prinz* signaled him aside and instead held out his hand for a flagon of dark, bitter ale. He sipped at the beverage, swaggered to the semiconscious prisoner and gazed at him appraisingly.

The man hung from the solid stone wall, clamps holding his ankles to the clammy surface. His wrists were suspended from chains so his torso hung a foot or more from the wall. His head drooped between his shoulders. Spittle hung from his mouth.

The floor beneath him was slippery with a mixture of blood, urine, and saliva.

Nikolauz spat a mouthful of ale, adding it to the puddle beneath the red man. What was his name? Yacabuchu or some other such barbaric jumble of syllables. The *Prinz* could never keep them straight. *Ach,* these Muiaians, who would ever think that such savages would possess the craft that they did? Clearly they were the heirs of a race of great magicians. Or perhaps they had managed, somehow, to *steal* the objects and tools of some superior people, likely some lost relatives of *Prinz* Nikolauz's own nation, Svartalheim.

The *Prinz* looked up into the face of this Yacabuchu. The savage's eyes were closed—or were they? Perhaps they were slitted open just the least bit. That was the kind of treacherous and cowardly deed that these Muiaian savages would attempt.

Nikolauz lifted his flagon, smiled momentarily at the traditional hunting scene embossed in the enamel, and filled his mouth again. He kept his face lowered to the flagon but surreptitiously he raised his eyes to glance at the red face above him.

Yes.

Yes.

The man's eyes were definitely slitted. He must be watching with envy as his captor sipped at the cool beverage in the flagon.

The *Prinz* lowered the flagon, raised his face and spewed a mouthful of ale onto the prisoner.

"You see, my good savage—I am not unaware of your needs. A little cooperation from you and a sip of this good ale might be yours. *Ale.* Understand?" He held the flagon so the savage could see it clearly. The man's eyes opened wide.

"You understand that, eh? *Ale?* What do you call it in your barbaric tongue?"

Yacabuchu's mouth moved, but only a series of garbled syllables emerged.

"*Vezza? Vezza?* Is that it, savage?" *Prinz* Nikolauz held the flagon of ale close to the red man's face, waited while he strained to reach it, then poured the remaining contents at his feet. He laughed, tossed the empty flagon to a waiting flunky. This time he accepted the chamois shirt, let the boy help him into the soft garment. Nikolauz smiled indulgently, smoothed the boy's soft, blond hair and patted him affectionately. The boy smiled coquettishly at the *Prinz* and slipped away.

The heavy door of the chamber swung open.

The commander of the watch stood there, followed by guardsmen in two ranks, their weapons clanking with each step. Between the ranks marched three strangers, one a strongly made man with a thatch of finely flowing hair, another more stockily built and hairless but otherwise resembling the first. And the third—a woman. The most beautiful woman *Prinz* Nikolauz had ever seen. Her face was thin and a pale milky shade. Her eyes were the blue of northern ice. Her long, pale hair hung like spun silver.

All three strangers wore bulky leather outfits. Those of the men were of dark colors, set off by turned linings of natural wool. The woman's was white. Despite the shapelessness of her outfit, it was obvious that she had a figure as slimly graceful as that of a young girl.

Prinz Nikolauz drew himself up, ready to demand the report of his guard commander. But before a word was spoken the woman stared wildly about herself, uttered a piercing scream and slumped against one of her companions.

The *Prinz* ordered her taken to a suitable chamber and placed in bed. The court wizard, Lodur, was as close to a physician as Nikolauz maintained in his establishment. He would look after the woman, assisted by a female servant.

The guard commander, Mider, described his discovery of the three strangers. "Two great lords and their lady," Mider asserted. Nikolauz watched the guard officer closely. He was neither the brightest nor the most aggressive of soldiers. A good man, reliable, and not a troublemaker. But he could be deceived, Nikolauz knew, and he could be cowed.

"How do you know they are not spies sent by the sub-men?" the *Prinz* demanded.

"But—but merely *look* at them, my lord. They are of the Svartalheim stock, are they not? And they speak—a sort of Svartalheimerisch. The *rot* Muiaianer," he shook his head, "there is no way!"

The *Prinz* nodded. To the strangers he said, "You two. How did you find your way into my Keep? Mider says you arrived with an explosion and fire. I almost think," he grinned frighteningly, "the poor fool thinks you are visitants from the god of storms."

The brothers von Richthofen exchanged a glance. There had not been time to develop a story to tell this little princeling. He seemed to be of Germanic stock and language, of some long-ago-separated branch of the great Nordic tree. If he could be induced to give help to the *Kondor* party, they might yet make a success of their venture. At best their situation was close to desperate. The *Kondor* itself was far off and—even if they could regain the aircraft—almost certainly unflyable without the parts destroyed in the explosion of the *Schwarze Adler*. And the Zeppelin itself was a total loss.

How could they reach either the *Symmeshoehle* or the Ice Rim? And, how could they pass back to their own hemidisk even if they did reach Hole or Rim? The case at the Hole was hopeless. But if they could obtain help and reach the Rim . . . and somehow make their way over or through it . . . Bodo would be waiting with the duplicate *Kondor*.

"May we first present ourselves." Manfred bowed. "I am Manfred *Freiherr* von Richthofen, Major of the King and Kaiser's Royal Prussian and Imperial German forces." He nodded toward Lothar. "And my younger brother, *Hauptmann* Lothar von Richthofen."

Nikolauz grunted noncommitally. "And the lady?"

"The Princess Irina Lvova, daughter of the Prince Regent Georgi Lvov and cousin of His Majesty Alexei IV, Tsar of All the Russias."

"I have never heard of your countries," Nikolauz said. "But you seem to speak truthfully. So—we will hold further conversation. Are you hungry? What, and drenched? A lovely storm tonight. Mider," he ordered, "take the Baron and captain above. Furnish them fresh clothing. I will await them in the hall."

The two strangers, dressed now in soft leather and cloth shirts, breeches and weskits, approached the *Prinz*'s table. He watched their progress, gnawing all the while on a haunch of mutton. When they stood before him he dropped the haunch back into the trencher that ran along the center of the table, lifted a wooden goblet and drank wine from it noisily.

"Welcome, *Freiherr*. Welcome, *Hauptmann*." He gestured expansively. "Sit. Eat. Drink. A mouthful of *gutem Rotwein?* Sometimes our vintage falls short of its name—the good, red wine. But that is our goal, at least." He smiled, then resumed.

"I suppose Mider has told you all about me by now. *Prinz*

Nikolauz von Svartalheim. *Der jungste Prinz von Svartalheim.* My eldest *Bruder* gets command of an army corps. The next, of a fleet. The third *Prinz* will someday become *Oberzauberer von Svartalheim.* Chief wizard.

"Eh?" He turned away, distracted from the brothers von Richthofen by his own train of thought. "Is that Lodur back from the Princess's chamber yet? I want him here for conversation. Hey! Hey! Page!" He stood up, lifted his goblet and drained its contents. Most of the wine made it down his throat, the rest spilled onto his doublet.

Again he called the page, uttered a curse and threw the goblet with perfect aim at the boy. It caught him behind the ear and the boy leaped erect, cursing.

"Hey, you! Go and fetch the *Zauberer* Lodur. Tell him the ice lady can recover alone. I want him at my table. Go!"

He picked up the mutton haunch he'd dropped and hefted it to fling after the fast-disappearing boy. But he thought better of that and slumped back into his chair. He gnawed in silence for a while. Then to Manfred and Lothar he said, "Well, what have you two to say for yourselves? Come crashing into my castle with a bang and a flash, like a pack of wizards yourselves."

He leaned forward, the haunch still in his fingers. "Say, you three *aren't*, are you? Wizards, I mean. *Zauberer.*"

The brothers exchanged a quick glance. Manfred prepared to answer the *Prinz* but was cut off by him instead.

"Say, you look a lot more presentable in decent Svartalheimerisch outfits. Not too bad a job. I think yours came from a man who fell asleep on guard duty the other night. He won't do it again, you can bet! *Zzzzzttt!*"

He drew a line across his throat with the mutton haunch, leaving a smear of sheep fat on his neck and his collar. "No, that's the last time he'll make *that* mistake!" He laughed.

"But what about you two? Never mind, have a bit of grub first. I want Lodur here when you tell your story. Sharp fellow. Best blasted court wizard I've ever had. Not that I've had that many, damn it."

He picked up his goblet and yelled for a fresh filling of the

Rotwein. He drank off half, held up the goblet to be refilled, suggested that Manfred and Lothar help themselves. "You boys have a lot of telling to tell. Might as well fill up your bellies and lubricate your larynxes before you start."

He looked around, leaped to his feet and pointed the mutton haunch—by now it was just a long bone steeped in grease with a tatter of gristle hanging from one end—toward the archway.

"Here he is! Here you go, my good friend! Join us, Lodur! Have a mouthful of food and a bladder full of wine. We're going to hear a tale and I want you to listen to it with your sharpest ear. Who knows who these foreigners really are?" He whispered the last question in a tone so low that everyone in the hall could hear it clearly.

The *Zauberer* wore the same soft garb as all the others, but his was a little cleaner than that of the *Prinz* and most of the men ranged up and down the table. He stood behind an empty seat next to the *Prinz*'s.

"Well, come on," *Prinz* Nikolauz demanded, "don't stand so on formality, you. You'd better introduce yourselves to one another. Here, never mind, I'll do it for you.

"This," he pointed with the haunch, "is Manfred von Richthofen. He's a real *Freiherr*. We don't get many Barons coming through here. Better be nice to him, eh? And this other fellow, the one with no hair on his head, this is the Baron's little brother. What did you say your name was, little brother? No, never mind, I remember now. It's Lothar, right? I have a lot of sympathy for you, little brother."

He paused and drank some more *Rotwein.*

"Yeah, we have a lot of little brothers around this dump." He wiped the corner of his eye with his sleeve. "Yeah, here we are scarfing down slop in *Prinz* Nikolauz's special dump, way the hell and gone up here in the boondocks, while the big brothers live it up with the gorgeous women and the fancy clothes. *Pfah!*" He spat on the floor.

"Siddown, Lodur!" He dragged the wizard into the empty seat. "Let me introduce the *Hauptmann.* As one little brother introducing another, Lodur, this is Manfred's little brother Lothar. See what a phenomenal memory I have? Mama always said I was a marvel. The youngest is always the brightest, Mama said. She always thought the laws of succession were ass-backwards. Maybe that was why Ottokar slipped that stuff into her food. Poor Mama!"

He began to cry in earnest.

The wizard put his arm around Nikolauz's shoulders. "*Freiherr* von Richthofen should be telling us his story, my lord, do you not agree? To arrive so suddenly, so spectacularly? One would almost think these strangers are wizards themselves, in the employ of our enemies."

The *Prinz* looked angrily at Manfred. "Is this so?"

Von Richthofen heard his brother whispering in his ear. "The man is a sot. This magician Lodur is the real power here. *Bruder*, beware!"

"Who are Your Highness's enemies?" Manfred asked.

Nikolauz pushed his goblet away and it toppled on the table, rolling crazily. It was empty. The *Prinz* laid his hands on the rough wood and shoved himself to his feet. He stood swaying.

"My enemies..." He paused and a convulsion shook his frame. "...are everywhere! Svartalheim is full of those who would destroy me! Why do you think I was sent to this stinking Keep? Who wants to live up here, posting guards against chipmunks and foxes, waiting for the war with Nuiaiaia..."

"Muiaia, my lord," the *Zauberer* Lodur murmured.

"*Ja*, Lodur, I said that."

"You said—yes, my lord, of course you did. I heard you wrong. I crave pardon."

"You see?" Nikolauz leaned across the table and gazed into Manfred's eyes blearily. "I don't want to talk to you! I'm sick of *grosse Bruder!* They're all the same, lording it over us *kleine Bruder*. You, little brother!"

He swung toward Lothar and started to slip forward. Lothar leaped to his feet and caught the *Prinz* before he could crash into the trencher of mutton slop.

"*Danke, kleine Bruder*. You see—we understand each other. We're the smart ones! You know why they made that rule?"

"What rule, Your Highness?" Lothar sighed.

"You know! Don't quarrel with a *Prinz*, Lothar!"

"Of course, Your Highness."

"Primo—primoginavere—what is it, my friend? You're my friend. You're a little brother just like me, Lothar. I'll bet that *Freiherr* brother of yours," he looked surreptitiously at Manfred, "I'll bet he gets all the gold, and the fine raiment, hey? And the ladies all flock round him, right? Just because he's the elder?"

Lothar grunted.

"What do you call that rule, Lothar?"

"*Ach, ja!* Primogeniture, Your Highness."

"*Ja*, prigovinature, that's what I said. Don't quarrel with me, Lothar my friend. We little brothers have to stick together. I'll tell you something. Hey, come over here where nobody can hear us. They all spy on me, you know, they all spy on me and report downstairs to the King."

He began edging his way along the table, leaning against the backs of his men, signaling Lothar to move with him.

Lothar cast a frantic look at Manfred. Manfred shrugged and tried to engage the *Zauberer* Lodur in small talk.

The *Prinz* Nikolauz dragged Lothar into an alcove. He peered out to make sure no one was eavesdropping, then leaned close so he could whisper in Lothar's ear. "I'll bet that ice lady of yours—you know, that Princess, what's her name?"

"The Princess Irina Lvova."

"*Ja*, that's the one I meant. I'll bet you she and your big brother—when you're not around to know about it—you know..." He made an ambiguous gesture.

"I don't know that, Your Highness," Lothar mumbled. "I think not. The Princess—"

"*Ja, ja*, Lothar. *Ja.* You're a good little brother, loyal to your big brother. Just like me. Good little brother Lothar and his big brother Manfred, good little brother Nikolauz and his big brother Ottokar. What does it get us, hey? Here's what it got *me!*" He gestured wildly and lurched against Lothar.

Lothar helped the *Prinz* regain his balance.

"What it gets us," *Prinz* Nikolauz said, "is sent up here to this damned cold heap of rocks they call a castle. Nikolauz's Keep.

Hah! Down home, my footman lived better than I do here. You ought to see the kind of place we have down below."

Lothar's brow furrowed. He shot a glance back toward the great hall. Manfred was sitting opposite the wizard Lodur. It was hard to see the expressions on their faces, but they did not appear to be engaged in animated conversation.

"Your Highness keeps mentioning *up here* and *down home*," Lothar told the *Prinz*. "Perhaps it is that the language has developed differently in our countries. In Germany we would say, *out here*, and *back at home*. Is the expression merely different in Svartalheim? Or do I miss a part of Your Highness's meaning?"

"Oho!" *Prinz* Nikolauz laid a greasy finger on the side of his nose. "You are a clever one, *Hauptmann* von Richthofen. You are a sly one! See? Another clever little brother, just like me. Your older brother can sit out there with his fingers in the trencher and his face in the *Rotwein* along with my official *Zauberer*. I'll bet they're exchanging one lie after another." He winked.

"*Ach*, but you and I, *Bruder* Lothar, we're too clever to try and fool one another, hey? *Nein!*" Suddenly his voice was angry. Suddenly he sounded far more sober than he had since leaving the table.

"When I say up and down, I mean up and down. Up here at Nikolauz's Keep, and down there in the *real* Svartalheim, where King Vithar rules and *Prinz* Ottokar wallows in luxury."

Lothar covered the lower half of his face with his hand. "Perhaps Your Highest would be so kind as to clarify for me his meaning. I have come from far away, and do not understand all that you say."

Nikolauz grunted. "Come with me."

He reached above von Richthofen's bullet head and pressed a series of stones high on the wall of the alcove. Then he tugged at a dust-impregnated wall hanging. Lothar could see only darkness behind the cloth. Nikolauz stepped into the darkness and drew Lothar with him. He reached back and shoved the false section of wall into place. The narrow crack of dim light that had penetrated from the great hall disappeared.

Lothar found himself in total darkness. He heard Nikolauz's

voice coming through the murk in a hoarse whisper. "Now stand still, at peril of your life!"

There was the sound of Nikolauz's leather-shod feet shuffling away for a dozen paces. Then the sound of flint scraping on steel. Lothar saw a small spark fly, then a fire flared dimly in the gloom. It seemed to rise through the air, then float toward him.

Nikolauz's face appeared, illuminated by the flame of a pitch-soaked torch.

"Now, take care. You see how narrow these stones are."

Beyond the stones lay only darkness. How far it reached, what might be beyond it—or below it—Lothar could only guess.

"Follow me," Nikolauz commanded.

He led von Richthofen along the narrow ledge. Eventually it turned into a steep flight of stairs that led downward into the basements of the Keep. They emerged through a concealed passageway and Lother found himself surrounded by a store of swords, halbreds, bits of armor, helmets and shields. He surreptitiously felt inside the borrowed clothing that he wore, assuring himself that his one lethal weapon—the Kaiser's dagger—was safe and available.

"Remarkable," Lothar commented softly to the *Prinz*.

"No, *Hauptmann*. This is nothing. I just didn't want that *Zauberer* to see us leave the great hall. Half the time I think he works for my brother the *Prinz* Ottokar. You know, our father, the *Koenig* Vithar, is getting old. None of us boys," he giggled, "really trust one another so much." He sniffled, then wiped his nose with the sleeve of his shirt.

"So everybody spies on everybody. And all our spies carry tales home to Daddy. Poor Daddy! He misses Mama so! I don't think he believes that Ottokar did the old lady in, either. So I suppose old Lodur'll get word back to Ottokar somehow, get word *down* to him, Lothar, about you three strangers. You never did tell me where you came from or how you got into my Keep. I ought to have you three up on the rack. Or you and your brother, anyhow. Daddy always said it was bad form to torture ladies."

The *Prinz* had been standing throughout his speech, holding the smoky torch. "Here, you take one of these damned things, Lothar." He picked up a dead torch and lit it from his own.

"Come on, earn your dinner, *Hauptmann!*" He thrust the torch into Lothar's hands.

"Now, come on with me. And you'd better tell me your story on the way."

They crossed the armory and moved on to another storage room. Here Nikolauz pulled an ancient and thoroughly threadbare tapestry away from the wall. Behind it was apparently blank stone, but as he had in the alcove off the great hall, Nikolauz pressed a series of stones. Nothing happened.

"*Ach, damm!* I can never remember. Is it *zwei-eins-eins-vier*, or *zwei-zwei-eins-vier?*"

He tried again. This time the wall swung open. The *Prinz* stepped through the opening, almost steadily, and drew Lothar through after him. They found themselves in a long corridor. There were two branches. The *Prinz* started down one of them. Lothar strode along with him.

"Never try this alone, little brother, *never*." The *Prinz* halted at a fork in the corridor, hesitated briefly, then stepped down one branch. After a few paces he said, "No. That's wrong. Come!"

He retraced his steps to the last branching, took the other direction, continued to lead Lothar through a series of turns and forks. As they strode along, the *Prinz* hummed a little tune.

Finally he halted before an iron doorway. He handed his torch to Lothar and dragged the door open on its rusty hinges. "Come on!" He stepped through, tugged the door shut, took back his torch from Lothar. "Now you will see, *Hauptmann kleine Bruder*. Now, I will show you why I say *down* to Svartalheim."

He tugged at a loose stone in the wall, reached behind it and moved a concealed switch.

Slowly, as *Prinz* Nikolauz withdrew his hand and slid the stone back into place, the floor began to descend.

At first the only light in the room was that of the two smoky torches, and the walls that slid by them were the same cold, gray, rough-hewn material as the Nikolauz Keep.

Then the walls changed to a different, transparent material. Through it, Lothar could see the lights and the fantastic, soaring architecture of the metropolis below.

Chapter 13

"Well, you look splendid," Lindbergh said, nodding approval at Amelia. She performed a pirouette, showing off her Muiaian finery. Howard Hughes added his admiration.

"I must say, you two look like a pair of splendid exotic creatures yourselves." Amelia grinned. "Here we are, all dressed up and nowhere to go! Feathers and gowns—not too many of them either! We could float onstage at the Folies-Bergère and no one would see anything amiss!"

"That's the only thing nobody would see," Hughes grunted. "I wonder if there's anyplace around here a guy could get a good cigar and a glass of hooch."

"I don't know about that," Lindbergh said, "but I know we're sitting here with these Lemurians or whatever they are, and the *Spirit* is up there on the roof." He jerked a thumb upward. "And we're not making any progress toward Symmes' Hole."

"Yes, that's true enough." Amelia was more serious now, her frivolity at the sight of herself and the others in their new outfits gone. "I wonder how our European rivals are doing!"

"Those Huns have good airplanes, you have to hand 'em that much," Hughes said. "Their *Jagstaffels* gave our guys one hell of a fight in the One Year War. They had good fliers and they had good ships. Lots of 'em, too! Fokkers, Albatrosses, Halberstadts. And those big Gothas! Flying battlewagons, is what those babies were!"

"What about their Woodhull Prize ship? That *Kondor* that we saw in the newspaper in San Diego." Amelia slipped into a glittering chair opposite Hughes. With Lindbergh beside her, and with her slim, almost boyish figure... with Lindy's light-colored hair that he wore on the longish side for a man and with Amelia's hair cropped almost as short as a boy's... they could have passed easily for brother and sister. Their Muiaian garb was revealing, but in their heavy flying suits they could even have passed for brothers.

Hughes called up the information he had on the Udet monoplane. "It's a powerful ship. They've advanced a lot since the war, I can tell you that much!" He filled in the background of Ernst Udet as aviator and designer.

"How do you know so much about the war?" Amelia asked Hughes. "You certainly weren't old enough to fly in it."

The Texan laughed. "Hardly. I was a leetle tyke back then, granny! But I got eddicated by the best. You ever hear of Jax Bullard, Amy? Charlie?"

They both shook their heads, *no*.

"Well, let me tell you about that fella. Eugene Bullard, but everybody called him Jax. What a guy! He was a black man, see, from Georgia. Only black aviator in the whole dang war. Crazy galoot! He used to go up with a live monkey inside his flying suit. Flew a Curtiss Ox against the *Jagstaffels*. Knocked down his share of Huns and then some. Lost a couple of ships himself, but he always walked away and flew again."

"Huh!" Lindbergh plunged his lanky form into a chair. "Sounds like a kid bragging about his favorite uncle! What's this Bullard to you, Howard?"

"Well, after the war, Jax had a hard time getting a decent job. You know, who's goin' to hire a black boy except for rough labor, or mebbe to be a servant or janitor, you know? Jax didn't want that, and he didn't want to go back to the farm and sharecrop.

"He come wanderin' across Texas, looking for something where he could use what he knew. Man had a good head and a pair of smart hands.

"My Dad was runnin' the machine shop by then, makin' drills and minin' tools and the like. Needed all the good mechanics and designers he could get. Jax come by, asked for a job, Dad give him a try and he got the job. Worked for us for five or six years. Could of stayed forever, far as Dad was concerned. But Jax just loved airplanes too much, couldn't stay in a machine shop.

"All the time he was there, I hung around him, I just couldn't believe a nigger that smart. I thought they was all dumb. But Jax Bullard, he was a wizard! Used to let me hang around with him, took me out to see barnstormers and his face would just light up when he got near an airplane. Took me up with him once, paid a barnstormer for a ride and set me right in his lap in an old Curtiss Ox and told me that he used to fly the things in the war. I guess he *was* like a favorite uncle to me, Charlie."

"Hah! What happened to him, Howard? You said he only lasted a few years at the tool works."

"Oh, I don't know. Drifted west, I think. Took a job as crew with some barnstormer passing through town. He was makin' a good living, probably had the best job any black man ever had, certainly in Texas anyhow. But he just couldn't stay out of airplanes. Had some wild theories about teeny little private planes, said someday anybody wanted an airplane, they'd be commoner'n Model T's. I dunno what ever happened to him."

"And that doesn't tell us where the Udet *Kondor* is, either."

"Yeah! I don't want to see them win the fifty thousand simoleons."

"I'm sure they're not in it for the money," Lindbergh said. "What a crew! The Russian Prince Regent's daughter and the two von Richthofens! The Romanov fortune is legendary. And as for the von Richthofens, they've been close to the Hohenzollerns for generations. One of them was foreign minister under the old Bismarck. The Kaiser's memory is long and his gratitude and generosity are famous.

"As long as you're useful to him! And flying the *Kondor* must be useful to the Kaiser's plans."

"I don't know," Hughes grumbled. "I can't figure out how Udet licked the fuel problem."

Hughes and Lindbergh, both decked in Muiaian finery, paced back and forth.

From her chair, Amelia suppressed amusement at the sight and said, "I wish you'd stop being mysterious and explain that remark."

Hughes faced her. "What I mean is this. With four engines, they're going to burn a lot of fuel. Of course, four engines can drive a mighty big airplane. So they can lift more weight, so they can *carry* more fuel. You know how the *Spirit of San Diego* labors under a full load. Think of what she could have done with three more Whirlwinds pulling her along!

"But more engines, bigger airplanc, more weight. That all takes more fuel to drive and you're back where you started from. What's the efficiency of it? What's the percentage? How does Udet expect the von Richthofens to do it? They have to be playing some kind of shell game!"

"No," Lindbergh disagreed. "How did *we* do it?"

"Hah?"

"How did *we* solve the fuel problem? How are we getting through the course with one load of juice?"

"We're not, Swede! We refilled three times just to get here. And we're getting close to empty again. If we don't refuel soon, we're going to be in bad trouble."

"Exactly."

Hughes stared. "I don't get it."

"Ah, Howard, Howard. Listen here, my friend. We have to get some gasoline for our ship. We're hoping these Muiaians can supply it, right?"

"Yep."

"If they can't—or won't—we're in the soup. What can we do? We'll have to abandon the *Spirit* and find some other way to reach the North Holc. And if we can do that—no small order, hey?—we still have to find a way through the Hole and back to civilization."

"Okay, Swede, okay. What're you driving at?"

"Just this. Our rivals face exactly the same problem. Unless

Herr Udet has made some incredible advance with his new ship—and I doubt it, I think we'd have heard at least some whisper of it if he'd discovered a way to burn water in his engines—then our rivals are in exactly the same trouble that we are."

He strode to the side of the room and stood gazing from a window. It was daylight now, and Lindbergh saw the magnificent city of Muiaia stretching before him.

"If I had a cartwheel in my pocket..."

"If these outfits had any pockets in 'em!"

"...I'd lay odds that our German colleagues and their Russian Princess are sitting somewhere, thousands of miles from here, trying to figure out just what we're trying to figure out. How to fill up so they can keep going."

"That's small comfort, Swede."

"It's better than watching them swoop overhead on their way to pick up Mrs. Martin's fifty thousand dollars!"

The doorway to the chamber split open. Old Icheiri entered, his iron-gray hair held away from his face by a small fillet of silver instead of the ceremonial plumes he had worn earlier. He spoke a sentence in the Muiaian *patois*.

Amelia translated. "He says, there is to be an emergency meeting tonight. He wants us to attend. He thinks we can save Muiaia from destruction."

"Destruction!" Hughes echoed. "This place is as solid as Dempsey's jaw! What's he talking about?"

"I don't know." Amelia shook her head. "But whatever it is, if we can help them, they'll help us back, don't you think? Otherwise, we're stuck. Isn't that what you and Charles were just talking about?"

Hughes gave in. "You're right, sister. Lead on, Chief."

The Muiaian council met deep in the heart of the brick-red ziggurat. The council room's floor was covered with a thick growth of grass and shrubs, standing amidst rocks and sand. Its roof was the blue of midnight. Hundreds of stars twinkled through wisps of cloud. There was the occasional flash of a falling star. Far to the end of the sky the moon gleamed an autumnal orange in brilliant edge.

Distant mountain peaks ringed the room. A small ceremonial fire burned in its center.

Icheiri spoke a low sentence to Amelia as they entered the room. Amelia laid her hands on the arms of her two companions. "Icheiri says they preserve the custom of holding council as their ancestors did. If we study this room, it might tell us where their 'old place' was."

"Yeah," Hughes grumbled. "That's uppermost in my mind, Amy." His tone turned the meaning of his words upside down.

Icheiri spoke again. Amelia said, "We have to be barefoot."

They left their footwear at the entrance to the room and advanced toward the fire. A dozen Muiaians sat on the ground around the flames.

Howard Hughes found himself looking harder at the campfire. He wasn't certain, but he thought that it was no real fire but a simulacrum of one. He held his hands toward it, sniffed the air for the odor of smoke but could not tell whether he really felt warmth and smelled smoke, or whether the illusion was so convincing that he made himself think he did.

Places had been held for them. Icheiri raised his hands and spoke to the council. There was a murmur of assent.

Lindbergh, seated between Amelia and a Muiaian woman whose features reflected the ruddy, flickering light, let out his breath in a long sigh.

The moon, moving from the false horizon of the remote mountains, was turning slightly, from absolute edge toward partial disk, adding to the light of the campfire.

Icheiri spoke again. At first he addressed his fellow Muiaians, then questioned the three strangers.

When he finished, Amelia told Howard and Charles what he had said. "He talked about our plane a little. Everybody knows about it anyhow—seems we're pretty big news around here. Now he wants us to tell them where we came from and what we want."

"I thought they had a prophecy about us," Lindbergh said.

"Thought they figured us as messengers of the gods or some such thing. Didn't you say that before?"

Amelia exchanged a few words with Icheiri. Then she said, "They have that tradition, and we seem to fit. You and I do, Charles, at least. Howard—your hair's the wrong color."

"Sure. A little rouge and I could pass for a siwash myself."

"Well, no matter. The thing is, Icheiri says they don't all believe in the old stories. Some of them think they're a nice tradition, or they take them for metaphors. Only a few of them would think that we actually came from heaven or anything like that."

"Makes sense." Lindbergh nodded. "If a white cloud drifted down in Times Square and some folks in long robes playing harps climbed off it, I don't know how many folks would really believe they were angels."

"Probably," Hughes said, "a publicity stunt for a new talkie!"

Amelia grinned at that. "Well, shall I tell them about the Woodhull Martin Prize and all of that? What do you think?"

Lindbergh rubbed his jaw. The blond whiskers were beginning to turn bristly. "Better find out if they have the same idea of the earth that we have. You know, it'd be hard to explain how we got here if they thought the world was spherical or something like that. We'd tell 'em about coming through the Ice Rim and they'd say, 'Well then you ought to have kept right on going and landed in Australia!'" He grinned back at Amelia.

She carried on a lengthy exchange in Muiaian *patois.* Several other members of the council joined in. At one point a woman took a stylized scepter like Icheiri's rod of office and used the glow of its tip to draw concentric circles in the sand. She pressed a stud on the rod and a red spot glowed at one point between the circles. Finally the discussion subsided and Amelia translated.

"This woman is their . . . chief geologist, is about as close as I can get to it. I think this supreme council, or whatever, works more like a faculty senate than it does like a government.

"Anyway, their understanding of the world is the same as ours. You see the map she made, and marked in Muiaia."

"That's good!" Hughes grunted. "Before we leave here we oughtta get a good map from these bozos. Put us a leg up on just pointing the ship north and praying!"

Lindbergh asked, "Do they know what's on our side of the disk?"

Amelia chattered with the Muiaians. Then she told Lindbergh and Hughes, "They don't know much more about our hemidisk than we do of theirs. They know that it's a world pretty much like their own. Part of their tradition is that their 'old country' may be on the other side of the disk. It's all tied up with their legends and their history. You know, a migration myth. I guess most peoples have them."

"Did she say anything about the Avenue of Sphinxes that we saw in the Halley Cleft? Did her people build those sphinxes?"

Amelia asked the geologist, got her answer, said, "They haven't explored the South Rim. They didn't come here that way. They've speculated on the possibility of exploration or commerce with our hemidisk, but they've never tried it."

Lindy shook his head. "Better tell 'em what we can. I don't see what use it'd be to them, but if they'll swap us information for information, we can use some ideas about the rest of this hemidisk."

"Where should I start?" Amelia asked him.

"Cripes!" Hughes burst in. "Don't let's just sit around beating our gums like this. If these guys want a geography lesson, let's give it to 'em!"

Lindbergh nodded. "Howard's right, Miss Earhart. You have had the most experience with teaching. Could you—oh, I suppose, give them a quick version of whatever those immigrant children are taught, up in Boston."

Amelia borrowed the Muiaian geologist's stylus. She drew a pair of concentric circles, representing the hemidisk they had come from.

As she sketched her map she spoke in rapidly improving *patois*. "Of course we all know that the earth is not really a simple disk. Our geologists calculate that it's really a torus, as much as a thousand miles thick at the equator, sloping to a much thinner crust before the Ice Rim. That's why most of the land area of our hemidisk is near the equator, and the northerly and southerly regions are mostly water."

She continued that way for half an hour, then halted.

"Another whole world," the Muiaian commented. She shook

her head in amazement. The firelight danced in her dark, clear eyes.

"What most amazes me is the colossal land masses in your equatorial regions. Here we have land distributed evenly, at least roughly so, across the disk," she told Amelia. "Well, like you we have watery zones at the North Hole and the South Rim. And I want to ask you about that odd other name you applied to the hole."

"You mean Symmes' Hole? It was named for a man who believed it existed when everybody else thought the earth was solid ice across the north. Symmes insisted there was an opening to the other hemidisk, and kept petitioning the government to finance an expedition there. They all laughed at him, and he died in disgrace, more than a hundred years ago."

She stopped and waited for the Muiaian to resume. Instead Icheiri spoke. "I think Cuchaviva wishes you to continue, and is too polite to ask," he smiled. It was the first time Amelia had heard the woman's name.

"That's about all," Amelia said. She held her palms up to show that she had nothing more to offer.

Cuchaviva smiled. "Well, two other things. We have not only the watery belts at the North Hole and the Ice Rim, but a third, the Great River, that circles the disk at the equator. That is odd, because by your scientists' theory, the river should be impossible. And by *our* theories, your great land masses should be impossible.

"The other odd thing is your fellow Symmes. You say he died in disgrace?"

Amelia decided to check with the others. Howard Hughes had never heard of Symmes. "I thought it was just a name," he said. You know—who ever asked if there was a real Mister Iowa or Missus Atlantic, who got a state or an ocean named for them?"

Lindbergh said, "Cuchaviva, is that her name?"

The Muiaian woman responded when he spoke her name.

"Well, Miss Earhart, yes, I know about Symmes because my dad was on a commission when I was a boy. They looked into private claims against the government. Symmes' great-grandchildren came before the commission and said that by refusing the exploration grant the government caused their ancestor to try and navigate the hole with inadequate equipment.

"Why, the poor simp fitted out a ship and set off without a navigator! Got turned around in a heavy storm and sailed the wrong way! His ship got lost and he disappeared with it and his whole crew, down near the Ice Rim. One old sailor was washed overboard and got picked up by a whaler. Government rejected the claim, said that Symmes would have to present it in person if he wanted to collect!"

Amelia, giggling, translated the whole story into *patois*.

Cuchaviva said, "But you see, we *do* have a story of a light-skinned man from the south, telling a strange story of traversing the ice. His name was Pymmes or Symmes." She queried other Muiaians. "Jurupari? Pachamac?"

"Just an old yarn," Pachamac said. He was a grizzled skeptic.

"You think that our Symmes," Amelia asked, "and your Pymmes were the same explorer?"

Cuchaviva shrugged eloquently. "Perhaps a coincidence. But don't you think it strange?"

"Hey!"

Everyone turned at the exclamation.

"Listen," Howard Huges gritted, "you gals can have your hen party some other time, if you want to cackle all night. I don't know what you're talking about, but it don't sound to me like we're making any headway about getting *out* of this dump!"

"Do we have to be in such a hurry?" Amelia asked.

"What's one-third of fifty gees?" Hughes responded.

Amelia said, "Well, I'll ask them what their emergency is. You know, that they said they hoped we could help them with." She switched back to *patois*. "Icheiri, Cuchaviva, Pachamac." She relayed the question.

Icheiri gestured Pachamac to reply. "Our country is an island. Here we have no enemies. Only our legends tell of men conquering other men, destroying nations, killing and making possessions of other men. We know nothing of these things."

As Pachamac spoke, Amelia translated for Lindbergh and Hughes.

Howard said, "Those little paralyzo-gadgets ain't so bad!"

Amelia translated.

Pachamac said, "Those are for hunting. No Muiaian kills for pleasure, but we capture wild beasts for our circuses. To capture a tiger—to train a tiger—those are feats!

"But we apologize for using the paralysis on your friends, Miss Earhart. Their behavior seemed like that of wild beasts. It was our shame to mistreat them, and we apologize.

"But our flying platforms," Pachamac continued. "You have seen our flying platforms. They bring us stories of far peoples. One in particular, from an icy land near the northern abyss. I can hardly pronounce the name of this land. I think, *Svartalheim*.

"Its people march, and kill. They seem to have no boats like those of our fishermen. And we have seen no flying devices over their land. Yet, somehow, they appear in country after country. And when they appear, they kill the leaders, they slaughter half the young men and enslave the rest.

"We send platforms to observe them and bring back information to us, and some of our platforms do not come back. So we fear that they have captured them and will learn to build their like—although they have conquered a dozen lands without them, anyway.

"We are afraid, Amelia Earhart. They are coming here—this we fear. We do not know even how they come, where to look, how to prepare for them. But Muiaia cannot flee again—there is nowhere left to go."

Chapter 14

"So," Nikolauz exclaimed, "what do you think of the *real* Svartalheim?"

Lothar von Richthofen staggered against the wall of the shaft; the rapid passage of the transparent surface knocked him forward so that he nearly collided with the *Prinz*. The aviator gathered himself. He shook his bullet head as if he were clearing away the lingering images of a dream.

"What is going on here?" he demanded.

"Just what you see."

Lothar thrust his jaw forward belligerently. "You aren't even drunk."

"Never was, *Hauptmann*. On that *Rotwein?* Do you know anything of the English language, by the way, *Hauptmann?* A marvelous pun there is. Our wine, they would call *rot*, *gut*—red, good, eh? But the words themselves have meaning, also. To the *Engländers*, it would mean *Magen krank*—belly-fouling. A good joke, eh?"

He burst into raucous laughter.

"Later," the *Prinz* resumed, "below, some *Schnaps* we can have, if we wish. And whatever other pleasures. The *Palast* is well stocked to provide the pleasures of those it houses."

"I do not—still do not understand." Lothar frowned. "*Erstens*—

firstly—you speak the English language. There are *Engländers* here? In Svartalheim?"

"*Nein, nein, mein Hauptmann*. But we travel. And we listen. The agents of the *Koenig* gather information everywhere."

Lothar pressed at his temples. For a moment he felt as if he was going to lose his balance.

Outside the transparent shaft he could see a landscape that stretched for kilometres; in fact, until it was lost in glowing mists. There was no visible horizon. He craned his neck upward. Perhaps he expected to see sky, or perhaps he expected to see some sort of man-made surface, the supporting structure upon which rested the land of Svartalheim where stood Nikolauz's Keep.

But the air was filled with a glowing mist; for a distance in all directions it was transparent, almost invisible. But when one tried to peer into the distance, the mist blocked one's vision; and when one tried to see above, the effect was the same. The mist was not of a uniform shade; rather, shards and streamers of blue, yellow, green, wove and slid around one.

And all the city, despite its soaring and curving grace, was built of the same dark stone or stonelike materials. From towers hung pennons bearing strange feudal totems. With neither sun nor stars, neither blue day nor black night, the city was wrapped in an eternal gloom. The mist, both illuminating by its glow and obscuring by its denseness, gave the city the appearance of a metropolis wrapped in eternal dusk.

Beyond the city lay a countryside of hillocks, bogs, stunted vegetation, forbidding bodies of water—

A winged horse, its rider dressed in coal-black mail to match the horse's coat and flying a small blood-red pennon that matched the radiance of the horse's red gleaming eyes, hovered momentarily beside the transparent shaft. The rider caused the steed to drop parallel with the falling platform, maintaining eye-level, for a matter of seconds. The pegasus sprang away through the misted air.

The last thing that Lothar saw of the rider and steed was the glow of red heat from the horse's hindquarters.

A cry of astonishment escaped Lothar's lips.

"What is the trouble?" *Prinz* Nikolauz asked.

"I have—I have either gone mad or have fallen asleep and cannot wake myself!"

"I do not see, *Herr Hauptmann*, the cause for your distress. Is it the city? Or the guardian?"

"The city—the city is amazing. This great town hidden beneath the medieval castle. But I can believe this is so. With difficulty, but I can believe.

"But that—that—" He pointed helplessly in the direction the black-and-crimson apparition had taken.

Nikolauz prompted. "*Ja?*"

"*Ein schwarzer Ritter auf einem fliegendem Pferd?* A black knight on a flying horse? I cannot—*it* cannot be! It—"

"*Herr Hauptmann.*" Nikolauz shook his head. "*Herr Hauptmann*, compose yourself, *bitte*. That was merely one of our Valkyrie. Svartalehim cannot leave herself unprotected, surely. Had the Valkyrie not recognized my personage, we would not have been left as we were."

With a hiss the platform came to a rest. The glasslike wall surrounding them rippled and drew away like a living membrane. As Lothar set foot on the flat blackness a chill passed up his leg to his whole body.

There was a humming sound and a flittering red vehicle shaped like a mad surrealist's version of a Nesseldorfer automobile approached. With its strange shape, like an ovoid covered with a nest of twisting snakes, the machine flowed along the ground, half alive.

It halted before the two men and stood waiting, still—or almost still. Lothar tried to tell whether the machine pulsed. He could not tell.

The side of the vehicle swung open. They climbed in. The seats were black and smooth.

Lothar tried unsuccessfully to relax.

Nikolauz spoke softly.

The vehicle accelerated.

Buildings passed like the elements of a dizzying black maze.

Shards of mist wove through the streets. A blue-gray rag whipped angrily around the black edge of a building and thrust like a living creature.

Lothar gaped. It was a mere blob of vapor, he told himself. Yet it seemed to move with volition. It was featureless, amorphous. But in its luminosity he thought he perceived malevolently glaring eyes.

As the car passed through the vapor, Lothar again felt the chill that he had experienced when he first left the sinking platform. An electrical tingling swept through his frame.

The car was out of the mist and plunging through the city's dismal districts.

Now Lothar began to perceive the people of this hidden Svartalheim. Their complexions were dark, their clothing unornamented, cut of a dark gray that approached the blackness of the buildings and streets. They moved in silence, huddling close to building walls, glancing furtively, darting across openings and squares.

The car reached a town plaza. Hundreds of flimsy folding chairs of dead, gnarled, dark gray wood were arranged in militarily precise ranks. An ensemble of musicians occupied a central stand. Their uniforms were black piped with dark, bloody red.

Their instruments were white, the only white things von Richthofen had seen in all of Svartalheim.

All was dim. Beads of moisture formed.

The blood-red vehicle spun on its axis and hummed between sections of wooden chairs. Von Richthofen gazed through the open windscreen. The audience was complete.

Faces turned toward Lothar, cold and expressionless.

A wisp of yellowish fog left Lothar with the feeling of chill dampness.

The vehicle halted. Its sides opened. The men climbed from the vehicle.

Von Richthofen felt the *Prinz* take his hand, holding his fingers gingerly in his own cold fingers, and lead him forward.

The conductor of the ensemble turned to face them. He wore drab formal garb. His baton was a needle of bone. His face was shriveled.

He bowed.

The *Prinz* signaled him to rise.

The conductor turned. His eyes locked with those of Lothar. Lothar peered deep. He saw Oswald Boelcke there. He saw Max Immelmann. He saw Vernor Voss.

The conductor bowed, dry lips moving. They formed a single phrase. Lothar's title and name.

Shocked, Lothar returned the bow.

The conductor mounted his rostrum.

The *Prinz* Nikolauz guided Lothar to his seat. They lowered themselves. Lothar looked at his chair, trying to understand the reason for its strange, discomfiting feel.

The music was peculiar and discordant.

Paralyzed, Lothar stared at the ensemble.

Their instruments, their white instruments, were of suggestive form.

The music became louder, or perhaps it was only the roar of Lothar's blood pounding through the arteries of his skull. The percussionist thumped thick mallets like ossae against the frightening parchment of kettledrums. Lothar's heart pounded. His throat constricted. A shrill reed chorus pierced his eardrums.

The music grew still louder. The audience behind Lothar rustled in their seats. He started to rise and flee, but felt the hand of the *Prinz* Nikolauz clutching his forearm.

The horns shouted at him.

The kettledrums rolled like thunder.

He turned to face the sky.

Moisture covered his face. He gasped. He struggled to his feet dragging Nikolauz with him.

He stumbled to the vehicle.

He grasped a segment of the sculptured exterior, felt it throb like a living aorta in his fingers. He plunged into the vehicle.

The *Prinz* spoke and the car, pulsing like something alive, spun and sped from the square.

The mist thinned. Buildings became visible. The streets were black and dull. The sky was a living mosaic of colors. Pedestrians turned frightening faces.

The road rose.

They crossed a river. The water was black but clear. Shapes

moved beneath its surface, pale as death. They moved rapidly. There were occasional flowerings beneath the water of ruddiness.

Ahead, a tall *Palast* threw angular towers toward the unfathomable sky.

The roadway led to a portcullis. Dim figures stood to either side. The portcullis loomed.

It was of black iron. Its vertical bars were shaped into a horrid face. Great eyes leered. The mouth gaped. The nostrils flared.

The red car pulsed.

Nikolauz spoke.

The vehicle plunged.

The portcullis opened its mouth and the vehicle plummeted through. It halted in the courtyard. Servants in dull livery bowed the *Prinz* and *Hauptmann* from the vehicle. Lackeys scurried.

A group of women, dark-gowned, dark-haired, turned toward them. They moved forward.

Nikolauz spoke softly to them.

One of the women detached herself from the group. She approached Nikolauz, spoke, awaited his reply, received it. She moved to Lothar, raised her eyes to his. He saw Immelmann, Boelcke, Voss. She laughed and turned away. Her hair trailed behind her like a mane; the train of her gown was like a tail. Her shoulders shook. She trailed faint perfume.

Nikolauz guided Lothar down a long corridor. Lothar experienced the sensation of having known the moment before, in the upper Keep. He blinked his eyes, shook his head. They reached a court chamber. Nikolauz presented von Richthofen to his father and eldest brother, the *Koenig* Vithar and the *Kronprinz* Ottokar.

"What do you, best of all things?" demanded the *Koenig*.

Von Richthofen studied the court through narrowed eyes, his mind racing. The family resemblances were obvious: Vithar's hair was white and his figure wizened; his features offered a glimpse of the Nikolauz of forty years hence. Ottokar was taller than Nikolauz and slimmer, but he had the same ruddy hair and moustache, the same rugged features.

Still another version of the family picture hovered about the throne, listening, watching, bending to whisper a suggestion to the *Koenig*. Unlike the others, this one was garbed all in a black cloth that shimmered like satin. Its lining was of a clear blue the color of lightning over the North Sea.

Surely, then, this was the *Oberzauberer*, the chief magician of the court of Svartalheim.

"*Ich fliege*," Lothar said. "I fly." Let these ones deal with that statement as they would.

The bold stroke brought a quick reply. The *Oberzauberer* stared at Lothar briefly. Clearly, he was startled.

"*Sie fliegen?*"

"*Ja.*"

"Very good, *Herr Hauptmann*. Let us see you fly, *bitte.*"

"Here?" Lothar waved his hand.

The wizard grinned hungrily. "Just a little, *Hauptmann*." The grin widened, showing long teeth. "Rise a short distance from the floor. Float a hair's breadth in the air."

The *Koenig* Vithar studied Lothar, chuckling.

"I cannot fly without my equipment."

"I see." The wizard circled his father's throne. He paused and muttered something to the *Kronprinz* Ottokar. Nikolauz, beside Lothar, shifted uneasily. If the stranger brought down the disfavor of the court, then Nikolauz had best be in at the kill, the captor of this menace. But if von Richthofen should win the King's approval, Nikolauz would do well to associate himself with the foreigner: the discoverer and sponsor of the new court favorite.

"Where," the *Oberzauberer* asked, "is your equipment? We sympathize, of course. We ourselves fly, on occasion—it is the privilege of sorcerers. And sometimes the duty, eh, *mein Herr? Ach*, but I thought you could," he made a flightlike gesture with one hand, "possibly raise yourself? Just a little bit, eh? By your own powers alone?

"*Nein?*"

Lothar took a step forward, gauging the reactions of the King, *Kronprinz*, court wizard. "Do not misunderstand me, *mein Herr Zauberer*. I am not a wizard like yourself. In my land, that is left to those who make it their lifework.

"In my land, I serve my *Kaiser-und-Koenig* in the *Armee*."

Ottokar reacted with a lifted eyebrow and a more attentive expression.

"In my land," Lothar continued, "the army has many . . . *ach*, you must not have such words. Machines—machines for flying. *Flugzeugen*, we call them. I, *ach*, ride such *Flugzeuge*, aeroplanes. With the others who remain at the Nikolauz Keep, I arrived in a *Flugzeug*. It was destroyed at the Keep."

The father and sons exchanged glances.

"Like the Valkyrie, then," Ottokar said. "You are a Valkyrie for your *Koenig?*"

Lothar considered. It was close. How could he explain to these men such a concept as the Luftwaffe? "*Ja*," he nodded. What puzzled Lothar was the Valkyrie he had seen from the tube connecting the upper and lower Svartalheims. Was he drugged? Mesmerized? Was he experiencing visions of madness, or had he somehow penetrated a realm of the supernatural? He had no belief in such—it contradicted his entire view of living.

But—?

"Men as Valkyrie," old King Vithar mumbled. "When men can fly as women, there is nothing stable in the world. Nothing. It is time for me to die."

"*Nein, Papa!*" his three sons chorused, each eyeing the other two suspiciously.

Lothar wondered where the fourth brother could be—probably at sea somewhere, plotting for advantage against those at home. How like the court at Berlin. At least these Svartalheimeren had no *alte Kaiser* living in exile to complicate matters.

"Well, fellow," *Kronprinz* Ottokar addressed von Richthofen, "if you can truly manage a—what do you call it? *Flugzeug?*—then perhaps you would demonstrate for us your skill."

"Gladly." Lothar stood to attention, made a quarter-bow and tried to click his heels. "Only, *mein Prinz*, I see no aircraft here in Svartalheim. If you could place workmen at my disposal, perhaps it would be possible to construct one."

A long chance, that. Lothar von Richthofen was an expert pilot and a good mechanic, but to design and build an aeroplane from scratch, in a foreign land like something out of ancient times . . .

. . . and yet, these people had an entire city, perhaps an entire country, built here beneath the earth. They had some sort of elevator for traveling between this Svartalheim and the Svartalheim of the Nikolauz Keep. What else might be within their abilities?

"Perhaps that might be arranged," Ottokar said. "If it should prove needful, *Herr Hauptmann*. But perhaps it would not be so."

Lothar's eyes opened wider. "Not so? Not needful? Do you have, already, flying machines?"

"*Hauptmann*," Nikolauz said, "you astonish me. You saw the Valkyrie as we descended from my Keep."

"*Ja*."

"What do you think she rode?"

"*Ein fliegendes Pferd*. A flying horse. That I do not understand at all. To me such creatures—pegasus we call them—have been always things of myth only."

"But to us," Ottokar took over, "they are not such. They are our own *Flugzeuge*. Our mechanicians build them. We fit them with engines . . ."

"Surely, *Hauptmann* von Richthofen," Nikolauz put in, "you saw the ruddy glow as the Valkyrie departed."

"*Ja, aber* . . ."

"Yes, but—yes, but what could you have thought you saw? The heat, the glowing exhaust of the engine."

"Come, come." Ottoker advanced from his father's side toward Lothar and Nikolauz. "Come, *Hauptmann*. We will escort you to the aerodrome, and you will show your prowess. We will give you a chance to ride one of our *fliegende Pferde*."

Chapter 15

Icheiri commanded a group of Muiaians to lift the tail of the *Spirit of San Diego* and roll the monoplane to the edge of the roof. The temporary crew of two were already seated in the aircraft. Others stood nearby, Muiaians, most of whom had participated in the council with Earhart, Lindbergh, and Hughes.

The pilot leaned from the Ryan's side window and waved to the makeshift ground-crew. The Muiaians lowered the ship's tail. The duralumin propeller began to swing smoothly. The Ryan's wheels were not chocked but the propeller was revolving so slowly that the monoplane did not creep across the stones.

The pilot slid the lever slowly to a new position. The *Spirit* lifted her tail until her fuselage was level with the roof. Her wings were set at their normal angle for horizontal flight.

Now the monoplane rose vertically until her black balloon tires lifted clear of the ruddy stones. Inside the cabin, the heavy hand crank was fitted to its socket and turned until the wheels were retracted into the boat-hull-shaped fuselage.

Amelia Earhart leaned out the window, looked straight down at the stone roof a few yards beneath, and grinned. She spotted Howard Hughes and Charles Lindbergh standing at Icheiri's side. She waved to the three of them, leaned back and said, in *patois*, "Okay, now—ready or not, here we go!"

She shoved the Ryan's throttle to its top position.

The monoplane surged forward silently and with a thrust like that of a roller coaster toppling into its dive—but the Ryan was moving straight ahead!

"It's eerie!" Amelia exclaimed.

In the copilot's seat, Cuchaviva shifted her gaze from Amelia's handling of the Ryan's controls. "Eh?"

"The sound," Amelia answered in *patois*. "The lack of it, I mean. There's always that engine droning away in any airplane. The only time you can be alone with the air, the wind, is when you cut your mill out and glide in for a landing. This is wonderful. Just the whisper of the wind in the struts. This must be the way it is for the birds."

Cuchaviva nodded. "I've always loved the platforms. When we fly for pleasure, often we remove the panels from the flier's cage. I, too, love the feel of the wind in my hair, on my skin. I'm glad we could fit your—what was the word?"

"Airplane."

Amelia sent the refitted Ryan into a steep climb. The monoplane behaved perfectly. The silent Muiaian engine delivered so much power that Amelia didn't have to rely on the plane's wings to make the climb—the propeller pulled the Ryan higher into the air!

There were few clouds, the sun was a sparkling disk nearing its zenith. A few Muiaian platforms hovered at varying distances, their pilots obviously fascinated by the strange aircraft that had risen from the roof of the brick-red ziggurat.

"You could simply have left your—airplane—" Cuchaviva said. "We would have let you take one of our platforms. One big enough to carry you, Amelia, and your two friends."

"Maybe we're being silly," Amelia said.

"Your scholars could study our platform, and we could learn from your airplane."

"Yes." Amelia leveled off and watched the airspeed indicator creep upward. "But as silly as it seems, we *are* in a race. And the rules state that we have to complete the course in one aircraft."

The *Spirit* had left the city of ziggurats and was darting silently over rich farmland. The sound of the slipstream passing over the monoplane's struts had risen to a shriek.

"The only thing I'm afraid of is putting too much strain on the wings. I heard too many stories when I was nursing in Boston. Pilots who'd seen their friends dive so hard in Morane-Saulniers or Nieuports that their wings just broke off when they tried to pull up. I never met anyone who had that happen to him. They never survived."

"I don't understand that," Cuchaviva commented. Her voice was lower than Amelia's. She had learned a few words of English—names for things that the Muiaians didn't have, that consequently were not named in their *patois*. Now the English words, mostly aviation terms, were being integrated into the *patois*.

The Muiaian pronunciation was liquid, musical.

Without warning, the Ryan began vibrating violently.

Amelia cut back on the throttle at once, noted the airspeed at which the vibration had commenced. "We can get up close to 190 with your engine, but that's cutting it too close. Anything over 175, I think, is going to be risky. When we get home, though, I'll bet the Ryan people will be happy to redesign the *Spirit* for higher speeds."

"Show me how you turn," Cuchaviva said. "I haven't seen any slide in your airplane."

"Slide?"

Cuchaviva cupped her hands, one over the other, mimicking a grapefruit-sized globe. She inserted her thumb into the imaginary globe and shoved a nonexistent control lever to various positions. "That's the only control we have on our platforms. You just slide it to whatever direction you want to move in."

She mimicked more manipulations. "Back to center to hover, forward to move ahead, up to rise. Or, turn the knob on itself to turn the platform itself."

Amelia watched Cuchaviva's hands. "This is a little more complicated," Earhart said. She kicked the Ryan into a steep bank. The plane swung into a curve, one wing tilted toward the green farmland, the other raised to the sun.

"Amazing," Cuchaviva murmured.

"Want to try it?"

"I've been hoping," Cuchaviva said.

* * *

"All right, they trust us." Howard Hughes ran his hand through tangled dark hair. "They let us wander around their streets after dark. Swell!"

"What's the trouble, then?"

"The trouble," Hughes gritted, "is that you two are acting like a pair of tourists. 'Oh, lookit the pyramids,'" he mimicked.

"Ziggurats," Lindbergh corrected.

"I don't care if they're Chinese pagodas!" Hughes yelped. "Don't you remember, we're in a race! Who knows where them krauts and that Russkie dame are by now? Maybe that's them up there!" He pointed at the star-specked blackness above them. Between the massive ziggurats a point of greenish light was moving across the sky.

"I doubt it," Lindy said.

Amelia shook her head, agreeing with Lindbergh. "That's one of the Muiaian platforms. They use them for their night patrols."

"Yeah, that's something else I don't catch onto. What are they patrolling about? If everything's so hunky-dory around here, how come everybody's so twitchy about patrolling? Their country's all one island, right?"

"Everything in this hemidisk is. There don't seem to be any really huge land masses on this side. Just big islands and smaller islands. Cuchaviva told me that there's a certain amount of trade between them, but each island is a country and their cultures are very different. Even their species differ, she said. Although they haven't explored their world as thoroughly as we have ours."

"Huh! You mean like Chinks, and Zulus, and siwashes?" Hughes grunted. "So what? I never saw nobody as red as these Muiaians before but I don't care. When I was a kid we all played together. I had a couple of nigger friends, besides Nig Bullard. And siwashes, too. So what—they all played the same."

"I don't mean that," Amelia said. They had halted at a great shining display. It covered one face of a ziggurat's entire ground level. Lines and broad stripes of colors like the new neon lights in New York and Los Angeles crawled over one another. They seemed actually to move before the eye, although it was impossible to tell whether the motion was real or illusory.

At both ends of the display, and at several points within it, vertical lines containing complicated knots pulsed out: white, gold, green, blue.

"You think this is their version of a Christmas tree?" Hughes grunted.

"Maybe a Fourth of July display," Lindbergh countered.

"Or a mural. Have you seen the paintings that Dali and Picasso are doing in Europe?"

"Huh! Probably an advertising sign. Those lines with the knots in 'em are their writing, right? I'll bet a half-eagle this thing says *Smoke Bulldogs* or maybe *Use Dinosaur Oil.*"

Lindbergh studied the lighted wall. "You're the only one of us who knows the lingo, Amelia. Do you think you ought to ask some passing citizen what this says? I don't know whether they're just being polite, leaving us alone, or whether they're really this blasé about strangers in the street."

"Don't you think we fit right in, wearing our borrowed feathers and finery?"

"If you put the Mikado of Japan down in the middle of Waco, Texas, he'd stand out, believe me. Even if he had on a pair of overalls."

Amelia stepped up to a passing Muiaian and spoke a few sentences. She gestured toward the glowing display. The Muiaian nodded and chattered back in *patois.*

"It's a newspaper," Amelia told the others.

"Too bad we can't read it, then." Lindbergh studied the moving colors. "You have no idea what it's about, Amelia?"

She laughed lightly. "It's about us. That's what our friend there told me. Partly about us, and partly about their problems."

"We keep coming back to that, don't we? I don't understand their problems."

"Come on, let's stroll," Hughes urged. "I'm gettin' itchy, standing in one place so long."

"Didn't Icheiri tell you anything while I was testing the *Spirit* with Cuchaviva?" Before they could reply, Amelia provided her own answer. "Of course he didn't. You don't know Muiaian. They don't know English.

"But Chuchaviva's learning a little English, and I'm getting comfortable with their *patois.*"

"And?"

Now they were well away from the glowing wall display. There were fewer Muiaians moving through the streets here, and fewer lights.

"They hardly even grasp the concept of war," Amelia said.

"But they're in one? It doesn't seem like it."

"Where were you during the One Year War?"

"Washington. My dad was in Congress."

"And you, Howard?"

"Home in Texas."

"Well, were there any trenches in Washington? Or in Houston? Horse-drawn artillery rumbling through the streets? Soldiers shooting and buildings being blown up?"

"Don't be silly. The fighting was in Europe."

"Exactly! And there's no fighting going on in the streets of Muiaia, either. And the Muiaians aren't exactly in a war. It's more like—well, look, Howard, Charles. This world is very much like ours, but it isn't identical to it."

"Could of fooled me. All them ziggurats on Division Street in Chicago, and bright-red siwashes in ostrich plumes sitting around the El Cortez bar in San Diego."

"All right." Amelia reddened. "You don't have to rub it in, Howard. But you understand, the geography itself is different. Instead of a few big continents here, they have nothing but islands. Hundreds and hundreds of islands. Their civilizations are much more varied than ours. And when I said that their species varied, I didn't just mean races with different color skins."

"Wait a minute," Lindbergh stopped her. "You mean actual different kinds of intelligences? Civilized creatures that—that aren't even human beings? Something like the Martians in Herbert Wells's book?"

Amelia shrugged.

"Well, what do you mean?" Lindbergh persisted. "You can't just leave something like that unexplained."

"Wait a minute yourself," Hughes interrupted. "Who's this Herbert Wells?"

Lindy shook his head. "Man wrote a story about creatures from the planet Mars traveling to earth. They looked like giant octopuses and were more intelligent than men."

"Crazy," Hughes grumbled. "Bunch of craziness."

"Anyway," Lindbergh addressed Amelia, "is that what you mean? Creatures with minds like ours, only not human in form?"

"I don't really know." Amelia held her hands out as if to capture the flow of ideas and hold them still while she studied them. "Cuchaviva promised to give us an earth-disk before we leave here. It will show the islands of this hemidisk, just as the ones we used in school show the continents and oceans of our hemidisk."

"Okay. What else?"

"They don't know what all the islands are like. There are hundreds of them. Maybe thousands. The Muiaians know that there are people with different colored skins on other islands. Their nations and languages and cultures, some of them, are as different from this one as Bombay is from Boston."

"But they're all still *people*, Amy, ain't they?"

"Howard, I don't know! I tried to understand everything Cuchaviva told me, but I'm not that good at the Muiaian *patois*. But I *think* she was trying to tell me that some of the remote islands are inhabited by—yes, intelligences that are not human!"

"Huh! Like Swede here's talking squids."

"I doubt that. But what if some of them are strange? What if some species other than Man *did* develop intelligence? How do beavers know how to build dams? How do passenger pigeons find their way over thousands of miles, twice every year?"

"That's just instinct, Amelia," Lindbergh said. "That isn't intelligence."

"Maybe so. But it's certainly highly organized behavior. It isn't just stimulus and response. It isn't just a simple matter of eating, fighting, and mating, that we usually attribute to animals. And if something else has intelligence, I have no idea what it might look like. I don't think I'd be too worried about any intelligent mammal. Well, rats might be creepy, but I don't think even that would upset me too much. Birds wouldn't bother me, certainly."

"But what if we met civilized spiders? Ugh!" Lindy kicked some bit of jetsam lying in the street. Or maybe something else made the slight scraping noise, a kind of scuttling noise. The street was deserted except for the three, and it was too dark to see very much.

"I don't think that's likely," Lindbergh asserted.

"Why not?" Hughes pointed a knobby finger. "You were the one talking about brainy octopuses. Why not talking tarantulas?"

"Because," Lindbergh said, "every living thing we've seen here—fish, people, trees—is the same as our own hemidisk. I don't think we're going to encounter any odd creatures now. But their geography and history are different from ours, so they might well have some very strange civilizations."

"I don't know about that." Hughes jabbed his finger toward Lindbergh. "You say everything's the same here as at home. How come they got red people? Really red."

"That's a trivial difference, Howard."

There was a noise above them. They halted and looked up. A dim form peered down at them, over the edge of the first level of the ziggurat.

"Oo-hay's at-thay?" Hughes whispered to the others.

"Nobody there but them chickens," Lindy whispered back.

Amelia walked to the base of the ziggurat. She peered up into the darkness. She spoke in a calm, low voice, using the Muiaian *patois*.

For reply, a dark circle hissed through the air. It descended over Amelia's shoulders, a net of heavy strands woven and anchored to a ring of rope. Amelia struggled to free her arms from the net. She cried out for assistance.

Two dark figures rushed from the shadows of the ziggurat, grabbed her arms and pinned them to her sides even as she twisted and strained to free herself from the net.

She kicked viciously at her attackers, felt a satisfying impact as her toe connected with a kneecap. Even in the instant of impact she felt the target yield sideways in the kind of injury that would have sent even Jim Thorpe or Bronco Nagursky to the sidelines.

She heard voices—Howard and Lindy yelling encouragement. She heard their shoes pounding on pavement stones as they ran to assist her.

She was knocked partway from her feet, saw in one frozen instant the black silhouette falling at her, seeming to tumble from the sky. At the moment she did not stop to analyze the sight; later, she realized that this must have been the observer who had watched them from the first setback of the ziggurat.

The tumbling figure had launched itself at Amelia, but as she fell away in the grip of another assailant the new one landed on her attacker and herself. Three of them sprawled together on the pavement.

More shadowy forms emerged from the gloom. They hissed softly to one another.

Amelia caught glimpses of light, of metallic glints as starlight and moonlight reflected from blades in the hands of the attackers. Obviously they were making every effort to maintain silence, to avoid detection by any passing Muiaian.

That was the advantage that Amelia and her friends possessed: they had no qualms about making all the racket in the world.

Earhart heard Hughes and Lindbergh shouting and grunting. There were sounds of flesh striking flesh, gasps of pain. At one moment Amelia felt a hot, moist rush onto her body. She didn't know whose blood it was—it might have been her own.

She struggled to regain her feet. A pair of arms were wrapped around her shoulders as someone strove to hold her down. She felt her legs grasped and lifted from the ground, then her torso. Two people started to carry her off. She writhed and cried out.

A lanky but muscular figure launched itself through the air like a tackler flying at Red Grange. But unlike Grange, the man carrying Amelia failed to elude the tackle. She felt the impact of Howard Hughes's 175 pounds of muscle and bone, the shock transmitted through the body of his target.

Two dark figures merged into one and tumbled away from her. She felt herself falling, her feet wrenched from the grasp of her second assailant.

She scrambled to a crouch. The impact of her body on the paving stones had knocked the wind from her and half-stunned her. Two men loomed darkly, moved forward to seize her. She saw one of them topped from behind by a taller, slimmer silhouette—Charles!

As the leading assailant reached for her, Amelia launched herself at him. She shoved against the paving stone with her hands and feet simultaneously, clenched her feet and tucked her chin against her shoulder-blade. With a distinct crunch she felt and heard the impact of her skull on the face of her attacker. Her head rang and points of light glowed before her eyes.

Staggering, she saw the man tumble to the stones with the slowness of glycerine moving through water. He made an animal sound, twitched and lay still.

Amelia scanned the scene.

Charles Lindbergh was locked in a wrestling and punching match with Amelia's first opponent.

Howard Hughes confronted two others. He had got a knife from somewhere—seized it from an attacker or picked it off the ground when it was knocked away from its wielder. Now he was feinting, first at one man, then at the other. They were armed as well.

Amelia positioned herself behind Charles Lindbergh's opponent, clenched her hands into a double fist and swung with all of her strength.

Her blow landed behind the ear of Lindy's opponent. The man dropped his hands to his sides and stood motionless.

Amelia swung again.

At the same moment, Lindbergh launched a solid right.

The blows struck simultaneously and the man slumped to the stones.

Lindbergh spun away and dashed to Howard Hughes's assistance. Amelia crouched over their fallen opponent and ran her hands across his garments, searching for a weapon.

One of Hughes's foes turned his head a few degrees to see what had happened between the other fighters. Hughes used the opportunity to lunge forward, bringing his knife in close at the waist. He ripped it across the belly of the other man, who staggered back and collapsed in a gush of blood.

Lindbergh kicked at the knife-arm of Hughes's remaining enemy. The man's knife flew in an arc, reflecting starlight. The rangy Hughes moved with astonishing speed, reversing his weapon, clubbing the knife handle and smashing its weight into the side of his opponent's head.

Without warning the square was bathed in a brilliant emerald glow. Amelia Earhart looked upward and saw a rectangular flying platform hovering above them. There was a hum and she felt, for the first time, the tingling helplessness of the stasis ray.

Chapter 16

For a strange, dreamy time, Irina was happy. She lay with her eyes closed, savoring the luxuriant feel of her satin bedclothes. She was warmed by what must be a quilt surmounted by a fur comforter. The remote bustling sounds of servants and attendants came and went. Her every need was cared for.

Someone—probably the court physician—lifted her hand. He held her wrist to take her pulse, then lowered the hand again to her coverlet. She felt a fluttering in her stomach as she imagined a handsome Russian doctor bending over her, then turning aside to whisper his heartfelt concern to her worried father.

She was a little girl once more, lying abed in the imperial Winter Palace. Graceful towers rose to meet the sky. Snow fell outside, and lackeys curried the horses who would pull her with her parents, their *troika* hung with merry sleighbells, the horses' manes and tails tied with gay ribbons in the colors of Christmas.

The little Princess sighed. Her father would be at her bedside, ready to lift her in his arms, encourage her to dress in her prettiest pinafore and descend for tea with her cousin, the little Tsarevich Alexei.

Ah, the poor little Tsarevich! How his parents doted on the fragile boy! God had first sent them four daughters—the Princesses Marie, Anastasia, Olga, Tatiana—and then the little Prince Alexei!

What joy at the birth of the future Tsar! And then what dismay as the family gradually realized how weak, how sickly the little boy was. His ailment was whispered in the palace corridors. *The Prince has the Royal Disease...the bleeder's disease...the slightest bruise could incapacitate him for weeks, poor little Alexei...the most trivial scratch and he might bleed to death....*

Irina was his favorite. For all that Alexei's sisters spoiled him, for all that his parents pampered him and his imperial father's ministers catered to their future monarch, still the little Tsarevich loved his cousin Irina, his precious Reenishka, the best of all.

And now that Tsar Alexei balanced precariously on the throne of imperial Russia, guided and propped by the Dowager Tsarina and the Prince Lvov, his precious Reenishka was sent off to Berlin to haggle personally with Prince Herbert von Bismarck, the Kaiser's chancellor, for a husband! She, the Tsar's own—

Indignantly she sprang upright in her bed, her eyes opened wide as she glared about the room.

"Princess, you waken. We are relieved."

The voice was a strange one, the language comprehensibly Germanic but far from the German she had learned from infancy at the behest of her tutors. This speaker had white hair and a moustache and beard to match; he was dressed in dark robes and wore the conical, pointed cap traditionally ascribed to wizards.

"This is not the Winter Palace!" Irina exclaimed angrily.

"No," the old man agreed. "That it is not."

"Then where—what—?"

"You do not remember?" This wizard kept speaking his strange language, so like the German. When Irina shook her head he continued. "This is Svartalheim, and you are in the Keep of the *Prinz* Nikolauz. I am the *Zauberer* Lodur. You were overcome at your first sight of the *Prinz.*"

She nodded weakly and rubbed her forehead. "I have no ladies here? No servants?"

"We are all your servants, Your Highness." The wizard bowed but there was a quality of mockery in his gesture, as there was in the expression on his face and the tone of his voice.

"Where are my pilots?" she demanded. "The *Freiherr* and the *Hauptmann* von Richthofen?"

"Ah," the wizard said softly. "The brothers, eh? Why, the one with the restless fingers is below, at table with the officers of the Keep. And the younger man, the one with the bald skull—our *Prinz* is showing him the lower reaches of Svartalheim. It may be some while before they return to the Keep.

"But now, Princess—I have your title correctly from the brothers?—you are Irina Lvova, Princess of All the Russias?"

Irina nodded. "*Da.*"

"Are you strong, Princess? We must speak, you and I. But first I wish you to regain your strength. It was unfortunate, your arrival just as Nicky was chatting with a red man visitor. I am sure that His Highness regrets," he paused, "upsetting the Princess.

"Well," he turned and gestured to a lackey, "bring for Her Highness a bowl of *Sauerweinsuppe.*"

The lackey scurried away. Until his return the wizard spoke with Irina as would a physician. Did she faint often, had she eaten regularly, was she accustomed to the rigorous climate of a place like Svartalheim? She nearly laughed at the questions, especially the last, thinking of the winters in Holy Russia.

The soup arrived. It reminded her of the hot, strong *schav* that was served to the servants at home and that she, Irina, used to beg from the chefs when she slipped away from her governess and ran to the kitchen as a child. The bread that came with this soup was more like the coarse black stuff eaten by serfs than the fine pastries served in the salons of Petrograd or Kiev. Still, it was filling.

"Now, Your Highness," Lodur told her, "maidservants will come and dress you. I regret that we have few garments suitable for a Princess, here at the Keep. At Svartalheim below, *ja.* Here, you will have to make do with what we can devise."

He rose without waiting to hear her wishes. Irina started forward, remembered that she was sick abed and permitted the wizard to make his departure. At the doorway he halted and looked back. "The maidservants will guide you to a suitable place for our conversation."

The *suitable place* proved to be a room large enough and gloomy enough to please a Bavarian noble. For a moment Irina wondered if it was worth her trouble to ally herself with a member of the imperial family—but here she was, in this awful Svartalheim place, on the far side of the earth's disk from home, and there was little she could do about it now.

She was garbed in soft, comfortable clothing of greens and browns. The *Zauberer* had discarded his own robes and tall cap, and wore informal clothing like her own. His costume was topped with an embroidered skullcap that gave him an appearance both scholarly and ecclesiastical.

A fire crackled steadily on a stone hearth, providing scant cheer and less warmth. The furnishings included a large, crudely hewn table, wooden chairs, shelves of books and a huge earth disk carven and painted and fully a yard in diameter.

"Your Highness." Lodur inclined his head to her. The gesture exhibited both economy and ambiguity: it could be interpreted as a small token of the *Zauberer*'s courtesy, or merely as a suggestion that the Princess seat herself in the chair as Lodur directed.

She took another.

"So. I trust Your Highness is refreshed."

"The fare was crude."

"The chef shall be punished."

Again, Lodur's speech contained a suggestion of mockery. The Princess held her tongue. She felt impelled to demand that he return her to the brothers von Richthofen, but she resisted the impulse. Better to say as little and hear as much as she might, with this difficult man.

"We are frankly puzzled, Your Highness," The wizard said. "Few strangers arrive here, and fewer still whose origins are a mystery to us. We are, as you may have inferred, a mere outpost. The poor little *Prinz*, you see..."

She waited for him to continue. When he did not, she prompted. "Yes, the *Prinz*—Nicky, you said?"

"Nikolauz. *Ja*. The old *Koenig* Vithar, may he enjoy more years yet of life." Lodur smiled cynically. "He was a virile young one in his day. Too many sons, you see. Or perhaps the blame attaches to Her late Majesty the Queen."

He leaned on the table with his elbows, steepled his fingers beneath his chin, fluffing his beard with his hands. What a splendid stage-prop was the facial hair of men, and how rare to find one who knew how to use it effectively!

Irina listened attentively.

"The eldest, the *Kronprinz* Ottokar, is kept busy with the army. The next, with the fleet. And the third, as *Oberzauberer*, chief wizard of the realm, is my own titular superior."

A slight emphasis on the penultimate word, and again that cynical turn of the mouth.

"But a fourth *Prinz. Ach*, what can the poor old King do with still another? Keep him around the house and he'll be nothing but trouble. So Vithar sends little Nikolauz up here to the damp cold woods to get him out of the way. And sends me—or has his *Hauptmann Zauberer* do it for him—to keep an eye on little Nicky!

"An eye! Give him a goblet of *Rotwein* and he'll take care of himself. Meanwhile, I shall surely curl up with terminal rheumatism before I get back below."

He levered himself from his chair and tottered across the room to stand before the fire. Had he moved so gingerly in the chamber where Irina had seen him earlier? Or was this more of the *Zauberer*'s stagecraft? She watched him holding his gnarled fingers to the fire for warmth.

"Well, Your Highness." He half-bowed toward her. "Enough of an old man's rambling." *(How old*, Irina wondered.) "We are so pleased to receive you here at the Nikolauz Keep. You must not withhold from us news of your home and travels. How did you come here, and why, and whither next are you bound? A woman's soft hand and sweet voice are precious to us here, and your news will surely keep our brains from atrophying for sheer lack of new things to think upon."

(And, who knows, may provide grist for your mill, Irina thought. *And when you have ground that grain, what kind of loaf will you bake of it, Wizard?)*

She rose from her chair and crossed to the earth disk. It was mounted in a ring so that it could be swung on its axis or spun on its center. Svartalheim was clearly marked on it in archaic script like that used on old German documents still sometimes to be seen.

Lodur stood beside her. Irina realized that he was very tall: she had allowed for the addition of his pointed cap, earlier, but even without it he towered.

"*Ja*, Your Highness." He pointed a long, bony finger. "We are here. And where is your home? Where is this place you call, All the Russias?"

Irina thought swiftly. She could hold back or try to mislead Lodur at this point, but he would penetrate her ruse in time—or might even, for all she knew, have learned already from Manfred or from Lothar the nature of their journey. Best to be truthful now, and dissemble when there was good reason to do so. And when she had won the confidence of the wizard.

With a dramatic gesture she shoved down at one edge of the earth disk. The heavy wooden torus swung in its mounting and the opposite hemidisk swung into view. Irina stopped the torus's motion and gazed at the newly revealed annulus with coldly smiling eyes.

The far hemidisk was painted with a weird melange of fabulous creatures and scenes. Just as she had herself feared that the *Hoehlar* maelstrom and Arctic icefields were a Hades inhabited by satanic demons and disembodied ghouls, so did these Svartalheimers seem to regard the entire opposite hemidisk as a region of supernatural terrors.

The annulus was divided into regions of flame and of ice, alternating as if separated by rays that spread from the *Symmeshoehle* to the South Rim. The ice was peopled by white hairy men, unicorns, fierce dragons that rose on webbed, ribbed, and claw-tipped wings and that spat lurid, sparkling flames. The regions of fire were inhabited by orange, red, and black creatures who glowed their malevolence and glared their rage at the beholder.

"There!" She pointed at the place where flame and frost converged.

"There," she repeated, "is my home. The region of All the Russias is great—the greatest empire of the earth." She sketched in its boundaries, imagining a map superposed upon the painted seas and flames and islands of crystal. "That is the empire of which I am Princess. And nearby," she sketched a smaller region to the arbitrary west of the Russian empire, seeing all the more clearly as she showed the world of her origin to Lodur, "is the home of the *Herren* von Richthofen. Not as much a place, you see, as is Russia."

Lodur stood stroking his beard. He gazed into Irina's face, the dancing flames of the fire-hearth flickering in his eyes. Irina found herself fascinated by their depth and darkness.

"You are from the land of devils?" he asked softly.

"There is no land of devils." Irina heard her own words with shock.

The wizard's eyes widened. Irina realized that they were usually shaded, that his bushy iron-gray eyebrows, peaked and rising to spikes in the middle, almost like the old German Kaiser's famous moustache, drew attention to them.

"No land of devils?" Lodur stroked his beard thoughtfully. He was almost a caricature of the archetypal wizard. "No land of devils? How did you get here, then, if you come from the other side of the disk?"

Irina described her journey with the brothers von Richthofen, the *Kondor*, the *Schwarze Adler*, the Zeppelin's crash and destruction.

The wizard was most interested in Irina's description of the great white ice-worm that Lothar had shot in the *Symmeshoehle*, and the pallid ghoul that had attacked her at their encampment on the ice floe.

"A ghoul... demon... imp." Lodur's thick eyebrows drew together. "Yet you say there is no land of demons."

"I'm afraid I am confused, myself," Irina conceded.

"You say that your side of the earth is a natural world of mountains and plains and seas. And we," Lodur's mouth quirked upward in a grin, "find our world quite comfortable and natural, and attribute wonders and terrors to yours. I perceive a certain symmetry there. Do you not the same?"

"You are the wizard, *Herr* Lodur, not I."

"Well taken, young lady. Er, Your Highness. Forgive me. Well, just between the two of us—" he looked around dramatically "—this wizardry business is mostly flummery, mixed with a bit of authentic lore. Fewer wizards believe in magic than do laymen."

"But what of the demon?"

Lodur spread his hands widely. "There are many wonders in the world, Your Highness. The earth is large, and we have not explored all of it by any means. Even the swamps and bogs here in high Svartalheim contain groves we have never penetrated. Places where men have disappeared. Probably lost, drowned, perhaps swallowed by quicksands. But who knows? There are tales of faeries and of beasts in the bogs."

"You do not believe in magic, then, *mein Herr Zauberer?*"

"What is magic but wonder unexplained, Princess? And what is lore but wonder explained? Maybe we perceive the same events in different lights, and call them wonders, magic—or merely lore."

He reached down and took Irina's hands, held them between his own. Lodur's hands were made on a scale larger than other men's. She looked up, into the dark eyes that saw the world from beneath those bushy brows. She wondered if Lodur was as old as his white beard and hair suggested.

"There are kelpies in the swamp and kobolds in the woods," Lodur said.

Irina gazed at him questioningly.

"Or are they merely serpents? Big reptiles? Bears?" The wizard released Irina's hands and made a shrug.

"Still, *Zauberer*, what was my white demon?"

"You say it was shaped like a man, but squatted rather than stood? Its face was flat and its mouth wide, it had no nose, its eyes bulged from their sockets? And you say that it hopped rather than walked?"

Irina nodded at each point.

"Well, then." The wizard walked to a row of books, drew down a heavy volume and laid it on a reading stand. He opened the pages to an ancient drawing. Irina stood at his side and peered at the yellowed leaves.

"*Ja, mein Herr Lodur*," she whispered, suddenly chilled to the marrow. "This is my demon."

"This is a toad, Your Highness."

"But a toad—" She held her hands up, indicating the size of a garden amphibian.

"A giant species," Lodur said. "Adapted to the Arctic region. Carnivorous—you were nearly its dinner, Princess. White—made to blend with the ice and snow, the better to conceal itself from its prey. And from its own predatory enemies. What eats a creature that eats men, eh?"

Irina shuddered.

"Come then," Lodur said. The tone of his voice was inviting. Irina's mind flashed to past moments spent with young Princes and Dukes in Petrograd, Kiev, Moskva, Odessa. In this the highest royalty were no different from the dirtiest of peasants. They courted the same way, flirted the same way. She looked at the wizard appraisingly. No, beneath that white beard he was not so old at all.

She smiled inwardly.

They stopped their horses at the crest of a hill and looked back, for a moment, at the Keep of *Prinz* Nikolauz. The sun was approaching the highest point in its track. Here in far northern regions the sun was as bright as it was in the tropics, yet the climate seldom warmed. Geographers wrestled with the puzzle and decided that the earth was thickest at the equator, subtly but steadily diminishing as one approached either the *Hoehle* or the Rim.

There were fires beneath the earth. Whether they were the work of Satan or simply of nature, the theologians might dispute with the geologists, but their existence was agreed upon by both. Where the earth was thickest, the fires were greatest, accounting for the greater heat of the tropics and the frigidity of the north and the south.

Even in late morning, the sky was more gray than blue and mists rose from the moat that surrounded the Keep.

"We won't become lost?" Irina asked.

Lodur shook his head.

"Do you often ride out *sans* retainers? In Russia, it would be unheard of. Always a squad of Cossacks would proceed first, to scout out bandits and subdue peasants. Else a noble would face mortal peril to cross the countryside."

"There are no bandits here," Lodur said. "Nor peasants. The Keep is Nikolauz's outpost. More—it is his place of polite exile. It is supplied from the lower Svartalheim. But does your homeland also resemble this one?"

Irina turned from the Keep to survey the land in the opposite direction. She had crossed the territory of Svartalheim one time before, aboard the Zeppelin *Black Eagle*, but that had been in darkness and in storm, when the airship had barely survived its crossing of the sea and the challenge of surmounting the cliffs.

Now Irina could look across the land without being shaken by storm and blinded alternately by blackness of night and by glaring lightning.

The Keep was built near the top of a slope of mostly naked rock. About it a few ugly trees and clumps of shrubbery clung to cracks in the granite. Snows and ice covered the peaks above the Keep. Their melting waters ran through a channel to feed the moat around the Keep, and from there drained away, through a narrow valley.

The valley—Irina could see it through drifting mists—continued into a bog, where the water disappeared in a gloomy mix of muddy islands and half-frozen pools. The cliffs they had crossed lay not far in another direction. If Manfred and Lothar had known, they could have directed *Schwarze Adler* a few kilometres down the coast and come in over low-lying boglands, without nearly dying against the rocky escarpment.

Lodur started his horse down the hillside. Irina's followed as soon as she permitted it to do so.

The wizard's mount was of a glossy black, its tack all of the same somber shade. Irina smiled—appropriate flummery. Her own horse was a richly colored bay, its tack of tan leather, silver, and cloth. The Princess leaned down and patted the horse on its neck.

"You see, Your Highness." Lodur swept one hand toward the swamp, holding the reins of his horse with the other. Small saddlebags hung at the horse's flanks, as black as the rest of its leather fittings.

"See what?" Irina asked.

"Through the swamp leads a safe trail. Anyone who did not know the way would never get through. But for one who knows, there is a path. And the path leads to a faerie castle older than Svartalheim itself."

Irina laughed nervously. The wizard had taken her off guard

this time: was he again reversing himself, to speak of wonders and mystification? Or was he mocking her own newly discovered skepticism?

"Who lives there?" she asked.

"That you will discover."

She hung back.

"You're not afraid, Your Highness? Not after slaying the demon upon the ice-floe?"

"A toad, you said."

"A toad . . . a demon. It would have eaten you in either case."

"Very well."

They spurred ahead. The wizard slowed and selected carefully an opening into the wood that loomed ahead. Irina looked once for the sun before sending her horse after Lodur's.

The sky had grown ever so slightly darker, and the sun's illumination was spread across it by a solid layer of overcast.

The trees were typical northern growth, firs and pines. The ground was deep with fallen needles and with moss. Irina could hear a trickle of water and the occasional call of unseen birds. Other mosses began to appear, on the trunks of the trees and then on their limbs, hanging in great beards and streamers.

A great scum-covered lake showed through an opening in the forest, and they turned to skirt it. There were patches of clear water visible through the scum, and as ever mists rose from these patches and wavered in the air.

Irina, garbed in trousers and soft boots, several layers of shirts made of thin leather and thick cloth, topped by a heavy fleece-lined coat and matching cap—still shivered. She had managed to retain her thin-bladed *Kaiserdolch* and its lacquered scabbard throughout her experiences at the Keep, and had transferred them to the inside of her jacket. She patted the scabbard nervously as she peered at the lake.

The *Zauberer* Lodur appeared as startled as Princess Irina when the water bubbled and hissed, and the kelpie arose with its disheveled hair, its slime-coated, ragged gown, its hate-filled gleaming eyes, and its long, dripping talons.

Chapter 17

"God damn it, that's twice!" Howard Hughes frowned his fiercest frown. "Besides, we had those bozos in hand. You guys show up like Nelson Eddy and the Canadian Mounties, just when we had 'em licked ourselves!"

Amelia tried translating that into Muiaian, completely failing when she came to the part about Nelson Eddy. Besides, she was laughing so hard she could scarcely finish.

Hughes got angrier yet, puffed out his cheeks, then found that he couldn't resist and joined in the laughter.

The Muiaians surrounding them watched in bafflement until Amelia tried to explain in *patois* what was so funny. The commander of the platform—Amelia's former copilot Cuchaviva—offered her explanations. "We did not wish to restrict your activities. You are our guests; we hope, our allies. We could hardly place you under arrest!

"But we were very worried." She indicated the still paralyzed forms lying on the deck of the platform. "We know there have been infiltrators. There have been acts against Muiaia—fields set afire, crashes of platforms, pilots killed. We have tried to capture those responsible, but until now we caught very few of them. And none who survived long—always they've been mortally wounded before capture.

"As for these, though—oh my, that one doesn't have much left of his face. What could have happened?"

Amelia blushed and ruefully rubbed the egg-sized lump on her head.

"*You* did that? With your *head?*"

Amelia nodded.

Cuchaviva shook her own head. "Best be more careful, Amelia." In *patois* the pronunciation was closer to *Ah*-mee-*Yah*. "Injuries to the head can be very dangerous. Well, this is important. If we can get some information from these evildoers, find out their homeland and their plans..."

She turned and spoke to the pilot.

Shortly the platform settled to the roof of the ziggurat that Amelia had started to think of as her temporary home. With armed Muiaians standing by, the paralysis of the raiders was released and they were turned over to healers, along with Amelia and Howard and Charles, all of whose hurts—even Amelia's swollen cranium—proved superficial.

The healthiest of the raiders was placed in a seat. He was a strongly built man with dark, short hair and angry eyes. His clothing was soft, plain, made of leathers and cloths in dark shades of green and brown. He'd managed, somehow, to retain his visorless cap through the melee.

Icheiri was present, and the others deferred to him. He spoke gently to the raider. Amelia translated Icheiri's questions for her companions. But there were no answers to translate.

Finally Icheiri turned from the raider and spoke to the others. Amelia told Howard and Charles what Icheiri said. That the man either did not understand Muiaian—or that he simply refused to communicate with them.

"Figgered that much for myself," Hughes grumbled to Lindy.

Icheiri spoke to a woman near his own age. Her name was Pachamac; her title, roughly, chairman of the Languages Department. When Amelia translated, Hughes grumbled, "This place is run like a big school!"

"Figgered that much for yourself, did yuh?" Amelia mimicked.

Pachamac spoke to the raider, first in Muiaian, then in a series of other languages that Amelia did not recognize. Finally Pachamac turned from the raider and spoke to a younger Muiaian.

In a moment Pachamac held a drinking mug. She extended it toward the raider. He reached for it eagerly. Pachamac pulled it away and asked a question. The raider glowered. Pachamac held the mug forward. Again the charade was enacted.

Finally Pachamac shrugged and began to drink, smacking her lips with pleasure and spilling blobs of water.

The raider, desperation on his face, uttered one word.

Pachamac ignored him but Amelia was startled to see the expression on Charles Lindbergh's face. He nudged Amelia.

Pachamac drank more.

The raider struggled for the mug.

Pachamac did not yield.

This time the raider spoke.

"He's pleading for a drink," Lindbergh whispered to Amelia.

"That's no surprise."

"But I understood him!"

"Are you a linguist, too?" She turned toward him, honest surprise in her expression. The movement made her head throb and she rubbed the swelling. "Wow!"

Lindbergh said, "When I was a kid. My grandpa was a minister in the Swedish court before he came to Wisconsin."

"I didn't know that. But so what?"

"So—he only knew a little English. He spoke Swedish, mostly. Some German. My dad knew the jargon. I used to understand it, too, from around the house. Came in handy in Washington, too. All the ambassadors' kids wanted to get into the gang that Quint Roosevelt and I had."

"And—and this man..."

Lindbergh spoke to the prisoner, bypassing both Amelia and Pachamac. The man made a surly reply.

"His name is Nikar. Something like that. He speaks a language a lot like German, with some Swedish and Danish and Norwegian mixed in. Not just that, either. It's a funny sort of old-fashioned German."

Amelia asked what Lindbergh meant, translating for Pachamac

as they went along. Even the raider was caught up in the excitement, throwing in words in his own language. Mostly they were requests for food and drink.

After a while Pachamac relayed the requests and helpers brought dishes and mugs for the raider.

"All right, this is what we know." Cuchaviva was speaking. Amelia translated for Lindbergh and Hughes, and translated their answers back to *patois* for the Muiaians Icheiri, Cuchaviva, Pachamac.

Dialogue with Nikar had to travel from the Muiaians to Amelia to Lindbergh to the raider, and back via the same circuitous route.

"What did Charles Lindbergh mean by 'a funny sort of old-fashioned German'?" Pachamac wanted to know.

When Amelia translated the question, Charles pondered for a moment. "It's like—look, in English, if somebody was reading the Bible, hey? There's an odd word once in a while, and a lot of theeing and thouing instead of just saying *you*. Or if you went to a Shakespeare play. You know what I mean?"

Amelia nodded.

"Well," Lindy said, "our friend Mr. Nikar talks that way. Partly it's a mixture of languages, but partly it's just that old-fashioned stuff."

Amelia transmitted that as best she could.

"All right," Pachamac replied in *patois*. She chattered quickly to Icheiri and Cuchaviva. Cuchaviva took up her summary. "At least we know a few things." She began ticking them off with her fingers.

"First, his name is Nikar."

The raider scowled.

"Second, he speaks an archaic form of some language that your Charles knows, that is spoken on your side of the disk."

Lindbergh nodded.

"Third, Nikar comes from a land called Svartalheim. He refuses to say where that is, and he threatens us with terrible suffering for forcing that information out of him."

She smiled sweetly.

Nikar's frown would have cracked a pier glass.

"I don't know about that bozo." Howard Hughes poked a long finger at Nikar. "Back in the war—"

"Oh, come on," Lindbergh cut in. "You and your war stories. Your friend Jax whipped the Hun singlehanded. If you'd been old enough to go along, you'd have personally brought the Kaiser back in handcuffs. Too bad President Roosevelt didn't have you to send instead of General Pershing."

Hughes's face matched that of Nikar for sourness. "What I started to say, Swede, was that a prisoner who couldn't stand up to interrogation better than *that* gink did, he'd have been a laughingstock."

"Well, he was hungry and thirsty. Besides, he must feel cut off from his people."

"Why? What about his buddies?"

"Didn't you catch that? None of the others survived."

"Aw, come on. We didn't handle 'em *that* rough. Maybe a couple of those bums could use some painless dentistry, but we didn't *kill* nobody!"

"No, we didn't," Amelia put in. "They killed themselves." She exchanged words with Cuchaviva and Pachamac. "They had poison. That's why they aren't trained to resist questioning. There's no need. If they're captured, one swallow and—*pow!*"

"So how come—?" Hughes gestured toward Nikar.

"However they kept the poison—probably in a hollow tooth. When I gave Mr. Nikar the billy goat treatment, his suicide kit must have gone flying."

"Poor simp." Hughes snorted in mocking sympathy. "Didn't know how to fight so good, didn't know how to win, didn't even know how to lose right. Haha!"

Amelia thought quietly, then spoke with Cuchaviva and Pachamac. Again a runner was dispatched.

"What was that about?" Lindbergh asked.

"We're getting a world disk. We have to settle a geography problem."

The world disk arrived. It resembled those Lindbergh had used in elementary school, except that the detailed side was the one they were on now, rather than the one where he'd grown up.

Amelia spoke to Lindy and Hughes in English, repeating her words to the Muiaians in *patois*.

Lindbergh didn't translate for Nikar. Let the Svartalheimer stew a little. The fact that he could see them pointing to areas of the disk, and that he could pick up references to himself and to Svartalheim, only increased his unhappiness.

"This isn't much more than a guess," Amelia said, "but consider this." She turned the disk onto its blank side and indicated an area south of the equator. "This is where the old Incan empire once flourished. And here—" she turned the disk back "—is Muiaia."

She glanced at the Muiaians. "We don't know really, when or how contact was made between the two. Or which was the original civilization and which the daughter, or colony."

"Those pyramids—" Hughes suggested.

"Yes. Pyramids in Egypt and Yucatán. Ziggurats in ancient Mesopotamia and now in Muiaia. Even some of the architecture they're finding in the jungles of Cochin. Plus the matter of language, of course."

"It's obvious," Pachamac offered in *patois*. "There was commerce, communication between the hemidisks. I heard your story of the Avenue of Sphinxes in the—what did you call it—Great Halley Cleft in the Ice Rim. There can be no question."

"That and our tale of traveling through a lake," Cuchaviva added.

"Well, what I was driving at," Amelia resumed. "Muiaia is roughly opposite the old Incan empire." She flipped the earth disk meditatively.

"Charles, here, is able to understand a little of Mr. Nikar's language. It resembles old German or Swedish. Two languages of our hemidisk. I don't know either, but I've *heard* them both and I can tell you that they *sound* a lot like . . . what should we call it? Svartalheimerisch."

Nikar glowered.

"Well, what I'm suggesting—" Amelia placed her fingertips near the representation of Symmes' Hole on the earth disk "—is that there's a similar relationship. Or was at one time. Between Svartalheim on this hemidisk, and the Nordic region, Scandinavia, Germany, the Baltic, on *our* hemidisk."

She looked at the others, noted their nods of agreement. "The question, then, is this. How much do you know about the Holar regions?"

"Not a great deal," Icheiri said.

Amelia waited.

Icheiri said, "You have told us that your hemidisk is made up of a few great land masses, and many smaller islands. How did you get your knowledge of the lands and the peoples of your world?"

Amelia translated for Howard and Lindy. Lindbergh offered a response. "Mostly by trade. Ships crossed the seas, horses and carts crossed the continents. Of course, that was before aviation."

"Yes, yes," Icheiri responded to Amelia's translation. "And what knowledge did that produce for you? Which regions are best known? Which are least known?"

Lindbergh pondered. "Okay, got your point," he said grudgingly. "We got to know the regions along the trading routes. Those are still the best known. Off the beaten trail, we don't know so much. Even now. Who knows what's in the middle of Tibet, or the Amazon jungle, or the Australian desert?"

Icheiri nodded.

"Just so. And in our hemidisk we have not your great bodies of land. Our total land area is great, but it is divided into so many islands. We have no—what was your term—continents. Yes. We have none."

Howard Hughes hummed a bar of a popular tune.

Icheiri resumed. "So our trade has been with the islands nearest our own. And consequently our knowledge is greatest, of lands nearest Muiaia. The farther an island, the less we know of it. If Svartalheim is near the North Hole, it is far from Muiaia. Not as far as the lands across the Hole—but far enough.

"Perhaps they know of Svartalheim in Haibrasl, though."

The other Muiaians nodded. "If anyone knows, they will know in Haibrasl."

Amelia translated the statement, then asked the obvious question. "What is Haibrasl?"

Cuchaviva took the world disk from Amelia. She glanced at Icheiri to get his agreement, then spoke. "The islands of our hemidisk are scattered across the world. But most of them lie in two great belts."

She pointed to the blue annulus, the circular band that split the world disk like a broadened equator.

"Dividing the island belts is the Great River."

"Okeanos!" Howard Hughes exclaimed.

"What?"

"Okeanos. The great world river."

"Howard, you continue to amaze me." Amelia laid her hand on his wrist, her fingertips brushing the heavy black hairs there. "I'd barely heard of Okeanos, and I attended Columbia. I thought you were a roughneck boy from Houston. Raised in a machine shop and all that fairy tale."

Hughes blushed. "I told you, a lot of us kids used to play together. All kind of kids. There was this Greek kid, he didn't talk English so good. But he used to tell great stories about Herakles and Jason and them. He told me about Okeanos. I allus thought it was a load of bananas, but look!" He pointed at the disk. "There it is!"

"Well, another mystery for us to carry home," Charles Lindbergh put in. "Let's get back to the business at hand."

Cuchaviva waited for Amelia's translation. Then she said, "As you see, Okeanos circles the hemidisk. It flows, although slowly."

"And there is, in the middle of Okeanos," another added, "Haibrasl."

Amelia looked up sharply. "You mean, the waters of Okeanos divide? They flow on either side of Haibrasl?"

"No. The island itself moves. Partly it is carried along by the motion of the water, and partly the people of that land, the Haibrasli, control its motion."

"Oh, no," Lindy commented. "That old saw! The famous floating island."

"Could be something like the Sargasso Sea," Hughes offered.

"That's just a bunch of kelp."

"But if enough built up. And if it wasn't anchored to the sea bottom. Couldn't it develop a kind of land surface? A crust of hardened mud? And if it got big enough, it could take hundreds of years..."

"I suppose," Lindy conceded, "it might be possible." But he was unconvinced.

"Because their land circles the hemidisk eternally," Cuchaviva said, "the Haibrasli have become famous traders. Their island is so fabulous that it was thought, for long, that it was a myth.

"But we know it's real! People travel there from all over the world. All of our hemidisk. Ships arrive there from many lands. And our flying platforms visit. And other flying craft from other countries."

Icheiri nodded. "If anyone knows where Svartalheim is, it would be the Haibrasli."

"I'm going there!" Cuchaviva said suddenly. She spoke to Amelia. "Will you go with me? If I can find Yacabuchu—I don't know where he is, but if he was scouting and found his way to Svartalheim..."

Hughes pounded his fist. "Just hold your horses for a minute! I dunno what the It Girl there was saying, but I can guess she was fishing us into some mess! Amy, are you getting us mixed into these bozos' politics or something?"

Amelia flushed. "I don't know what Cuchaviva has in mind. She's looking for someone called Yacabuchu."

"Well, whatever. They're all the same to me. Look, Amy, these galoots been nice enough to us. Heck, they put us up, they fed us, they give us fresh outfits to wear—"

"Don't forget, they fitted the *Spirit* with one of their engines," Lindbergh put in. "That's worth a lot more than a tankful of gasoline would have been. It should be worth a fortune when we get home. The beginning of commerce between the two hemidisks, after thousands of years of separation!"

"Holy cripes, Swede, no wonder your old man was a politician! You sound like you're running for President. Don't you like Jimmy Walker no more?"

"What are you getting at, Howard?"

"Well for Pete's sake let's not get off the track and get all tangled up in these jaspers' problems. If these Svartalheims or whatever they call 'em and these Muiaians are gettin' revved up to have a war, that's their problem. Don't you two remember what we're here for? Don't you remember Mrs. Martin and the fifty grand we're racing for?"

"There may be some things more important than that prize," Amelia said softly.

"Little Miss Social Worker! You ever hear the one about charity begins at home?"

Lindbergh gestured the others to an at-least-momentary pause. "Listen here. We have to get to Symmes' Hole. If we can make the trip by way of this Haibrasl place, and then do some errand at Svartalheim, we're not even going off our route. Besides," he rubbed a bruised cheekbone, grimacing, "I think we may have a little score to settle at Svartalheim."

Amelia said, "Then let me ask Cuchaviva how quickly they'll be ready to leave. We do owe them a favor, in exchange for refitting our plane with the magnetic engine."

She turned to Cuchaviva. Lindy and Hughes, unable to follow their dialogue, watched the expression of Nikar. He, too, followed the gestures and intonations of Cuchaviva and Amelia. He was very unhappy.

Amelia turned back toward the men. "Her husband is a scout. An aerial explorer for Muiaia. They've been getting reports of conquerors from the north. That's probably Svartalheim. Cuchaviva's husband, Yacabuchu, is overdue from his last flight.

"Now that they know the Svartalheimers are after them, Cuchaviva's pretty sure that's where her husband is. She wants him back!"

Lindy nodded. "When does she want to start?"

Amelia shot the question at Cuchaviva. She got her reply. "She wants to take two aircraft," Amy said. "We can go in the *Spirit* and—wait a minute."

Another quick exchange with Cuchaviva.

"The Muiaians are willing to send Nikar back to Svartalheim, in exchange for Cuchaviva's husband. It'll take some negotiations before they can get him out. But the idea, anyway, is to take the *Spirit* and one of their platforms. We'll divide our party. There should be two of us with Nikar, two on the other craft. I'd think..."

* * *

They lifted into the dawn, circled around a few squalls that were moving in from the northeast, and headed for Okeanos. The motion of the earth brought sunrise from the north today, and the *Spirit of San Diego* was painted golden by the early rays.

She was a silent gilded bird, her propeller whirling with a ghostly smoothness, the slipstream whistling past open cabin windows like twin wendigoes.

Howard Hughes and Amelia Earhart shared the controls of the Ryan. Lindy had threatened hysterics if he were denied the opportunity to pilot a Muiaian platform. The two craft were within radio range of each other, but there was no need for communication as yet.

The two expert navigators, Amelia Earhart and Cuchaviva, had estimated the flight at twelve hours' duration. If they arrived anywhere near Haibrasl after dark they could establish communication, then home in on the island's lighted landing field.

Meanwhile, each craft was equipped with a Muiaian navigation aid unknown on the other hemidisk—a small metallic earth disk attuned to a signal generator that ran off the craft's engine's magnetic field.

A glowing spot appeared on the model disk, corresponding to the location of the aircraft. Any time they needed to orient themselves, they had only to refer to the disk.

They passed over a series of islands separated by broad lanes of water, throughout the day.

Amelia peered from the cabin of the *Spirit*. "I'd give anything to know what it's like down there. What kinds of people, what kinds of countries? It's another whole earth, Howard!"

Hughes grunted.

"That's another thing that makes the Woodhull Prize unimportant," Amelia said. "Think of it! Columbus wanted a new route for the silk and spice trade, and he found the New World. We're after Mrs. Martin's fifty thousand dollars but we've found a new world too!"

Hughes remained uninterested, gazing abstractedly from the Ryan's window.

He gasped in surprise and horror. "What's going on over there!

Look at that, they're twisting and shaking like they was going to bust!

"Holy cow, look at 'em now! That thing's in a power dive! Oh, gosh, that's just like Jax Bullard described Al Ball when he smashed up at Strasbourg! Oh, my God, Amy!"

There were tears in his gruff, throaty voice. "Oh, my God, there they go into the drink!"

Chapter 18

Freiherr Manfred found himself seated opposite a familiar figure. It was the guard commander who had first approached the *Schwarze Adler* party after the crash of their Zeppelin. The man had a brutal countenance, broad shoulders, a heavy, muscular body running badly to fat. The *Truppenführer* Mider kept careful watch on the others at the wooden table, and Manfred kept equally careful watch on the *Truppenführer*.

Clearly Mider was fond of filling his belly. One hand steadily grabbed greasy morsels from the trencher. The other, he seldom removed from the thick stem of his crudely carven goblet, yelling to servers every time his drink needed replenishment. Mider seemed hardly to care what was put into the drinking implement—the Svartalheimers' heavy-bodied, slightly sour wine or their strong and almost syrupy mead. Red fluid or golden, Mider would empty the goblet and shout for more, stuffing his mouth with gobbets of dripping meat between.

Von Richthofen limited himself to a rough sandwich, slapping as nearly manageable a chunk of roast as he could find between two slabs of rough, black bread. The only eating implement he used was the *Kaiserdolch*, the Emperor's dagger presented him by Chancellor Prince von Hindenburg in Berlin—how long ago?

How long ago? It could not have been more than a couple of

days, yet the Baron felt as if it had been years since that incident in another world, in another life. And such it was. He accepted a glass of the heavy red wine and permitted himself to gaze into it, the image of the room around him blending into the scene conjured by his imagination.

The men at the table were dressed in rude cloth and leather, their tabards stitched with roughly made coats-of-arms, baldrics slung over shoulders supporting crudely made swords. Beyond them, the stone walls were hung with dusty tapestries and arms antique even by the standards of Svartalheim. Slovenly dressed halberdiers stood guard at the entryway.

Manfred might as well have slipped backward through time to the fourteenth century, instead of traveling through the *Symmeshoehle* here in the twentieth.

Von Richthofen's attention was seized away from his reverie by the thump of a beefy fist on the table. He blinked and looked into the grease-coated face of the *Truppenführer* Mider. "Say, fellow, I am addressing you!" The guard captain roared. Obviously he was becoming more confident with the consumption of mead and wine.

Manfred decided to play cautiously. "What was it you asked?"

"I said, you never did account for your arrival here in the Keep. Where did you come from? And how did you get over the battlements?"

"I'll answer to your master, *Truppenführer*. I'm more interested in your statements than in your questions."

"Is that so?" Mider was growing belligerent.

"You know my rank, and the deference due it. I understand that your master is a *Prinz*. That, as well as my host. Certainly I defer to him. But what is your rank? And what do you think is the proper form of address to a Baron?"

"A Baron? *Ein Freiherr?*" Mider laughed until he hiccoughed.

Meanwhile, Manfred was assessing his situation. The *Prinz* Nikolauz was nowhere to be seen. He'd disappeared with Lothar, gone off to some unknown place and purpose. Manfred was as happy to be rid of his brother, at least for the time being—Lothar had been a brilliant swordsman and a daring aviator, two skills which Manfred himself had taught him, and in which Lothar threatened to outstrip his elder brother.

He was an invaluable ally—as long as he could be relied upon. In the sky, flying against an enemy *Escadrille*, he could not be beaten. But here, in this remote Keep, with the Russian Princess lying abed and no other European within thousands of kilometres...

It would not be beyond Lothar to turn on his brother. The death of Manfred would bring the title of *Freiherr* von Richthofen to Lothar, and with it the powers and estates of the family. Manfred was best off by himself in this confrontation.

Mider's laughter and hiccoughs had turned to a fit of coughing. One of his men was thumping him on the back. Ultimately the source of the problem appeared. A hearty thwack on the baldric coincided with a final convulsive cough and a chunk of meat dislodged itself from Mider's throat. It flew across the table and bounced off Manfred von Richthofen's cheekbone.

The guard captain stared at Manfred. The table became suddenly silent. The only sound was the scrape of rough wooden chairs on crude flagstones as men slid their seats to free their knees. From Mider's side of the table there was an uncomfortable stirring of cloth and leather on wood: that side of the table was fitted with a single long bench, shared by diners of lesser rank.

"I *may* be prepared to accept your abject apology," Manfred hissed at the *Truppenführer*.

"Ap-ap-apology?" Mider echoed. Tics crawled through the muscles of his face as he attempted to decide whether to offer regrets, to bluster through the incident and establish himself as top man present, or to laugh the matter aside. The second choice was most appealing. Both the *Prinz* Nikolauz and the *Zauberer* Lodur were absent, Lodur in his role as court physician having left to care for the foreign *Prinzessin*. If Mider could establish dominance over this self-proclaimed *Freiherr*, his own status as *Truppenführer* would rise.

Still, there was a dangerous look to the *Freiherr*'s eye. Mider essayed a laugh that came out a nervous giggle. He darted a glance along the table. "Come, brothers, let's show this arrogant nobody how to exercise some humility!"

The men stirred uneasily but none rose to Mider's cause.

Mider slid his hand toward the scabbard that hung from his baldric.

Like a bolt of lightning the foreigner had kicked his chair back from the table and launched himself through the air. A blade glinted in his hand.

The stranger's feet seemed to fly over the trencher before Mider could shove himself from his position on the bench. In an instant Mider saw three things coming toward him: the foreigner's two feet and the flashing blade held in a hand arcing low over the trencher and aimed at Mider's torso.

The most that Mider could do was shove himself away, dropping backward, downward, sideward all at once. He was fortunate enough to avoid the slashing blade, but felt the impact of the stranger's feet, one thudding solidly into his shoulder, and the other glancing from the side of his head.

In that same moment, Mider realized that he had made a dreadful error in challenging the *Freiherr*, and that he had compounded it by drinking enough wine and mead, first, to make himself tipsy. There was a ringing in his ears, the room went out of focus, and a terrible cold fist seemed to have clenched itself around his belly.

Even so...

The foreigner had passed over Mider and landed on the floor behind him. Mider swung his legs over the bench. The guard seated beside him had placed distance between them—he wanted no part of this tussle.

Mider's boots hit the flagstone floor with a double thump. He shoved himself upright by placing his hands on the table-edge behind his bottom and pushing off. He spread his feet for better balance, shaking his head to rid it of the wooziness that his drinking had provoked and the foreigner's kick made worse, and at the same time he reached for his sword.

He drew it and held it before him. The stranger danced almost effeminately away, keeping his eyes on Mider's sword and his hands. The *Truppenführer* hefted his sword and swung it at the foreigner. Von Richthofen hopped backward easily, avoiding the swing. The weight of the heavy sword drew Mider partway round. As he recovered himself he felt a jolt from behind, as if he had been kicked lightly in the rump, and a slight pricking on his upper arm.

He turned and saw von Richthofen grinning and holding up his puny dagger. The tip of it was reddened. Mider looked at his arm and saw that the sleeve had been sliced and a little wound administered.

He hefted his sword and faced von Richthofen. Again Mider swung the heavy blade in a horizontal arc that would sever an opponent at the waist. But again von Richthofen dodged the blade, this time by dropping flat to the flagstones as the sword passed above his head.

Again Mider was swung around by the weight of his sword. He heard his opponent move behind him, felt a stunning impact against the base of his skull. He stumbled forward, crashed against the end of the dining table and avoided falling.

He turned to face von Richthofen. The foreigner held his dagger hilt upward, indicating that he had used its solid handle to deliver the blow to Mider's skull.

"You men!" the *Truppenführer* roared. The score of men-at-arms and halberdiers scattered throughout the hall seemed to shrink away from Mider. "You men!" he repeated. "Capture this foreigner! Disarm him! He has attacked your guard captain! Capture him!"

The men shuffled and shifted, each trying to make himself invisible by standing behind another.

"Very well," Mider growled. "I shall take care of him, and then of you others!"

Von Richthofen's grin was chilling.

"Woman!" Mider shouted at him. The Svartalheimer's head was clearing. If he could play for time, meanwhile taunting von Richthofen into some error...

"Woman," Mider said again, "you fight with that little woman's dagger. That little tooth like a burgher gives his daughter in hope of defending her petty virtue. Fight like a man, you coward! Pick up a man's weapon—if you can lift one!"

Von Richthofen stood his ground, legs apart, knees bent, his arms at his sides and his little dagger held close at his hip.

"Come, *Truppenführer*, let us see how you defend the honor of the Keep. Make your master proud of you, dog. You've yet to even nip my ankles!"

Mider hoisted his heavy blade, wrapping both his fleshy hands around the hilt, feeling the grease from his interrupted meal as he closed the one hand beside the other. He lifted his sword over his head and advanced against von Richthofen. "All right, *Herr Baron*. I'll nip your heels for you—starting at the top of your louse-bitten skull!"

He launched himself at a run, swung the sword with both his hands, hard enough to cleave the foreigner from scalp to crotch. He grunted with the effort. Then his sword struck—and von Richthofen wasn't there! Faster than Mider could follow, he'd thrown himself forward and wrapped his arms around the Svartalheimer's shins.

The sword struck the flagging with a jolt that vibrated up Mider's arms to his shoulders, and a clang that reverberated off the great hall's gray stone walls. Mider felt the heavy sword leap from his grasp like a living thing, saw it clatter and bound across the flagging to lie inert at the foot of a tapestry.

Von Richthofen uncurled himself from around Mider's legs.

The *Truppenführer* gawped down at the foreigner, baffled by such bizarre conduct. Mider's hands were numb and his head still rang from the impact of his blade against the stone.

Von Richthofen sprang to his feet, lifted his little dagger and poked with it. For an instant Mider thought that it was aimed for his eyes but there was a flash before him, a searing pain, and something flew across the room and landed on the floor. There was a sudden gout of redness in front of Mider. He raised his hands toward his face and saw that they were drenched.

"Now, you bleeding pig," Mider heard von Richthofen's voice coming as if from an immense distance. "See how you snuffle without your snout." Von Richthofen stood before Mider. Mider groped for him with his tingling hands but von Richthofen danced away. Mider took another step. Von Richthofen moved aside. Mider tried to lunge for von Richthofen but he felt himself sliding on his own blood.

He fell for what seemed eternities while the dark floor grew closer and closer. Finally his cheek smashed into stone. Flashes of light filled his fuddled skull. Blood still gouted from his face, from the place where his nose had been. It was forming a puddle with his face in the middle of it.

From above him he heard a voice, saw a foot advance, felt it shove him from his side onto his back. He looked up and saw von Richthofen, tall as an oak, swaying rhythmically over him. "If any of you care for this piggy's life, you'd better burn his wound before he bleeds to death."

Mider couldn't tell whether anyone responded or not: a storm was pounding in his ears and von Richthofen above him was whirling in circles as his world faded into blackness. Such was his good fortune, for his pain would only have begun.

Von Richthofen spurned the bleeding *Truppenführer* with his boot, bent and cleaned his *Kaiserdolch* on the man's baldric, then returned it to its scabbard. He strode to the halberdier nearest the entryway of the great hall and commanded the man to lead him to Princess Irina's chamber.

The man scurried to obey.

As they exited from the hall von Richthofen could hear the remaining men-at-arms milling about, engaged in low conversation. He chuckled to himself.

The halberdier led him along a corridor and up a circular flight of stairs, then down a passage to a sumptuous bedchamber. The Princess Irina was absent. Only a woman servant sat in one corner of the room, patiently stitching at a contrivance of heavy cloth.

Manfred demanded to know the whereabouts of the Princess.

The woman servant curtsied clumsily and spoke with uncertainty, saying that she did not know where the Princess had gone.

Von Richthofen pressed her.

The servant told him that the *Zauberer* Lodur, the court wizard and physician of the *Prinz Nikolauz Schloss*, had come to see her, and the foreign lady had gone with him.

Where?

To the *Zauberer's* chambers.

Again von Richthofen was off. At Lodur's place—combination

workshop, library, dwelling—there was sign of Irina's presence. A scarf that the woman servant identified as having been used by the Princess lay across the arm of a chair. The wizard's chair, too, had been moved from its usual position. And a book lay open on the wizard's reading stand. Von Richthofen leaned over the volume. His eyes widened at the illustration he beheld.

"Where would they have gone from here?" he demanded of the halberdier and of the woman.

The two of them looked at each other.

"I do not know," the woman said.

"Perhaps..." The halberdier hesitated.

"Quickly!" von Richthofen thundered.

"We should, sir, at least check the stables."

"*Ja, gut!* You will come with me, then. Bring your weapon. What is your name, man?"

"Balor, sir."

"Lead the way!"

At the stables they found two empty stalls. "Can you trace their path, Balor? Has the *Zauberer* a regular retreat where he would have taken the Princess?"

The halberdier's face clouded in concentration. "I—I think, sir—the *Zauberer* knows a trail through the marsh."

"We will follow. Mount!" Von Richthofen selected a horse, commanded the halberdier to fit it, leaped upon its back.

Quickly they were out of the stables and away from the Keep, following the trail of the *Zauberer* Lodur and the Princess Irina. The sky was darkening and the mists rising. The sun would shortly set and plunge the countryside into a darkness intensified by the thick layer of mist.

"*Mein Herr,*" Balor pled, "I don't know this trail very well, and in the darkness..."

"Ride!"

"There are bogs, *Freiherr*—"

"Ride!"

"And—"

Manfred yielded to curiosity. "*Ja, Balor.* There are bogs and—what?"

"Monsters, *Freiherr.*"

So. Like the toad. Irina's demon, Lodur's tome had identified as a species of pallid Arctic batrachian. And this simple spear-carrier's monsters—pure superstition, or some ordinary creatures of the swamp, magnified by tale-tellers holding forth on late watches at the Keep.

Bears, wolves, lizards became trolls, *loup-garous*, dragons.

Fafnir the size of one's hand, sitting on a limb awaiting a horsefly for its dinner.

"Ride."

Their course led down a grass-covered hillside. Beneath them von Richthofen could see the top of a sea of mist, wisps licking upward like hungry waves lapping from the sea. As the two horses plunged into the mist side by side, it was as if they had actually entered water. Von Richthofen could feel the sudden attack of cold and dampness through his borrowed garments. Instinctively his hand leaped to the hilt of his *Kaiserdolch*. He should have armed himself with a more substantial blade before leaving the Keep.

He yelled to Balor and asked how he was armed. The man had yet his halberd. Also, strapped to his baldric, a heavy iron-bladed sword and scabbard.

Von Richthofen commanded the man to slide the baldric from his shoulder and pass it to him. Then he slipped it over his own torso, felt the heavy sword bumping rhythmically against his leg with each stride of the horse beneath him.

"How far?" von Richthofen demanded. "How far could they have gone?"

Balor had no idea.

"Think, you pig! Where would the *Zauberer* have taken Her Highness? Surely not for a picnic here in the muck! Is there another Keep nearby? A chapel? Think!"

"*Ach, ach, mein Herr . . .*"

As the other man pondered, von Richthofen could hear the sounds of their horses: no longer was there the clean, pleasant sound of hoofs on turf. With each step, now, there came a splattering. At the beginning of each successive stride there was a moment of hesitation, then a wet, sticky sound as the hoof was pulled from the muck. Then the splattering noise again, as the hoof descended.

Now the muck must be deepening, and water actually accumulating on its surface, for von Richthofen could feel his horse's slight hesitation as it dragged its feet from the muck. And he could feel cold moisture on his feet and calves as the icy water splattered with each step of the horses.

"There is no other Keep nearby," Balor said at last. "*Mein Herr* Lodur keeps a place out here, though. I think, *Freiherr*, only. Never I have seen the place. But in the Keep the men talk, you know how, sir." He laughed nervously.

"The men talk sometimes," Balor resumed. "On watch, late, *Freiherr*. And they say that Lodur goes, sometimes, to hell. Yes, to hell. Other times they say, he goes to heaven. That he has a magic room that carries him to heaven or to hell."

Von Richthofen gritted his teeth. What truth lay under the heaps of superstitious rubbish the man was spouting? "Where is this magic room of Lodur's?"

"No onc knows, *Freiherr*. Some say it's in the Keep itself. Others say it's here in the woods somewhere. Maybe we'll find it, if the quicksand does't suck us under first, or the monsters get us."

Von Richthofen sncered.

"Monsters, *Freiherr*, I swear it. There are goblins here, and trolls, gnomes, faeries, kelpies..."

"*Halt!*" von Richthofen commanded.

Balor and both horses drew up. Von Richthofen reached again for a weapon, this time for the heavy sword he had taken from the other man.

There were voices. Distinctly, three voices speaking.

Von Richthofen cupped his hand to one ear. *Ja, ganz bestimmt*, three voices. He couldn't distinguish words, but one voice was that of a man. The others secmed to be women's, and yet—and yet there were tones in onc of those that he could not categorize as human. They were speaking—he strained to hear—some mixture, some dialect.

Definitely it was Germanic, possibly it was Svartalheimerisch.

"Come!" he commanded Balor. "It is the Princess! We have found her!"

"But the bog, *Freiherr!*" The halberdier's voice was strained, fearful. "My horse—I think we're in quicksand!"

As if on cue the horse shrieked, an almost human outcry of terror. Von Richthofen turned to see the other, but all he could see was a wall of mist. From Balor and his horse came sounds of panicky struggle. The creature's hoofs splashed in water. Manfred himself dripped with icy splashings. The water dripped from his hair and face onto his borrowed clothing.

It stank.

"*Hilfe!*" Balor cried out. "*Gott! Freiherr! Helfen Sie mir!*"

Again the horse shrieked. The horseman's voice blended with that of the animal. There was a final scream, a horrid sucking sound, and nothing further.

Manfred edged his horse a little bit in the opposite direction. With each step the beast found firmer footing. Finally it was able to stand and to move its feet without the sucking and splattering of muck and water.

Slowly Manfred urged his horse forward. Without a sound he inched the borrowed sword from its scabbard and held it in his free hand, point forward. It was heavy, clumsy, ill-balanced. Especially so, to the hand of one accustomed to fine fencing blades imported from Spain. But it gave him a sense of adequacy nonetheless, a feeling that he could not get in this dark swamp from his *Kaiserdolch.*

The voices ahead were nearer. Von Richthofen urged his horse forward. He could see the light of a flickering flame. He could hear the voices raised in disagreement. He called, "Irina! Princess!"

"Manfred!" The reply was in her unmistakable voice.

"Manfred!" Stay away! Is too late for Princess and wizard! Save Baron only! Go away, Baron Manfred! Go! Go!"

Chapter 19

"What—what's going on?"

Cuchaviva turned helpless eyes toward the light-haired foreigner. She tried to tell him what had happened, but they shared no common language. She struggled with the controls of the platform, desperately working to bring it back to level flight. Or at least to soften its impact on Okeanos.

Charles Lindbergh turned to the Svartalheimer Nikar and did his best to get the information he'd failed to get from Cuchaviva. This time he used the old Swedish-German mix he'd learned as a boy in Wisconsin.

Nikar's expression made it clear that he understood Lindy's speech, but for an answer he merely laughed. He might have failed in his mission, his fellows dead or imprisoned in Muiaia, but he'd get his vengeance now!

Cuchaviva yelled. The dark water was rushing up to meet them. It could be only a matter of seconds before the platform crashed with an impact that would kill them all.

Lindy spun around, hoping against hope that the Muiaians fitted their aerial platforms with parachutes—if they'd ever discovered the principle of parachuting. Jumping out of disabled aircraft would certainly be no new experience for Lindy: he'd earned his Caterpillar Club credentials as an air cadet and renewed them twice while flying the mails between St. Louis and Chicago.

But there was no sign here of 'chutes. Lindbergh realized that he might have radioed to Amelia in the *Spirit* and had her translate back to Cuchaviva, but there was no time left for that. The water couldn't be more than ten seconds away from their platform. Lindy kept his eyes open, braced himself in his seat, counted, counted . . .

Cuchaviva grasped the control globe firmly, twisted the upper and lower halves in opposite directions. The top of the globe swung aside and the bright yellow button inside glowed at her. She shouted a warning to her two passengers, for all that she knew neither would understand her words, and shoved down on the button.

There was a surge and a thump as the spring-loaded housing of the passenger cube, in a single motion, uncoupled from the flying platform. Had the platform lost power in level flight and the pilot been unable to glide to a landing, the springs would have thrust the cube straight into the air.

As it was, with the platform in a near-vertical dive, the cube shot forward instead of up. Lindbergh could see black Okeanos a few yards beneath them all.

The gyrolizers in the base of the cube whirred into life and altered its attitude so it floated levelly, just above the water.

Nikar uttered a series of angry syllables.

Cuchaviva reclosed the control globe and set the platform on course for the final approach to Haibrasl. Operating only on its gyrolizers and emergency power units, the passenger cube limped slowly toward land, wavelets lapping at its lower surface.

Cuchaviva flicked on the radio device and signaled the *Spirit of San Diego*. Speaking in Muiaian *patois* she conducted a brief exchange with Amelia Earhart, then handed the apparatus to Lindy.

"Cuchaviva says you had a close call," Amelia told him.

"Close! I was already filling out my application blank for the airman's Valhalla. What happened?"

"How do I know, Charles? From here? All I know is, we were flying along smooth as whipping cream, and suddenly Howard yelled and pointed."

"Yes—and—?"

"And there was your plane—your platform—headed for the drink."

"Could you tell anything from our appearance?"

"Well—you know, those cup-shaped things around the perimeter, that give off the rays that keep the platform aloft..."

Lindy grunted.

"Half of 'em *weren't* glowing! In the dark, it's lots easier to see the glow. It looked as if all the cups along the front edge of the platform had cut off. And a few of the others.

"That made you tilt. Then the rest cut off. Else the platform would have spun. Or maybe flipped tail-over-nose."

"Yeh. I think it would have. That's what it felt like."

There was a pause, then Howard Hughes's voice took over. "Swede, I figger your kraut pal there must have something planted on him that did it."

"Like what? Didn't the Muiaians check out those raiders? They all had those hollow teeth, and they all used them except our boy here. What could he have had that nobody found, back in Muiaia?"

Hughes didn't reply at once. Lindy scanned the sky above the cube, looking for the *Spirit of San Diego*. He spotted it.

"Howard? You lose me?"

"Uh, that was a shrug," Hughes's voice returned. "Sorry."

"I didn't hear it."

"Yeah. Anyhow, glad you guys came through it okay. Looks like we're going to be welcomed right ahead. I'll get off the line so Cuchaviva can talk to these Haibrasl cookies in her own lingo, or whatever they use around here."

Lindy handed the radio gear back to Cuchaviva and listened with half an ear to the exchange between her and the—he couldn't help thinking of it as the control tower—at Haibrasl. Meanwhile, Lindy stared at Nikar. If the Svartalheimer had really caused the crash of the platform, and it seemed almost certain that he had...

The craft had seemed reliable enough until the near-crash, and it was asking too much of coincidence to assume that a random failure would occur during the one flight with a Svartalheimer prisoner on board.

But if Nikar *had* caused the crash of the platform, how had he done it? And why had he *not* wrecked the passenger cube as well, when it converted into an escape machine? Was the thing he'd used—whatever it was—good for only one mission, like an artillery shell? Or did it need time to regain its charge, like some electrical gadgets?

"I don't suppose you feel like telling me how you did that," Lindy addressed Nikar in old Swedish-German.

Nikar laughed.

Cuchaviva brought the cube in over the waters of a harbor. There were scores of ships present, none of them exactly of types Lindy recognized but many of them vaguely suggestive of types he had either known or at least seen in pictures. Some were sail-powered, resembling anything from Chinese junks to Phoenician traders to Spanish galleons. Others looked more like modern metal-clad steamers, save for their lack of smokestacks.

The cube hopped over the harbor and came to a modern-looking landing field. Cuchaviva set down with a sigh of relief. Clearly, flying the escape device was a nerve-stretching job. Lindy looked overhead, scanning the sky for Amelia and Hughes. He'd spotted the Ryan earlier by its running lights, and now he saw it picked out in ground-mounted spotlights.

The Ryan circled the field, then whispered in eerily for its landing.

Lindy saw Amelia and Howard climb from the Ryan. They embraced and then headed toward the cube. At the same time, a party of individuals left the largest building near the runway and headed for the two aircraft.

They were dressed in white one-piece costumes, men and women alike. As they drew closer, Lindy saw more details. The outfits could have passed for a cross between grease-monkeys' overalls (although sparkling clean ones!) and a grand admiral's summer whites.

They wore boots. Their skins were a sort of suntanned brown. And most of them carried writing-pads. Well, of course: if Haibrasl was a floating trade center there would be forms to fill out and probably customs to pay. Lindy tried to imagine what would happen if he and Earhart and Hughes—and their Ryan!—wound up impounded by Haibrasli customs inspectors because they couldn't pay the fees!

Hughes and Earhart reached the cube before the Haibrasli.

Cuchaviva swung back a translucent panel and the four of them hustled Nikar out of the cube and onto the tarmac.

The Haibrasli halted and their spokesman, a pudgy, officious man with the mannerisms of Oliver Hardy, started to scold. His language was new to Lindy.

But Cuchaviva seemed to comprehend. She spoke to the man in a broken form of his language and he switched to the Muiaian *patois*. Well, that was something: at least Amelia would understand what was going on. As Cuchaviva and Oliver Hardy—Lindbergh had to look away from the man to keep from giggling—carried out their conversation, Amelia translated for Lindy and Hughes.

Apparently the Haibrasli were piqued that the Ryan and the Muiaian platform hadn't radioed their full intentions before landing.

Cuchaviva explained that they'd been sabotaged over Okeanos. She laid the blame on Nikar and asked the Haibrasli for navigation data to get them to Svartalheim.

The Haibrasli complained, questioned, handed Cuchaviva forms to fill out.

"This fellow's really being sticky," Amelia told Howard and Lindy. "When Cuchaviva told him that Nikar wrecked the platform, Cruach—he's the fatty—said it took place over the high seas, wasn't his problem. Cuchaviva carried on a lot about that. Cruach said, well, did we want him to intern Nikar. Cuchaviva said, no, we needed him for later on, when we get to Svartalheim."

"Wait a minute. What's going on now?" Lindbergh asked.

Cruach—the Oliver Hardy man—was gesticulating. Cuchaviva sounded thoroughly upset.

Now Cruach called one of his underlings from the party behind him. A short-haired woman in a less elaborately decorated set of coveralls stood beside him. Cruach spoke rapidly to her. She addressed Nikar.

"She's speaking Old Nordic or whatever they call the language," Lindy volunteered. "Oh-oh. Look at that, now Nikar's feeding her a cock and bull story about—oh, boy!"

He turned from Hughes and Amelia, started speaking Nordic to the short-haired woman. She responded sharply. Nikar laughed and addressed another sentence to the woman.

The conversation turned into a complicated exchange in Muiaian among Amy, Cuchaviva, and Cruach, Nordic among Lindbergh, Nikar, and the short-haired woman. Her name was Wyddan.

Lindbergh and Earhart provided translations between the groups while Hughes fumed and followed along as he could.

Finally Hughes exploded with a roar of frustration. "You can't mean that! These—these headwaiters or whatever the hell they are—they're turning that creep Nikar loose?"

"Howard," Lindbergh said, "we came within a hair's breadth of winding up in the clink ourselves. Nikar wanted to prefer charges against us! For kidnapping, assault and battery, false imprisonment, extortion, and spitting on the sidewalk!"

"They don't care that he's a spy? That he attacked Amy in Muiaia? Sabotaged the platform and nearly killed Cuchaviva and me?"

Lindy held up his hands. "Cruach, here, and his helper Wyddan—they say that whatever happened in Muiaia is our problem, not theirs. So is anything that happened over the water.

"But here in Haibrasl, the only thing resembling a crime that they've seen is us trying to hold Nikar against his will. So, now, we can't hold him. We can't make him come along when we leave here. And if we try to drag him against his will, they're going to throw us in the hoosegow and lose the keys."

"It ain't decent!" Hughes sputtered.

He launched himself through the air at Nikar, shouting. "You rotten S.O.B.!"

Nikar dodged behind Cruach.

Hughes had his hands in front of him, fingers extended to close around Nikar's throat.

Cuchaviva, who had been watching the exchange between Hughes and his companions, shot out one hand in a vertical chop, catching Hughes across both wrists. At the same moment Lindy launched himself through the air in a flying tackle. He caught Hughes around the waist, Lindy's muscular shoulder poking into Hughes's rangy midriff, knocking the man sideways and off his course for Nikar and the latter's human shield.

Lindy and Hughes rolled on the tarmac, grabbing and pummeling each other like a pair of street brawlers. Hughes's body, lanky but muscular, gave him the advantage of leverage. But Lindy had greater agility, and his training included a Tunneylike calculation that held Hughes's Dempsey-style ferocity at bay.

Somehow the frustration and tense energies of their trip, ever since leaving the El Cortez in San Diego, were directed against each other.

Hughes landed a solid left to Lindbergh's ribs, felt the smaller man jerk almost double with the impact of his bony fist.

Lindy reached up and smashed a hard right to Howard's head. Hughes winced—there would be a glorious shiner to show for that moment.

Hughes rocked Lindbergh back with a hard blow to the chest.

Lindy countered with a distancing punch aimed at Hughes's face.

They rolled onto the tarmac again, fetched up against the heavy rubber wheel of the *Spirit of San Diego.*

"Wait a minute, wait a minute," Lindbergh gasped.

Hughes grunted. "Hah?"

"What are we doing?" Lindbergh managed breathlessly. "Why are we fighting?"

They released their grasp on each other, disentangled their long legs. Hughes climbed to his feet and helped Lindbergh to his.

Lindy was still half breathless from the hard shot he had taken in the ribs. He stood leaning against Hughes, panting for his breath. Hughes had one hand against his eyes, gingerly testing the results of Lindbergh's hard punch.

"Here's a quarter, boy," Hughes said. "Go fetch me a beefsteak to put on this shiner."

Lindbergh managed a sickly laugh. It faded when he caught sight of Nikar, no longer hidden behind the overgenerously proportioned Cruach, standing beside the Haibrasli now and looking like a rat beside an Iowa porker.

"Catch a glim of that bastard," Hughes grumbled. "Why'd you stop me from wringing his scrawny murdering neck, Swede?"

"I can see your point. I'd have liked to get at that rat myself.

But these Haibrasli are sticklers, and we're already on thin ice with all their rules. From what Amy says..."

He drew a better breath and managed to stand without support. "...Haibrasl is some sort of home base for this whole crazy hemi-disk. Soon as we set foot on Haibrasli soil it was Ollie-Ollie-Oxen-Free. Anything Nikar did to us back in Muiaia or over Okeanos, they don't want to hear about it. Cruach's a little bit out of sorts over our not making the right kind of landing or something, and if you'd done assault and battery against old Nikar there, Cruach might just have stuck us in the pokey."

"Yeah," Hughes grumbled. "That's the second time you said that."

"Because it's important!"

"I'd still like to—" He stopped and turned to face Nikar. He strode across the intervening space and halted, nose-to-nose with the Svartalheimer.

Hughes stood with his feet apart, fists on his hips like a drill-sergeant preparing to ream out a recruit, and gave a loud and lengthy raspberry.

Nikar stood in startled silence while the Haibrasli looked on, puzzlement on their features.

Hughes walked back and stood between Lindbergh and Earhart. "Maybe that creep never heard of a Bronx cheer before, but he knows what one is now. And I feel a lot better."

The Haibrasli lodged them in quarters that were adequate if spartan. Their problems, among others, included the fact that the Haibrasli expected payment for the lodging, landing fees for the *Spirit of San Diego* and the passenger cube from Cuchaviva's lost platform, and for any other services the travelers utilized.

They wanted payment for food consumed. And they wanted payment for any navigation aids they provided, including simple information.

Cuchaviva set out to find a way to make good.

Wyddan showed up unexpectedly, and asked to talk with Lindbergh. He was happy that somebody actually wanted to see him—he'd felt that Amelia had become the brains of the *Spirit* expedition, and Howard the muscle, leaving himself as little more than a passenger.

It developed that Wyddan's interest in the travelers was mainly in the *Spirit of San Diego*. Wyddan herself was a technician. She knew every vessel that tied up at Haibrasl's port. And her conversation, conducted in Old Nordic, convinced Lindbergh that the variety of these ships was even greater than he had thought.

Now Wyddan was investigating aircraft, and she found the exotic *Spirit of San Diego* irresistible.

Lindbergh and Hughes took her happily for a ride in the *Spirit*. After a while she asked to try the controls and piloted the monoplane over miles of Haibrasl. Lindbergh sat in the copilot's seat beside her. Hughes crouched behind them at the navigator's station, leaning from the window to watch the landscape below.

"Look at that!" he exclaimed, "It really *is* moving!"

He pointed down at the shoreline of Haibrasl. From high above, it was possible to discern the wake of the island as it ploughed slowly and majestically through Okeanos.

"Nobody ever messes with you guys?" Hughes asked Wyddan.

Lindy translated the question and she explained that, No, Haibrasl was universally respected territory. That was the island's greatest protection. She was natural prey for scores of potential enemics, but each of them knew that to attack Haibrasl would mean branding as an outlaw nation, the foe of all.

"That's why we had to make you free that Nikar person," Wyddan added. "We understood what he'd done. The Svartalheimers have a reputation for their treachery and for their works of conquest. They don't appear often at Haibrasl, because their country is at the edge of the northern ice zone, near the North Hole. It's just too far from here.

"But word reaches us. They keep popping up. Every few years, we hear that an army of Svartalheimers has suddenly appeared in some other country, and conquered it, and made it a vassal state to Svartalheim."

Lindbergh frowned. "You mean straight-out invasion and conquest? They land an army on ships, and conquer another country?"

Wyddan made a negative sign. "They have a navy, but they

use it chiefly to cut off their victims from help. Or from escape! But that isn't how they accomplish their conquests. Nor do they fly their armies in. They're known as an almost primitive people. Nobody knows how they get there. Maybe by sorcery."

"Come on!" Lindbergh translated for Hughes, and Hughes sneered at the suggestion.

Wyddan shrugged. "Then I don't know how they do it. And of course, the word that comes to us is always vague. But they do manage to get an army into the middle of another country, and then they take it over. Maybe they grow soldiers like wheat!"

Back on the ground they were greeted with good news. Cuchaviva had found a Muiaian merchant ship docked at Haibrasl. It was unloading grain and furnishings, taking on minerals and furs. The captain agreed to transfer the passenger cube back to Muiaia, and to put up the fees the Haibrasli demanded. Cuchaviva wrote out chits to be paid when the merchantman returned to Muiaia.

"Then we can provision and clear out of here, right?"

"Right. Only—do we need Nikar with us? Do we need him to navigate us to Svartalheim?"

Lindy rubbed his chin. "Turns out we have a pretty good friend at court. Wyddan swapped us info for info. She wanted to learn about the *Spirit of San Diego*. Howard and I took her up for a hop, let her handle the ship for a while, and she repaid us with navigation data. You know that earth disk we've been using? She marked in Svartalheim!

"I think we can reach there all right. Question is, would we be better off if we brought Nikar with us? And would he go with us? I doubt it, after what went on back in Muiaia, and especially after that stunt of his, to try and crash the platform. Besides—we couldn't trust the guy!"

Amelia looked troubled. "Aside from all of that, you know—I don't really understand what Nikar and the others were after, in Muiaia. Why did they attack us in the street?"

"I think Wyddan had the answer to that one, too. The Svartalheimers are expanding their realm. They have some way of sneaking an army into somebody else's country, and once they're in, they just take over. It's very neat. However they get in, that must be how they got into Muiaia. Somehow they might have got wind of some strangers in town—*us.*"

"*Hmm*—yes," Amy nodded, her light curls bobbing. "They seem to have a first-rate intelligence service, no denying that. We were a new factor, an unknown quantity. So—we were invited back to Svartalheim to help 'em figure out what *we* were up to!"

"Then, what next?" Hughes asked.

"I think we get ahold of Nikar and—"

"That's what I wanted to do all along. Why'd you stop me?"

"That isn't what I meant, Howard." Amelia reached to touch his face gently. "Oh, my, you really are getting to be a sight! Well, we offer Nikar a ride home..."

"What about Cuchaviva?"

"She says, she thinks her husband is in Svartalheim. Possibly as a prisoner. She wants to go and find out, and get him back."

"And we just drop everybody off and head for Symmes' Hole and the prize money."

"You think that?"

"Sounds looney to me. Kind of like walking into the lions' den."

Amelia shrugged ingenuously. "*Flying* into the lions' den," she said.

Chapter 20

It was the training method of a Boelcke. You show the student the controls, put him in the *Flugzeug*, the aeroplane, and off he goes. True, the method is costly in training craft and in student aviators. But it is fast and effective. And those who survive become competent *Flieger* in short order.

Doubly escorted by the *Kronprinz* Ottokar and the younger *Prinz* Nikolauz, Lothar von Richthofen reached the barracks of the Valkyrie all too quickly. These were an astonishing lot. All of course were female. What else would one expect—as the *Koenig* Vithar had asked jocularly of Lothar.

They even wore the costumes that one expected—helmets shaped like artillery shells, chain mail of darkened steel, gauntlets, boots. There were even stylized spurs, vestiges of the days when real Valkyrie rode real horses.

Well—Lothar wondered about that last. Real Valkyrie? Best reserve judgment in this strange land. If anyone had described for him, before the *Kondor* had rumbled from the ground at Tempelhof, the experiences of these days...

As for the Valkyrie themselves, they ranged from the typical Wagnerian embodiment of the legendary women—bulky, ungainly females both overweight and overage in service—to some remarkably *wohlgestaltet* and altogether appealing. The commander of the Valkyrie was of the former class. She waddled from her quarters as rapidly as she could propel her bulk, to greet the two royal visitors.

She permitted herself the form of being introduced to the *Hauptmann* von Richthofen, then turned the *Prinz* Nikolauz and the *Hauptmann* over to the ministrations of an underling while she herself hustled the *Kronprinz* Ottokar away for a tour of facilities.

Nikolauz turned and leaned toward Lothar. He expressed himself, *sotto voce:* "On occasion, my fellow little brother, our mutual status has its reward, hey? Poor Ottokar! He avoids that fat she-leech at every chance, but she manages to outwit him time after time. *Ha-ha!*"

"*Prinz... Hauptmann...*" The Valkyrie commander's assistant inclined her head toward Nikolauz and Lothar.

"*Fräulein.*"

She gave her name as Arawn, her grade as *Leutnant* of the Svartalheimer Valkyrie. She led them to a row of the astonishing metal horses and permitted Lothar to examine one. At close range it was obviously not a living creature, but the detail of its manufacture made clear the reason why he had mistaken it for one.

Each muscle was represented beneath the rippling black skin, and each hair was separately represented in the false coat of the machine. Thc *Leutnant* Arawn laid aside her metal helmet and gauntlets for easier movement in explaining the mechanism to von Richthofen. Her hair was the color of wheatstraw, braided into long queues and wound like a crown to fit beneath her helmet. Her eyes were a shade of brilliant aquamarine. Her hands were strong and graceful: Lothar watched them as she demonstrated the workings of the *fliegende Pferd.*

The contrast with the hands of his brother Manfred was striking: where the *Freiherr*'s long, spatulate digits writhed and leaped constantly, as if animated by a will all their own, Arawn's graceful, oval-tipped fingers seemed always at peace. They moved with unassuming efficiency at the will of their mistress. Each motion, however slight, was purposeful, efficient, attention-holding.

The *Leutnant* Arawn helped Lothar to climb aboard one of the mechanical horses. He was an experienced rider. The feel of this metal beast between his legs was a strange combination of the familiar and the odd. He leaned forward and patted the creature—no, the *machine*—on the neck. He was startled, not by the realization that he had foolishly treated a mechanism like a living creature, but by the fact that the neck had felt like warm, living flesh rather than like metal.

"Are you ready, *Hauptmann?*"

"*Ja, Leutnant. Fertig.*" He glanced over his shoulder at Nikolauz. The *Prinz* was gazing almost paternally at Lothar and Arawn. The *Kronprinz* Ottokar and his overfleshed Valkyrie commander were nowhere to be seen. Lothar grinned inwardly.

"Off we go!" cried Arawn.

Lothar slid forward a lever on the control panel of his machine. It was set like a pommel on the front of the saddle. He moved another lever.

The machine moved its legs like a living horse, walking leisurely forward.

Lothar glanced sideways. Arawn had redonned her helmet and gauntlets before mounting her own *fliegende Pferd*. The Valkyrie wore sidearms as well, the functioning of which was a mystery to von Richthofen. Arawn's *Pferd* moved ahead of Lothar's. The Valkyrie was expert with the machines while Lothar was clearly a novice.

He watched her set more of the pommel-mounted controls, then take the mechanical creature's reins in hand. Once going, the machine could be controlled by its reins, and with pressure-plates set into its sides like the sensitive points in a living horse's flanks. Arawn gave a twitch of the reins and her *Pferd* broke into a trot, then launched itself into the air.

Lothar gathered his resolve and imitated the Valkyrie. His mount followed hers. The sensation was astounding. Once at a hunting lodge, Lothar and a group of other young Junkers had drunk themselves into a state of high intoxication on hot *Schnaps* spiked with opium shipped home from the Prussian concession of Shantung.

They had mounted horses and gone riding through the forest, calling to one another, hounds tracking and baying. In a moment of strange apotheosis Lothar had felt a mystical union with his mount. It was as if he, *Hauptmann* (or had he been, back then, a lowly *Leutnant?)* Lothar von Richthofen, had become one with the beast: a centaur, six-limbed, fierce, his lower torso not balanced upon the leather saddle but grown into—growing from!—the back of the pounding horse.

The forest had been lighted by the lingering glow of a long summer evening, but now mists rose and the sun disappeared beyond distant slopes. He had felt no cold or dampness from the mist, nor any sense of panic at the notion of being lost at night in the woods.

As if they had been of a single mind, he gave the beast its head, patted and spurred it to move though the woods as fast as it could make its way. The wind was on his face, the sounds of the horse's hoofs and the unseen forest creatures were in his ears.

His companions were nowhere in evidence.

Time lost its meaning. He could not tell whether he had been riding for moments or for ages. The mist penetrated his clothing and his body. He felt that he could open his mouth and drink in the very essence of the forest. With his thighs he could feel the play of the horse's flank muscles.

He could not tell whether he was rising or descending. The trail through the woods wound past echoing mysterious lakes and dark glades where glowing eyes peered out at him. The sound of a distant hound's cry echoed through the wood. Lothar felt every vibration of the air.

The man-and-horse had halted before a gnarled tree where an owl sat staring solemnly. Lothar had spoken to the owl. The owl responded. Each, speaking his own language, had seemed fully to understand the meaning of the other. Finally the owl excused himself, rose and flexed his wings, then departed on a mission of his own.

Lothar had turned his horse back toward the rural *Schloss*. At the stable he had parted fondly from his equine half, embracing the horse for a moment almost as lover to lover, then strode slowly to the hall. His fellows drifted back one by one. A few made feeble attempts at light comment regarding their ride.

Then all sat quietly, some smoking meerschaums or brandy-soaked cheroots, gazing into the fire, and then retired not long before the dawn.

Next day none of them spoke of the experience, nor had Lothar ever mentioned it, even to his older brother.

"*Hauptmann!*"

He jerked back to reality.

"*Hauptmann* von Richthofen," *Leutnant* Arawn cautioned, "please try to keep close. One can become lost in the mists. Are you doing well with your *Pferd?*"

"*Ja, Leutnant.*" He brought his mind halfway back to the job of learning the use of the flying horse. He watched Arawn sweep the sky on her mount, swooping in great, banking circles, dipping and soaring again. From the rear he could see the glow of red that marked the power plant of the flying machine, the *Flugzeug*.

The Valkyrie had explained it to him, vaguely. Something about the conversion of heavy materials into their lighter parts, and the liberation of energy in the process of unlocking. It was all very hard to follow, especially in the archaic tongue of the Svartalheimers with its odd usages and gaps in vocabulary. But, Lothar deduced, it was something like the energies described by the French family Curie, those strange experimenters.

They flew over the plaza where Nikolauz and Lothar had attended the weird concert. The bandstand was deserted, the rows of seats where the audience had sat were vacant.

They approached the *Palast* of the *Koenig* Vithar, circled once about the upper reach of a dark, battlemented spire. Lothar could envision medieval warriors, men of the time of Barbarossa, crouching in the bartizans.

Their bows were nocked and ready to shoot down at their attackers. Franks from the west, Slavs from the east. Sub-men all. Searing pitch fell from the tower, burning away assaulters, sending them screaming and tumbling from wooden assault-ladders to land with thumps on the heads and spears of their fellows.

"*Hauptmann!*"

Lothar spurred his *Pferd* until he overtook the *Leutnant*'s mount and they rode side by side away from the *Schloss*, toward the edge of the city. In the distance Lothar briefly glimpsed a gigantic cylinder rising transparent toward the sky, disappearing into the mists that overhung this lower Svartalheim. Somewhere above must stretch the titanic roof of this hidden world, and above that the upper, primitive Svartalheim where Nikolauz's Keep stood outpost against the barbarians of the darkling world.

There, Lothar pondered, *Freiherr* Manfred and the Princess Irina still were. Had the *Hauptmann* and the *Prinz* been missed? Were those upper Svartalheimers searching for them now? Or were the disappearances of Nikolauz, alone or in company, commonplace?

Beneath the two riders the city was growing thin. Buildings were fewer and smaller; open patches, more numerous. The colored, quasi-living mists of this lower Svartalheim wound and swirled over the riders. An almost solid rag of moisture shot from a larger mass of the stuff, wrapped itself around Arawn, seeming to draw a suggestion of color and essence from her, then whipped away and ploughed into Lothar.

It slid across his saddle, circled once around the body of his horse, then crept up his leg and torso, clung to his face like the breath of a maiden.

Then it swept away and was lost.

He looked at Arawn. She caught his gaze and smiled at him enigmatically.

Gradually she accelerated the pace of her *Flugzeug*. From a trot to a canter to a full gallop it advanced its speed.

With each increase of Arawn's speed, Lothar altered his own. The beast—no, the machine!—he had been given, was capable of matching anything done by the Valkyrie's mount.

They rose.

Arawn disappeared into a bank of mist, then emerged again from its upper surface. There was no sun in this lower Svartalheim. The mist itself glowed, and the glowing moisture clung to Arawn's figure as she mounted from the mist-bank. It curved away slowly beneath her like glory trailing from the hands of an angel.

Lothar urged his mount after Arawn's, plunging into the bank of radiant mist. At once his eyes were dazzled by a spectrum of colors. The mists that had swept past him previously now danced and filled his vision with scintillant points of light in every tint from garish primaries to subtle lavenders and turquoises. The stuff filled his lungs and his nostrils and his mouth with a riot of flavors and scents. It smote his eardrums with a noise like a thousand musical instruments sounding at once.

His head swung from side to side involuntarily. His kinetic sense alone told him that his mount, true machine, was immune to the overwhelming hallucinatory onslaught of the glowing mists.

With a suddenness that startled even him, Lothar burst from the cloud. He looked at his hands holding the reins of the *fliegende Pferd* and saw that they were trailing wakes of color. He raised one hand and held it before his eyes. It glowed like a creation of a religious painter.

He looked ahead, saw Arawn on her own *fliegende Pferd.* She halted the machine in the air, spun it about, toward him. The mechanical horse reared, pawing misty air with its forehooves. Lothar's own ears provided the wild neigh that the silent machine did not utter.

"Arawn," von Richthofen cried, "we have reached the very heavens! Are we creatures of flesh or of spirit now?"

She laughed at him and called back, "We are flesh, the same as ever. If you doubt it, climb from the back of your horse. You'll come back to earth fast enough—but rather too forcibly for enjoyment!"

He spurred his horse and drew alongside her.

"Still," von Richthofen said, "behold the glory!" He swung his hand before him, sweeping across the view. Mounds and crevasses of mist, like clouds above the trenches of Europe, spread away from them. But where other clouds were only white or gray except in the distant tint of sunrise, here they glowed with every color imaginable. Their shapes were fantastic, beyond the grasp of imagination.

Gryphons, whales, hippogriffs cavorted before their eyes. Great masted ships rose and swayed across sparkling seas. Castles to shame the *Palast* of King Vithar reared their towers, swayed, leaned, tumbled.

Lothar reached for the hand of Arawn. She took his also. This first touch of her flesh told him that she was as warm and as vital as a woman could ever be. No cold warrior-maiden, this Valkyrie. He looked into her eyes: she smiled.

He suppressed again the impulse to dismount. For all that these clouds of glowing mist seemed solid he knew he would plunge to his doom.

"Come, Lothar," Arawn called. She withdrew her hand from his and spurred away, not rapidly.

He followed. *Is this real?* he wondered. *Is this another flight of fantasy? Is this lower Svartalheim real, with its futuristic automobiles, its surreal architecture, its ghoulish orchestras?*

Regal courts straight from Bayreuth.

Valkyrie mounted on flying horses powered by glowing radium.

"Come, Lothar."

He thrilled at the sound of her voice. He envisioned the body beneath the coat of chain mail. He imagined Arawn nude against a cloud of glowing, piebald mist. He squeezed shut his eyelids, shook his head like a hound clearing pond-water from its coat.

He followed her.

The mists grew darker.

Above them the vista grew vague.

Beyond the piebald clouds a new vista appeared, a green landscape dotted with trees whose branches reached clawlike toward him. Mosses and undergrowth covered the ground.

Dizzily, Lothar realized that he had lost all perspective, all sense of distance, even the knowledge of which way was up, which down. The feel of his own body in the *Pferd*'s saddle told him that the clouds were beneath him, the landscape above. But the evidence of his eyes was completely the opposite.

He could not see Arawn.

He looped his pegasus so the ground was beneath him—and felt himself tugged halfway from the saddle up toward the clouds.

Perspiration burst upon his brow.

He guided his *Pferd* to earth. He had to use the machine's levers to hold it to the grass, to keep it from tumbling into the air with him still on it.

A hillside rose before him, its shape half-hidden by forest-green shrubbery and trees. He guided his mount into a copse of dim evergreens. Before him opened the dark mouth of a cavern.

Half in a fugue he rode his horse into the cavern. He was literally lightheaded. Redness swam before his eyes and his ears roared.

The cavern was dimly illuminated by banks of glowing mist. He heard muffled, distant sounds. He called, "Arawn!"

His *Pferd* stepped daintily, as if walking on the ceiling.

He guided it through passageways that wound and divided until he was hopelessly lost and could only continue in hope of chance salvation.

The cavern rose and dipped, its floor tilted crazily. Somehow Lothar's disorientation lessened. His sense of up and down, at least, grew more nearly normal.

A dim opening appeared ahead. Lothar spurred his mount. It trotted smoothly ahead. Lothar emerged from the cavern's mouth.

He closed his eyes, struggling to grasp the meaning of up and down, the direction of earth and sky.

All about him, through mist and cloud-dimmed forest, he thought he saw hints of treetops, leaves almost black and so thick that little if any light could penetrate them. Where the trees were not, patches of broken land appeared, chiefly flooded into bogs or ponds.

There was a flash of greenish brilliance as lightning crackled between a black clot of mist and a tall and tortured treetop. With the clap of thunder that followed, a cold gust swept over Lothar. The stink of ozone assaulted his nostrils.

He peered ahead seeking Arawn. She was again in sight, but far from him. Her back was to him, and she was galloping across—across what?

He could not tell.

Was it a solid layer of mist? Or was it earth? Was it a span of dark, swampy soil? He tried to pick out the hooves of her *Pferd.* Did they splash with each stride, as if she were galloping across a span of mud-flat?

"Arawn!" he cried.

His voice echoed like the howl of a wolf.

"Arawn!"

She glanced over her shoulder, then turned away.

He spurred. Ahead, and downward, ahead, and downward. He felt the horse's hooves jolt as they made contact with a solid or nearly solid surface, after the long ride across the mists.

He looked about. He was in a copse of woods. Trees towered overhead. They reached for him with long, taloned branches. They looked like monstrosities out of an illustrated Grimm.

"Arawn!" he cried.

He heard the voice of the Valkyrie call back his own name, and suddenly he realized that the voice of Arawn had awakened in his being responses that no voice had ever before aroused.

And he heard another woman's voice echo his name as well. A voice he had heard before, the voice of a woman he had known in Europe, a woman with whom he had traveled these thousands of kilometres.

Irina!

"Lothar!" her voice cried. "Lothar! Where—?"

The landscape became a madhouse, a nightmare of darkness, of cold trees dripping with moisture, his horse's hooves splatting in mud and standing water with each step, of wisps and chill, pallid mist that floated and blinded.

He urged his horse forward slowly, trying to find the Valkyrie Arawn. An opening appeared between the trees. He spurred his horse a few final steps and halted it, facing the opening.

Arawn was not to be seen.

Instead there spread before him the surface of a stagnant pond some fifty or sixty metres in breadth. To one side, rising gray through the clinging mists, was a strange, high house, its roof pitched steeply, gabled, dripping.

Far closer to Lothar, rising from the center of the pond, was a parody of womanhood. She had her back to him, but even from this angle he could see that she was inhumanly tall, shockingly emaciated. A shapeless gown of grave-white cloth hung from her shoulders, and down the center of her back, a long tangle of green-black hair spread wildly.

She held one hand high in the air, and with it was pointing across the pond.

The hand pointed at—the Princess Irina Lvova.

A second figure stood near the Princess, and between them two horses blew white clouds from nostrils aquiver with fright.

"Irina!" Lothar cried.

She trembled visibly and started to call to him, but the woman in the center of the pond gestured imperiously and Irina subsided. Without moving her hands from their posture of command the woman turned her head slowly, slowly, until she gazed directly at Lothar.

Red eyes glared hatred at him. Lips thin and pale as snow moved silently. Lothar felt himself seized by a force he could not comprehend. He was frozen in his tracks.

The woman turned away. She moved one hand, drawing clawed fingers through the air as if carefully sweeping some polished jewels across a tabletop, toward her body.

At the edge of the pond Irina, terror in her features, raised a soft-booted foot and thrust it forward. She lowered it into the pond. The water, there at its edge, covered barely the sole of her boot.

The naiad, water-witch, kelpie, reached out toward Irina and again drew its claws slowly through the air.

Again Irina lifted one foot, stepped slowly forward, lowered her foot into the pond. This time the chill water covered the leather upper of Irina's boot.

The horses' nostrils steamed. Clouds of vapor rose from their sweating flanks. One of the beasts shivered visibly with cold.

The witch gestured again.

Irina responded. Lothar peered into her face. In her eyes he saw only fear, yet her hands hung limply at her sides and her feet obeyed the unspoken summons of the witch. The water was deep over Irina's ankles.

Lothar shifted his gaze from the confrontation of the women to the Svartalheimer still standing beside the horses. He recognized the figure as that of the court sorcerer, the *Zauberer*, of Nikolauz's Keep.

Lodur.

The man's beard fringed his face like a white ruff. He had lost his cap, if one he had worn, and his hair completed the circle of white surrounding his features. He seemed fully aware, yet strangely passive, observing the drama of the women.

Lothar's attention was captured by a sound. Somewhere a chorus of banshees wailed. Lothar discovered that he could move, could turn in search of the source of the strange harmony. It was weirdly pitched, a sound composed in part of shrieking and in part of humming.

It came from the sky.

He gazed above. It was night. What light might fall from moon or stars was blocked by the endless, restless mist. A flock of harpies might circle overhead, or a squadron of evil angels. He tried to pierce the darkness with his eyes, to see midnight-robed figures bearing smoldering ruby torches, hovering on wings of jet-black feathers, softly.

Was the hellish harmony their voices?

For an instant Lothar saw the glow of a torch.

He dropped his glance to the pond.

Irina had advanced a third of the distance to the water-witch. Greenish scum floated on the frigid surface, waist-deep now on Irina. Her face appeared calmer, the terror in her eyes not departed but lessened, like that of a child eager for, yet frightened of, some unfamiliar experience.

On the shore a horse snorted, jerked its head sideways. By apparent accident the horse jolted the wizard Lodur. The *Zauberer* started visibly. His eyes bulged and his mouth fell open. But no sound emerged.

He seized his own hair in both hands and tugged at it as if to bring himself fully from the grasp of a dream. He clambered onto the back of the horse with an agility that startled von Richthofen.

Lodur spurred forward, into the icy water. Trembling, his beast responded. The wizard held the reins in one hand. The other worked the clasp of a saddlebag. From von Richthofen's vantage point, the *Zauberer*'s actions with the saddlebag became masked.

The horse plunged past Irina, its splashing legs throwing fist-sized blobs of scum onto her face and body.

The water-witch looked from the Princess to the *Zauberer*. She gestured to him with both hands. Lodur covered his face with his palm. His horse halted, midway between Irina and the kelpie. Water rose over the chest of the beast, over the stirrups, over Lodur's feet.

The *Zauberer* drew a heavy clay jug from his saddlebag. He smashed its mouth across the pommel of his saddle. He cast a fistful of some glittering powder into the air before him. It began slowly to drift downward toward the scum-covered pond. He spurred his horse forward, guiding it in a circle, half swimming, throwing the powder into the air until the kelpie was surrounded by a shimmering curtain of motes.

The *Zauberer* halted again, beside the Princess Irina.

She stood entranced.

Lothar von Richthofen looked upward as he heard the scream of banshees closer than ever. A beam of demonic light flashed downward.

Lodur raised his hands and extended them toward the shimmering wall. A lurid stream of energy flowed from the tips of his fingers to the wall of fog and it burst into wild flames of lurid jade.

From within the circle of flame the voice of the kelpie rose in a shriek of frustrated rage.

Lodur seized the Princess Irina by one hand and led her back toward the edge of the pond.

Gradually the dancing jade flames fell. The voice of the kelpie ceased.

The beam of satanic light appeared once more from above the pond, and the band of screaming demons brought their shrieks slowly downward, downward, downward toward the scummy pond.

Chapter 21

Less than an hour earlier the *Spirit of San Diego* had tilted its wings, its duralumin propeller whirling silently, powered by the almost inaudible Muiaian magnetic engine. The shores of Haibrasl and the waters of Okeanos were far behind.

Moonlight glinted on the *Spirit*'s aluminum skin. The ship's landing wheels were retracted. A thousand feet beneath its boat hull rolled layers of clouds.

Amelia, in the pilot's seat, concentrated on the instrument panel. At her side, Cuchaviva studied the world-disk they had brought from Muiaia. Behind them, Howard Hughes snored softly while Charles Lindbergh stood guard above the Svartalheimer Nikar.

"Here *we* are," Cuchaviva said in *patois*. She pointed at the glowing speck that represented the monoplane.

Amelia glanced at the disk. The glowing speck showed them three-fourths of the way from the Ice Rim to Symmes' Hole.

"The only trouble," Amelia nodded, "is that we don't know where *here* is. And we don't know where Svartalheim is, either."

Cuchaviva balanced the world-disk on her lap and laid one hand gently on Amelia's jodhpur-clad leg. "It can't be far. Somehow I can feel it. I know it!"

"At least we won't run out of fuel," Amelia ventured. "But I feel as if we're in a test chamber. Just flying, flying. Not getting anywhere."

She peered through the windscreen, studying the cloud bank beneath them. She dropped the *Spirit* until it was enveloped by clouds, then down through a layer, hoping to make a visual fix on a landmark.

"I—well, what good is it all? Look out there." She waved her hand at the windscreen.

The sky was completely gray. Divided into layers, one an unbroken cloud bank that hung lifelessly above the monoplane, the other a billowing, impenetrable floor beneath, the whole world was two heavy leaves in some malevolent volume, ready to slam closed, squashing this doomed gnat into nothingness.

The Ryan's running lights were blazing and a directional spotlight mounted on the edge of the metal cowling stood ready to flare into life. But there was no purpose in shining the spotlight now onto mounds and billows of featureless mist.

"If only Nikar would speak," Cuchaviva mourned.

"I don't understand him." Amelia glanced briefly over her shoulder. The Svartalheimer, at the sound of his name, stirred, recognized Charles Lindbergh's close surveillance, subsided again.

"If he'd tell us where Svartalheim is, he could get home. I suppose he's afraid to face his superiors. They seem to be a pretty ruthless bunch! But then—why did he leave Haibrasl with us? He could have refused. He could have stayed there, or signed on as crew on some freighter. You saw that labor exchange! Cruach certainly didn't force Nikar to come with us!"

She shrugged helplessly. The Ryan drove on, through the doubled layers of gray. Amelia found herself, on occasion, still starting at the realization that the familiar drone of the Wright radial was absent. There was only the gentle hum of the Muiaian engine that had replaced it, and the high-pitched scream of slipstream over the Ryan's metal and fabric surfaces, her streamlined braces.

Amelia raised her hand and rubbed her eyes.

The steady rush of the monoplane between the layers of cloud, the constant hum of the power plant, the high harmonies of the slipstream had lulled her into a state more nearly akin to hypnosis than to slumber. But then—

She blinked, pointed, called to Cuchaviva. "Look!"

Howard Hughes stretched and scrambled forward to crouch beside the pilot's seat.

Lindbergh shifted, maneuvering Nikar between himself and the others. Over Nikar's head he could see out the windscreen.

"Could be a reflection," Hughes ventured.

The light was red. Against the backdrop of featureless gray it was impossible to determine its size and range. It could be a speck a few dozen yards from the *Spirit* or a conflagration miles away.

It was definitely a glow. There was none of the flickering associated with open-air combustion.

It disappeared.

"It could of been a reflection," Hughes reiterated. "Our running lights. This rotten soup..." He made an angry pass at the fog.

"Could have been," Amelia conceded.

"What *else* could it have been, though?" Lindbergh asked.

Amelia waited for somebody else to answer. No one did, so she volunteered a guess. "The Udet?"

Another silence, while Amelia translated for Cuchaviva.

Cuchaviva hummed noncommittally.

"Maybe we ought to try the radio," Lindbergh said. "Although we might not want to identify ourselves to the *Kondor*, if that was who it was. We're way ahead of 'em, if that was the *Kondor*. We should be within hours of the Hole now, and they're just starting for the Rim. How'd we get so far ahead?"

"Hah!" Hughes braced himself against the cabin wall and faced the others. "What if that *wasn't* the Udet ship? Maybe it was a Svartalheim pursuit ship. We don't know what those bozos got in the air. That might be their version of a Fokker Tripe. Maybe they got better night navigation than we do."

Lindy clenched his jaw. "Good point, Howard. For that matter, if we try to contact the ship, we could be picked up by ground stations. It *is* risky.

"Still—I think we should make our move. We have some high cards to play." He jerked a thumb at Nikar. "And there's no point in just flying around in these clouds for days on end."

All to no avail.

The radio apparatus received only the crackle of static and a latticework of remote voices, distant crosstalk and incomprehensible signals that might be anyone, anywhere, and certainly was of no use to the Ryan monoplane.

"I'm sure I saw that glow," Amelia insisted, in English and in *patois*.

"I saw it, too," Cuchaviva affirmed.

"Can't we get anything out of the disk?"

Cuchaviva shrugged. "It shows our own position. But it can't show us the ground because we don't know the ground configuration here."

"So it gives us our position relative to a blank!"

"I'm afraid that's so."

Amelia translated for Lindy and Hughes.

"Can't say we'd do any better on our side. The earth inductor compass works the same way. If you have good charts, you can plot your position. If you don't, you know where *you* are but you don't know where you *are*." Lindy glared through the windscreen.

Howard Hughes burst into laughter. The others demanded to know what he found so funny.

"It's like the little kid who got turned around down at the zoo in Sam Houston Park. Kid went up to a guard and asked him for help. The guard said, 'You lost, sweetheart?' And the kid said, 'Shoot, no, your honor, I know where *I* am, I'm right here by the monkey house! It's Ma'am 'n' Pap I've mislaid somewheres.'"

Lindbergh snorted.

"There it is!" Amelia pointed again. The red speck was visible for a moment, then was gone.

"Did you see where that went? Did it just wink out, or did it *go* somewhere this time?"

"I saw it! I think it dropped before it disappeared," Lindy said. "I'm almost sure it was diving."

"Damn," Amelia grumbled. "One thing we should have done was get an airplane with windows that point *down*. We can see everywhere but under us, and that's where we need to see!"

"Okay, Amy, we ain't licked yet!" Hughes was struggling into a heavy flying jacket. He drew a leather helmet over his thick shock of hair, pulled a pair of goggles down over his dark eyes.

"You look like a recruiting poster, Howard."

"Yeah. Sign up and whip Kaiser Bill. Flick on that outside spotlight."

"What for? What are you—?"

He was already sliding open the window in the Ryan's cabin door. "Me and Lindy done plenty of wing-walking stunts back on the barnstormer circuit. Right, Swede?"

"Maybe you ought to let me handle this, " Lindbergh offered. He started to move toward the window himself.

Nikar heaved against the cabin floor and launched himself. A split second more of patience might have brought success to the Svartalheimer, but he moved too soon. Lindbergh caught a glimpse of him from the corner of his eye.

As Nikar lunged, Lindbergh swung around, dropped his hands and caught Nikar by the shoulders, adding a downward impetus to the Svartalheimer's forward motion. Simultaneously Lindbergh drove his right knee upward. He caught Nikar under the jaw, the man's new downward momentum countering the upward force of Lindy's knee.

There was a thud at the moment of impact, then a second dull sound as Nikar slumped to the floor.

"Damn. He should have been tied up," Lindbergh said.

"Look," Hughes said, "I've had a nice rest. You've been busy playing lockup with that bum. I'm going outside."

He hoisted one foot over the windowsill. "Keep 'er steady," he told Amelia. "Keep the light on. Keep an eye on me—I dunno if I'll be able to yell loud enough, so watch me for hand signals, okay?"

Cuchaviva stared as Hughes lifted himself through the window, then disappeared from the airplane.

Howard grasped the edge of the cabin tightly with one hand. The full blast of the slipstream nearly tore him loose from his handhold. For the moment he could feel the Ryan quiver in response to the sudden drag on one side of its fuselage. Then Amelia compensated for the imbalance and he felt the plane settle back to a smoother course.

The spotlight was ahead of him, mounted high. He ducked

under it easily. His booted feet were resting on the D-rings that had served back at Halley Cleft for starting the radial without having to swim for it.

He moved his hands cautiously, like a mountain climber. Methodically, he assured himself of each new handhold before he relinquished an earlier one.

The cold, damp air swept across his face, misting his goggles. Before he could wipe the mist away the water had accumulated to the point where he didn't need to wipe it off—it was like peering through an automobile windshield in a heavy fog.

He looked back toward the cockpit and signaled to Amelia that he was all right. He reached up with one hand to see if he could aim the spotlight from his perch on the D-rings.

The spotlight swiveled smoothly.

Hughes scanned the sky ahead of the Ryan, straining to see through the shimmering disk of the propeller. Nothing. He tried peering to the side, then up and down.

Nothing but gray . . . gray . . . gray.

And then—a speck of orange ember glowing in the air. He tried to focus on it and it was gone. But he knew it was lower than the Ryan.

He leaned back so Amelia could see him clearly and signaled to her to take the *Spirit* down.

He crouched against the fuselage, his feet planted firmly on the D-rings, right hand clutching the metal cowling-edge, left hand directing the spotlight.

Earhart threw the Ryan into a bank and circled downward through shards of mist. She kept the angle of descent slight. The altimeter showed a safe distance above sea level, but a mountain might lurk in that fog, ready to smash the Ryan like a sledgehammer.

Hughes swung the spotlight, probing the mist. The clouds were turbulent—in part, at least, due to the Ryan's slipstream. Wisps and shards swept past Hughes. His face and hands were dripping. He shifted his position on the D-rings.

So far the Ryan had escaped the perils of ice through most of her journey, but he could see the sinister line of white behind him, creeping along the leading edge of the wing. He dropped his focus to the D-rings and found that they too were becoming coated with frost.

He tightened his handhold.

There was a rent in the mist beneath the plane.

Hughes peered down, swinging the spotlight through a narrow arc. Then he pulled himself erect and swung his arm, signaling to Amelia.

She cut the Ryan's forward motion. With its new Muiaian power plant it came to a nearly perfect hover. She peered through the window and saw Hughes gesture again. She followed his signal and double-checked the Ryan's landing gear, found that it was safely wound to the retracted position.

"We're over water," she informed the others.

Hughes sank to a crouch.

Beneath him there was a sudden crackle. A bolt of electricity snapped through the darkness. Then there was a sudden flare of light and a gust of warmer air. A circle of flame blazed upward, illuminating a pond of scum-covered water. There was a loud splash inside the circle of flames, then the water quieted.

Shortly the flame, also, died away.

Hughes reached up and signaled to Amelia.

She brought the Ryan lower.

With a gentle splash that sent ripples coursing through the scummy water, the Ryan settled onto the surface of the pond.

Hughes rose to his feet, swung the spotlight horizontal.

It picked out a strange, high house in the mist. The building showed no sign of habitation. Hughes turned the spotlight. At first he could see nothing but the dismal pond surrounded by a wall of eerily dripping trees and wandering mists.

Then he saw—a woman.

He exclaimed—and she returned an inarticulate gasp.

He stood dumbfounded. He could now make out, in the circle of illumination offered by the spotlight, a woman's figure and that of an elderly man with white hair and a flowing beard. Between them stood two dark-coated horses, blowing pale clouds into the chill, moist air.

From the cabin of the *Spirit*, Hughes could hear the voice of the Svartalheimer, Nikar. Obviously the man had recovered from his encounter with Lindbergh's knee.

He was shouting.

"Lodur! Zauberer! Helfen Sie mir!"

The man standing on the shore swiveled his white-framed face. He reached for the saddlebag of the horse nearest himself, opened a flap and withdrew something.

Before he could see what the man did next, Hughes was distracted by a sound beside him. Water splashed. There was a half-audible sound, as of a man in concentrated effort, then a quick *swish*.

In one motion Hughes ducked, whirled, launched himself from the D-rings where he stood balanced in flight boots and jodhpurs. There was a sharp pain in his shoulder.

The icy envelope of water closed over him. The pond was terribly cold. He wondered if it were brackish. Fresh water this cold must surely have frozen.

But that thought was a fleeting irrelevancy as Hughes stroked his way beneath the surface. It would have been useful, also, to know how deep the pond was. But there was not time to investigate that.

He broke the surface, treading water in a low crouch. The spotlight on the fuselage of the *Spirit of San Diego* still illuminated a circular area on the surface of the pond, as well as reflecting off the metal fittings and fabric covering of the airplane itself. Hughes knew that he made a black silhouette and he wanted to minimize the size and conspicuousness of that shape.

No one was visible ahead, but with mists curling over the surface of the water and the light coming from behind him he knew that peril was still at hand. He reached gingerly over his shoulder to investigate the source of his pain. His fingers closed on the hilt of a dagger.

With a single effort he drew it from the fleshy area outside his shoulder-blade. That instant of warning, then, that had prompted him to shift away from the D-rings had saved his life. A second or two longer and the dagger would have found its mark between shoulder-blade and spine. He would have suffered a punctured lung, maybe a punctured heart!

With a start he realized that he'd been holding his breath. He let it out silently. With the next inhalation he realized that the scum-coated pond stank. Ahead of him he caught a glimpse of light. He recognized the shape ahead of him: another man.

The stranger was watching. No! He was searching. He must be the one who had thrown the knife. He'd seen Hughes bound from the monoplane at the instant of the dagger's strike. But if he had failed to pick up Howard's silhouette as he emerged from his subsurface swim, then he was at a disadvantage.

And he was standing. The water barely reached to his waist!

As silently as possible, Hughes drew another breath. He transferred the dagger from his hand to his clenched teeth. He must be bleeding steadily. He offered a silent prayer that there was nothing in the water to be drawn by the scent of blood.

He lowered his face, held it to the merest fraction of an inch above the scummy pond. He could see the other man now, scanning the pond in search of him.

Hughes dropped beneath the pond's surface, found bottom and launched himself into a submerged breast-stroke. He wondered what Amy and the others were doing in the Ryan, and what the two figures on the bank with the horses were up to.

He counted strokes, closing the distance between himself and the man who had thrown the knife he now gripped in his teeth. He tried to see the man's legs through the scummy water but there was nothing but blackness.

He halted, calculating that he was only feet from the man. He braced his toes and his fingertips on the pond bottom, broke water as gently as he could with his head and shoulders. He still wore his flying helmet and goggles. The goggles had kept his eyes clear of pond-water and this gave him a momentary advantage.

He saw the other man as if he'd been peering through a rain-streaked window. The man had a bald skull and a thick, brutal face. His eyes flew open in startlement as he saw Hughes plunge forward. He had time for a single exclamation—*Teufel!*—before Hughes closed with him.

The two men grappled. The bald man was apparently unarmed, now, and struggled with his bare hands.

Hughes kept the dagger clenched in his teeth. He wasn't eager to kill. He knew that the man had attempted *his* life and failed, but it had been a strangely impersonal attack. Alive, the bald man might be a source of information. Dead he was worthless.

The bald man grasped Hughes's right hand with his own left.

Hughes landed a punch with his left, but it wasn't a strong one. His left arm wasn't working properly. He could move it okay but the strength was gone—the wound behind his shoulder-blade was responsible for that.

The bald man uttered a laugh of triumph. He swung a hard right. Hughes managed partially to slip the punch, but it caught him behind the ear and sent flashes of light through his head.

With a wrench he managed to free his right hand from the other's grasp. He shoved it under the man's chin. He caught him with the heel of his hand and half-punched, half-shoved upward and away. He could feel the man rise as his feet lost their purchase on the mucky pond bottom.

The man flailed wildly.

Hughes shoved his weight forward, struggling to keep the man off his feet and to flatten him on the surface of the pond.

The bald man swung his right hand wildly and Hughes felt it connect, hard, with the side of his head. His teeth rattled. His jaw popped open involuntarily. The razor-sharp dagger arced away from both men and disappeared into the scum.

Simultaneously the bald man howled. He staggered, clutching his right wrist with his left hand. A wisp of fog blocked Hughes's vision, then he could see that the bald man had ripped his hand open on the blade. Blood gouted blackly from his palm.

Hughes moved forward, shouting at the man to give up. He didn't know whether he was understood, but the man halted, ignored Hughes. Clearly he was out of the fight. He stood holding his wrist, staring at his pouring blood. Again he howled mournfully.

With his uninjured arm, Hughes reached for the man's wrist. He took it and led the man slowly back toward the *Spirit of San*

Diego. With each step the light grew clearer and the going easier. Hughes reached up with his injured arm and managed to swing the goggles back onto his forehead.

Inside the Ryan he could see the others peering anxiously after him.

From the far side of the monoplane he heard a sound—a horse's whicker. He halted, startled, then heard more sounds from the far side of the plane.

"What's going on?" he called. "Amy, Lindy! Lend me a hand with this bozo!"

He heard stirring inside the plane. He couldn't tell what they were doing.

From the far bank he heard voices. A young woman's, and an older man's, and neither of them speaking English.

The man's voice rose in command.

As if in response, the shards of mist floating at random over the face of the pond began to move in more orderly fashion. They formed themselves into a spiral, whirling coldly. They formed a wall of living mist.

Hughes was frozen in his place.

The wall of mist revolved more rapidly.

The Ryan's spotlight glared wildly in Hughes's eyes. The bald man whose wounded arm he still held was transformed into a statue of infinitely heavy marble.

The wall of mist revolved.

Hughes found himself turning, also. Slowly. Slowly. The Ryan moved past him. Then the bald man. The figures on the far bank of the pond. Then the dripping woods, the swirling mist.

The strange high house loomed over him, almost as if it were growing where it stood. It was like a fairy-tale house, like some witch's stronghold in a Grimm volume illustrated by Edmund Dulac.

Fires of greenish lightning flickered around the house's eaves.

The door was opening.

Slowly.

Chapter 22

Dumm, selbstsüchtig, holzköpfig, eitel.

Stupid, selfish, blockheaded, vain.

That was the Princess Irina Lvova. Yet, not entirely consistent. She had defended herself against the monster of the ice, thinking it a demon, not recognizing it for a mortal beast. And yet, if anything, that required more rather than less courage of her.

Mager, bleich, blass.

Scrawny, bloodless, pale.

Yet she carried herself with a certain possession. She had an air of aristocracy that could never be acquired unless it was expected—demanded!—from the cradle onward.

And in this moment of madness and peril she had called to him. Not to save her, but to save himself.

Manfred leaned across his horse's neck, peering into the mist. The horse stirred nervously, blew breath in pale streamers. He laid his hand against its neck, comforting the animal.

He could hardly believe that his surroundings were other than the dream of a diseased mind. He might have fallen into the screen of a bizarre photoplay by Murnau or Wiene.

Castles. Wizards. Horsemen.

Swamps. Bogs. Mists.

In the center of this vision, beyond the Princess Irina and the

Zauberer, in the center of the dark and brooding pond, there arose a creature of terrifying familiarity to the boy who had been raised on the gloom-ridden fantasies of his ancestors. Here in this strange land of Svartalheim the gothic trappings of a thousand years ago seemed more the framework of reality than any diplomatic machination of *Kanzler* or Kaiser. The dark, trembling beast between his knees was more real than any aeroplane or Zeppelin, any *Kondor* or *Schwarze Adler*.

The *Zauberer* cast some powdery stuff at the kelpie before Manfred. There was a duel of sorceries, and it was won by Lodur. Then madness fell upon sanity—or sanity upon madness.

The twentieth century descended upon the twelfth.

An hour ago this sequence had begun with the arrival of Manfred von Richthofen and the unfortunate halberdier Balor.

Warned back by the Princess Irina, Manfred had watched as Lodur and the Princess Irina had faced the terrifying, pallid kelpie. It had been, yes, as if the modern aviator-warrior had fallen into an earlier and more sinister age.

And then, bafflement upon bafflement, from above the pond a modern aircraft had descended, spotlight flaring through the gloom.

More furious struggle, and yet more, had taken place before Manfred's amazed eyes.

And again the *Zauberer* Lodur had taken a hand in the course of events, before Manfred von Richthofen's eyes, and by the time the scene had quietened the aircraft stood abandoned, rocking gently as misted breezes tugged at its surfaces.

Von Richthofen urged his horse forward. It was reluctant to approach too close to the pond. He bent forward and clucked reassuringly in its ear.

The horse obeyed.

Von Richthofen straightened himself, sitting astride his dark horse, his hand still grasping the heavy sword he had taken from his lost companion, the soldier of the Nikolauz Keep. Too bad that the fellow's mount had stepped into quicksand and been lost. The man might have known more of these woods than he revealed, and an obedient soldier might prove useful in case Manfred came upon enemies.

Still, there was no undoing what was done.

From the bank of the pond he could see the aeroplane more clearly than he had from his place beneath a tree. It was of a highly advanced type. Manfred's eyes narrowed as he studied its configuration. He could not make out the nature of its engine, but the design of the fuselage and wings were clear enough marking, even had it not been for the identification numerals painted on its flat surfaces and the name that stood out in clear script upon its nacelle.

The aircraft was American.

It must be—there was no other answer—the aeroplane of the Woodhull Martin competition party from America.

Von Richthofen shook his head slowly, a feral grin spreading across his face. After a time he let out a soft chuckle.

He climbed from his horse and led the beast to a nearby fir, tied its reins to a low-hanging limb. By all odds he would not need the creature again, but in case he should, it would remain where he tied it.

Manfred crept softly to the edge of the pond. He estimated the distance from himself to the aeroplane. He would, of course, prefer to avoid a dousing in the pond. But if it were needful in order for him to gain his object he would swim the North Sea.

He searched along the bank and found a stone the size of a hen's egg. He hefted it and tossed it close to the aeroplane. It splashed into the scummy pond, creating a broad, lazy ripple. There was no clue as to the depth of the water, nor as to whether dangerous creatures might lurk in the pond.

What had become of the kelpie after its disappearance?

There was nothing for it but to undertake his task.

Von Richthofen lifted one foot and held it over the scum. He heard a voice and raised his face to look for the source.

The sky was a patchwork of cloud and blackness studded with glittering points of light. Shards of pale mist wove. The points of light were tiny, faint, remote. Their colors were white, yellow, blue.

A single lurid point glowed ruddy and malevolent.

Mars.

It could be no other.

It moved.

Von Richthofen blinked, drew back his foot, instinctively raised his sword to position across his body.

Mars moved. It seemed to be swinging in a broad arc across the sky. It disappeared behind a patch of mist, then reappeared farther away. Its course described a narrow curve. It seemed, in fact, to be circling above the pond.

Its attitude was—but this was insane! The planet Mars was separated from the earth by scores of millions of kilometres. It moved in its orbit as the earth did in its own, and as the courses of the worlds drew closer or farther, and as their rotation on their axes brought them into disk or into line with each other, they appeared to vary widely in brightness and size.

At least, so Mars behaved with regard to observers here on earth. How the earth would appear to some hypothetical Martian astronomer, von Richthofen was willingly prepared to leave for others to ponder.

But it could not circle above a pond like a firefly in the night. That was impossible!

The glow flickered into darkness.

Manfred blinked his eyes.

Against the background of glittering stars and pale gray mist the silhouette of a horse and rider became visible.

The rider—Manfred squeezed his eyes shut and muttered an oath—seemed to be a woman wearing the oval helmet of the legendary Valkyrie.

The horse halted in midflight, hovering on black-feathered wings. It pawed stiffly at the air. It floated above the aeroplane, illuminated from beneath by the reflected glare of the aircraft's blazing spotlight.

The rider urged her horse back and forth, striding on mist and empty air as confidently as ever horseman urged a mount on turf. When the horse halted briefly with its hindquarters toward the Baron, he saw again the ruby glow that he had taken at first for the light of the planet Mars.

It came from the horse.

Finally the rider urged her horse to movement again. She trotted in a circle above the pond, then slowly descended until the horse's hooves landed with soft sounds on the mucky bank not ten metres from von Richthofen.

"*Gnadige Frau*," Manfred called softly.

"*Mein Herr?*"

Valkyrie or not, at least the woman spoke with a human voice. And she spoke, in the same manner, the Old Nordic tongue that the denizens of the Nikolauz Keep had used.

"*Kommen Sie hier*," von Richthofen commanded.

He heard the hooves of the woman's horse striking the soft, cold soil. His deliberate choice of tone in addressing her, commanding her obedience, had succeeded.

The shape of the horse and its rider loomed over him. The woman's horse was a larger one than von Richthofen's borrowed mount, and she sat astride the beast while he stood beside his own. That was an error. He should have remounted his horse before confronting her. The advantage of eye-level was now hers rather than his. And it was too late to remedy that.

He demanded her identity.

"*Leutnant Arawn*, *Valkyrie*, *mein Herr.*"

Leutnant? Valkyrie? More puzzlement.

He identified himself. "*Freiherr Major von Richthofen.*"

There was momentary silence. Von Richthofen's eyes swung from the woman to the aeroplane. The spotlight still illuminated a cone of brilliance from the aircraft's engine cowling to the scummy water. Mist-demons danced.

"Von Richthofen?" the Valkyrie echoed at last.

Angrily the *Freiherr* gave affirmation. "*Ja*, *ja*, *Freiherr Major Manfred von Richthofen*, *Jasta elf*, *Geschwader ein*, *Koeniglich und Kaiserlich Luftwaffe!*"

"*Ach*, *ja.*" The Valkyrie seemed to be taking the odd confrontation with astonishing equanimity. With more, in fact, than von Richthofen himself was able to muster.

"I think I have met your brother," the Valkyrie said. "He is *Hauptmann Lothar*, *nein?*"

"*Ja.*"

"In fact, I was showing him the use of these *fliegenden Pferder.*"

She reached down and patted her flying horse on the neck. "Only, the *Hauptmann* seems to have disappeared."

"How can horses fly?" von Richthofen demanded.

"*Ach.*" The Valkyrie laughed. "Anyone knows that *real* horses cannot fly. Even if they had wings like this one. *Himmel!* The wing-loading problem alone would be insurmountable. Wild stories, legends, *mein Major*. Faerie tales. But unless one believes in magic, no horse could ever fly.

"These are machines. Here, I will show you. *Ach*, the *Hauptmann* was using a *fliegendes Pferd*. I hope he is not injured. An inexperienced rider could get himself killed. A moment. Let me see..."

She fiddled with the pommel before her. The woods and the lake were silent. The water beneath the aeroplane's spotlight seethed almost audibly as figures of mist rose from the scum, whirled their languorous dance beneath the spotlight and passed from sight.

There was a sound of another set of hooves and a second horse, identical to the Valkyrie Arawn's, trotted across the bank of the pond. It halted and stood motionless beside Arawn's.

"Here, *mein Baron*," Arawn invited. "Come and help me to search for your brother. I seem to have lost him. He was using this *Flugzeug*." She patted the newly arrived winged horse. "This flying machine. Now, here is his machine. Where is the *Hauptmann* Lothar?"

The Baron shook his head, baffled. He crossed to stand beside the Valkyrie, to examine the pommel on her horse.

It was a control panel. The dials and levers differed from those with which he was familiar, those of aeroplanes and Zeppelins and automobiles. But the difference was in the detail, in the technology employed by these Svartalheimers. The *Begriff*, the conception, was by no means strange.

"You set the controls here," Arawn was explaining, "and then you guide the flight of the *Maschine* with the reins and by pressing on its flanks."

"And my brother?" His long fingers, acting with a life of their own, were moving across the control panel on the pommel, not yet altering the position of any control but familiarizing themselves with the arrangement of the knobs and switches. A good fighter pilot need no more look at the controls of his aircraft than a concert pianist need stare at the keyboard while he plays. The mechanical aspect of flight must become as much a part of the subconscious as breathing.

The true *Totschläger*, the killer-aviator, was a creature of instinct and of cold hatred.

"I asked the *Hauptmann* von Richthofen to remain nearby as we flew. But we became separated in the mist."

Another matter bothered Manfred. "Flew from where, *Fräulein Leutnant?*"

"Svartalheim Aerodrome, *Herr Major*. Where else?"

"Of course." Despite practice in the concealment of feelings, he was relieved that she could not see his face. Nikolauz Keep gave the appearance of a medieval castle, a society of serfs and bumpkins, a continent of petty kinglings that would have made Bismarck rub his hands in eagerness to be at work. Bismarck, the *real* Bismarck, the *Eisenkanzler!* Not this ruddy little Herbie who sat on the edge of his Papa's great mahogany chair and dangled his boots above the carpet!

Here was this young woman, an aviatrix. Despite its whimsical form, her mount was nothing but an odd sort of aeroplane. How it rose and advanced through the air with its birdlike wings and its lack of propellers was a mystery, but surely not one so great that an engineer like Manfred's friend Ernst Udet or the Russian genius Sikorsky could not unravel it.

"The aerodrome," von Richthofen asked Arawn, "is it near the Nikolauz Keep?"

She looked puzzled for a moment, then burst into laughter. "The Nikolauz Keep? *Herr Major*, what would those upper folk know of aviation? Or any other modern development? We do not even tell them about the *Untergrundwagen*, except those whom we place in positions of authority over the others, like the *Truppenführer*. We have to do all our testing and training down below, or else out in the haunted swamps, like here."

She smiled ironically as she spoke the word *Spukensümpfe*, haunted swamps.

And what was the *Untergrundwagen*, the under-earth-car?

In any case, Manfred felt that he was getting into more complications than he wished. Yet there seemed no clear way out for him. Von Richthofen's whole instinct was to act immediately, directly, against the enemy.

But who was the enemy?

Surely not this Lieutenant Arawn, this Valkyrie. He studied her face from beneath heavily lidded eyes, felt the fingers of one hand creep unbidden to his belt and rest there, giving him a posture of command. A woman bearing officer's military rank was a strange notion. Von Richthofen felt uncomfortable in this situation, but he held the double advantage of his noble rank and his superior military grade.

Something strange had happened to the Princess Irina. What it was, what the *Freiherr* von Richthofen could do about it . . . what he *wished* to do about it, he did not know. The woman was in fact a cold and self-seeking creature, determined to win her way into the highest ranks of the royal and imperial household. She had no real use for him, a mere *Freiherr*, other than as a steppingstone to the altar-rail of some princely chapel.

For all von Richthofen cared, he could abandon the scrawny Irina here in Svartalheim, rescue his brother Lothar and return to the home hemidisk to the welcome of heroes. A welcome that would be tempered by a suitably melodramatic mourning for the poor lost Russian Princess who had died a martyr's death in the terrible lands of the far hemidisk.

But that would not do. The Kaiser and the *Kanzler* were both interested in strengthening Germany's ties to the Russian empire. The Dowager Tsarina was herself a German. She and the Prince Lvov, not to mention the Tsar Alexei, would look with disfavor upon the loss of Irina here in Svartalheim. And any weakening of the alliance of Tsar and Kaiser would only undercut the strength of the already tottering Kerensky government, and enhance the prospects of support in the Duma for the dangerous Bronstein.

Ach! Why did politics have to come into every situation? "Just hand me my gun and show me the enemy!" von Richthofen snarled involuntarily.

"*Major?*"

He blinked. How long had he stood in reverie, wondering what to do, while the Lieutenant Arawn had stood waiting, her hand on the pommel of her *fliegende Pferd.*

"*Leutnant*, I beg your pardon. I was thinking about other matters. Political problems."

"I did not know that the Baron was interested in politics."

"I am not. It seems, instead, that politics is interested in me. I wish it would go away and leave me alone. I am interested in flying, in fast and powerful machines, in war."

"So you wish your gun, Baron."

He jerked his head once, forcefully, in affirmation. Then he pointed to the American aircraft floating in the center of the pond, its spotlight providing the chief illumination for the scene. "That *Flugzeug*, that flying machine, belongs to the enemy."

"What enemy?" Arawn asked.

"You would not know. Not in Svartalheim. What about the *Untergrundwagen*, *Fräulein Leutnant?*"

"A simple vehicle," she smiled. "Our soldiers train in them all the time. We may be able to see some even here, even at this hour."

"*Ja.* And their use?"

She moved her hands through the air, indicating first a level course, then a nearly vertical dip. A horizontal motion once again, and then a precipitous rise. She moved her fingers like a child playing the game of worshipers leaving a church.

"*Soldaten*," she said simply.

"You have used the underground cars in war against—whom?"

Arawn rubbed her forehead. "Such matters are for the *Koenig* Vithar and the *Prinz* Ottokar to decide. Utgard. Altheim. Helgard. Muspellsgard." She shrugged. "What am I—a lowly *Leutnant* of Valkyrie. I take my orders from my *Kapitan*, *mein Hauptfrau*, and she from hers. You understand, *Herr Major*, things military."

He nodded his head. "That I do. And you say there are *Untergrundwagen* exercises in this area?"

"Not far."

"Then, *kommen*. We will observe."

"By *fliegendes Pferd?*"

He pondered that. "I think there is room..." He inclined his head toward the amphibious monoplane.

"You can fly this *Maschine?*" Arawn inquired.

"If a *Maschine* can be flown, *Freiherr* von Richthofen can fly it." To himself: he would have to study the controls, of course. One did not simply climb into a strange aircraft and proceed. There was also the problem of a cold start for the engine, having only this Valkyrie lieutenant as ground-crew. But he could do it, he was certain. The monoplane, at least, had a propeller on its nacelle!

The two *fliegenden Pferde* did fit into the cabin of the aeroplane. Their passage across the pond, a distance of only yards, had been an eerie one nonetheless. For Manfred, the sensation of sitting astride the black winged horse, its flanks and coat almost indistinguishable from those of a real beast, yet knowing all the time that the *Pferd*, the horse, was no more alive than a wooden one on a *Karoussel*, was disorienting.

Yet his sure instinct for flying machines of any description had not failed. He had floated across the pond on the back of the borrowed *fliegende Pferd.* Getting the two mechanical beasts into the cabin had been a delicate task. Their dimensions were not designed for such cramped quarters. But Manfred and Arawn had managed, and now he sat at the controls of the aircraft, the Valkyrie at his side.

He studied the controls. The instruments and their knobs and dials and toggles were for the most part familiar in design. There had apparently been a recent modification in the craft's power system, and von Richthofen was somewhat leery of trying the plane without instruction. But there was no choice.

He flicked off the outside spotlight. The reflected glare ceased and the cabin darkened. He slid the throttle a notch from its position and was astonished to hear a gentle hum, and in the dim light outside the aircraft—the light reflected from the aeroplane's own lights—to see the propeller begin silently to revolve.

Within minutes he had raised the monoplane from the pond, set it moving on a course that carried it in an ever-widening spiral over the area from which it had risen. "This is amazing," he said to *Leutnant* Arawn. "Never have I come across such a machine! This will revolutionize the field of aviation!"

"And to where will you fly now?"

"To see this *Untergrundwagen* you spoke of. Will you direct me?"

She gave directions. He consulted the Ryan's earth inductor compass, the ship's altimeter as well, and set a course that brought the Ryan skimming low over banks of mist. He flicked on the outside-mounted spotlight and by its illumination caught sight of the swamp through occasional breaks in the mist.

Arawn pointed through the window. "There, *mein Herr*, you see?"

Von Richthofen brought the monoplane to a halt; with the throttle down and the newly installed devices activated, the plane hovered silently, even better than the Spanish Cierva's autogyro was reported to do. He adjusted the spotlight with care.

A mound of earth like a mole's telltale burrow erupted in the clearing. The prow of the *Untergrundwagen* shoved clear of the ground, thowing clots of earth to either side. It was shaped like a great screw that revolved, channeling through the soil.

The ground that it chewed away was carried along the bulletlike body of the *Wagen*. The hull was streamlined, lubricated with periodic pulses of gleaming oil. Stabilizing fins with knife-sharp edges prevented the hull of the *Wagen* from spinning dizzily as it progressed.

The machine burst fully from its channel and lay on the ground. Its stern was rounded and flattened. It folded inward like the irising shutter of a fine camera.

Squads of soldiers poured from the opening.

Unlike the halberdiers and guardsmen of the Nikolauz Keep these men wore strangely modernistic garb. They carried weapons of a nature unfamiliar to von Richthofen. As they tumbled from the rear of the *Untergrundwagen* they scurried about, pointing into the air at the hovering monoplane.

Von Richthofen reached to flick off the telltale spotlight just as the first of the soldiers aimed his weapon upward and began to fire.

Von Richthofen was almost, but not quite, quick enough to avoid a hit.

Chapter 23

There were no days or nights for Yacabuchu. Once there had been, but there no longer were. From Muiaia to Haibrasl he had traveled as a common sailor on a trading ship. At Haibrasl he had disappeared into the anonymous and ever-changing world of longshoremen, merchants, sailors, smugglers, and thieves that forms around the docks in every trading port.

From there he had managed to sign onto a Frieslandisch trireme bound for Quivira with a load of angora from the Rhipaean Mountains. In Quivira he jumped ship, made his way overland to the port of Tiguex and signed on as a sail-rigger and mast-fitter on a Felgardisch trader bound for Svartalheim.

Along the way he had applied his talents as observer, supplemented by his considerable abilities with language, to gather intelligence against his return to Muiaia.

Only it looked, now, as if there would be no such return. Caught by the *Truppenführer* Mider's men, turned over to the *Prinz* Nikolauz, Yacabuchu had languished since in this dungeon somewhere beneath the Nikolauz Keep. He could take the pain inflicted by Nikolauz and his torturers better than he could endure the disorientation of being cut off from sunlight and darkness, the weakness induced by hunger and thirst.

But he had not yielded. He had not even hinted to Nikolauz

that he spoke any language but that of Muiaia.

And it seemed that the end was near.

The style of the house and its furnishings was a tantalizing blend of the familiar, the almost-familiar, and the alien. Its walls were of wood and plaster, their exposed beams suggestive of Tudor England. The floors were of closely fitted dark stone, like the floors of Machu Picchu. The huge fireplace with its ornately massive mantel resembled those of a typical Nordic castle.

The fireplace held a roaring blaze. What burned could hardly be determined through the crackling, dancing flames. But the flames themselves were of a livid ultramarine. Their glow was so intense that it seemed one might carry it away in one's hands.

There was little smoke. What there was filled the room, strangely, with the salty tang not of stagnant pond water but of storm-lashed, rock-edged seacoast.

Charles Lindbergh regained the ability to move.

He found himself slumped in a highly carved wooden chair. Its tall back and massive arms suggested the tangled bodies of writhing snakes—or perhaps the lithe necks and scaly heads of some hydra-like dragon.

He rubbed his tingling face, ran hands through his tangled blond curls, pushed himself groggily to his feet.

He stared into the blaze, trying to fathom the nature of the burning material. It might have been a thick log, happenstantially formed in its suggestive shape. Or it might have been—he preferred not to consider the alternative.

His attention was wrested away from the livid flames by the figures flanking the hearth. They might have been the king and queen of a fancy dress ball. A man tall and slim, his face wreathed in flowing white hair and beard, his body covered by a dark robe marked in enigmatic and shuddersome symbols. Opposite him a woman, or a semblance of woman, equally tall, slim to the point of emaciation, her skin as pale as a corpse's, her hair as long and straight as a witch's, blacker than coal but highlighted with glints of a definite bluish green.

The white-haired man watched Lindy rise. He inclined his white-fringed head in a gesture of courtesy—or mock-courtesy.

Lindbergh returned the nod. He leaned against his chair.

A huge table stood nearby. It was carved in similar fantastic fashion so that its entire length was a continuous mass of writhing serpents or dragon's necks. Fearsome fringe-framed faces peered from the tangle.

Other figures were ranged around the table. One by one, Lindy saw, they stirred. He gazed at one face, then another.

Amy! Thank heaven that Amy was here and safe.

And Hughes. Good old Hughes, Lindy's diamond in the rough. Howard's clothes were drenched with blood, but whatever wound he might have suffered must be closed now, for there was no more apparent bleeding.

There was their friend from Muiaia, the geologist Cuchaviva. She was rubbing herself, restoring her circulation, looking around.

And there was Nikar, slumped in his place, flicking furtive glances from person to person, calculating his chance to turn the bizarre situation to his own advantage.

Two others were strangers to Lindbergh: a bull-necked, bullet-headed man with one hand wrapped in blood-soaked bandages, and a slim woman with hair the color of pale yellow diamonds and eyes the shade of faintly bluish ice.

"*Willkommen*," the white-maned man intoned from his place by the hearth. "Can you understand me?"

He spoke in Old Nordic.

"I understand you," Lindbergh said. The eyes of the other brightened at his statement.

"*Ein unbeholfenes Vefahren*," the man said. *A clumsy procedure*. But it would have to do. He introduced himself by title as well as name: the *Zauberer*, the wizard, Lodur. The dark-haired woman did not speak. She understood, Lodur said, but she would utter no word.

They must confer. All would consider themselves, the old man said, his guests here at his little *Waldhaus*, his woodland retreat.

There would even be refreshments should anyone care...

Lindbergh turned and looked at the table. There were pitchers and goblets, loaves and platters of cold meats. He lifted a goblet and sniffed. He hadn't noticed anything on the table a moment ago. And he hadn't heard anyone enter the room to lay out the things on the dragon-wood.

He sipped at his goblet, gingerly. It contained a sparkling wine. In the room's silence he realized that through some tacit procedure he had been chosen spokesman.

The bullet-headed man with the bandaged hand rose. He said, not in Old Nordic but in modern German, *"Ich bin Hauptmann Lothar von Richthofen, koenigliche und kaiserliche Luftwaffe."*

Howard Hughes leaped to his feet. "Von Richthofen!"

The men stared at each other speechlessly.

The ultramarine flames sent weirdly colored shadows dancing across the walls. Two of them, Hughes's and von Richthofen's, moved toward each other. As if choreographed they halted. Von Richthofen lifted his bandaged hand contemplatively. Hughes moved gingerly, testing his freshly closed wound.

Again they advanced.

Halted.

Saluted.

Shook hands—gingerly, for it was von Richthofen's right hand that was so heavily bandaged.

Embraced! Also, gingerly, for it was Hughes's lacerated back that was so recently closed up.

And the laughter of the two men echoed from the beam-raftered shadows of the *Zauberer* Lodur's *Waldhaus.*

"Lindy! Amy! Listen, you guys! Don't you know who this feller is? You should hear the yarns old Jax Bullard spins about this guy! This here is Lothar von Richthofen! Hottest Fokker-jockey who ever handled a stick!"

"Jax Bullard! Der schwartze Flieger! Er flog nach Douai und Lille! Bullard is ein Freund von Dir?"

"He says," Lindy began.

"Damn, Swede!" Hughes was flushed. "I know where Jax flew! What a crazy thing, I must've rooted for Jax to flame this chump twenty different times..."

Lindy kept up a running translation for von Richthofen.

Von Richthofen spattered gutturals and Lindy translated for Hughes.

"And I him, an equal number!"

"You never scratched Bullard but you almost got me today in that stinking puddle outside!" Hughes jerked a thumb toward the front of the *Waldhaus*. The room was sealed and there was no seeing the pond where the Ryan had set down, but they all understood the reference.

Von Richthofen wanted to know if Hughes had ever met Frank Luke, Eddie Rickenbacker, Roy Brown.

Hughes wanted von Richthofen's assessment of different Fokker aircraft. If the D-7 tripe was really so hot—

"*Ach, ja, ja! Ein liebliches Flugzeug!*"

"He says, 'Yes, a darling—'"

"It's okay, Swede, that much I can get myself. Ask him, How come Tony Fokker went to a single-winger with the D-8?"

Von Richthofen followed that unassisted. "*Das eindecker Flugzeug, Howard, war—*"

Lodur interrupted. "I'm sure you have much to discuss, you fliers." He smiled enigmatically. "But we all have much to discuss together. This is the sacred land of Svartalheim. We have been *angegriffen.*"

Invaded.

"By whom?"

"By you, *Herren und Damen.*" He wagged a finger. "You come from such far places, except for the woman Cuchaviva. Her home we have heard of, at least. But you others are from—where?"

They told him.

"*Ja, so, Amerika,*" he nodded. "*Und Russia.*"

Irina sat as icily silent as the kelpie beside the hearth. She acknowledged Lodur's mention of her homeland with a barely visible nod.

"And of course," Lodur continued, "the *Hauptmann* von Richthofen from *Deutschland.*"

"I wouldn't call it an invasion, *mein Herr Zauberer.*" Lindbergh repeated his statement in English.

"We're here for different reasons. Miss Earhart and Mr. Hughes and I are in a race. As soon as things are settled we'll be more than happy to leave Svartalheim behind us. In fact, we'd be happy to go right now, only Cuchaviva helped us and we feel that we owe her something in return.

"As for Captain von Richthofen—why, it happens that he's one of our honorable competitors. And Her Highness, I understand, is a member of Captain von Richthofen's group too."

The Russian nodded.

"And, of course, your "*Herr* Nikar," Lindy said.

The former raider snarled.

"We'll have to decide what to do with this fellow. Maybe we could work out a swap. How about *Herr* Nikar for Cuchaviva's husband?"

The wizard's eyes, flashing beneath bushy brows, darted from Lindy to Nikar.

There was a tense silence, broken only when von Richthofen changed the topic. "I must apologize to *Herr* Hughes," Lothar said. Lindy translated for him. "The incident in the pond—it was a moment of highest desperation. I attacked *Herr* Hughes in dishonorable fashion."

Hughes grinned. "Forget that. The old bozo's stickum fixed it up quick. But we're going to whip you in the air, Lothar. I can see old Mrs. Martin's greenbacks right now!"

The *Zauberer* took back the conversation. "I wish to understand your route, your origin, you aviators. America, Russia—yes, but where are these lands? And where lies your destination?"

Lindy shot a glance at his partners. Was there a danger in revealing too much to this Lodur? Did Svartalheim, for instance, represent a threat to their own hemidisk?

Svartalheim had magic—or seemed to, anyway. Lindy didn't put much store in hocus-pocus. He was a hardheaded midwestern materialist to start with, and he'd seen people like Blackstone and Carter and the great Houdini himself debunking spirits and spooks often enough to remove any doubts he might have held.

Surely the *Zauberer* had pulled some mighty impressive tricks. And if that kelpie woman wasn't a goblin of some sort he'd eat his skimmer. But weird creatures didn't have to be supernatural.

What could a bunch of medieval weirdos like these Svartalheimers do against a modern country like the U.S.A.? Swordsmen against army tanks? Kelpies against battlewagons? *Zauberers* against Douglas B-2 bombers?

Mider lay on his straw pallet, the half-empty jug of *Rotwein* close at hand. He brooded miserably on his state.

His loss of blood had been stopped by the only means available, cauterization of the terrible wound left by the foreign *Freiherr*'s blade. But he was left hideously disfigured, a huge scar glaring from the center of his face where his nose belonged. A scarf wrapped around his face, covering all beneath the line of his eyes, served in part to spare him the humiliation of being seen by others and the horror of glimpsing himself in any burnished blade or goblet of wine.

The *Prinz* Nikolauz, returning to the great hall after his departure with the *Freiherr*'s brother, had personally saved Mider from death by blood loss—but upon hearing the narrative of events had added to Mider's loss of his nose the loss of his rank as *Truppenführer* and reduced him to common soldier.

Mider lifted the jug and swigged deeply at the wine, half-choking and sputtering it over his already stained tunic when he failed to pause for breath.

He heaved himself to his feet, bent to retrieve the jug and made his way groggily from the room. He proceeded through little-used passages of the Nikolauz Keep, burrowing into the earth. At length he emerged in the building's cellars and made his way to the dungeon where prisoners were kept.

A single *Rotmann*, the spy Yacabuchu, hung by chains from the wall. He appeared half-dead, three-fourths delirious.

Mider stood before the *Rotmann*, gazing into his brick-colored face. "Red man! Red man!" Mider took the jug in both his hands and sloshed a spray of wine across the prisoner's face.

Yacabuchu opened his eyes and looked down at his tormentor. He said nothing.

"Hey, red man! They've been very unkind to you!" Mider laughed drunkenly. "Me too. Me too, red man. Say, let's get even with 'em! You want to get out of here, don't you? What about heading for the swamps? Want to see what it's like out in the swamps? You came here to spy out Svartalheim, I know that. I'll give you a chance to see it, all right. Come on!"

He staggered to the wall of the dungeon, found a dark crevice in the stone, a dark crevice hidden by the dim, flickering illumination of the dungeon, a crevice the size of a man. He slipped within its shadows, glanced back at Yacabuchu. "What's matter, you like it here so much?"

The *Rotmann* moaned and struggled feebly against his metal bonds.

"Oh, you're stuck there, hey?" Mider drew an iron poker from a charcoal fire and crossed to Yacabuchu with it. The tip of the poker faded from a white heat to lurid orange, then to black.

The *Rotmann* cringed.

"Oh, don't be so damned womanish," Mider grumbled. "Say, do you understand me at all, red man?"

Yacabuchu muttered a single word. To Mider it sounded almost like *Wein*. "All right, all right, just have a li'l patience, red man."

He inserted the poker between the prisoner's metal bonds and the stone to which they were attached. Laboriously he freed the spy, one limb at a time.

The red man collapsed to the dungeon floor. Mider held the jug for him and the man swigged greedily at it. He almost dropped the jug but Mider saved it. The red man seemed to turn gray. He broke into huge beads of sweat, then puked all the wine back onto the dungeon floor.

Mider hummed, then held the jug for the spy again. This time he took a single, small swig and handed the jug back.

"Come on, red man, now I'll show you something you've never seen."

Mider took the *Rotmann* by the elbow, raised him shakily to his feet, guided him to the black opening in the stones.

From the dank blackness of the passageway they emerged, a few score paces later, into the *Untergrundwagen* hangar.

Mider ushered Yacabuchu into a small *Wagen* designed for staff visitations and inspections of training exercises.

* * *

Lodur stroked his beard. "Well, I suppose you may as well go on your way."

"What about Cuchaviva?" Amelia put in. "Howard, Charles, we're not just going to hightail it home and leave her here!"

"What does *she* want?" Lindy asked. "Not to come with us, I'd think."

Amelia exchanged words with Cuchaviva. Then she said, "Charles, she wants her husband and she wants to return to Muiaia. She has no interest in coming with us. And she certainly doesn't want to stay here."

Lindy grunted. "Swell with me. But I hope she doesn't expect us to hang around here while everything gets unraveled."

Hughes put in, "What about those two joes?" He indicated Lothar and Irina. "Ask 'em what *they* want, Swede!"

Von Richthofen and Lvova had left their places and gone off to a remote corner.

Cuchaviva, distraught, caught Amelia's hands. She exploded in a single, lengthy series of words. Among those emerging were repetitions of a phrase something like, "*Blamos, blamos, lamenteh mash'do, mash'do.*" She dropped Amelia's hands, pounded her fist on the tabletop, stalked toward the door of the *Waldhaus*.

The others stared after her. Only Howard Hughes moved. He started after Cuchaviva but before he had taken two strides Amelia caught his arm, looked into his face and shook her head.

When Amelia dropped Hughes's arm he stood silently, watching as Cuchaviva pulled the door open, disappeared through it and dragged it shut behind her.

Hughes walked to von Richthofen's side and they resumed their aviators' shoptalk, von Richthofen speaking a mixture of German and English, Hughes using his hands primarily to make his points. Soon they were facing each other at one end of the dragon-table, swapping propwash over goblets of wine.

Up the table from them, Irina sat sulking.

Lindbergh and Earhart pulled out chairs, joined Hughes and von Richthofen. Lindy offered space in the *Spirit* to von Richthofen and Lvova. "The Ryan'll carry five easily, especially with the new magnetic engine. Of course," he smiled wryly, "you'd lose the Woodhull Martin Prize. But it doesn't look as if you have much chance at it anyhow."

Lindbergh smiled. "Whatever happened to your aircraft?"

Von Richthofen growled. "The Udet *Kondor* is north of here, *mein Herr*. All safely covered and dogged down. But it is disabled. Parts."

Lindy shook his head in the sympathy of airman for airman. "But how'd you get here?"

Von Richthofen's bullet head grew crimson with emotion. "We had also a Zeppelin on board. But it was destroyed. Exploded and burned in the Nikolauz Keep. *Kaputt*."

Lindy covered his mouth with one hand, trying to look contemplative while he hid his growing grin. "Well, you're welcome to hitch a ride with us. You'll probably get a hero's welcome in the U.S. anyhow. We're like that, you know!"

"Wait a minute! Wait a minute!" Hughes gestured frantically. "Ask him where his brother is, Swede! There was three of them just like us. Where's old Baron Manfred?"

Lothar's face showed comprehension. He ground his teeth but before he could speak, Irina did.

"Princess is not going!"

The others gaped at her.

"Not going!" she repeated. "Sick of being Prince's daughter, playing harlot for weakling Tsar, haggling for husband like kulak buying sickle!

"Will stay in Svartalheim! Will find job for self and become citizen!"

There was a crash as Lothar von Richthofen smacked his goblet down on the dragon-table. "*Bei Gott!* A good idea, Princess. I, too!"

She glared at him suspiciously. "Why?"

"Why? Because *I* am sick of being the younger brother. Manfred is the Baron, I am simply *Herr* von Richthofen. Manfred is the *Major*, I am merely the *Hauptmann*. He commands the *Jasta*, I merely fly the aeroplane.

"Here, you see, I will no longer be the little brother," Lothar reiterated. "Here *I* am von Richthofen. *There*—in the Fatherland—I am von Richthofen's *Bruder*."

Lothar turned to face Lindy. "*Herr* Lindbergh, I beg to decline your kind offer. And to request of you a great favor."

Lindy lifted an eyebrow.

"When you return to our hemidisk you will please say nothing of this matter. You did not see us. You did not encounter the *Kondor* or its crew, and you know nothing whatever of any Zeppelin.

"The world will believe us dead. They will mourn us briefly, but will remember you long. Such is the reward of victory."

Lindy conferred briefly with Earhart and Hughes. Then he said, "All right, Captain. But will you answer one question for us: Where is your brother?"

A look of anguished loss passed over Lothar von Richthofen's face. "*Ach, mein Bruder, mein Bruder!* Our little emergency craft, our Zeppelin—it crashed in the Nikolauz Keep. An explosion, a terrible fire. Poor, poor Manfred! Never will we see him again."

He broke down completely, burying his face in his hands.

At first the Svartalheimer Mider was unwilling to let Yacabuchu sit beside him at the controls of the *Untergrundwagen*. But the Muaiaian persisted, and after a while Mider tentatively yielded.

Yacabuchu studied the instruments and Mider's use of them. The *Wagen* was an ingenious and highly advanced mechanism, certainly an astonishing achievement for a people as seemingly primitive as the rude Svartalheimers. But as he was accustomed to Muiaian science and experienced at piloting the magnetic platforms of Muiaia, the *Wagen* was not long a mystery to Yacabuchu.

Mider guided it through carefully laid subterranean channels until it was—it must be—well away from the Keep. Then he set it onto a side passage that rose abruptly to the surface.

When the *Wagen* broke surface, Yacabuchu could hardly tell. Through the small transparent ports of the machine, all that he could see was darkness anyway.

Mider guided the machine a fair distance across the mossy, wooded surface of the land, then brought it to a halt.

Yacabuchu gazed through the port. A faint light had begun to filter through the thick trees. Night was giving way, grudgingly, to dawn. The Muiaian gestured at the port, getting his message to Mider easily.

The Svartalheimer unlatched the heavy iron disk that served the *Untergrundwagen* as entry and exit hatch. The interior of the *Wagen* was fairly lined with armament, but the two men climbed out unarmed.

Yacabuchu felt ravenous hunger and thirst. He found a small, fresh stream and knelt beside it to slake his thirst. The water was cold, clean, the most delicious beverage he had tasted in his life. After drinking a few cupped handfuls he rinsed his face and neck for the first time since his capture by Nikolauz's guards.

Refreshed, he looked up from the stream and saw his wife Cuchaviva approaching through the woods. He dropped his face to his hands and wept.

Dawn had broken also at the *Waldhaus*.

Amelia stood framed in the doorway. She smiled and inhaled rich morning air, moist and heavy with life. She raised her face to the sky, brushing light curls away from her cheeks, sensing Howard Hughes and Charles Lindbergh close behind her.

The only clear opening to the sky was that directly above the pond.

Leaving Lothar von Richthofen and the Princess Lvova together in the *Waldhaus*, unhindered by the *Zauberer* Lodur and the dark-maned kelpie of the pond, Amelia and Howard and Charles advanced to the edge of the water and gazed at the glorious sky overhead.

The sun was bright, and a few tiny white clouds floated gently, high above the gloom-ridden trees.

There was a faint whining sound. Amelia turned and followed it until she caught the brilliant glint of sunlight on the brushed aluminum engine cowling of the *Spirit of San Diego* as the monoplane circled overhead.

Chapter 24

This American monoplane was no warship, but after piloting the heavy *Kondor* and the clumsy, slow-moving *Schwarze Adler*, it had been exhilarating to man these controls. The monoplane was quick and it responded well to the pedals or the stick.

That had saved them.

The Ryan was of course unarmed, and when the troops leaving the *Untergrundwagen* began firing, it had taken all of von Richthofen's skill to evade destruction. Fortunately the plane's cowling and wings were of metal. From the pilot's seat he could observe charred spots on the underside of the wings, and in the fuselage, small holes where the ground troops' weapons had burned through the skin.

It was a lucky stroke that the heat had not set off the Ryan's fuel tanks. Or was there even petrol in the plane's tanks? It was obvious that the monoplane's radial engine had been removed and replaced with an unfamiliar power plant. From its silence and smooth operation he could only infer that it was an electrical motor of some sort. But if so, where were the batteries, and how great a charge could they hold?

Next to the tank of compressed hydrogen, the batteries for *Schwarze Adler*'s propellers had been the heaviest and bulkiest objects in the entire Zeppelin. And they had produced relatively little power, and held only a sorely limited charge. *Gott*, who had designed the mill of this monoplane?

Von Richthofen cast a sideward glance at the Valkyrie. She had managed finally to call to the ground soldiers and get them to hold their fire. Another blessing of the silent engine.

Now she turned her face toward von Richthofen and asked, "Where are you headed, *Freiherr?*"

"I wish to test this aircraft," he replied.

"But what about your *Bruder?*"

Well, what about his brother, indeed? Von Richthofen stared ahead, conspicuously absorbed in the handling of the Ryan. Of course, he was not truly answerable to this woman. As major to lieutenant he could simply announce that the subject was closed.

But she had planted the question in his mind.

Lothar was not really a bad fellow, in his way. Certainly a good pilot and a good fighting man, even though his style was a bit wild. By Manfred's lights, Lothar was controlled too much by his passions, not enough by his mind.

And there had been a thread of resentment in Lothar's conduct for as long as Manfred could remember. Lothar had never reconciled himself to the role of *kleiner Bruder*, younger brother. Manfred held the title of Baron, the military grade of major. Lothar was merely the brother of the Baron, and a captain.

Was that Manfred's fault? If *he* had been the younger brother, and Lothar the older, their roles would have been reversed. Why couldn't Lothar come to terms with reality?

And as for the Princess Lvova...

Manfred had never cared much for Russians anyway. He had admired the engineer Sikorsky and his giant aeroplane *Ilya Mourometz*. It was a virtual flying battleship, with its multiple engines and gun emplacements and racks of aerial bombs. Not the kind of plane for von Richthofen: to ask him to fly a heavy bomber was like asking a knightly horseman to drive an armored diligence.

Still. it was a splendid weapon in the hands of the proper crew.

Ach, but Russia was a terrible country. Half Asiatic barbarian and half decadent liberal. No wonder she had crumbled in the One Year War. If the war hadn't ended, German troops would have poured through Poland and Byelorussia. They would have battered down the very gates of Moskva in another year. It was only the mad turnabout of politics in America and that country's adventurist President Roosevelt that had ruined Germany's bid for continental hegemony and sent the *alte Kaiser* into exile!

Who cared for an alliance with backward Slavs, anyway? It might be the *Kanzler*'s plan, but von Richthofen didn't care for it. And he cared less for that *Eisberg* the Princess Irina.

"*Herr Major?*"

This time he responded to Lieutenant Arawn's question. "I suppose we ought to find the little brother, *ja*. You have a suggestion, *Leutnant?*"

"I would start back at the pond, *Herr Major*. I last saw the *Hauptmann* there. Do you think we can find the pond?"

"Certainly." He read the earth inductor compass on the Ryan's panel, set a back-azimuth and sent the monoplane coursing over the swamp.

The sky had lightened and the treetops beneath the aeroplane were clearly visible. The sun was well above the horizon, the gray mists were clearing rapidly and the world was turning into a vivid duotone of bright blue above and dark green below.

The pond appeared suddenly, a patch of black liquidity dotted with blobs of jade-green scum. A tall, archaic structure stood upon one bank. Its doorway swung open.

Von Richthofen pulled back on the stick, hit the rudder pedal, shoved the stick hard over and threw the monoplane into a steeply rising spiral. He pulled out the throttle to give the prop enough power to avoid a stall.

Through the wide window he could see the figures pouring from the doorway. They were pointing upward at the plane. He thought he could identify some—not all—of them.

"*Leutnant Arawn!*" he snapped.

"*Mein Herr.*"

Von Richthofen thought with the speed of lightning. He did not wish a confrontation with these—certainly not at this moment, not while flying an unarmed aircraft.

"*Die Amtsgewalt übernehmen Sie!*" He commanded her to take

over. Before she could protest he slipped from his seat, crossed the cabin to the two *fliegenden Pferde*, the two mechanical horses. He activated one of them, maneuvered it to the dogged-shut door of the cabin, climbed into the saddle, shoved open the door.

"*Auf Wiedersehen, Leutnant!*"

The *fliegende Pferd* plunged away from the aeroplane, von Richthofen at its controls. The ground leaped to meet him, individual trees thrusting pointed peaks out of the mass of dark-green vegetation.

Von Richthofen stabilized the *fliegende Pferd*, overcoming its wild tumble. He was still diving toward the treetops, but he was gaining control of the horse. He pulled on the reins. The *Pferd* lifted its nose. He could feel its muscles—no, he corrected himself, its spring-metal rods—move between his calves.

The *Pferd* folded its forelegs, extended its hind limbs, spread its wings to guide itself. Only a few yards from the treetops it leveled off and shot across the surface of green.

Von Richthofen looked above for the first time since he and the *fliegende Pferd* had hurtled from the cabin. He could see the Ryan silhouetted against the now-bright sky. Arawn had obviously got the aeroplane under control. As he had expected. She had brought the Ryan out of its climbing spiral, leveled off, and was now running a low-altitude pattern, searching for the pond.

That was not Manfred's problem, then. At least, not for now. He was more interested in testing the capabilities of the *fliegende Pferd*.

He held the reins loosely in his right hand, used his left to adjust the controls on the pommel. The *Pferd* was instrumented. Its scale of measurement was unfamiliar to von Richthofen, but he quickly estimated the values. He took the *Pferd* to a safer altitude and ran it through a speed test.

As nearly as he could tell, the machine was able to attain a speed in excess of three hundred kilometres per hour! When he had it up to speed he had to crouch low over its neck, his cheek pressed to the animal's—the machine's!—coat, its mane whipping the back of his neck. He expected to smell the strong odor of a sweating horse.

Instead, he detected only that of hot machine oil.

He slowed the *Pferd*, put it through a series of aerobatic exercises that would have done Max Immelmann proud. As he ran the *Pferd* through its paces, a plan took form in his mind.

The pommel contained a kind of cumulative distance metre and a variation of the familiar earth inductor compass. He read the distance metre, then returned his attention to testing the *Pferd*'s capabilities and familiarizing himself with its operation.

After he had completed a new and complex series of aerobatics, he examined the metre again. It showed a lower reading than previously. What could that mean? He studied the instrument. Yes. The metre must have been set at its upper limit, when last the *fliegende Pferd* received its fuel or charge of power.

The lower figure represented remaining power.

He translated that into range, sucked his teeth in pleasure. If the *fliegende Pferd* could travel that distance without another charge, his plan was feasible.

Looking down, he saw his fingers dancing across the instrument panel as if they were celebrating a triumph.

He took the horse up several thousand metres. He was most accustomed to seeing the earth from an altitude of five thousand to seven thousand metres, and he was most confident of flying well at that altitude. He took a last downward look at the pond.

Arawn had landed safely. Well, that was fine. He had no particular interest in the Valkyrie, but neither did he bear her ill will. It was not Manfred von Richthofen's way to wish others evil, unless they interfered in some manner with his reaching his own goals. Then, let them beware!

The monoplane floated near the edge of the pond, apparently in enough water to keep it safely level. Von Richthofen was too high in the air to see objects the size of human figures on the ground.

His long fingers danced up and down the neck of the *Pferd*.

He took a reading on the magnetic compass, adjusted the earth inductor and headed northward.

The warmth of the machine between his knees kept him half comfortable. He set a fair speed, crouching low in the saddle to minimize the discomfort—and drag—that would come from exposure to the slipstream. His eyes stung and watered. Even with its heater roaring, the *Pferd* began to ice up on its ears and mane and wingtips. Von Richthofen dropped to a lower altitude. He reached forward and knocked away some of the ice with his knuckles.

Beneath him the forests and swamps of Svartalheim spun past, like images on a screen. Except for the wind, he could imagine that he was standing in midair, the *Pferd* hovering like a super-autogyro while the tree-covered landscape unrolled. The swamps were fewer now, giving way to meadows and rolling hills.

He surveyed the sky around him, his heart leaping and his lungs filled with the clean morning air. There were a few black dots in the distance. They seemed stationary, but von Richthofen knew better. There was not a cloud visible.

Ahead of him the rolling hills gave way to a range of low mountains, old mountains, worn down by millions upon millions of years of snow and rain and wind.

Somewhere there is a mountain a thousand kilometres high...

He wondered where he had picked up that notion. Probably from one of the Kaiser's effete philosophical cronies.

And once every thousand years a little bird comes to that mountain to sharpen its beak by rubbing it on the peak...

Von Richthofen squinted against the slipstream and studied the black dots hovering ahead of him, above the mountaintops. They were no more than specks. But they were larger specks now than they had been.

And when the little bird has completely worn away the mountain by sharpening its beak, a single moment will have passed in eternity.

Von Richthofen made a rude sound with his mouth, and his fingers lifted from the horse's neck to make an angry gesture. Where had he accumulated such intellectual rubbish, indeed!

He slapped himself on the chest to set the blood flowing, the skin tingling, to keep from going stale in the saddle. He dropped his free hand to his side, slapping his leg. His fingers, like independent creatures, checked to ascertain that he still wore his borrowed sword tucked in his belt in lieu of a scabbard.

Borrowed? Well, the owner of the sword—what was his name, Mider? No, that was the unfortunate *Truppenführer*. No, it was Balor. *Ja*, and he was now at the bottom of a lake of quicksand near the wizard Lodur's pond. Manfred decided that he could forget about returning the sword.

He laughed.

Those fingers of his closed around the hilt, drew the sword and hefted it. *Ach*, it was an ungainly piece of workmanship. But, *ach*, it was good anyway to hold a sword in his hand, feel a horse—even a metal one—between his legs. Like this he could be a knight of the days of Barbarossa.

The mountain range was drawing close, and the hovering black spots above it had grown large. Von Richthofen could make them out, now, as birds. Definitely, birds of prey. Well, that was natural. The lower slopes showed a definite timber line, and lower still the timber gave way to grassy slopes. Perfect home for small game, and where there was game there would be predators.

Such was nature's plan.

One of the birds swooped downward. It was close enough that he could make out its shape. It tilted, held out its head, tucked its wings against its body and plummeted. Once it unfolded its wings, altered its course, swept the air to increase its speed, then plummeted again.

Von Richthofen tried to see its prey. Was some hare or wild sheep grazing stupidly on a meadow? No! There was another bird, flying perhaps a thousand metres lower. The predator—at least a large falcon, possibly a mountain eagle—was aiming at it.

What eyes, to spot a victim at such range!

The intended victim sensed the presence of its enemy. It tried to evade the diving predator, but it was too late. The eagle—von Richthofen decided that it was indeed an eagle—struck like a blacksmith's hammer.

The victim had no chance.

A few feathers flew.

The eagle rose, its prey in its talons, and drove for altitude. It headed back toward the mountains, toward its nest, for a feast. Perhaps to share its meal with young.

Something made von Richthofen snap his eyes away from the successful hunter, and look above his own head. Something black and frightening was dropping toward him. He had time only to jerk his body sideways. Reflexively, he tugged on the reins.

The attacking eagle glanced off the side of the *fliegende Pferd*. The sound of razor-sharp claws on fabric-covered plates was like that of a railroad train's metal wheels screaming over frozen iron tracks. A wolfish expression crossed the Baron's face.

He scanned the sky in all directions. Perhaps this bird was the mate of the first he had seen. They seemed to hunt separately; no other bird was nearby.

The hunter that had attacked him skittered and tumbled through the air, then quickly righted itself. It was shocked but uninjured.

Von Richthofen steadied his horse, leveled its flight, drove toward the bird. He held his sword at the ready.

The bird swung around and stared at him, unafraid.

They flew at each other like jousters in a tourney.

At a distance of only a few metres the bird swung up, presenting its vulnerable underside to von Richthofen. He lunged at the bird to spit it on the tip of his sword.

The bird slipped sideways, raked at his arm with its claws as they whizzed past each other.

A searing pain streaked up von Richthofen's arm and he dropped the reins from his other hand, clutching at his wound. The eagle's claws had ripped through his sleeve and torn a row of red furrows up his arm. He was fortunate that the bird's claws had gone no deeper. As it was, he would lose a little blood and would be sore once the wound began to close, but he had not lost the use of his arm. Or of his sword.

He swung the *fliegende Pferd* around.

The eagle had recovered also, had regained its steady course and was already driving toward him. This time, as the bird approached, von Richthofen jerked back on his horse's reins instead of lunging with his sword.

The *Pferd* jolted back and up at the impact of the eagle on its belly. Again there was the screech of claws against fabric-covered metal.

Von Richthofen flicked the reins. The *Pferd* nosed over. As he expected, the eagle was tumbling helplessly, thirty metres below him. He dived, calling on the full power of the machine.

As he drove past the bird he would swing his heavy Svartalheimer blade, using it this time to slice rather than to spit. The bird had nearly recovered itself. A shred of fabric hung from one talon. It had leveled off and spread its wings to regain lost stability.

Von Richthofen swung his sword.

The bird yielded with a crunch that filled von Richthofen's ears and a jolt of impact that ran up his arm and shuddered his torso.

The bird tumbled away, cut neatly in two.

Now von Richthofen drew level, watched the black speck of the eagle disappear beneath him, tugged back on his reins to regain his former altitude.

The duel had carried him into the mountains. He examined both compasses, directed his mount through a pass between two snow-covered peaks. The air was chill here, and a few clouds drifted among the mountains. Von Richthofen plunged through one such. He had cleaned his heavy sword as best he could, and sheathed it again in his belt.

As the *Pferd* emerged from the vertiginous pass he saw the land below fall away toward a field of white. It was the frozen sea where the *Kondor* was staked down!

Manfred von Richthofen stood in the cabin of the giant plane. He pondered briefly what he would do if the aeroplane were in working order. Continue the circumpolar flight, even though he knew there was little chance of victory? Turn back toward the *Symmeshoehle?* Fly to Svartalheim and persuade the Princess and his *Bruder* Lothar to return with him to Tempelhof?

No matter. It was all idle speculation. The *Kondor* was as hopelessly unflyable and irreparable as if it had smashed against a mountainside or disappeared beneath the waves.

Still, what could not be repaired could at least serve as a source for salvage.

He searched the cabin carefully and found a fresh set of warm flying clothes for himself. There was even a leather flying-helmet, complete with goggles!

He set these things aside, located the *Kondor*'s medical kit, and set to work on his arm. He stripped away his torn shirt, swabbed the wounds with disinfectant. A gasp of pain escaped his lips as he cleaned out the gashes. He took bandages and wrapped the arm carefully. It was clumsy work, acting as doctor and patient at the same time, but he got the job done.

He had deactivated the *fliegende Pferd* and tied its reins to the *Kondor*'s wing-strut. The only danger there was that the horse's warm hooves might melt into the ice, then freeze in place. But he did not plan to remain here long enough for that to happen. It was already late afternoon and he wanted to arrive at the *Symmeshoehle* at dusk.

With his arm disinfected and bandaged he sat down to a meal of leftover supplies. He downed a hearty belt of *Schnaps* to keep him warm. Then he climbed into the flying suit. He pulled the leather helmet over his head, slipped the bottle of *Schnaps* into his pocket and closed the flap to keep it secure.

Then he made his final, vital search of the *Kondor*'s interior and found what he knew he must: a Mauser pistol, clean and oiled, and a box of ammunition. He loaded the pistol, strapped its holster to the leg of his flying suit, dropped extra ammunition into his pocket. He fixed the heavy Svartalheimer sword to his side also, swung open the door and stood—aghast!

His *fliegende Pferd* was gone!

He leaped from the *Kondor*, ran clumsily to the place where he had left the *Pferd*. There were parallel furrows in the ice, showing where the *Pferd* had been dragged away.

Von Richthofen set out at a trot, following the trail. His head spun. He dared not run at top speed. He didn't know how far he would have to pursue the machine and those who had stolen it from him. There was no point in racing until he fell exhausted.

And yet he must overtake the thieves! Without the *Pferd* he was lost—stranded. The *Kondor* could not fly again, and he had no other means of escaping the ice.

The trail of the machine led through a region of uneven ice, jagged hillocks and broken floes. In places the trail became confused. It disappeared, reappeared, doubled upon itself.

Where it swerved around a greenish ice-hill he climbed to the peak instead of following the track. From the top of the hill he could see the shadow of the *Pferd* and of the thieves in the afternoon sunlight. He half-slid, half-rolled down the farther side of the hill and jogged after his prey.

He shouted after the thieves. "*Halt! Halt!*" They turned to look at him. Men all in white, dragging the dark-hued *Pferd* away from him. He drew his pistol and brandished it so they could see it.

"*Stehenleiben!*" he commanded. *Stay there!*

When he had halved the distance between himself and the thieves he realized they were not men but demons—the white demons that Irina had encountered during her visit. The giant batrachians that she had confronted and one of which she had slain with nothing more than her *Kaiserdolch*. If a woman could defeat one of these monsters with only a dagger, surely the great Baron need not use a firearm against them.

He slid his pistol back into its holster and drew his sword.

The closest demon turned and launched itself at him.

Von Richthofen greeted it with a great sweeping underhand blow of his weapon. Thc bladc caught the monster beneath the ribs and tore upward, spilling viscera and pale juices.

The creature collapsed at von Richthofen's feet.

A second monster came at him. Clearly they possessed little intelligence, and no notion of military teamwork. The Baron met the charge of the creature with a downward stroke, splitting its skull and spilling its small brain onto the snow. The creature ceased its charge and began to wander aimlessly. The destruction of its brain had robbed it of its purpose but not of its life. It waved its webbed hands senselessly, walked a few paces past von Richthofen, turned and wandered in another direction, halted, turned around in circles, finally wandered away.

The remaining monsters stood beside the *fliegende Pferd* watching von Richthofen. He raised his sword, swung it around his head so its blade caught the declining sunlight. He roared at the pallid demons, then ran at them. In panic they dropped to their haunches and sprang away in great bounds. They emitted a bass thrumming as they went.

He shoved his sword back into his belt, examined the *Pferd* and found it undamaged. He climbed into the saddle, studied the compasses. There was no need now to return to the *Kondor*. He activated the *Pferd*, trotted across the snow briefly, then leaped into the air.

When he reached the *Symmeshoehle* he soared toward the center of the opening, then sent his *fliegende Pferd* into a dive. He needed to reach the midpoint as quickly as possible. Once there, he slowed the *Pferd* and set it to circle the circumference of the *Hoehle*. Soon the sun would rise in his home hemidisk, and soon the *Spirit of San Diego*, he expected, would become visible, rising through the *Hoehle*.

Von Richthofen gazed back. The first gray dawn had already appeared beneath him. By the time the Ryan monoplane drew near, von Richthofen would be waiting, hidden in the glare of the sun. It was a tactic that had served him well in the time of the *Einjahrkrieg*. The American crew would not see him, but he would see the Ryan, sunlight glancing back from its metal wings.

They would never know he was coming for them.

Chapter 25

"Why do you think Lodur let us go? I don't particularly like that gink, and I sure don't trust him any farther'n I can throw him!"

Lindbergh, seated beside Hughes, said, "Why shouldn't he let us go? What does he care about us?"

Before Hughes could answer, Amelia Earhart said, "What does he care? I'll tell you what he cares *about*. First of all, these Svartalheimers are a throwback to the Germanic tradition of centuries ago. Sorcerers, gothic chalets, knightly traditions. We were a fly in their ointment. We introduced new factors, we messed things up. If Lodur is as much of a bigshot around here as he seems, he'll be pleased to be rid of us."

"Yeh," Howard snorted. "But I think he'd be more inclined to stick a knife between our ribs and get rid of us that way."

"And bringing Cuchaviva with us," Lindy added, "and that rascal Nikar. You see, we involved ourselves in his country's affairs. Even if we didn't mean to, we got ourselves in deep."

"That's right," Howard conceded. "But what about Cuchaviva? Where'd she go? I've never seen a frail take a powder faster than she did. One minute, in the thick of things in that creepy witchhouse. The next—*whoosh!*"

Amelia said, "I can answer that one, Howard. She went to look for her husband."

"Just like that? In a foreign country, thousands of miles from home, all alone? She just went looking for the guy?"

"She's a determined woman. I feel guilty about it, about letting her go like that. But she had made up her mind, and somehow . . ."

Lindbergh and Hughes turned expectantly toward Amelia.

"Don't laugh at feminine intuition, you two swashbuckling he-men. Somehow, I know she's going to find him."

Hughes said, "Okay! But *I'll* tell *you* guys something. I wouldn't trust them Svartalheimers. They're just a bunch of krauts as far as I'm concerned, and I still think they're out to take over the whole damn disk!"

Amelia's grin was sour. "You seemed to hit it off very nicely with *Hauptmann* von Richthofen, Howard. If he was just a kraut, and you think he's out to conquer the disk. You managed to overcome the language barrier and the difference in your ages very nicely."

Hughes reddened. "We was just swapping propwash, that's all. Don't mean I trust the gink any. It was just a lot of fighter-jockey talk. Born ten years too late, that's me. Man, if I could only have swapped places with Jax Bullard in the big war!"

"Tell you what, Howard. Why don't you swap places with me right now. You lost a lot of blood and you need to rest." Amelia took Hughes's seat, nodded to Lindy and concentrated on flying the Ryan. The night sky was clear and bright. The outside air was bitterly cold. Even now its bite penetrated the Ryan's fabric skin and chilled the fliers even through their padded suits. But the air was as dry as bone. There was no present risk of icing, and that was important.

"Do you think Lothar was telling us the truth about his brother?" Amelia asked. "He certainly put on a convincing show of grief, I know. But still . . ."

"I know," Hughes grumbled, "feminine intuition. What do *you* think happened to Manfred?"

"I have no idea. I'm just not convinced that he's dead."

Lindbergh said, "You don't think we ought to look for him?"

Hughes growled. "Don't anybody remember, we're in a race? You two can play lord and lady bountiful if you want, but *I* got my eye on sixteen thousand, six hundred 'n' sixty-six fish, courtesy of Mrs. Victoria Woodhull Martin. I can just see her front man standing there when we hit the strip in San Diego. And all this other stuff can wait, as far as I'm concerned."

"That's fair enough, Howard. But you know you're being short-sighted. Those greenbacks will be nice, but they're nothing compared to what's going to happen, once we open up commerce between the hemidisks."

"Huh! Tourists!"

"Well, tourists, yes. But what's important is their science. What they have that we lack, and vice versa. Look at the way the Muiaians modified this aircraft. If we can import their magnetic engines, or get a license to build our own, think of what it will mean to aviation! The world will be spanned with safe, quick, cheap airliners!

"And as for your so-called dumb krauts, Howard . . ." He reached back and patted the *fliegende Pferd* that still stood in the Ryan's cabin.

"They're no bunch of medieval peasants, Howard!"

"Aah, they sure looked like it."

"Then explain the horse. An artificial beast with a self-contained power-plant. Capable not only of locomotion but of flight. There's a lot more to those folk than meets the eye. We haven't heard the last of Svartalheim.

"And as for the rest of this hemidisk—think of it, hundreds of different countries, each with its own history, its own science—we've found a whole new world!"

Over the barely audible hum of the Muiaian engine and the high harmonies of the slipstream, an almost subsonic rumble had become audible.

"I think we're near the Hole," Amelia said.

"Okay." Lindbergh shifted his weight. "The ship should be able to handle that. We planned it with Bowlus and Hall."

The Ryan sped through the night, white ice-fields beneath its metal wings reflecting the bright moonlight. The monoplane's running lights resembled brilliant shooting stars. Her silent engine ran smoothly. The whine of the propeller and the night air singing in the struts rose over the rumble of the maelstrom like a soprano choir over a great bass organ.

Close to the Hole, winds buffeted the monoplane. "I think I'd better take her up," Amelia said. She pulled back on the stick and the Ryan raised its nose toward a distant glimmering spark. She throttled up to prevent the *Spirit* from losing airspeed.

"Wow, look at that!" Hughes pointed down.

The waters swirling around the lip of the North Hole were visible by moonlight, occasional chunks of ice the size of small glaciers spinning in the rushing brine. Through the five hundred miles of space in the center of the Hole, mist and clouds drifted leisurely, but there were sufficient rifts in the vapor to show a dim gray background.

"It's early morning over there," Lindy commented. "By the time we get through the Hole it should be high noon! Home in time for lunch, eh?"

He grinned happily. Then, more seriously, "Amelia, did Cuchaviva give you any idea how long we're good for? When do we have to refuel, or charge up, or whatever you do?"

"No time soon. If ever. These engines draw power from the earth's magnetic field. As long as it's there, we can fly."

"Holy smoke," Hughes grimaced. "Perpetual motion! Next you'll buy the Brooklyn Bridge or tell me that the earth is a sphere instead of a disk!"

"Not quite, Howard. But you can never tell." She laughed. She dropped the Ryan's nose and cut power to the prop so it did little more than windmill. She swung the craft into a long, gentle bank above swirling brine. The water rushed beneath the Ryan's hull, green-blue, spotted with chunks of floating ice the size of Kansas barns. She checked the instruments and leaned back in her seat.

"Nothing to do for a few hours. Then we'll have to flip and climb again."

The opening of the North Hole, now far above them, showed a circle of night sky, its blackness dotted with stars. A moon should be high over the hemidisk they had left, but it was not visible from deep in the Hole.

Beneath them the opening to their home hemidisk grew brighter, its misty gray turning gradually to a pale blue.

Occasionally some great sea animal surfaced in the swirling brine. They passed an iceberg where a family of sea lions cavorted. The largest of them, a huge-bodied old male, halted in his tracks and reared back, gazing after the *Spirit of San Diego*. Standing upright the creature was nearly twenty feet tall. It opened its great-tusked mouth in a roar of defiance as the Ryan swept past.

Howard Hughes rummaged through their supplies, slid open a window and flung a scrap of food down to the lions. The monoplane was past their floating iceberg before the animals had time to retrieve the tribute.

Now there was more ice and less clear water with every minute. After a time they were circling past unbroken—but uneven—fields of ice.

Lindbergh leaned from his seat and stared. "*Brrr!* We don't get winters like this even in Minnesota! I wonder if any Esquimaux ever get swept over the edge and wind up here."

"Huh!" Hughes grunted. "Don't suppose they'd last very long if they did! But, say, take a look out there! *Somebody* lives on this ice. Or some *thing!*"

A great white creature, a worm or centipede or caterpillar, reared blindly, groping toward the *Spirit*.

"Keep 'er up, Amy, unless you want to be worm food today!"

She slowed the *Spirit*'s descent, then ceased to drop altogether. The slowly turning propeller continued to pull the plane in a great, gentle, circular path.

"Bargain basement," Amy announced. "Men's braces, shooting sticks, superhets, and ladies' unmentionables."

"I'm glad you mentioned unmentionables," Hughes said. "But now that you mention it, how do we handle this? Coming through the Rim worked okay, we just kept going. But how to navigate through here?"

"Just hang on and watch my smoke." She wound up the silent power plant until the Ryan's struts were screaming through the cold air, then executed a perfect Immelmann turn. When she leveled off again the Ryan was back in its long, gently-banked course.

"Hey, hold on!" Hughes complained. "How'd you do that? You

didn't do *nothing!*" He peered through the windscreen, then out the side window. "Wait a minute, you *did* do something. Only what the hey did you *do?*"

When she didn't answer he stared through the windscreen longer, then through the window in the Ryan's roof, frowning. "O-o-o-h-*kay!* I see what you did!"

Lindy prompted him. "What, Howard?"

"Look up there." Hughes pointed. "It's blue. It was night above us when we went into the Hole, now it's night down there." He pointed. "And blue up there!"

"That's right!" Amelia beamed. "When we finish climbing we'll be over the Hole and ready to head south."

Later the ice turned back to swirling brine. The circle of blue grew larger. The sun peeped over the edge of the Hole, proof that it was high noon where they were soon to emerge. The brilliant illumination, reflecting off the blue-green brine, filled the Hole with weirdly dancing lights and images.

Lindbergh leaned over the instruments. "We should be out in another minute," he announced.

"What!" Strangled gasps escaped Earhart and Hughes at once. A chunk of blackness, silhouetted against the glare from above the Ryan, swooped at the monoplane. There was a thump and a shudder. The black object was gone. The monoplane settled back onto its course.

"What was that?"

There was another thump and the Ryan shuddered again. This time the black object swept past from rear to front. Through the Ryan's windscreen they could see it, a shape like a horse and rider. The horse was dead black, winged, and left a redly glowing trail behind it.

The rider, even more incredibly, seemed to be a knight in armor, complete with shining sword.

"Holy cow!" Hughes jumped to his feet. "That's the mate of our toy horse! How the hey? Swede, what'd that Rhine maiden gal tell you about them things? Whatever it was, there's our answer to what happened to Manfred. He wasn't killed in no explosion. He's got a sword in his hand and he's after us!"

"Oh-oh, more trouble!"

The aerial horseman had swung about and was charging the Ryan from a half-mile's distance. "He'll kill himself," Lindy exclaimed. "Arawn told me that the other *fliegende Pferd* was missing. That means flying horse. But what's the man *doing?*"

"He's chopping at our control surfaces," Amelia shouted. "If he gets a cable—"

"Can't we fly like an autogyro, with the new engine?"

"I'd hate to risk it! And he could just keep attacking!"

"And we got no weapons on this ship! Damn, if only Jax Bullard was here!"

"We *do* have weapons." Lindbergh slipped out of his seat. "Howard. take my place. You're Miss Earhart's copilot now. Just hold on and try to evade him, Amy!"

He scrambled to the rear of the cabin, opened the Ryan's big tool locker, rummaged inside. "Here's what I wanted! Couldn't ask for more—a crowbar!" He hefted the heavy metal rod. "Come on, Howard, lend a hand before *mein Herr Baron* gets us for good!"

Hughes grabbed Amelia's shoulder. "Got him in your sights?"

"There he is," she pointed. The black *fliegende Pferd* was climbing again, its widespread wings and bulky-suited rider silhouetted against the glaring sun. The mouth of the Hole glittered blue-green and white.

"Okay. Just keep us airborne!" Hughes made his way back to Lindbergh and the second *fliegende Pferd.* Lindbergh was already sliding the machine toward the cabin door. "You've never flown one of them things," Hughes charged. "What do you know about it? You won't have a chance!"

Lindbergh shook his head. "Arawn gave me a briefing back in the swamp. And the instruments are marked in Old Nordic so I can read 'em, at least. I'll manage. I'm a quick study. Besides, von Richthofen can't have had much practice either, and he seems to be doing all right."

"Yeah. How many combat missions did *you* have in the war?"

"As many as you, Howard! So just get the door!" Lindbergh climbed into the saddle of the *Pferd*, activated its power supply, began setting controls.

"God bless you, Swede," Hughes muttered. He had the door

unlatched. Impulsively he turned and hugged the blond flier. "Give him a kick in the ass for me!"

He slid the door open.

Lindy inched forward. He held the reins in his left hand, the crowbar in his right so it lay lightly across his lap.

The *fliegende Pferd* slid from the cabin. For a fraction of a second it seemed to hover outside the door, then tumbled away.

At the same moment the other *fliegende Pferd* completed its climb and circled, and dropped once more from out of the blinding sunlight. Von Richthofen headed at the *Spirit* from one o'clock high, a black silhouette of a balloonlike man sitting a coal-black, winged horse.

His heavy sword glinted in the sunlight.

Earhart watched von Richthofen's dive as Howard Hughes struggled with the door. She couldn't tell whether von Richthofen had seen Charles Lindbergh dropping away from the *Spirit of San Diego.* Von Richthofen headed straight for the airplane. If he had seen Lindberg, he ignored him.

At the latest possible moment, von Richthofen pulled up and passed above the Ryan's wing. Earhart lost sight of him but thought, *He must be going for the tail.* She pulled the Ryan into a nearly vertical climb. There was a bump and a shudder. She kept the stick pulled all the way back and power at its maximum.

"Either he got us or we got him!"

The Ryan held its posture for a moment. Then it tilted over and fell backwards, belly up.

"You should of warned me," Hughes yelled. He clung to a cabin-brace.

The plane slipped past the horizontal, into a dive. "There. Look! Our elevator-plane must have caught his horse's legs!"

Earhart pointed.

The *fliegende Pferd,* von Richthofen still in its saddle, was tumbling. A similar figure of horse and rider circled warily a hundred yards away.

"At least we bought Charles a little time. Now it's up to him." Amelia brought the Ryan through the last few degrees of its inside loop and leveled off. "I'm glad this ship can stand up to aerobatics. I was afraid we were going to lose our wings."

* * *

Seated on his *fliegende Pferd*, Lindy let go his breath, relieved at the escape of the Ryan from von Richthofen. He watched the Baron get his horse under control and level off. If von Richthofen didn't see him, and returned to attack the *Spirit*, Lindbergh could come at him from the rear...

He rubbed the back of his hand across his forehead, still gripping the crowbar. That would be a cowardly way to fight. He'd have to challenge von Richthofen, face off against him.

No! That wasn't right either! This wasn't any knightly joust. It was bloody war on a miniature scale, the loser to forfeit his life!

Well, that was academic. Von Richthofen had spotted him. The Baron turned his mount and faced toward Lindbergh. Lindy couldn't see the other man's expression. His face was partly coverd by a flying helmet, and the distance was too great. That glint might have been from bared teeth for all Lindbergh could tell.

Lindbergh raised his crowbar and waved it.

Von Richthofen did the same with his sword. He kept his other hand in his lap, holding the reins of his *Pferd*, just as Lindbergh did with his. Von Richthofen started forward.

Lindy watched, then drove his own *Pferd* toward the enemy. He held his crowbar at the ready. The *Spirit* was circling somewhere nearby. Lindy caught a glimpse of the plane from one corner of his eye. There was nothing that Howard or Amelia could do for him now.

The black silhouette of von Richthofen grew as it raced toward Lindbergh. There was misty darkness beneath his horse's hoofs, blue brilliance above, green rumbling brine to the side.

The horses approached left-to-left. Was that the way they did it in the feudal tourneys, Lindy wondered. Before he could give the matter thought, von Richthofen was upon him. Lindy saw the heavy sword descending, raised his crowbar and deflected its slash.

There was a shock in Lindy's arm, and the other horse and rider were gone. His *Pferd* swerved, plunged toward green water. He pulled back on the reins, managed to get the horse's nose up and headed away from disaster.

He swung around.

Von Richthofen had swerved in the opposite direction, toward the center of the Hole. Lindy saw him circle and head for him again. He headed out toward the other *Pferd.*

For an instant the two horses hovered, their riders holding back on their reins. Von Richthofen raised his hand to his brow. Was he wiping moisture from his goggles, or—?

Lindy realized that the Baron was saluting him, mimicking the gesture of a jousting knight as he raised the visor of his helmet.

Lindbergh responded.

They dropped their hands, lifted reins and moved toward each other again. Lindy leaned over his horse's neck, reducing the air resistance and offering a smaller target for von Richthofen's sword.

Like a pair of speeding locomotives approaching on adjoining tracks, the two metal horses sped together. Lindbergh kept his eyes trained on von Richthofen's sword and on the arm and hand holding the weapon, alert for any sign of the other's intent.

Von Richthofen held the blade level with the plane of his charge, like a jouster's lance.

Lindbergh knew that this would make a tougher attack. The onrushing sword offered a small target for any deflecting blow, and if it reached his body with the combined force of the two machines there was no question that he'd be spitted like a chicken.

He leveled his crowbar. Its tip was divided like the claws of a hammer, and while the bar had no cutting edge it could be used as a piercing weapon as effectively as von Richthofen's sword—possibly more so, thanks to its massive shaft.

The horses were twenty yards apart now...

Ten...

Lindbergh gave a tiny tug at the reins of his *Pferd.* The horse swerved a few inches, sideways and down.

The two riders flashed past each other.

Lindbergh lunged upward with his makeshift spear. At the same time he saw von Richthofen swing his sword, readjusting his aim for Lindy's maneuver.

The sword's tip missed Lindbergh by a fraction. Its edge caught the fabric of his flying jacket and tore away a chunk of sleeve. At the same time Lindbergh felt an impact and a hot pain in his thigh.

He heard an explosive, momentary roar, felt a terrible wrench as his crowbar struck not von Richthofen but von Richthofen's *Pferd.*

The crowbar was torn from Lindbergh's grip. It went tumbling away, back down the North Hole toward the ring of ice that marked the halfway point of transit. As it fell the bar was a simple black line twisting against the grayish mists and the black sky of the far hemidisk. It glinted once as it caught the rays of the overhead sun and was turned for a part of a second into a glowing golden hyphen.

Then it disappeared.

Lindbergh looked at his injured arm. The wound seemed to be a clean slice, not deep. It bled spectacularly but Lindy knew just enough about anatomy and of first aid to realize that no major blood vessel had been cut. The question was whether his nerves and muscles still functioned.

He moved his arm, wriggled his fingers.

They obeyed.

He scanned the Hole for von Richthofen, spotted him a quarter-mile away performing his own damage inspection. Lindbergh bared his teeth. There was a hot, throbbing pain in his leg a few inches below the hip. He looked at von Richthofen again to make sure he wasn't charging.

In fact, the Baron was having trouble with his *Pferd.* It would make a short charge in one direction, then halt suddenly, twist, leap sideways, charge again.

Von Richthofen had his hands full.

Lindbergh inspected his leg. There was a small hole in his flying suit. Its edges were blackened and still smoking slightly. He probed through it with one finger, winced and jerked his hand back.

That hurt!

He tried again, gently, carefully, and confirmed what he by now had deduced. He'd been shot. Obviously, von Richthofen had held a pistol across his lap, in the same hand that grasped the reins of his *Pferd.* As they passed, Lindbergh concentrating on von Richthofen's sword, the Baron had shot him!

Lindy swung his *fliegende Pferd* around, searching for the *Spirit of San Diego.* If only there were some way to use the Ryan as a fighter! He spotted it, circling overhead. But it was useless, unarmed.

He searched for von Richthofen. The Baron was still having trouble with his *Pferd.* It shuddered visibly, tipped forty-five degrees and circled slowly.

Now what to do? Before Lindy could decide, von Richthofen took action. He slid his sword into his belt, raised both hands pointing a tiny black object toward Lindbergh. There was a puff of smoke from the muzzle of the weapon and a bullet whizzed past Lindbergh's head. The sound of the explosion followed the bullet by a fraction of a second.

Lindy put his *Pferd* into a dive, headed toward the swirling brine of the Hole, then realized his mistake and cut back for the center of the shaft. If von Richthofen pursued, Lindy didn't want to offer a silhouette against white ice. Better to hope for concealment in the thick mist.

He looked back over his shoulder. Above him von Richthofen struggled with his horse. Higher still the *Spirit of San Diego* circled silently.

Von Richthofen got off another shot. It missed.

The *Spirit* banked, pointed its nose at von Richthofen and dived.

Von Richthofen's horse spun on its own long axis and Lindbergh could see the rider clinging desperately. The *Spirit* swooped past him and another puff of smoke sprang from the Baron's weapon.

The *Spirit* zoomed past von Richthofen. His *Pferd* swung more wildly than ever. Lindy realized what Amy was doing: using the plane's wash to throw von Richthofen into wilder and wilder gyrations.

The Baron partially steadied his horse, swung his Mauser and fired at Lindbergh. He missed. The Ryan climbed, banked, then dived.

Lindbergh saw von Richthofen struggling with the pommel of his *Pferd.*

The Ryan shot past him.

The Baron's horse shook violently. He pulled back on the reins but instead of responding the *Pferd* dipped and plunged at Lindbergh. Lindy pulled his own *Pferd* sideways.

The Baron toppled.

Lindy knew that the other man was doomed, there was no way he could survive a crash of his machine into the brine or onto the ice.

He cupped his hands around his mouth and shouted at the top of his lungs.

"*Springen Sie! Springen Sie!*"

The Baron seemed to understand. It was a desperate chance, to leap from his own *fliegende Pferd* to Lindbergh's as he flashed by, but the alternative was certain doom.

Von Richthofen raised himself in the stirrups, placed one booted foot in the saddle, launched himself toward his enemy.

Lindbergh dropped his reins, rose in his stirrups, leaned and held out his arms to catch the flying body.

Von Richthofen raised his pistol and pulled the trigger.

The shot clipped Lindbergh's flying jacket and grazed his ribs.

It also sent von Richthofen tumbling with its recoil. The Baron and his useless *fliegende Pferd* rushed past Lindbergh. Von Richthofen, fury in his features, hurled the pistol at Lindbergh.

It fell short and tumbled toward the swirling brine.

Lindbergh watched the three figures falling. The Mauser disappeared first. Von Richthofen and the *Pferd* dwindled more slowly.

Lindy thought he could see the horse shaking, tumbling, starting to glow. The horse and tumbling rider dwindled further. They were two specks against the mist, then one speck.

Then a blinding glare like a miniature sun bloomed in the center of the North Hole. It glowed for a few seconds, or perhaps that was merely an afterimage seared into Lindbergh's vision.

He blinked, blinked, seeing nothing but the glowing dot, cold white against greenish-black. He leaned over the neck of his horse and hung there, pressing his face deep into the creature's artificial mane. His stomach heaved but nothing came up.

He leaned back and found that he had recovered enough vision to recognize the *Spirit of San Diego*.

He raised the nose of his *Pferd* and climbed carefully back toward the *Spirit*. By the time he had drawn level with it, Amy had halted its circling and was using the Muiaian power plant to make the plane hover. He could see her face through the Ryan's windscreen. Howard Hughes was signaling.

The reaction to his adrenaline-jag started to settle in. The Ryan wavered before his eyes but he managed to steer the *fliegende Pferd* to it. Howard Hughes had the cabin door open for him. Lindbergh maneuvered the horse through the opening, then sat still in the saddle, too weak to speak or to dismount.

From behind him he heard Hughes grunt as he dogged the door shut. Then those strong, calloused hands were lifting him from the saddle and laying him gently on the floor of the cabin.

Amelia's voice, from the distance of a million miles, floated to Lindbergh. "Take the controls, Howard," she said. "Let me get at Charles's wounds. I'll bring the first-aid kit. Just get us over the edge and head for home. It should be as simple as flying the mails, from here."

Lindy let his eyes slide shut. Not that he had any choice in the matter, not by now.

Chapter 26

Ernst Udet and *Graf* Hans Bodo von Alvensleben were comfortably settled in plush chairs, a polished table between them, cigars and brandy in hand, when the message arrived. It was brought by a consular employee who coughed politely to gain their attention, clicked his heels and bowed, once recognized.

"*Mein Herren*," the worker said, "word from the radio room." He bowed a second time, more stiffly than the first, and extended to them a sealed envelope.

Bodo waved the man away. With Udet in close attendance he opened the envelope and spread a sheet of flimsy. From inside his morning coat he extracted a small alligator-covered code book and gold pencil. After a few moments of work he looked up. Udet met his eye.

"*Schlecht*," Bodo muttered, "*Sehr schlecht!*" He turned the flimsy so Udet could make out the message, its translation from code penciled now beneath the original.

"*Wirklich schlecht*." Udet agreed. "Bad indeed! No sign yet of the *Schwarze Adler*. And now Novaya Zemlya reports that the enemy plane has been sighted emerging from the North Hole! The race is lost, *mein Herr*. Even if our people cross the Rim now, it will take them longer in the duplicate *Kondor* to reach Tempelhof, than the Americans to reach San Diego!"

He strode to the fireplace where a crackling blaze strove to dispel the chill of Buenos Aires in autumn. He threw his cigar into the flames and gazed moodily after it, then spun and faced Count Alvensleben. "There is hope yet, *mein Herr*. If you will authorize me to act—"

Alvensleben looked up. He spoke no words, but an upraised eyebrown and a shoulder lifted in a barely perceptible gesture commanded the aviator to continue.

"We can leave Buenos Aires at once in the second *Kondor*. I will pilot it myself. I did so enough times in testing. The aeroplane is fully fueled. Our staff here efficiently purchased petrol from the American fleet at Tierra del Fuego. Their Captain Jarrold was happy to provide it. A gesture of good will!"

He laughed mirthlessly.

Alvensleben frowned. "I fail to see the point of this exercise, *Herr* Udet."

"The point is this, Count. There is a little surprise awaiting on board the second *Kondor*. By personal authority of the *Kanzler*, there is installed a light cannon in the plane. We can leave Buenos Aires and refuel at Guayaquil. *Herr* Hentsch and *Monsieur* Chirol will provide us with all that we need. From there it is one more hop to San Diego."

"*Ja*." Alvensleben nodded. "And once there? Are you going to blow up the city? Lay siege to the U.S. naval base there?"

Udet returned to his seat. Although there were no others in the room, he leaned conspiratorily toward Alvensleben and glanced around before speaking. "It would be better, of course, if we knew exactly the Americans' route and their schedule. We may have to intercept the enemy before they reach San Diego. We have no proper combat aircraft available, but with the weapon mounted on my ship, we will blow those fools from the sky!

"Then . . ." He leaned back in his chair, laced his fingers in his lap, continued in his low voice. "Then we continue on to Tempelhof. The Americans, tragically, were lost just when triumph was within their reach. Such incidents are not unprecedented. Think of the unfortunate Frenchmen Nungesser and Coli!

"And our *Kondor* lands in triumph. Germany has won the great circumpolar air race. Think of it, *mein Herr!*"

Graf Alvensleben rubbed his chin meditatively. He dropped his hand and sent Udet a piercing look. "There is one small problem, Ernst. Where are our gallant adventurers? Everyone will want to see the two noble aviators and their beautiful royal passenger. What do we tell the press? Who stands to accept the prize money from *Herrin* Woodhull Martin? Certainly not you?"

Udet shook his head. "A good point, *Graf*. But surely it can be met. It can be arranged for the *Kanzler* to receive the prize money and present it to the fliers. Perhaps even for the Kaiser himself to do it!

"In the meanwhile, the three travelers are exhausted from their heroic ordeal. They have faced glaciers, mountains, deserts. They are in seclusion. They need to regain their vigor. Before they emerge, who knows what can be arranged? The cream of Berlin's theatre and *Kino* studios are available."

Now it was Count Alvensleben's turn to rise and cross the deep carpeting, to stand before the hearth. Unlike Ernst Udet, Alvensleben did not gaze down into the flames. He turned his eyes to the gilt-framed portrait that hung above the fireplace, a portrait of the present Kaiser similar to that which hung in the office of *Kanzler Prinz* von Bismarck ten thousand kilometres away.

The Count gazed upward, peering into the face of the slim, erect figure. He could almost—almost—feel those pale, hard, cold eyes boring back into his own.

"Very well," he whispered.

He spun on his heel and snapped the words a second time. "Very well, Udet. Telephone the aerodrome and command that the *Kondor* be prepared for flight."

"Such is the standing order, Count. The aircraft is kept in readiness constantly, by my personal instructions to the crew."

Bodo nodded and puffed at his cigar.

At the aerodrome the chauffeur maneuvered the Durkopp touring car to the closed hangar where the Udet *Kondor* was kept under armed guard. *Graf* Alvensleben dismissed the car and with Udet entered the huge building. Shortly, the two men stood beneath the wing of the *Kondor*. They were garbed now in standard flying suits of thick leather and heavy wool pile. Both wore warm boots, but for the *Kondor*, thanks to its closed cockpit, aviator's helmets were unnecessary. Instead, each wore a fleecy astrakhan cap.

At Bodo's insistence, both he and Udet climbed aboard the aeroplane before it was wheeled to the runway. The chance of their being seen by anyone who ought not to know of their presence was remote, but Bodo sought to remove all possible risk to their enterprise.

A few hours later the *Kondor* approached Guayaquil.

The airborne cannon had been tested as the giant monoplane crossed the high spine of mountains that runs from Ecuador southward to Patagonia. *Graf* Alvensleben had expressed concern at the jolt to the ship's frame with the firing of each round, but Ernst Udet assured him that the *Kondor*'s all-metal fuselage could withstand all demands placed upon it.

When the *Kondor* was still several hours' flying time from Guayaquil, *Graf* Alvensleben himself spoke with *Herr* Hentsch by radio. There would be no difficulty, Hentsch hastened to assure Alvensleben. M. Chirol would certainly furnish petrol as needed. And he, *Herr* Hentsch, would be honored to provide a basket of food for the Count and *Herr* Udet to carry with them, if they had not time to pause for a meal at Guayaquil.

The great monoplane droned in over granite peaks. It circled above the Pacific briefly to permit a low-altitude run at the makeshift landing field, then dropped toward the ground. Ernst Udet, humming as he handled the controls, sighted on the hastily abandoned soccer field. He laughed as squads of schoolboy athletes scurried to the sidelines, then stood gaping at the buzzing, silvery *Kondor*.

"That will be Hentsch," Alvensleben said, pointing from the copilot's seat. "He is the only one properly attired."

Udet glanced briefly at the dark-coated figure next to the soccer field. He grunted in satisfaction, less at the sight of *Herr* Hentsch than at the white-coveralled man beside him, and the khaki-garbed workers and the row of fuel drums nearby.

"*Herr* Hentsch," Alvensleben added, "will be more than eager to assist us, I am sure, in view of his failure with the enemy."

The *Kondor*'s large wheels touched ground briefly, bounced, then rolled smoothly along the soccer field. The zone-stripes of the field ticked past the cockpit as the aeroplane slowed. Smiling, Udet cut the two port engines, revved the starboard pair and swung the *Kondor* through a perfect ground loop. Behind the monoplane its tailskid left a furrow marking the plane's progress.

Graf Alvensleben and *Herr* Udet climbed from the aeroplane, accepted the greetings of Hentsch, commanded him to have their ship's fuel tanks filled at once. Hentsch signaled to M. Chirol. The Frenchman, without a word to Hentsch or the newcomers, turned to his crew and issued orders in heavily accented Spanish.

While the tanks were being filled with petrol, Hentsch delivered his report to Bodo. No, he had not succeeded in his mission against the enemy. No, he had no excuse to offer. He had thought his plan appropriate. A stroke of ill fortune. How could anyone have anticipated that a *goat*...

Bodo told him that no action would be taken just yet. Decisions would be made at home. But it would be well for Hentsch to prepare himself for recall. Yes, Alvensleben was aware that Hentsch had been in place for a decade and a half. He remained subject to command, would be ill-advised to add insurrection to his charge sheet.

As soon as the aeroplane was ready to depart, Alvensleben and Udet climbed aboard. Hentsch they left staring morosely after them.

The *Kondor* taxied to an advantageous position. Udet gunned the engines and the aeroplane roared forward, lifted from the ground and rose heavily into the air.

Swinging again over the cold Pacific, Udet maneuvered the *Kondor* to a northwesterly course. In time the Panama Canal glinted beneath the plane's starboard wing. With instructions from Udet, Count Alvensleben operated the *Kondor*'s radio beacon homing device, locating the transmitter at Colón in the Canal Zone.

They continued, following the shoreline as it marked the small nations of Central America, then Mexico. More radio transmissions were picked up at Zihuatanejo and Tomatlán. Then there was open water to the mouth of the Sea of Cortez. The *Kondor* settled into its final long approach, Baja California beneath the port wing, Sinaloa and then Sonora beneath the starboard.

The four heavy pusher engines droned smoothly.

Turning from time to time, Udet saw *Graf* Alvensleben dozing in the copilot's seat. Udet made no effort to waken the Count. Let him sleep.

Dusk was approaching as the *Kondor* once again passed over land. Ernst Udet peered through the windscreen, then at the plane's compass. He nudged Bodo Alvensleben awake.

"*Was? Was?*" Alvensleben rubbed his eyes and peered around.

Udet pointed ahead, suggested that the Count try to find a San Diego beacon.

Bodo fiddled with the radio gear, tuned in not a directional beacon but instead a commercial broadcast from San Diego. An excited announcer was delivering news bulletins, all of which concerned themselves with the approach of the *Spirit of San Diego*, winner of the Woodhull Martin prize of fifty thousand dollars for the first circumpolar journey.

"Not so quick," Bodo grumbled. "They do not win until they return to their point of departure. They left from San Diego and they must reach San Diego again or they have not won!"

Sunset tonight would be in the west. Ernst Udet glanced from the window beside his pilot's seat and gauged the distance from the sun to the horizon. It would be a while yet, possibly half an hour, before darkness descended.

The radio was still crackling, the news announcer's voicestill giving excited details of the Woodhull Martin race. Incredibly, the *Spirit of San Diego* had not refueled once since emergingfrom the North Hole. The crew had radioed word to the ground of a change of power plant on the far side of the disk. The newmagnetic engine of the *Spirit of San Diego* required no refueling.

There was word also of an aerial battle in the Hole, reminiscent of the dogfights above France in the *Einjahrkrieg*. The American pilot Lindbergh had been wounded but was still aboard the

Ryan. The other members of the party were flying the plane to its destination. There was no word—yet—of the rival party since their departure from Novaya Zemlya.

Udet and Alvensleben exchanged glances in silence.

The sun was now nearing the surface of the Pacific. The westerly sky glowed with flaming orange and lurid purple. The land beneath the *Kondor* was dark. Far ahead of the monoplane a glimmering of lights appeared as the city of San Diego grew close.

The news announcer's voice rose to a new pitch of excitement. Word had been received that the *Spirit of San Diego* had been sighted approaching the city from the northeast.

"Too soon," *Graf* Alvensleben grumbled. "What is this new engine of theirs, that requires no refueling? They will arrive before we do!"

Udet glanced at the fuel gauges and smiled frostily. He shoved forward the throttles of the four engines. Their droning increased in pitch and volume alike. The *Kondor* surged forward, pressing against the backs of its two occupants.

The lights of the city now resembled a scattering of cinders that glowed against the near-blackness of the landscape. The sun had reached the horizon. A stripe of flame marched from it to the edge of land. Overhead the sky shaded from dark blue toward evening blackness.

Ahead of the *Kondor* a flat illuminated area was visible. This was the city's airfield. Its runway was ablaze with floodlights rigged to assist in the landing of the approaching Ryan monoplane. Searchlights, placed at the edges of the landing field, probed the sky, seeking the silver craft.

From the *Kondor*'s radio set the voice of the news announcer continued, delivering details of the circumpolar race. Behind the one staccato voice there rose a hum, nearly a roar, of uncounted others. Thousands had gathered to welcome the *Spirit of San Diego* and squads of police were striving to keep them from blocking the runway in their eagerness.

Graf Alvensleben pushed himself erect and stepped to the cannon. The weapon's muzzle projected a quarter of a metre through a gasketed firing port in the nose of the aeroplane. The cannon itself was bolted to a shock-absorbing mount beside the copilot's seat.

Bodo slipped the canvas covering from the cannon. He opened the breech, worked its mechanism a few times, then proceeded to load a high-explosive shell.

"You are ready, Excellency, to serve as gunner?" Udet asked.

Alvensleben snorted. "I have not spent my entire career bowing to visitors and examining documents in the *Kanzlei*, *Hauptmann*." He patted the cannon affectionately. "It will be my pleasure."

Simultaneously a roar arose from the crowd and a speck appeared in the northeast, visible from the *Kondor* only as a tiny spark reflecting the last rays of the sinking sun.

"Here she is," the news announcer gushed, "The *Spirit of San Diego*, our own Americans, the greatest aviators, the greatest explorers since Christopher Columbus ventured..." The rest of his voice was drowned by the cheering multitude. With an angry grunt Bodo snapped off the radio apparatus.

The Ryan aeroplane approached, slowly taking distinctive shape. A second tiny, glowing speck rose from the ground like a spark rising from a bonfire.

Graf Alvensleben stared. "What is that?"

"It might be—" Ernst Udet shook his head. "I cannot tell. Not yet. Maybe nothing. Maybe—"

The *Kondor* droned along its northeasterly course, headed from sea to land, while the *Spirit of San Diego* whirred silently over rolling hills, approaching the city at the end of its own long flight.

Udet leaned toward the windscreen, squinting as if to focus upon the newest speck in the sky. "If you please, Excellency. Again the radio. It may tell us what that is."

Alvensleben complied.

The excited voice resumed:

"... Mohawk *Pinto*, welcoming the heroic trio at the end of their historic journey, before they even set foot on good American soil once again. If you can see the two planes, ladies and gentlemen, you'll probably be able to see the Ryan waggle its wings in response to the little *Pinto*. That's the plan, we've been informed. Even though we can't see it, the *Pinto* will waggle its wings when it gets close enough to the Ryan, and by the airman's code, the Ryan will return the gesture.

"We should be able to see that, because the Ryan is so much bigger than the little *Pinto!*"

"So!" Alvensleben frowned. "A further complication. Do you know this Mohawk Pinto, Udet? He is an American aviator?"

Udet suppressed a snicker. "The Mohawk *Pinto*, Excellency, is an aeroplane." He inclined his head. "It is a miniature. A tiny thing. A joke. They must have sent it up to give everyone a laugh!"

Bodo did not laugh. "It could be armed, *Hauptmann*, could it not? A small fighter plane?"

Udet shook his head. "There is no chance, *Herr.*"

"Then we will ignore it until we have finished off the main enemy. If possible, we will destroy this *Pinto* also. If not, too bad."

The *Kondor* skirted the landing strip, avoiding the searchlight beams that swung inland, probing the sky, seeking the Ryan monoplane. First one light, then others found the Ryan. It was caught in a nexus of white, glaring beams. The silver skin of the aeroplane shone like glittering mercury in the dancing searchlights.

The tiny *Pinto* swung past the *Spirit of San Diego* and above it, like a sparrow daring an eagle to take note of its passage. The pilot of the Ryan must have seen the *Pinto*, for the larger plane waggled its wings just as the news announcer had predicted.

The Ryan dipped toward the landing strip. Astonishingly, like one of the experimental autogyros of the Spaniard Cierva, it seemed to descend almost vertically, maintaining its stable orientation all the while.

The tiny *Pinto* had disappeared somewhere in the darkness.

Bodo tapped Ernst Udet on the shoulder. He pointed through the windscreen of the *Kondor*.

Udet nodded.

He pointed the nose of the giant *Kondor* straight at the *Spirit of San Diego*.

Graf Bodo von Alvensleben stepped to the cannon, sighted carefully on the Ryan monoplane, and fired.

The *Kondor* shuddered at the recoil of the cannon despite its special mounting. Then the *Kondor* droned steadily onward.

Chapter 27

For all that anybody cared about him, Eugene Bullard could have grown feathers, put on an angel robe, flapped his elbows and flown into the sky under his own power. Thousands of people had gathered at the airstrip. Floodlights brightened the tarmac and spotlights probed the sky. But all they cared about was the *Spirit of San Diego*.

One balding, middle-aged black man making his way into a secondary hangar with a couple of helpers in tow could hardly have been less significant.

At Bullard's direction his helpers wheeled the tiny Mohawk *Pinto* from the hangar—actually, little more than a glorified shed—and out to the end of a vacant taxi-way. The taxi-way was feebly illuminated by the final ghostly gray of dusk, and by spillover illumination from the main runway.

Bullard's helpers chocked the wheels. Eugene climbed into the *Pinto*'s cramped cockpit and began setting switches. One helper fetched a can of aviation fuel and filled the little plane's tank. The other stood before the plane. At Bullard's signal he swung the wooden prop. The *Pinto*'s sixty-horsepower Vélie radial coughed once, sputtered into life, then settled to a high-pitched buzzing.

Bullard grinned. He pulled on his leather aviator's helmet, slid the goggles over his eyes and gunned the Vélie. His helpers pulled the chocks and the tiny *Pinto* leaped forward. Rapidly it picked up taxiing speed. Eugene held the ship on the taxi-way as long as was safe, then pulled back on the stick and felt the light monoplane jump from the tarmac.

The *Spirit of San Diego* was visible to the northeast.

Bullard swung the *Pinto* in a circle above the milling crowd as a mixture of good-natured shouts and laughter rose to greet him. He pushed the Vélie to its maximum power and sent the *Pinto* into the steepest climb the little plane could manage without losing airspeed.

High above, the *Spirit* was caught in the bright beams of probing spotlights, first one, then another. It glowed a whitish silver against the now-black sky.

The *Pinto* carried no radio equipment. Eugene hoped that someone with a ground-mounted apparatus would inform the Ryan that his light plane was rising as a greeter. He could hardly have been prouder of his former protégé Howard Hughes and Howard's two friends.

He reached the altitude of the *Spirit of San Diego* and leveled off. He flew his *Pinto* toward the Ryan, waggled his wings, then swung away as he saw the larger plane return the gesture.

Then the Ryan did something very strange.

It seemed almost to halt in midair. It was still high above the landing strip, and it seemed to be sinking, slowly and gently, straight toward the tarmac. The Ryan's prop slowed until it hardly moved. The plane *must* stall and tumble into a perilous dive. But instead it hung there, descending slowly, as if the searchlight beams were solid columns of light holding it up.

Eugene cut back on the *Pinto*'s radial, dropping speed. He swung past the almost stationary Ryan, pulled his helmet from his head and waved it like a flag.

As he passed the Ryan he caught a glimpse of its occupants. There was no sign of Charles Lindbergh, the congressman's son. But he could see the tall, dark-haired Howard seated beside a slim, short-haired woman who must be Amelia Earhart.

Hughes started uncertainly to wave back, then recognized Bullard and grabbed Earhart's shoulder with one hand, pointing at the *Pinto* with the other. Bullard could see Hughes's mouth working, but the Vélie's buzzing was all he could hear.

A sudden *whoomp* jolted him, shaking the whole *Pinto*. Eugene looked around, frantically seeking the source of the sound and shock.

Another airplane was approaching. A monstrous metal-bodied monoplane with four great pusher engines mounted on its wings!

Inside the *Spirit of San Diego* there was a moment of confusion. Howard Hughes had just exclaimed, "That's Jax Bullard, Amy! It's Jax in the little puddle-jumper!"

Then from the southwest there had come a flash of flame, a whistling noise, the loud report of cannon-fire.

"What?"

Hughes and Earhart gasped in unison. Behind them, as comfortable as they could make him, Charles Lindbergh sprawled on the floor of the cabin. Hughes and Earhart had tried to get Lindy to let them land and get help, but he'd insisted on their completing the flight to San Diego first.

Beside Lindbergh stood the inactive mechanical horse, twin to the one Manfred von Richthofen had ridden to his doom.

Earhart pointed through the windscreen. "Look at that!"

Hughes followed her pointing finger. He saw the giant *Kondor* circling to get into position for a second round from its cannon.

"Holy cow!" Hughes hit the controls. "We're sitting ducks for them bozos! We better get the hell out of here!"

The Ryan's duralumin propeller spun into life.

The Ryan leaped forward. Hughes was in the pilot's seat. He swung the plane upward sharply, banked and turned out toward the sea.

The *Kondor* had circled and was lining up for another shot at the Ryan. There was a second blast and a shell screamed past the Ryan's tail empennage, missing the fabric-covered framework by inches.

Hughes dived.

The *Kondor* roared overhead and again swung around for another pass at its target.

"They're firing a fixed gun!" Hughes shouted. "They can't track with it! They have to fly straight at us to fire!" He leveled off, then banked back toward the mainland. "I think we can outmaneuver them and buy time while they swing back after us!"

"Can we land?"

Hughes wiped sweat from his forehead. "Tricky! I don't think we can buy *that* much time!"

Amelia swung in her seat, peered up through the ceiling panes. "Here they come again! Wait a minute! That little plane—"

"Jax!"

"He just buzzed them. Like a gnat! Their pilot must be scared, their whole plane dipped. Now I can't see the little plane. No—there it is! Now they're after him! They've fired again!"

There was another *whoomp!*

"Missed. Howard, what can we do? They'll kill us all!"

"No they won't. Take the controls, Amy. I'm going after 'em on that crazy horse thingum!"

For a moment silence fell between them.

Then Amelia broke it.

"Like hell you are, Howard! You grew up in a drill-bit factory. I had a pony between my legs before I was out of diapers!"

She moved toward the iron pegasus.

Hughes started after her. "Come back here, Amy! Hang on! I can't just let you—"

She lunged and whipped the wheel-crank from its brackets, whirled back toward Hughes. "Sit down, God damn you! Sit down and fly this damned airplane!" She brandished the crank at him like a copper's billy.

He looked stunned, but he subsided.

She felt hot streaks on her face. She crouched on the floor, shaking Lindbergh, one hand on each side of his head, the wheel-crank still in her grasp.

"Charles, help me!"

The *Spirit of San Diego* shook. There was a crash followed by the too-familiar *whoomp*.

"We just lost a wingtip!" Hughes shouted.

"Fly her, Howard! Swede, I need you! How does this thing work? How do I turn it on?"

Lindbergh stirred. He groped for Amy's shoulder. She helped him to the pegasus.

"Activator," Lindbergh grunted. He pointed to a toggle switch on the pommel. "Speed, altitude. See—controls, gauges. And it—and it—responds to reins—pressure on flanks—like real horse." His eyelids slid closed. She let him crumple gently.

She leaned over the pegasus, flicked it into life, tugged open the cabin door and climbed onto the horse's back. She guided it forward carefully. "Howard—you'll have to get the door closed behind me."

He grunted assent.

As the pegasus's forefeet tipped over the edge of the doorframe the machine toppled. It struck at the rim with its hind hoofs. Amy clutched at its mane. The pegasus tumbled from the Ryan, spinning end for end through blackness.

Amy struggled desperately at the controls, managed to level off a few hundred feet above the ground. The three-way dogfight of Ryan, *Kondor*, and *Pinto* had carried them back over the landing strip and the searchlights beside the runway danced and probed crazily, catching the three planes and losing them again as they maneuvered.

High above Amy's head the *Kondor* was now charging bull-like at the slow *Spirit of San Diego.* The *Spirit* was in a climbing turn as Hughes attempted to get above the *Kondor* and out of line of the enemy's cannon. Amy could see that the Ryan's starboard wingtip was missing, the carefully smoothed end now a tattered shambles.

A tiny speck was visible, higher then either the *Kondor* or the *Spirit of San Diego.* Must be Jax Bullard in his little *Pinto*, Amy thought. He'd wanted to be part of the welcoming party for the Ryan. Now he was getting his wishes and then some!

Amy pulled on the pegasus's reins, kicked at its flanks, felt it swoop upward as its wings cleft the air and its engine thrust it ahead.

Bullard tilted his little plane into a dive. It seemed to be headed straight for the *Kondor*. The pilot of the *Kondor* was intent on lining up his shot at the Ryan.

The *Spirit* climbed.

The *Kondor* roared after it.

The *Pinto* spun down from above.

At the final possible instant the pilot of the *Kondor* noticed the little plane. The giant monoplane swerved. Flame lanced from its firing port as the cannon unleashed another round. It missed its target.

The *Pinto* swept past the cabin of the *Kondor*, passed under its wing. The two great pusher props on that side missed the *Pinto* by a hair. The little ship danced and quivered in the *Kondor*'s great slipstream, very nearly capsizing in the turbulence.

While the *Kondor* and the *Spirit of San Diego* maneuvered still again in their murderous gavotte, the climbing pegasus and struggling *Pinto* drew level. Amy flew alongside the light plane. She could see Bullard clearly, just feet away from her.

She tried to shout at Bullard but her words failed to reach him over the whistling of the slipstream and the buzzing of his ship's Vélie engine.

Bullard spotted Amy and shouted at her, also, but she couldn't hear him. He pointed up at the larger planes, then back at himself. His gestures made his intention clear.

He was going to ram the *Kondor*.

Amy shouted, "No! No, Eugene!" But he didn't hear, or he didn't pay attention.

He put the little *Pinto* into a steep climb.

Amy urged her horse upward, upward, found that it could keep pace with the climbing *Pinto*. For twenty seconds they climbed.

Thirty.

Forty.

They were almost level with the two larger planes.

The *Kondor* had got behind the *Spirit of San Diego* and was closing in, its pilot working to get close enough for a sure shot. It would be the final stroke of the aerial duel, one ordained from the outset.

The two big planes had moved far to the northeast again.

Then Hughes had swung the Ryan back toward the city. On

their last lap the *Kondor* had overshot the more maneuverable Ryan and had had to swing around to pursue the Ryan back toward the airport.

Now the iron pegasus and the light plane had reached and surpassed the altitude of the two larger craft, and headed toward the charging aerial duelists.

With a rush the *Spirit of San Diego* sped past the pegasus and Bullard's *Pinto*, its propeller whirring but its only sound an eerie whine. The *Kondor* like an angry bird of prey roared after.

Eugene Bullard kicked his *Pinto* into a sharp turn to pursue the larger planes.

Amelia Earhart pushed her iron horse into a shallow dive. There was no way she could outspeed the *Kondor*. But now she closed with it, diving toward the big monoplane's enclosed cockpit. Seconds stretched into eternities.

She could see two men in flying suits inside the huge plane's cabin. One of them was hunched over the ship's controls. The other bent over the breech of a cannon, sighting in on the fleeing Ryan. The man at the controls of the *Kondor* waved to the cannoneer, pointed up at Amelia.

She swung the iron wheel-crank.

The pegasus and the *Kondor* rushed past each other.

Amelia's blow, delivered as they passed within feet of each other, was aimed at the head of the cannoneer. He already had his hand on the firing mechanism of the cannon. As the pegasus flashed by the cabin of the great plane, Amelia tugged back on the reins, kicked the pegasus into a steep climb and swung the crank.

She felt a terrific impact that left her right arm quivering and numb.

The pegasus responded to her command, swooping through a high-arching inside loop. From its peak Amelia could look straight down at the *Kondor* and the *Spirit*. Sometime in the few seconds following the impact of the crank with the cockpit glass, Amelia was vaguely aware that she had heard the *whoomp* of the cannon's discharge.

But the only sign of the encounter showed on one pane of the

Kondor's windscreen. It was completely cobwebbed by the impact of the blow. Apparently the cannon shell had gone wide, thanks to Amelia's effort. Her right hand was so numb that she had to look at it to tell whether she still held the heavy crank. She did not. The crank was gone, sent tumbling to the ground at the moment of impact.

At the top of her inside loop Amelia kicked the horse into a half snap-roll, converting the loop into an Immelmann. She leveled off, banked, found herself flying side by side with Eugene Bullard.

They glanced at each other and for an instant exchanged fierce comradely smiles.

The *Spirit*, under Howard Hughes's guidance, had emulated Amelia's maneuver. The *Kondor*, too massive to tolerate the stress of the inside loop, had had to bank over the city before resuming its pursuit. The *Spirit* was not at the same altitude as Earhart and Bullard. It flashed past them, headed inland.

The *Kondor*, following, had to climb at the same time, losing speed as it did so.

Bullard gestured, pointing to himself and to the Udet monoplane. He repeated the movement. His intention was again clear: an attempt at an aerial ram.

It was certain suicide.

The Udet roared toward them.

Amelia saw Bullard dip the nose of his little ship and start down an invisible chute leading straight to the giant *Kondor*.

With a shout Earhart kicked her pegasus into a course parallel to Bullard's. The pegasus power-dived; its greater weight and power brought it flashing past the *Pinto*. Amelia screamed at Bullard, waving frantically as she sped by him, crying a prayer that he understood.

She could see the two men in the *Kondor* gesturing and shouting at each other, struggling with the controls of the big ship.

Amelia swooped to a halt and stood hovering, the pegasus's wings moving constantly, artificial jet-black feathers furling and turning to maintain its stability. Amelia peered upward, saw the little *Pinto* plunge for the *Kondor*. The *Pinto* made a tiny cruciform silhouette in the sky. A still tinier silhouette separated itself and tumbled away from the airplane, made visible only by the stars it blacked out as it fell.

There was a deafening crash.

Orange flame gouted in all directions.

A blast of withering heat swept over Amelia.

A body hurtled past her, nearly close enough to touch. It did touch—or tried to. The falling man stretched desperate arms toward Amelia as he tumbled past.

Outstretched fingers failed by inches to reach outstretched fingers.

Amelia could see Bullard tumbling, illuminated against the glaring spotlights that still probed upward.

Desperately she shoved her iron mount into a top-speed power dive. The pegasus's wings clove the air, driving it earthward. Its hot glowing engine shoved it down like the fist of a volleyball player spiking a shot.

Wind whipped past Amelia's face, snapped her short hair back. She pressed her cheek against the iron horse's neck.

Beneath her the floodlit landing strip with its throngs of milling curiosity-seekers glowed like a furnace.

Ahead of her, Eugene Bullard tumbled helplessly. As he spun through the air he caught sight of Amelia plummeting after him. He was seized by an idea. Amelia saw him go spread-eagle in the air, maximizing the atmosphere's resistance and slowing the acceleration of his fall.

They were only a few hundred feet above the tarmac, mere seconds from certain death. Amelia urged her horse to a final burst, shouting into its ear as if it were a living thing.

She clutched the pommel with her right hand, still half numbed and weak from the blow she had delivered to the *Kondor*'s cabin window. With her good left hand she reached for Bullard. Their fingers met, this time. They clenched. She tugged.

He spun in her grasp and plastered himself against the pegasus, belly pressed against its broad iron chest, arms and legs wrapped around it like a starfish on an abalone. The impact of Bullard's body as he struck the pegasus drove it sideways by fully a foot.

Amelia's hands were free again.

She jerked back on the reins, swinging the pegasus out of its dive. She could see individual faces in the milling crowd beneath her. The horse had actually come level with the wind-sock mounted atop the field's main hangar. Amelia grunted with the shock of suddenly multiplied forces as the pegasus pulled out of its incredible plunge.

Her face still pressed against the horse's neck, Amelia locked hands with Eugene Bullard. There was a glint in his eyes that she could not read. For a fleeting instant she had the insane notion that it was the glint of laughter. She could manage no response at all.

The pegasus flew level over the top of the hangar, leaving behind the airfield, heading toward the Pacific, gradually slowing as it traveled.

There was a roar overhead as the *Kondor*, its cabin utterly demolished by the impact of the *Pinto*, its four pusher engines screaming, completely out of control, barreled past. The *Kondor* crossed the city weaving erratically. Then before Earhart's eyes it nosed up into a power stall, dipped and plunged.

There was a moment of suspenseful silence... a single crashing impact... then a cloud of steam mixed with black greasy smoke arising from the ocean.

There was an open grassy field beneath the pegasus. Amelia managed to land on it safely. Eugene Bullard loosed his desperate embrace of the iron horse, staggered to his feet, then stood leaning against the machine. Amelia slumped wearily in the saddle.

Bullard looked into her face. Blood was pouring from inside his nose where small vessels had ruptured. He ignored the bleeding. Amelia's reflexes, developed caring for the wounded in Boston, came into play. She raised her good hand to wipe away the blood.

Bullard said, "Thank you."

Amelia straightened. She drew a deep, shuddering breath of night air. "Can you climb up?" she asked Bullard. "We should get back to the airport."

He managed to climb on the pegasus and perch behind Amelia. She started the pegasus back toward the landing strip. She kept the machine on the ground this time, riding it through quiet streets as if it were a docile livery hack.

Ironically, no one paid attention. Hardly anyone was in the

streets. An occasional flivver chugged past, still headed toward the airport, hoping to arrive before the climax of the night's events.

The police had succeeded in clearing the crowd from the landing strip. The throng now lined its edges impatiently.

A flying squad of police met Amy and Bullard. They broke way through the crowd, helping the two fliers. The pegasus was placed under guard in a hangar. By the time they reached the end of the landing strip, the *Spirit* was into its final approach, coasting in, dead-stick.

Amy clutched Bullard by the arm. "The crank!"

Bullard looked at her in puzzlement. "What?"

"The wheel-crank! I took the crank from the cabin. There's no way Howard can get the wheels down, now. They'll have to land on the bay."

But Hughes, flying the *Spirit of San Diego* while Lindbergh lay semiconscious behind him, did not make a sea landing.

He brought the Ryan in low, nearly flat, its propeller merely windmilling. The monoplane whispered across the landing strip, moving so slowly it seemed it must stall out at any moment and fall to the ground.

The ship nosed up slightly, halted and hung a few yards above the runway.

"Of course! I forgot! The magnetic engine!" Amy relaxed, realizing that she had been unconsciously holding her breath.

"What magnetic engine?" Bullard asked. "How in blazes did they do *that?* I taught that Howard boy everything I knew about flying, but *nobody* can make an airplane just stand still in the air like that!"

"The engine—we got it from a country on the other hemidisk. They have—"

"Never mind." Bullard let out an explosive breath. "Why should I be a skeptic? You saved my life with that flying horse of yours. I *have* to believe in that! I've gotta get my hands on it and that magnetic engine both!"

A few hours later Charles Lindbergh lay in a white-sheeted hospital bed, his wounded leg thickly bandaged where surgeons had dug out von Richthofen's bullet. Lindy was pale and weak from the wound and from loss of blood, but he had taken nourishment and his head was clear.

In the same room, Eugene Bullard sat in a straight-backed chair. His ribs had been strapped. Tufts of cotton showed from his nostrils.

Amelia Earhart's right arm, splinted, rested in a sling. The diagnosis was a cracked bone and a dislocated shoulder, both resulting from her attack on the *Kondor*.

Only Howard Hughes, showered and dressed in fresh clothes that came within inches of his ankles and wrists, was totally uninjured. He and Eugene Bullard were engrossed in plans for the devices brought back from Svartalheim and Muiaia.

There was a knock at the door. Before anyone could move, the door opened and two well-dressed men entered.

"Bill! Don!" Hughes exclaimed. "How'd you two devils get past those dragons in the lobby? They weren't letting anybody up here!"

He didn't wait for their answer. "Amy, here's a treat," he said. "This here's the Ryan men that built the *Spirit of San Diego* for us!" He turned back to Bowlus and Hall. "Amy here saved the day for us more times than I can count! She's a champ! And, say, do you guys know Eugene Bullard?"

Bullard said, "We've met."

"We've been trying to hire Eugene," Don Hall said. "He came by the airplane works for some parts for his little Mohawk. I've never met a man who knows aircraft like him. But he wouldn't sign on."

"I've been waiting for you, Howard," Bullard said. "These fellows have a nice little shop going, but I've been thinking about another scheme. Now that you've won the Woodhull Martin Prize, what are you going to do with your share of the money? You weren't thinking of starting a West Coast operation, were you? And maybe concentrating on aviation out here?"

The moustachioed skull gave its grin again. "Funny you should mention that. I had something like that in mind. And I'll need a chief engineer. Matter of fact, if you had the capital, Eugene, I'd rather have a partner."

"Hah! I'm afraid all of my capital was wrapped up in that *Pinto*."

Bullard shrugged.

The door swung open again, and three more individuals entered the room.

"What is this, Union Station?" Lindy managed from his bed.

"You remember me, Swede?" One of the newcomers crossed and carefully shook Lindbergh's hand. "Your doc said we could only have a few minutes. But we figured the *Union* was entitled to an exclusive. Here's my photographer."

From behind a heavy four-by-five Press Graphic, the photographer nodded a greeting.

"And Mr. Austin." The final arrival nodded. He wore a natty business suit and carried a slim briefcase. "Mr. Austin is Mrs. Woodhull Martin's personal representative. We want to get some photos when he presents the prize to you heroes. The *Union* already has an extra on the press, with shots of your landing, and the crash of that warplane that attacked you. We'll want your exclusive stories for the paper. There are already representatives from half a dozen book publishers waiting in the lobby with contracts for you!"

Austin laid a slim cordovan briefcase on the table beside Lindbergh's hospital bed. "I have spoken with Mrs. Martin, using the new transoceanic trunk. Mrs. Martin was most thrilled by your triumph.

"In fact, she expressed her regrets that she could not join you today, but as you know, she is very old and has difficulty traveling. She is ninety years of age. But still fully alert."

He slipped immaculately manicured fingers inside his jacket, withdrew a leather key case and carefully selected from it a small silver key. "Mrs. Martin asked me to say that she has waited since 1912, when she first offered her prize for the circumpolar flight, in hopes of seeing the money claimed. I daresay that those hopes have kept her alive these fifteen years."

Unlocking the cordovan briefcase, he extracted a small sheaf of envelopes, then carefully relocked his briefcase and returned the key case to his jacket.

"Mr. Lindbergh."

Flashpowder exploded as Austin handed the envelope to the aviator.

"Miss Earhart."

"Mr. Hughes."

More flashes as the San Diego *Union* photographer shot pictures.

"Each of you will find a check in the amount of $16,666.67," Austin said, "totaling $50,000.01." He smiled diffidently. "Mrs. Martin authorized me to round your checks to the next higher cent. Mrs. Martin will absorb the extra cost herself."

He faced Eugene Bullard.

"Mr. Bullard. I explained to Mrs. Martin your role in the safe return of the *Spirit of San Diego*. In appreciation of your deed, Mrs. Martin has also authorized me to disburse an additional $16,666.67."

He handed a fourth envelope across.

Bullard took the envelope, then grabbed Howard Hughes by both arms. "There's my share of the capital!" he exclaimed.

"Uncle, you got yourself a partner," Hughes said.

Chapter 28

Amelia Earhart turned the corner and dodged between two sightseeing sailors dressed in summer whites as she approached the hotel marquee. She paused for a moment to savor the relief that the overhang offered from the blazing San Diego sun.

Fancy ironwork spelled out *U. S. Grant Hotel.*

Amelia stepped back into the bright sunlight. She paused before the inviting frosted-glass doors to the hotel's bar and grill. A large plate-glass window beside the doorway offered an inviting glimpse of the interior with its dark woods, white linen, polished brass. Waiters in waist-aprons scurried beneath green-shaded electric lights and slowly revolving overhead fans.

In a corner of the plate-glass window a neatly lettered sign informed passersby that the ladies' entrance was around the corner.

Behind Amelia the mixed noonday crowd of businessmen and secretaries, off-duty seamen and dockhands, tourists and vacationers, moved in the slow-paced bustle dictated by the strong subtropical sun.

From the blacktop street automobile horns sounded raucously as two drivers, disputing a right-of-way, left their vehicles and stood toe-to-toe, gesticulating and threatening each other with beefy fists.

Amelia turned her back on the scene and, ignoring the hotel's advice concerning a ladies' entrance, pushed open the doors to the bar and grill.

Inside she was shocked momentarily by the darkness and calm. As soon as her eyes had readjusted she looked around for an open table.

A tall, curly-haired man wearing an immaculate business suit stood up suddenly. He waved to Amelia, then dropped his napkin on the table and almost ran the length of the grill. He swept Amelia into his arms and planted a kiss on her cheek.

"Amy! Amy! What a surprise! What are you doing here?"

He held her back at arm's length.

"Charles!" Amy reached to touch his cheek. "You were limping."

He laughed ruefully. "A souvenir of my brief encounter with *Herr* Baron von Richthofen. I can also tell whenever it's going to rain.

"Amy, are you meeting somebody? Do you have an appointment?"

She shook her head.

"Then come on." He took her hand and led her to his table as a child would lead his mother. "Do you want some lunch? This place has the best food in town!"

"Let me get my bearings first!" He held the dark bentwood chair and she slid into it. "Maybe just a glass of beer to cool off. It's broiling out there."

"Anything!" He signaled to the waiter, pantomimed tilting a stein to his mouth, then turned his attention back to Amelia.

"I thought you'd gone home to Kansas. I never expected to see you in San Diego again. How come you didn't write to me, or wire?"

"I didn't know I was coming out here myself. It was just an impulse. You know, Muriel's been just wonderful to me. She and George have put me up at the farm, protected me from curiosity-seekers, given me everything I could ask for."

She halted as the waiter placed a sweating stein in front of her. She smiled gratefully at him. "I may want some food in a little while, but nothing yet."

Lindbergh nodded encouragingly. "It sounds idyllic."

"I suppose it was. You know, Muriel has a husband and a house full of children. The farm is going well. They have more than enough money. It seemed to work out fine for me to play the role of Aunt Amy. Your ears should have burned, Charles. You were in the bedtime stories I told them every night. You and Howard and the *Spirit*, the von Richthofens and that Russian Princess and the people we met in Muiaia and in Svartalheim, and that terrible battle when we got home and how Eugene Bullard flew up in his little airplane and saved us."

"Yep. So—how come you're here? Not that you're unwelcome, understand."

"Oh, ever the diplomat." She grinned to take the curse off her words. She took a deep draught of her beer, then gazed into her stein as the liquid cooled her.

She looked up, into Charles Lindbergh's eyes.

"I'm bored, Charles."

He raised his eyebrows.

"You remember after the One Year War, for a while there was a rash of news stories. *Doughboy Robs Bank*. That kind of thing."

"Sure. The President even appointed a commission to look into it. They found that soldiers who'd got used to the excitement and danger of war couldn't just go back to being farm hands or factory workers. They missed the sense of adventure."

Amy nodded.

Lindy unconsciously rubbed his game leg. The wound in it had healed completely and he kept von Richthofen's flattened bullet on his key chain for a souvenir.

"I see what you mean. It's been a bit of an anticlimax for me, too."

Subtly their roles shifted. "I didn't think you could be bored," Amelia said, "with the life you've been leading. I see your name and your photo in the newspaper all the time. Shaking hands with Jimmy Walker, signing a contract with Mr. Griffith to appear in films . . ."

"It sounds wonderful, doesn't it? As wonderful to you, as your happy life back in Kansas seemed to me when I thought about it."

"I guess I can try some food now," Amy said. "What do you recommend?"

Lindy signaled the waiter again and soon Amy was attacking a portion of lamb chops with sliced green beans and baby potatoes. Lindy had already finished a corned-beef sandwich. He ordered them another round of beer.

For a few minutes Amy dined in silence while Lindbergh looked on.

Finally Amelia said, "What are we going to do, Charles? If I had to milk one more cow or collect one more egg, I think I would have gone mad. Muriel and George and their children are happy and fulfilled, but it was driving me crazy.

"Charles, I've ridden the *Spirit* as an ice-boat down the Avenue of Sphinxes. I've seen the ziggurats of Muiaia and ridden the aerial cube to Haibrasl. I've met the wizard of the swamp and naiad of Svartalheim, and flown through the maelstrom of the North Hole.

"How can I ever be happy again, feeding chickens and baling hay?"

"Amy, I know what you mean, but it's over. We've had our adventure, and now it's over. Howard and Eugene Bullard are developing magnetic engines for the world's air fleets. I've been doing publicity work for the Ryans. If you don't want to stay on Muriel's farm, I'm sure you could line up something. Didn't the Hollywood people approach you, for that matter?"

"I sent 'em away. They said I could be the next Pearl White. I don't want to be the next Pearl White. I want to be Amelia Earhart!

"Besides..." She picked at a lamb chop, then shoved her plate aside and took another sip of beer. "Besides, I can't help worrying about my friends. What ever happened to Cuchaviva? Did she find her husband and get back to Muiaia? Are they all right? And what are the Svartalheimers up to? They reminded me of the Kaiser's Junkers. I didn't trust them and I worry about what they're up to.

"I can't just live a quiet, happy life. Not any more. I have to *know*. I have to *do*."

Lindbergh signaled the waiter. "An iced coffee. Amy?"

"I'll stick with beer."

The waiter cleared her dishes.

"Well, I might as well be square with you, Charles. I didn't quite expect to run into you this quickly, but I knew you were in San Diego. I read where you were doing design and consulting work for Ryan. I'm checked in upstairs. If we hadn't met by accident, I was going to call Ryan's in a day or two and talk to you."

"Okay. I kind of suspected as much." He grinned wryly. "But just what is it that you want, Amy?"

"I want to go back. And I want you to go with me."

She sat in silence as he thought that over. The bar and grill was still jammed. Customers and waiters bustled. But a silence had fallen over and around their table.

"I donated the *Spirit of San Diego* to the city. That is, the newspaper agreed to donate it when I suggested as much. They fitted it out with a Wright engine again, restored the original state. Howard and his friend Eugene Bullard have struck a bargain with the Ryans and they're out there together, studying the silent mill that Icheiri's people put in for us."

"You mean we can't take the *Spirit* back with us."

"In a word, yes. That's what I mean."

"We can get another plane. With what we learned, we can write up specs, we can get a plane that's better than the old one. Something bigger and stronger. If Howard and Eugene can really dope out the principles of the Muiaian power plant, we can fit up a new ship with magnetic engines.

"Charles," her eyes were glowing, "Charles, it will be the grandest airplane ever built. We can find out what happened to Lothar von Richthofen and the Princess Lvova. Charles—we'll be alive again!"

Lindy stared into his tall glass of iced coffee. After a long while he looked up. His eyes were fixed on Amelia's. "You have a room here in the Grant?"

Amelia nodded.

"Could we go there? Could we go there now?" he asked.

"Oh—well, I had no special plans for the afternoon. But I—"

"I could go down to Ryan's to do it," Lindbergh said. "Or get a ride up the hill to the El Cortez. I'm staying there. I'd walk, but this bad leg, you know—the hills can get steep."

"Well—"

"I need to place a trunk call," Lindy explained. "I need to phone Mr. Griffith in Hollywood and tell him I won't be available for that film after all!"

ABOUT THE AUTHOR

An Adventure, Richard A. Lupoff's first book, appeared in 1939 in an edition of one copy, crayon on construction paper. Unfortunately, *An Adventure* is now out of print. The author remembers little about that first effort except that it involved a visit to "the Stachyou of Liberty." In forty-five years, Lupoff's spelling has improved considerably. Or maybe it's his editor who has become more diligent.

While still in high school, Lupoff wrote for the sports pages of *The New York Times*, *Philadelphia Inquirer* and other newspapers. In college he edited a short-lived independent newspaper, one of the forerunners of the "underground press" of the 1960s and '70s.

Since the 1950s he has written for scores of magazines and newspapers including the *Washington Post*, *San Francisco Chronicle*, *Army*, *Ramparts*, and *The Magazine of Fantasy & Science Fiction*. Several of his stories have been nominated for literary awards, and his novel *Sword of the Demon* was a finalist for both the Nebula Award and the Hamilton Memorial Award.

Lupoff's works have been published in Great Britain, France, Spain, Germany, Italy, Greece, Israel, Brazil, Argentina, and Japan. He has worked in radio, television and film, and has taught at the University of California, the College of Marin, and at other universities.